Janet MacLeod Trotter was born in Newcastle and grew up in Durham. She has been editor of the Clan MacLeod magazine, a columnist on the *Newcastle Journal* and has had numerous short stories published in women's magazines, as well as a novel for teenagers. *A Child of Jarrow* is her eighth saga. Her first, *The Hungry Hills*, gained her a place on the shortlist of *The Sunday Times'* Young Writers' Award. Janet MacLeod Trotter lives in Northumberland with her husband and their two children. She has an author website on the internet. Find out more about Janet and her other popular novels on: www.janetmacleodtrotter.com

Praise for Janet MacLeod Trotter's previous novels:

'Not only a good read but a vivid picture of the coalfield . . . You'll believe you're there' Denise Robertson

'Well-researched, highly readable . . . compelling and utterly convincing' *Northern Review*

'A tough, compelling and ultimately satisfying novel . . . another classy, irresistible read' *Sunderland Echo*

A Child
of Jarrow

Janet MacLeod Trotter

headline

First published in 2002
by HEADLINE BOOK PUBLISHING

First published in paperback in 2003
by HEADLINE BOOK PUBLISHING

10 9 8 7 6 5 4 3 2 1

ISBN 0 7472 6741 3

Typeset in Times by Avon DataSet Ltd,
Bidford-on-Avon, Warwickshire

Printed and bound in Great Britain by
Mackays of Chatham plc, Chatham, Kent

HEADLINE BOOK PUBLISHING
A division of Hodder Headline
338 Euston Road
London NW1 3BH

www.headline.co.uk
www.hodderheadline.com

For all my special and talented nieces –
Noelle, Sophie, Fiona, Annabel, Isla,
Skye, Lorna and Susan
– with much love

Chapter 1

1902

By the time they struggled down the hill into Jarrow, one daughter either side of their wheezing mother, the Coronation celebrations were half over.

'You should've gone on ahead with our Mary and Jack,' Rose panted, stopping once again to catch her breath. Her legs were already swelling up in the heat. 'I could've stopped at home.'

'And miss the party? Don't be daft, Mam!' Kate exclaimed, squeezing her arm. 'It's not every day we get a new king.'

Rose grunted. 'We haven't yet. Lying in some palace with bits of his insides missing, isn't he? May the saints protect him!'

'Don't you start,' Sarah muttered, her broad face perspiring in the sudden summer heat. 'You sound like Father.'

'Aye,' Kate laughed, then mimicked their stepfather's gruff speech. ' "What they want to have a Coronation festival for? The bugger's not even being crowned! What if he never recovers from his operation? Might as well crown the next one!" '

1

Sarah burst out laughing 'Didn't stop him ganin' off at the crack of dawn to start celebratin', mind, did it?'

'That's enough,' Rose said sharply, regaining her breath. 'Show some respect for your father.'

Kate felt familiar rankling at her mother's insistence that their cussed stepfather, John McMullen, was their father. He was notorious around Jarrow for his foul-mouthed ranting and drunken brawling, for his defence of all things Irish and contempt for all things womanly.

Kate remembered little of her own father, William Fawcett, except for fragments of memory that warmed her heart: piano music and lusty singing, a gentle voice telling her tales of the saints. She remembered sitting high up on strong shoulders so she could look out over a vast sea of hats and caps. She could recall a smiling fair face and a large hand wrapped around hers, pulling her down the lane. They were running faster and faster, her father crying out, 'Race the moon, Kate! See if we can beat it!'

But consumption had killed him, just as it had Kate's eldest sister, Margaret. To save the remaining four girls from the workhouse her mother had married the stern, volatile John McMullen and achieved a precarious semi-security for them all. Or not quite all, for their sweet-natured sister Elizabeth had died of the measles soon after young Jack had been born. And there had been dark years of no work and aching hunger when she and Sarah had been forced out to beg on the streets for food. Kate still felt sick at the memory of the terror and humiliation.

'Respect!' Sarah spat out the word.

Kate gave her older sister a warning glance. She did not want past miseries to spoil their present enjoyment. Yet she knew Sarah hated their stepfather even more than she did, and for good reason. It was only two years since he had nearly whipped her to death for missing the last tram home from Newcastle. Since then Sarah had worked up river in Hebburn and returned home as seldom as possible. But they had both been given the day off for the Coronation festival and neither of them was going to pass up a rare holiday and the chance of a free tea. She and her sisters loved a party, and Sarah had come home safe in the knowledge that John McMullen would be occupied inside some public house, boozing until sundown or the landlord threw him out.

Kate was glad the dignitaries of the town had decided it was too late to call off the celebrations at this late hour. The processions, brass bands and entertainment in the park would go ahead as planned, despite the luckless King Edward's coronation being put off until he had recovered from an appendix operation. But looking down the bank from Simonside, they could see that the processions were over. Bunting flapped irritably in the hot breeze and twists of paper from penny sweets scudded across the cobbles.

'I can still hear the bands playing,' Kate said eagerly, chivvying her mother forward.

'Where do you think our Jack's got to?' Rose fretted.

'He'll be in the park watching the soldiers. You know he's daft about uniforms.'

'Aye,' Sarah laughed. 'Better find him before he joins up.'

'Don't say that!' Rose gasped. 'He's still just a bairn.'

'She's teasing, Mam,' Kate reassured, knowing how Rose doted on her shy, serious-minded son. 'Haway and let's find the fun.'

They linked arms and bustled their mother into the dusty town, the sisters singing as they went. It was only after they reached the crowded park and the tea stalls, and spotted Jack's

3

slim figure and dark head close to the running buglers of the Durham Light Infantry, that Kate remembered Mary. No one had thought to ask about their youngest sister – quick-tempered, petulant, restless Mary. But Mary had always taken care of herself and, at fourteen, took little heed of what anyone said, not even her stepfather. She was the only one of them who showed him no fear and walked a tightrope between his indulgence of her and his quick-fire temper.

As a small girl, Mary had been brought up by their Aunt Maggie and had always been closer to her than her own mother. John, in his own gruff way, had tried to spoil Mary, make up for Rose's neglect, but to no avail. Mary seethed with resentment and impatience at them all. She hated living in the old isolated railway cottage to which Rose had moved them a year ago, and chaffed at the restrictions imposed by her parents.

'Jack's allowed to wander where he likes!' she would rail. 'Why can't I go into town?'

'He comes to no harm round the fields,' Rose would defend, 'and he brings home food for the pot.'

'You let our Kate go!'

'She works in the town.'

'It's not fair!' Mary always ended up screaming. 'I hate it here! I wish I still lived with Aunt Maggie!'

Kate saw how this wounded her mother but if she leapt to Rose's defence, Mary accused her more shrilly of being the favourite daughter. It was Mary's beloved Aunt Maggie offering to take her and Jack to the festival that had allowed Mary her freedom today. Kate caught sight of her sister now, arms linked with her young cousin Margaret, who allowed herself to be bossed by Mary. They were gazing at a display of glass birds and china vases that were prizes at an archery

4

stall. Mary turned and Kate waved her over, but her sister ignored the gesture.

'She'll be off to get Jack to win her one of them birds,' Sarah commented. 'Anything fancy and our Mary's got to have it.'

'Let's get Mam a cup of tea,' Kate said brightly. She preferred to be snubbed by Mary than be the focus of her waspish tongue. Let her sister spend the day how she wished, for Kate was determined to enjoy herself too.

They found Rose's sister, Maggie, picnicking on the edge of the field. She quickly shared out her paste sandwiches and rock buns and they caught up on each other's news.

'Danny's doing canny at the Works.' Maggie spoke of her husband. 'Good regular work this summer. How's John? Still celebratin' the end of war with the Boers?'

Rose snorted. 'He's not signed the pledge, that's for certain. I'm just glad the troops are coming home and Jack's too young to join up. He's had me that worried these past couple of years with all his talk of soldiering – and running around pretending to shoot at imaginary Boers.'

'Just lads' games, Mam,' Kate assured. 'He's not even out of short breeks.'

'Aye, let the lad play while he can,' Maggie agreed. 'He'll be out to work and at the beck and call of the bosses soon enough.'

'Is Aunt Lizzie coming over the day?' Sarah asked.

They were all fond of Rose's youngest sister, who lived beyond Gateshead on the grand Ravensworth estate where her husband, Peter, was a gardener.

Maggie shook her head. 'Have you not heard? She had a bad fall – ankle's up like a balloon. Peter sent word a couple of days ago that Lizzie wouldn't be across. Didn't Mary tell you? I told her when she came down yesterday.'

5

Rose gave an impatient sigh. 'No she didn't! That's half the reason I've bothered to come out the day – the thought of seeing our Lizzie.'

'How will she manage with the bairns?' Sarah asked.

'Aye, it's a busy time of year for Uncle Peter an' all,' Kate added.

Maggie nodded. 'I said to our Mary, "Why don't you gan over to Ravensworth to help out for a week or two?" But she didn't seem that bothered.'

Rose snorted. 'No, she wouldn't. Not if it means keeping an eye on Lizzie's wild boys. She'd rather be at home, even though she complains at the little I tell her to do.'

'Well, who can blame the lass?' Maggie said in defence of her niece. 'She's more delicate than your other lasses – more suited to shop work than skivvying, I'd say.'

'Work-shy, more like,' Rose said bluntly. 'She didn't last with the Simpsons more than a few months. Spent more time looking through Mrs Simpson's wardrobes than polishin' them.'

Kate wished that she could go and help her aunt, for she had loved her one visit to the countryside when her cousin Alfred had been christened. She had glimpsed the towers of Ravensworth Castle glinting mysteriously above the wooded hillside above them and passed one of the lodges with its impressive wrought-iron gateway. Her Uncle Peter had given them rides in a handcart and picked strange furry fruit growing against a warm brick wall that had tasted sweeter than plums.

But she knew that her mother needed the wages she brought in from working as a general maid in a prosperous part of South Shields. Her stepfather's wage as a docker was as unsure as the seasons, its size dependent on the number of stops he

6

made to quench his thirst on the long way home up Simonside bank. So Kate kept her secret yearning to herself.

'Wait till I have a word with Mary,' Rose determined. 'Might be just the answer – get her out from under me feet.'

They stayed on to watch the children's races and special tea laid on by the borough council. Later, Kate slipped away with Sarah and they wandered round the town, arm in arm.

'I've met this lad,' Sarah told her abruptly.

'Lad?' Kate asked, her blue eyes widening in surprise. She saw her sister's plump fair face colour. 'You're never courtin'?'

'Keep your voice down!' Sarah hissed, looking around her anxiously.

Kate too glanced over her shoulder in familiar fear, as if their stepfather would suddenly burst out of a nearby pub and harangue them for being out alone on the street.

'It's all right, he's drinking down Tyne Dock with Uncle Pat,' Kate said, reading her sister's thoughts. 'So who is this lad? And where did you meet him? Why didn't you tell me before? Eeh, fancy you courtin'!'

'I didn't say I was walking out with him – I've only just met him,' Sarah said, flustered. 'I shouldn't have told you.'

'Haway,' Kate grinned. 'You can't keep secrets from me – I'll not tell a soul.'

Sarah gave a self-conscious smile. 'He comes into Hebburn on a Saturday to sell veg from his da's allotment. I answered the door to him once and now he comes regular. Always stops for a bit chat.'

'That's canny,' Kate encouraged. 'Is he bonny-looking?'

'Aye,' Sarah said cautiously. 'He's smaller than me, mind, but he's got a grand smile.'

'So where does he live?'

'Gateshead way.' Sarah shrugged evasively.

'What do they call him?'

Sarah shrugged again. She caught Kate's sceptical look. 'But he said he's coming to Hebburn for the fireworks the night.'

'The night?' Kate exclaimed. 'So what are you doing in Jarrow? Get yourself back to Hebburn before he finds another lass to share his cabbages with! You'll never find a man round these parts with Father watching like a hawk. I just have to look at a lad and he's calling me worse than muck!'

'Do you think I should?' Sarah asked, unsure.

'Aye, course I'm sure!' Kate insisted. 'Gan back before it's all over.'

Sarah still looked undecided. She took Kate's arm. 'Will you come with us? I can't go looking for him on me own.'

Kate felt tempted. How she would love to go to Hebburn and watch the fireworks light up the night sky. Fireworks always reminded her of her real father and being carried in his arms as the heavens above them exploded with light. Rose had once told her the event had been for the old Queen Victoria's Jubilee, but forbade her ever to mention it in front of her stepfather. Kate had learnt long ago that any mention of their past life as Fawcetts always enraged John McMullen.

The other thing that fuelled his jealous temper just as much was the thought of his stepdaughters attracting the attentions of men. He was more possessive of their virtue than their own father ever could have been and was forever lecturing them on the dangers of lust. Even to glance at a man or exchange a casual word was a crime. John would accuse them of encouraging men and berate them in foul language. It mattered not

8

how old or ugly the man. Even portly Harry Burn, their married neighbour, provoked John's jealousy for calling by with a gift of vegetables and a cheery word.

'You ever get into trouble with a man and I'll skin the hide off you!' their stepfather often threatened. Kate never doubted that he would. 'No one disgraces the name of McMullen, do y' hear?'

It was because of their father that she could not go with Sarah. Secretly she yearned for the chance to meet young men, just to chat with them and maybe have a dance or two. She was almost twenty and had never been courted. Her own mother had married at such an age, but Kate hadn't even held a lad's hand or walked out with a man on a summer's evening. Tonight, in the warm evening breeze under a canopy of glittering fireworks, would be just the night for meeting a lad and falling in love. Kate burnt with frustration that such a time might never come for her.

'It would be canny,' Kate said with longing, 'but it'd bring more trouble than it's worth.'

Sarah nodded in understanding.

'You can go with that lass who works next door,' Kate suggested, quelling her own disappointment. 'Bel, isn't she called? She's good company, from what you say. Gan and enjoy yourself!'

Sarah smiled, encouraged by Kate's enthusiasm. 'But what about Mam?'

'She'll not stand in your way. And me and Mary can see her back up the hill. Don't you worry about Mam.'

Sarah needed no further persuasion. The sisters returned to the park and Sarah said a hasty goodbye, promising her mother that she would visit again within the month. The rest of the family lingered for another hour, enjoying the late afternoon sun, but as the heat went out of the day Rose began to fret.

'Haway, it's time we made for home – your father will likely be back wanting his tea.'

Mary protested at once. 'I want to stay for the bonfire!'

'He'll not be back for hours yet, Mam,' Kate added, reluctant to return too.

'It'd be just like him to come back early and catch us out – then we'd never hear the end of it,' Rose said with a bitter laugh.

Kate thought it was far more likely that her stepfather would stay out until closing time, then wake them all up with his noisy singing and banging about as he staggered drunkenly into the furniture in their cramped kitchen. Sometimes a madness would grip him when in drink and he would order them up out of bed and make them stand to attention, shivering in their nightclothes while he swung the fire poker over their heads and roared orders as if they were his soldiers.

It was best to humour him and play along with his deluded games, where he thought himself the famous General Roberts, marching them through the hell of an Afghan war. It was only in drink that John's tongue was loosened about his experiences as a foot soldier in India and their gruelling battles with Frontier tribesmen. When sober he would say nothing, except to spit in the fire and curse the British Army for its ingratitude to Irishmen like himself.

As a small girl, Kate remembered him coming to court her mother dressed in a smart army jacket. She had gazed up in awe at his stern, handsome face and felt a mix of fear and admiration. For a while she had been desperate to gain the approval and love of this tall, godlike soldier who had come

10

to save her mother from servitude in the puddling mills and them all from the workhouse. But nothing Kate ever did seemed to please him and she had given up trying.

'Haway,' Kate sighed, seeing her mother's mind was made up, 'we'll get a good view of the bonfire from up the hill, Mary.'

'I'm not going!' Mary said stubbornly.

'You'll do as you're told,' Rose snapped, her face lined with fatigue. She had been too long standing on her swollen legs and yearned for the peace and threadbare comfort of their old cottage. Increasingly she disliked large crowds and the company of anyone outside close family. For too long she had had to put on a tough front, fending off rentmen, bailiffs and indignant neighbours that John had offended. Now she was weary of the world and wanted nothing more than to hibernate in her dilapidated railway cottage above the scruffy overgrown embankment and tend her small garden.

Kate, quick to avoid a row in public, turned to her aunt. 'Why doesn't our Mary stay over with you the night, Aunt Maggie?'

Maggie nodded with a cautious look at her older sister. 'That's no bother.'

'Jack can help us up the road,' Kate added. Her half-brother was tossing a stone and catching it, hovering on the fringe of the dispute, keeping out of the way. But his pennies were long spent and the military bands gone, and he was restless to be off.

'Please, Mam?' Mary said, her look suddenly sweetly pleading. 'I'll be back in the morning to help with the Sunday dinner, I promise.'

'Very well,' Rose acquiesced, quickly losing the appetite for confrontation.

11

With the argument averted, Rose struggled to her feet and held out an arm to Kate and Jack. Together they made the steep haul out of Jarrow town, the River Tyne and its forest of cranes and chimney stacks to their backs. Kate heard her mother's breath come more easily the further away they travelled from the smoky, dusty air of the town and the closer once more to ripening fields and the hazy distant hills of County Durham.

As they approached the straggle of cottages at Cleveland Place, their neighbour, Harry Burn, hailed them. He was sitting outside his cottage on a low stool enjoying a bowl of tobacco.

'A grand day, Mrs McMullen!'

'Aye, grand.' Rose paused to catch her breath.

'Win any prizes, Jack?'

Jack looked bashful as he held up a stuffed bird in a glass jar.

'You'll not get much feeding off that,' Harry teased.

'He won it for our Mary,' Kate smiled, 'but she made him carry it home.'

'And what are you doing back so early, young miss?' he winked. 'No canny lad to walk you home yet? By, the young 'uns today are slow ganin' about things, aren't they, Mrs McMullen? We were wed and knee-deep in bairns at their age, weren't we?'

Rose looked flustered but Kate stifled a giggle.

'Plenty time for all that,' her mother snorted.

'Lads of Jarrow must be daft in the head for not courting this young lass. If I was ten years younger—'

'Ten!' Ena Burn brayed from the cottage door. 'More like fifty.'

Harry chuckled and nodded his head in agreement with his wife.

Ena beckoned them to the door. 'Come and have a glass of me home-made lemonade. You look all done in. Never mind my Harry's nonsense. Here's a stool, sit yourself down.'

To Kate's surprise, her mother plonked herself down on the upturned half-barrel by the doorstep.

'Just for a minute then,' she sighed. 'I'm partial to your lemonade. Jack, run in the house and fetch a bottle of me ginger wine. We'll share that out an' all.'

They all knew Rose hid her small store of home-made wines and cordials in the wash house where John would never deign to go. They were hardly alcoholic but when John returned home drunk and thirsty for more he would drink anything fermenting in a bottle.

As the neighbours sat on in the warm evening sunshine, Kate hovered on the edge of the conversation, half wanting to sit with them and half yearning to chase Jack around the soot-covered elms at the end of the lane where he had gone off to play. Her restlessness got the better of her. Picking up her skirts she ran off after her young half-brother, her petticoat flapping around her ankles.

'I'll keep an eye on our Jack,' she called over her shoulder.

'Don't let him climb too high!' Rose shouted.

Kate ran with a quick loping stride. Since birth her left foot had been turned in awkwardly, but she was light on her feet and still able to catch Jack over a short distance. She ran up behind him where he was throwing sticks into the high branches and grabbed him round the waist.

'First to touch the lovers' tree!' she challenged, spinning him round and setting off before him.

Jack recovered from his surprise, dropped his fistful of sticks and chased after his sister into the small copse above the railway line. They arrived at the old oak simultaneously,

Jack knocking into Kate and pushing her to the ground, so she couldn't touch the tree first.

'I won!' he cried. They both lay on the ground, panting and laughing.

'Cheat!' Kate gave him a playful shove.

'You had a head start.'

'You don't have to wear long skirts.'

'You're just a lass.'

Kate rolled over at the provocation and began to tickle him until he giggled out loud and begged her to stop. This was how she loved him, exuberant and wiry as a young pup, not the subdued loner who avoided company and scowled under dark brows at his family. She knew that his father frightened him and that he was growing tired of his mother's protective fussing, but she at least could make him smile. To Kate he was still the small boy who used to pad around after her like a shadow. She could remember him as a tiny sickly baby whom they all feared would die, and recalled a time when John had rocked Jack in strong arms and sang Irish songs, when he had stayed up all night keeping him alive. Kate knew John had loved his son deeply in those days and wished Jack could remember that too. But since the bad times when they had been forced on to the streets to beg, Jack had seen enough of his father's violent temper and felt the sting of his thick leather belt too many times to believe he was loved.

Jack sprang up and began swinging from a gnarled branch. Kate stood and shook the soil from her skirt. She began to hum as her fingers traced the weathered carving on the tree: two sets of initials set in a heart. W. F. and R. M. Who had they been? Kate enjoyed musing about the mysterious lovers who had left their mark. She liked to think it had been her parents, William Fawcett and Rose McConnell, but her mother had been dismissive.

'I never came here with your father – and don't you dare mention such a thing in front of your da or we'll all be swinging from that tree!'

But Kate still liked to guess. 'Winifred Foster loves Ralph Marshall.'

'Wilfred Frankenstein loves Ruth Maggots,' Jack mocked.

'Walter Fisher loves Rachael Manners,' Kate smiled.

'Bet they weren't even friends; bet they're dead now.' Jack jumped down, tiring of the game already.

Kate gave him a shove. 'Course they were friends – sweethearts,' she declared. 'Bet they married and lived happily for years and years.'

'You're just soppy!' Jack said in disgust, kicking savagely at an exposed root. 'I'm never getting married. I'm going to join the army or run away to sea.'

'Not if Mam catches you first,' Kate laughed.

'I'll do what I like when I'm older. I'll climb up to the top of the mast just like this, watch!' Jack swung himself up by a low branch into the tree and grabbed a higher one.

'Mam says you're not to go too high,' Kate warned.

'You're just scared 'cos you can't do it,' Jack called down. 'Lasses don't climb trees.'

Without a thought, Kate unlaced her boots and kicked them off. She hitched up her overskirt and tucked it into her belt.

'Watch me!' She hauled herself up after him. But straddling the second branch she looked down and felt suddenly dizzy. Jack laughed from high up, still visible in the ailing half-bald tree.

'Coward!'

15

'Jack, I'm stuck, come and help us!'

After a pause she saw her brother descend. He guided her down backwards.

'Don't look down, just feel with your feet.'

Kate slipped gratefully to the ground. 'You'll make a canny sailor. Or chimney sweep!' she added with a broad smile.

'Race you back!' he grinned, picking up her boots and running off with them.

She screamed after him out of the thin trees and down the rutted lane. Kate was so intent on sidestepping the nettles and potholes that she did not see Jack stop abruptly as he reached the corner of the outhouse, or notice her mother's frantic waving over the wall.

Too late she looked up and almost collided with the tall gaunt figure standing, hands on hips, by the broken garden gate. With a gasp of shock, Kate stared into the angry bloodshot eyes of John McMullen.

Chapter 2

John grabbed Kate by the arm and yanked her in front of him. His grip was vicious but his eyes seemed glazed and unfocused as he looked her over.

'Look at you! Running around like a gypsy in bare feet and all that leg showing. What you been doing in them woods, eh?'

Kate braced herself for a slap on the face. 'Nowt, Father, honest. I've been keeping an eye on our Jack.' She looked for her brother but he had slipped past them. She could sense Rose standing tensely beyond them on the brick path.

John swung round unsteadily, still keeping his hold on her. 'Jack, where are you?' he growled. But the boy did not answer.

'I've sent him to fill the hod,' Rose answered in a calming voice. 'Kate's been a grand help today. Came back early, we did. Sarah left early for Hebburn an' all.'

'Where's Mary?'

'Stoppin' with Maggie – just for the night.'

John grunted and turned back to Kate. He leant forward so that the stink of his stale whisky breath overwhelmed her. It was always worse when he'd been on the whisky. Beer made him loud and occasionally hearty; whisky inflamed him or made him maudlin. She tried to hide the distaste she felt.

'You don't look like you've been looking after Jack,' he said, his voice strangely low and threatening. 'Looks like you've been rolling around on the ground like a bitch on heat.'

There was spittle on his wiry moustache and his slack colourless lips. Kate could not imagine how her mother could bear to kiss such a man. There was something odd about the way he was looking at her that set Kate's heart thumping.

'Come away inside, John,' Rose beckoned softly. 'Haway and sit by the fire. You look tired.'

John turned, momentarily distracted by her reasoning tone. 'Eh? I'll come when I'm ready. What sort of mother are you, letting the lass run around like a dirty little—'

'John!' Rose stopped him quickly. 'She's been playing with Jack, that's all. Let's all gan inside and Kate can fetch you a bite to eat.'

Kate knew her mother was desperate to avoid a scene in front of the neighbours. Rose came forward and put a hand on John's arm. He threw it off, but released his grip on Kate, pushing her ahead of him.

'Get yourself inside before I change me mind and skelp ye for being so shameless.' Kate hurried into the cottage. Behind her John shouted at Harry Burn, 'And what you staring at? Don't you look at my missus like that or I'll knock you into next week! That scarecrow wife of yours not enough for you, eh?'

'John!' Rose hissed. 'Come inside.' She almost dragged him in the house, mortified at the abuse he hurled at their affronted neighbour.

The happiness of the day dissolved as John's moodiness settled on the low-ceilinged kitchen. He went to sit in his chair by the fire, which Jack was stoking up with coal, and

18

Kate hurried into the pantry where her mother was hacking into a loaf of bread.

'Pull your skirt down!' Rose hissed. 'And tidy your hair. You're too old to be messing around with our Jack. I knew we should've come straight home – should never have stopped for that drink with the Burns. Lucky I saw him staggering up the hill and left sharp. What you have to get in such a mess for?'

She turned and looked Kate over. Her thick brown hair was dishevelled, snaking down her neck and sticking to her glistening pink cheeks. Her large blue eyes were troubled under dark curving eyebrows, like limpid pools reflecting her mood. How beautiful she had looked hopping down the lane with slim legs showing, her full lips parted in laughter. Kate had the curved body of a woman but with a girl's quick unselfconscious movement and lack of inhibition.

'Sorry, Mam.' Kate gave an anxious smile. 'It was just a bit carry-on. Let me take that in for Father.'

Rose was about to hand her the plate of bread and cheese, then changed her mind.

'No, I'll do it. You stay in here and start peeling the potatoes for the morrow.'

Kate was baffled, but a little relieved. She scraped back her hair and pinned it up again, then rolled up her sleeves and went out to fetch potatoes from the sack in the outhouse. By the time she returned with an armful of potatoes she could hear John's voice raised once more.

'Is it too much to expect to have me family at home waiting for me? And a holiday at that! But no, they're all gallivantin' round the town, gettin' up to mischief!'

'They're not in the town,' Rose pointed out. 'And me and Kate and Jack are here.'

'Where's the lass?'

'Fetching tatties.'

'I want her in here. It's a bloody holiday! We should be singing and dancing – aye, and drinking.' Kate heard him aim his boot at Jack, for her brother gave out a yelp. 'Gan and fetch me a jug of beer from the Twenty-Seven – tell 'em I'll pay for it the morrow.'

Kate's heart sank at the mention of that terrible pub. Its real name was the Alexandria, but it was known locally as the Twenty-Seven because it served as the next stop after the twenty-six staithes along the docks, nestling among a row of mean, soot-blackened houses in Leam Lane. In the bad times, she and Sarah had hung around its doors, begging the scraps from the bait tins of men still earning enough to drink there. They had been grateful for the blasts of warm air from inside and the crusts handed out to them like dogs. Kate forced the fearful memories from her mind.

'Kate!' John bawled. 'Stop hiding out the back and get yourself in here!'

She hurriedly dropped the potatoes into the stone sink and brushed the soil from her bodice. She saw Jack give Rose a questioning look and her answering nod, then the boy ran thankfully from the room. Kate could tell by her mother's set expression that she had gauged John's mood to be too volatile for argument. It was better to go along with his wild notions than risk riling his temper further. The more he drank the sooner he would pass out and the sooner they could all go peacefully to bed.

'Come here and sing with me, lass!' he ordered her over. 'Sit at me feet. And you, woman,' he glared at his wife, 'sit yourself down and cheer up your miserable face. You'd crack a mirror with that look.' He laughed. 'Haway, lass, and sing.'

Kate slipped cautiously to her knees by the hearth, wary of his sudden joviality. It could change back in an instant to aggression. He began to sing of sweet Molly Malone and she joined in the chorus, her voice rising clear above his deep tobacco-husky tone. Rose picked up some mending and settled in the chair opposite, while the two singers went through John's Irish repertoire. By the time Jack returned with a half-jug of beer Kate was on to the local songs she had picked up as a child and her music-hall favourites. John grumbled about the small amount of beer, but drank it straight from the jug while Kate carried on singing.

She loved to sing and felt her high spirits return with each song. Jack edged close to her but sat in the shadows just beyond the ring of firelight.

'Sing "Thora"!' John demanded between slurps, shaking her shoulder roughly. It was a sentimental song about a lost child, but Kate loved its haunting melody and its picture of a land of snow and magical starry skies. She imagined it was somewhere up on the moors above Ravensworth where Aunt Lizzie lived, those blue shimmering hills she could glimpse in the distance on rare clear days from this home at Simonside. One day she wanted to reach them and explore beyond the mysterious hazy horizon.

She began to sing it softly, gazing into the blue-tinged flames of the fire that mesmerised. Rose put down her sewing to listen and even the restless Jack was stilled. Kate's voice wrapped around them all, her hair glinting like bronze in the firelight.

When she finished, the room was bound in silence as if she had cast a spell. Then John put out a hand and ruffled her hair in a rare gesture of affection.

'You're a bonny singer,' he murmured.

21

He took a large swig from the jug, sloshing the last of the dregs on to his moustache and down his stubbled chin. His fleshless cheekbones stood out in the firelight, his once-vivid blue eyes bleary with booze and fatigue.

Rose stirred. 'Jack, Kate. Time the pair of you were off to bed.'

'Bed? It's hardly dark!' John complained. 'We'll have more singing till the sun gans down. Haway, Kate, sing us some more.'

Kate had risen at her mother's words, but now stood undecided. John grabbed at her skirt and held on.

'Another song!' he commanded. 'And sit down the rest of you.'

When she saw her mother pick up her mending once more with a stifled sigh, Kate sang on. Jack squatted on the floor, yawning and fighting sleep. She sang until she was hoarse, repeating songs from earlier in the evening. Whenever she thought John had dozed off she tried to move away, but he kept a hold of her skirt and stirred at the movement.

Darkness fell and the fire died down, so that they could hardly see each other. Kate sang softly until she was sure her stepfather slept. But as she put out a hand to release her skirt from his grip, she felt it tighten. In an instant he pulled her on to his knee and in a befuddled voice said, 'Rose, me bonny Rose.'

'It's me, Father,' she whispered, trying to pull away. 'Kate.'

'Just sit for a minute,' he mumbled.

Kate sat as still as could be, waiting for her mother to remonstrate. She held her breath but was only too aware of John's hands on her. One lay heavy on her lap while the other he slipped around her waist. His callused fingers were stroking and probing, his thumb edging up the curve of her breast.

Kate's heart thumped hard. She wanted to jump up and run from him, but she sat frozen on his knee, wondering what to do. She peered through the dark at Rose but could not see her face. Could her mother see her predicament or had she fallen asleep? Kate could just make out the sprawled figure of Jack beyond the hearth mat. She pushed out a foot to try to stir him but he slept on.

All the while John's fingers fumbled over her body, his breathing coming hard on the back of her neck. His other hand squeezed her thigh.

'Bonny lass,' he whispered, 'bonny as my Rose.'

Suddenly his hand moved round to grab her inner thigh and at the same time he nipped her breast. Kate gave out a startled cry at the unexpected pain and leapt up.

'Don't, Father!'

'What's that?' Rose said sharply. She had dozed off to Kate's singing. Kate stumbled towards her in the dark, breathing fast.

'Mam—'

'Has he touched you?'

'He thought I was you, Mam,' Kate hissed.

'Wha's that? Wha's all the fuss?' John slurred. 'I was asleep.'

Kate knew he was lying, or maybe he had been half asleep and dreaming of Rose. Either way, she would not let that happen again. She shuddered to think of the way his hands had been pawing her. She kissed Rose good night and fled up the ladder to the bedroom in the loft she shared with Mary.

Kate got under the blanket fully clothed, still shaking from the incident. A short while later she heard Jack climb the creaking ladder and fall on to the mattress in the curtained-off section that served as his room. She was thankful that her

23

parents slept downstairs in a boxed-in bed in the kitchen alcove. Rose was no longer fit enough to climb ladders and John was too tall and often too inebriated to attempt such a feat.

Below she could hear Rose coaxing John to bed, and his lurching footsteps across the floor. She could not make out his mumbled grunts, but she heard the noise of their efforts to climb into the bed. There was a short exchange of words; John insistent, Rose wearily accepting. Then Kate heard the squeaking of the bed boards that Sarah had once told her was the sound of consummation. It was short, sharp and rhythmic as if someone was bouncing on the bed. Soon afterwards it stopped and she heard John's snoring like the sound of bees swarming.

Kate huddled under the blanket to block out the sound. It made her feel nauseous to think of her mother doing intimate things with John's whisky breath hot all over her and his rough hands kneading her flesh. Never would she choose such a man for a husband! She would marry a gentleman with good looks and charm, who would sing with her in harmony. A man more like her real father who could play the piano and be accomplished at a trade. She would never reduce her children to begging in the street or suffer the shame of a husband who broke rocks at the workhouse for a pittance as John had once had to do.

She lulled herself to sleep with romantic thoughts of this future man. Later, in the early hours of the morning, she woke, still cocooned in pleasant dreams. She flinched at the touch of a warm body next to her. Kate recoiled at the thought John might have climbed up to lie beside her. But in the grey pearly light through the skylight she saw Jack curled up like a mouse in the space where Mary usually lay.

Kate relaxed and snuggled back beside him. She felt comforted by his warm breath on her cheek and his smell of hay and earth.

'My little soldier,' she smiled to herself.

Slipping an arm over his body she drifted off to sleep again.

When she woke a second time, Jack was gone and motes of dust were dancing in the strong beam of sunlight flooding the room. Kate heard her mother moving around downstairs. She got up quickly and went down to help, noticing John's bulking shape in the bed beyond, still snoring.

Rose said nothing as she handed Kate a cup of weak tea she had poured from the pot keeping warm on the stove. Her broad face looked pasty and creased with lack of sleep.

'Do you want me to start on the dinner, Mam?'

They had got out of the habit of going to Mass since Rose had found the trek down to St Bede's in Jarrow too much for her swollen legs. There had been periods during the bad times when lack of decent clothes or boots for their feet had kept them away from church.

'In a minute,' Rose said quietly, giving a brief glance to her sleeping husband. Then she nodded silently for Kate to follow her outside.

They went out through the pantry to the yard with the wash house, where Jack helped John keep a couple of mangy hens. One of them flapped up on to the wall at their sudden appearance. Rose led the way out into the lane. They stood sheltered from the railway embankment by overgrown nettles and hawthorn bushes.

'I've been thinking about our Lizzie,' Rose said abruptly. 'She'll be needing help.'

25

Kate watched her mother's tight expression. 'Aye, she will.'

'I think you should gan and help your aunt – give a hand with George and Alfred.'

'Me?' Kate gawped at her. 'But what about me job in Shields?'

Rose continued to look out over the embankment as she spoke. 'You can sharp pick up another skivvying job. You're hard-working and eager to please.'

Kate was foxed. 'But what about me wages? How would you manage?'

Rose turned and faced her. Her eyes were dark-ringed but glinting.

'It might just be for a couple of weeks – maybes a month – just while Lizzie gets back on her feet. We'll manage.' She put out a hand and touched Kate's arm. 'Take this chance. Ravensworth's a big estate and there might be a place for you permanent.' There was an urgency in her voice. 'Sometimes I wish I'd had such a chance instead of our Lizzie. But we each have a different lot to bear and mine hasn't killed me yet.'

Rose gave her a brief wistful smile. 'Your da wanted you to have the best start in life – and I don't mean that old lump lying in his bed yonder,' she said with a curt nod at the cottage. 'I haven't been able to give you much, but maybes now you can make some'at of yourself. You've got the best looks of all me bairns, alive or dead, and a nature to suit.'

Kate felt herself colouring at her mother's words. She had never heard such praise from her lips.

'Mam—'

Rose gripped her hand. 'I want you away from here. Father will never let you near another man – least not the type who'll make you happy.'

Kate swallowed. 'Has he agreed to me going?'

26

'Not yet, but leave him to me. I know how to get round him.' Rose gave a short bitter laugh.

Kate thought of last night and the creakings from the box bed, and felt uneasy. Is there anything a mother wouldn't do to protect her children? she wondered.

'So will you go?' Rose demanded.

Kate was filled with sudden excitement. Her dream of going to Ravensworth and the mysterious blue hills beyond was almost within her grasp.

'Aye, willingly,' she smiled.

Rose patted her arm in relief and turned quickly, so that Kate would not see the gleam of tears in her eyes. She had no idea how deeply she would be missed, how hollow her mother's heart would be if she never came back. But Rose, who had lost two daughters for good a long time ago, was used to a heavy heart. Yet she would never have the words to describe such desolation, and it served no purpose to try.

'Get the brisket on, lass,' was all Rose said and Kate followed her back inside, her mind already racing ahead to the future.

Chapter 3

Kate heard later that the arguing started during Sunday dinner. But by then she had escaped to the house in South Shields where her employers were hosting a large lunch party. During the week she was general maid, laying fires, cleaning brasses, washing and ironing. She had been given the day off for the Coronation celebrations, but ordered to be back before luncheon on Sunday to help in the kitchen.

It was late in the evening when she made the two-mile walk back up the hill to Cleveland Place, and her limbs ached from heaving cast-iron pots of food and cauldrons of hot water around the kitchen and carrying trayloads of food up and down stairs all afternoon. She approached the cottage warily, wondering what she would find.

All was quiet in the kitchen, with John's chair empty and only Rose sitting close to the fire, trying to mend a tear in Jack's shorts by the dim light.

'The calm after the storm,' Rose said drily.

'Where is everyone?' Kate discarded her jacket and loosened her chafing boots.

'Father's asleep – stomach playing up as it always does after a day on the whisky. Mary's gone to bed – tired herself out with all her rantin' and cryin'.'

'About me ganin' to Aunt Lizzie's?'

'Aye.'

'But she didn't want to gan. She hates the country.' Kate flopped on to the horsehair chair she'd bought in a sale for her mother but which Rose found too uncomfortable.

'Well, now she does. Our Mary's as changeable as a weathercock.'

'Only 'cos you've chosen me to go. She can't bear to think she's being left out of some'at.'

'Father told her to stop bawling like a bairn or he'd put her over his knee like a bairn. Said she was too young to be going so far from home and that it might do you good to have a bit of Lizzie's firm hand – high time you stopped playing in trees like a boy.'

'He's agreed to me going then?' Kate sat up in expectation.

'As long as Lizzie and Peter cover the cost of your keep – and you send back your wages if you pick up work. So you can write a note for me and send it ahead to let them know you're coming.'

Kate leapt up and gave Rose a hug. 'That's grand. Thanks, Mam!'

Rose shrugged her off. 'Now go and call for our Jack – he's been out since tea time.'

Kate went out into the chill night air. There was no sign of the boy in the back lane and she imagined he was lying low in one of his many dens along the embankment or in the copse. The moon was hidden by a blanket of cloud but there was still a lurid smudge of daylight on the far horizon that helped her pick her way among the potholes.

'Jack? I'm back. Time to come in. Jack!'

No reply came. She edged further up the track towards the trees. It was cold without her jacket and she rubbed her arms.

'Jack! Come home now. Mam wants you. You know how she frets. Haway, Jack, show yourself.'

Still the boy did not answer and Kate wondered if he had gone off on one of his rambles, forgetting the time. He could disappear for hours, stalking the unkempt embankment for birds' eggs and berries, or pestering the nearby farmer to let him help shoot the rooks.

She turned to look back towards the railway cottages. In an instant, somebody jumped out of the long grass and grabbed her from behind, clamping a dirty hand over her face.

Kate gave a muffled scream and tried to wriggle from his hold.

'You're captured!' Jack cried in triumph, tightening his wiry grip.

'Jack man, leave go. You're hurting me!'

Abruptly he let go and pushed her away.

'You little beggar!' Kate gasped. 'I nearly died of fright!'

'I'll make a canny scout, won't I?' he crowed.

Kate smoothed down her clothes as she eyed him. He had unexpected strength in his slim gawky body. He gave her one of his resentful looks from under puckered dark brows.

'What's wrong, kiddar?'

He hunched his shoulders and began to walk away from her.

'Tell us, Jack,' Kate said, catching up.

'What you have to gan away for?' he accused.

'To help Aunt Lizzie, of course.' They carried on walking. 'It'll not be for long, maybes a month.' She swung an arm round him but he shook her off.

'You'll not come back,' he said.

'Course I will.'

30

Jack shook his head. 'No you won't. You want to gan away – just like Sarah. Everyone wants to gan. You're leaving 'cos of me – Da said so. You're not to play in the woods with me no more.'

Kate took hold of him. If only she could tell him that it was John she couldn't wait to get away from. She was running from his critical words, his smothering strictness and now that lustful look in his eye, the memory of his predatory hands. From these she had to escape and she suspected that was why her mother was so keen for her to be gone too.

'Not because of you! You're me little soldier and I'll miss you, honest I will. But it'll not be for ever, I promise. Bet I'll be back by the time you finish school for the summer. We'll gan picking wild raspberries together, eh?'

But he just looked at her as if he did not believe in her promise. Then he turned away and ran home without her.

Mary's reaction was much more vocal. She tossed on the flock mattress they shared and dug sharp feet into Kate's back.

'It's not fair! Why can't I go? You've already got work in Shields. Why should you get to go?'

' 'Cos Mam said,' Kate sighed. 'Any road, you'd hate being stuck in their tiny cottage, washing dirty gardener's clothes – and you don't even like George and Alfred.'

'Only 'cos they put a worm down me back and blow their noses on their sleeves.'

'See, you'd not be there five minutes before you'd be crying to come home.'

'No I wouldn't!' Mary wriggled and poked her sister.

Kate shifted in irritation. 'Leave off and get some sleep. I've got to be up early, even if you don't.'

31

But Mary wouldn't be quiet. 'Why should I be the one stuck out here in this mucky little hovel at Mam's beck and call all day long? It's just not fair.'

' 'Cos she needs your help. She can't be doing all the fetching and carrying with her bad chest and swollen legs. And there's Jack to give a hand.'

'Jack,' Mary gave a petulant snort, 'he's never here. Might as well build himself a house in those trees and go and live there.'

'Well, at least you get along with Father more than the rest of us. You know how to get round him when you want. You have an easy life of it here, if you ask me.'

'I'm not asking. I hate it here, I never wanted to come. I wish we were still in the town.'

'What? Choking to death next to the chemical works? If Mam hadn't moved us up here where the air's fresher, our Jack would be dead by now.'

'Aye, it's always Jack, Jack. Mam only cares for him – and you – Mam's little pet. No one thinks about what I want. The only one who looks out for me is Aunt Maggie. I wish she were my mam.'

Kate kept silent at the provocation, for maybe there was some truth in it. There had been hard times after their father died when Maggie had taken in baby Mary and brought her up as her own. She still remembered the day when the resentful young Mary was brought back to live with them, kicking and wailing and destroying the family harmony. Only John had any patience with her; for her sisters it meant less food on their plates and less room in the bed. She wondered if Mary would ever be happy. It was just in her nature to hanker after what she couldn't have, or want to be somewhere other than where she was.

Kate rolled to the edge of the mattress, thinking how good it would be to get away to Aunt Lizzie's. She sank into an exhausted sleep long before Mary's unhappy mutterings ceased.

But when the day of departure came, Kate was suddenly tearful at leaving her family behind. She had given notice in Shields, the note to Lizzie had been sent and a small wicker basket of possessions packed. Jack was going to help her carry it down to the railway station in Shields before going on to school and Mary was coming for the outing.

John was sitting slurping tea at the table, dressed for work. He had avoided her all week, hardly giving her a glance, and Kate wondered what he recalled of the previous Saturday. Something about his awkwardness towards her suggested that he was eager to be rid of her; she was a thorn under his skin.

'Kate's off then, John,' Rose said stiffly.

He looked up and nodded. 'You behave yourself and work hard. Don't do owt to bring shame to your mother or me, do you hear?'

'No, Father, course not.' Kate hesitated. A week ago she would have dashed forward and planted a kiss on his hollowed cheek, but now she was wary. 'Ta-ra then.'

She clattered out of the cottage with Rose following into the dewy morning light. Her mother pressed a parcel of jam sandwiches wrapped in brown paper into her hands.

'Take care of yoursel', hinny.'

'Oh, Mam!' Kate flung her arms around her mother's neck, squashing the bundle of food. 'Will you be all right?'

'Aye, don't fuss.' Rose pushed her away gently. 'Tell Lizzie I'm askin' after her and let us know when you're settled.'

Her words sounded final, as if she did not expect a swift return. Rose's wistful look and the way she fondly adjusted her daughter's straw hat was too much for Kate. The tears that were stinging her eyes flooded down her pale cheeks.

'I won't go if you don't want me to!'

Mary huffed down the path. 'Well, I'll go then.'

Rose thrust a rag of pocket handkerchief at Kate. 'Course you'll go. Wipe your eyes and let's hear no more wailin'. Now be off with you or Jack'll be late for his lessons.'

Kate blew her nose and tried to quell the sobbing she felt welling up inside. She did not attempt to kiss her mother again.

'I'll write. Mary can read it to you.'

Rose nodded and waved her away. Kate gave one last look at the cottage as they turned into the lane. Rose was still standing in the doorway, her face in shadow. The brooding cooing of hens broke the early morning quiet and the smell of damp earth and wet grass was strong. She waved and just as she turned away she caught sight of John's tall figure come to the door to watch.

'Tak' care, lass,' he called.

Kate felt a sudden pang that she hadn't said a proper goodbye. Her feelings for him were so mixed at that moment. She remembered how it felt as a small girl to be desperate for his attention. There was a time when he had laughed easily, teased them and taken them to the circus. How had that man turned into one with such a ferocious temper and a raging anger against the world? But part of her would always be frightened of him. Like a simmering pot that might boil over, he could never quite be trusted. She waved back and linked arms with Mary and Jack.

They said little to each other as they walked down to Tyne Dock, though Mary made comments about people as they passed and her mood lightened the nearer they grew to the streets, with their bustle of traders and workers. She was happy to hang around for the train and spin out her jaunt to the station, but Jack was edgy and eager to be gone. He hovered impatiently while Kate bought her ticket to Lamesley.

Then he dumped down Kate's basket. 'I'll be late for school if I wait any longer.'

Kate knew that he wouldn't, but didn't argue. It would only embarrass him if she hung on to his arm and begged him to stay.

'Ta-ra, kiddar.' She smiled and ruffled his hair. 'Promise I'll be back soon.'

He hesitated a moment, his dark blue eyes unsure, then nodded and turned on his heels. Her half-brother sprinted away without a backward glance and disappeared into the smoky street.

'Pity they don't teach him to speak at school,' Mary said drily.

Kate sighed. 'It's just me and you then. You don't have to stay if you don't want.'

Mary snorted. 'You're not getting rid of me so quickly. I'll say the train was late and have a bit look round the shops before I go back up that muddy lane.'

Kate could not help laughing. She swung an arm round her contrary sister.

'Eeh, Mary. I think I'll miss you too!'

Mary snorted. 'No you won't. Anyways, I'll not miss you. I'll have a whole bed to myself and maybes Mam might notice I'm there with you gone.'

Kate gave an impatient sigh, but knew there was no point arguing. Mary thought she was hard done by, and once she had a notion about something there was nothing anyone could say that would change her way of thinking.

The train pulled in with a squeal of wheels and sigh of steam. Kate picked up her basket and gave her sister a quick peck on the cheek.

'Take care of Mam – and our Jack.'

Mary pursed her lips, but nodded. Kate thought she would say nothing, so she turned and clambered into the nearest carriage.

As she turned to get a glimpse out of the window, Mary called out, 'Write and tell us what it's like – what the gentry are wearing. Bring me some'at back, won't you? Don't forget.'

Kate nodded and waved. She had no idea what she was supposed to bring back, but she would try to find something to please her sister. A moment later the train was jolting into movement and pulling away from the station. Kate peered through the blast of smoke for a final glimpse of Mary. Her heart hammered in sudden panic at what she was doing, leaving the familiar surroundings of Jarrow and South Shields for an unknown life in the countryside. At that moment she wanted to hang on to her sister and not let her go. She waved frantically, but someone had shut the window to keep out the smoke and the moment to shout a farewell was gone.

Kate squeezed into a seat in the middle of the carriage but craned for a view out of the grimy window. It all passed so quickly and the smoke was still thick around them, but she thought she recognised the stretch of embankment at Cleveland Place. She wondered if her mother paused in hanging out her washing to come to the back fence and watch the train go by.

When the rows of blackened terraces and spires of Jarrow gave way to the sprawling village of Hebburn and its docks, Kate thought of Sarah. There had been no time to see her older sister to explain what she was doing. Mam had said she would tell her on her next visit. Kate determined she would write a letter when she was settled.

Then all the familiar landmarks were past and the train hurried on into the towering tenements of Gateshead, where she had to change for her train south to Lamesley. By the time she was boarding the second train her nervousness was changing into excitement at her new adventure. She gazed out of the window as the train took her out of the teaming metropolis of Gateshead, heading south , and abruptly plunged her into a world of ripening corn fields and undulating hills.

That day at the docks, men knew by the brooding look on old McMullen's pasty face not to speak to him or get in his way. When the dark moods took a hold of him it was best to let him work in silence. Some said he'd been like that since his army days in Afghanistan, about which he refused to talk. Others murmured he must be suffering from too long a night in the Twenty-Seven. Many wondered if there had been trouble at home, but it was pointless to ask. John McMullen was too proud to admit there was anything wrong, and what went on in a man's home was his own business.

Mary hummed to herself as she dawdled along the street, watching the shopkeepers winding out their faded canopies against the July glare. She peered into shop windows, yearning to touch the soft fabrics in the draper's, smell the soaps in the chemist's and listen to the soft rustling of tissue paper in the haberdashery. She would be a collector of beautiful things to guard against the drabness of the world. Aunt Maggie's love of books had shown her that there could be gentility in Jarrow, even among the dirt and poverty that were ever present like inferior neighbours.

Mary smiled as she suddenly remembered that Kate had not taken her winter jacket with the blue velvet collar that she had coveted for three winters. Kate had said she'd be back long before it grew cold enough to wear. Mary would have it. It suited her better and she would wear it whatever the weather. Kate wouldn't mind, and besides, she, Mary, deserved something in compensation for being the one left behind to slave for the family.

On the point of turning for home, Mary caught sight of a stall selling second-hand books and periodicals. She hesitated. There was money in her purse to buy suet, but she had a sudden desire to treat her favourite aunt to one of the battered novels. She would call on Aunt Maggie before facing her mother. Maggie would give her a bacon knuckle or some split peas to make a soup that would compensate for the lack of suet. Rose would scold her but she did not care. Mary had learnt how to close her ears to shouting and threats until they subsided. Her mother was too crippled to run after her with a rolling pin, and nagging Kate was gone. She would do as she pleased. Mary went inside and bought a book.

Left behind, Rose stabbed at the flapping shirts on the washing line with thick wooden pegs. Her arms ached from the savage pounding of washing in the poss tub that morning, but her face to her neighbours was expressionless. Only the redness of her eyelids betrayed the tears she had shed in the privacy of the wash house.

Along the embankment, Jack threw stones on to the empty track, his face disconsolate in the silvery glare of a hazy sky.

The scream of the train's whistle still echoed in his ears like a tune that lingered in his head and would not be quiet. He would be late for school or maybe he would not go that day at all. He would be strapped, but he did not care. He would grit his teeth and not flinch. Jack could bear physical pain, would welcome it. Anything would be better than the strange aching in his chest that felt like suffocation. His eyes felt itchy as if he would cry, but only bairns and girls cried.

He retreated to the oak tree and climbed into its comforting arms. Jack scraped at the lovers' etched initials with his dangling boot.

'Williamena Ferret-Face loves Richard Mudpie,' he muttered.

Then suddenly, bewilderingly, the leaden lump in his chest heaved and tears flooded his eyes. Jack gave out a sharp yelp. He curled into the tree, buried his face in his arms and wept.

Chapter 4

Alexander felt a familiar boyish rush of excitement as the horse and trap turned under the castellated gateway and waited for the lodge keeper to emerge. Impatient, he leapt down from the passenger's seat.

'I'll walk up to the castle,' he smiled at the coachman who had brought him from the station. He paid him his fare, waved away the change the man tried to give him and lifted down his leather case.

'Good afternoon, Mr Bates!' he called to the stooped retired gardener, whose sole responsibility now was to open and close the high wrought-iron gates at this seldom-used entrance to Ravensworth. Most of the many visitors who came and went from the bustling estate did so by the broad entrance and sweeping driveway to the north. The south lodge was almost obscured by foliage and the narrow turf drive was roofed by massive oaks and elms, creating a green mossy tunnel. But it reminded Alexander of childhood visits and on the spur of the moment he had got the coachman to stop.

'Mr Pringle-Davies?' The old man grinned with pleasure. 'Good day to you, sir.'

'Grand day, Mr Bates. You look fighting fit as ever.'

The keeper chuckled as he moved slowly to unlock the rusting gate.

'Aye, grand day. Are you here for long, sir?'

'A few days of business and a few more of pleasure, I should think,' Alexander answered with a swift smile, clasping the man on the shoulder as he stepped through the gate. 'Is Lady Ravensworth at home?'

'Don't rightly know,' he wheezed. 'I'll ask the missus, she knows it all. If the cat sneezes in the castle kitchens she's the first to hear it. Mrs Bates!'

A tiny woman with an old-fashioned cap on her head and an even more bent posture than her husband came bowling out of the stone cottage. She looked up sideways and cried in delight at the sight of the tall young man.

'Master Alexander! Come here and let me look at you. By, you're as tall as a tree – and still your mother's fair face, so you have. Such a bonny face!'

Alexander blushed and laughed aloud. 'You knew her better than me. I bow to your superior knowledge.'

'Listen to you,' she crowed, 'words coming off your tongue like a proper gentleman. I don't care what they say about you being a common Pringle, your mam was a Liddell as much as His Lordship's a Liddell – and she was a real lady. I used to fill her bath for her and I can tell you—'

'That's enough, Mrs Bates,' her husband coughed in warning. 'Mr Pringle-Davies doesn't want your life story, just wants to know if Lady Ravensworth is at home.'

Mrs Bates clucked in disapproval. 'No, she is not. Gone somewhere foreign – the Continent or the likes. Left His Lordship to his hunting. Not that he does much of that these days at his age – sleeps a lot in the library so I hear. Eighty-one. Still a handsome man, mind. And there's the old dowager still at Farnacre, and she a hundred! They're long-lived the Liddells – excepting your poor dear mother.'

41

'Mrs Bates!' her husband cautioned her again with one of his embarrassed coughs.

'Thank you for your information,' Alexander said with a reassuring smile, touching the old woman on the arm. 'It's good to see you're still keeping a watchful eye on the place as ever, Mrs Bates. Just like you did when I was a boy.'

She clung on to him. 'Always enjoyed your visits, Master Alexander. Not the same without children about the castle – you were always the liveliest, a right little handful, but a loving nature. Didn't I always say that, Mr Bates? A loving nature. Now there's no children – just parties and balls and the like when the mistress is at home. Crying shame His Lordship has no son and heir—'

'Mrs Bates!' Mr Bates growled.

Alexander tipped his hat at them both, waved a cheery goodbye and strode off up the track before Mrs Bates could waylay him with offers of tea and a further hour of gossip. She had been equally garrulous as a housemaid, easily distracted from her work when he had stayed at the castle as a boy. The orphan. 'That poor bairn', as he had often overheard the staff describing him within earshot.

Nobody had known quite what to make of him, Alexander thought with familiar discomfort. He was a Liddell through his mother. But she had eloped with a handsome Scots coachman, been outcast and then died, leaving the itinerant Pringle with a small boy on his hands. His father had handed him straight back to the Liddells and disappeared out of his life too.

Alexander did not like to remember the painful, confusing years of being tossed around his mother's family like a hot coal that no one wanted to handle. He had felt like one of the gentry, but the world had looked on him otherwise. He was classed as a wild Pringle and had played up to their disapproval, behaving as badly as he knew how. Only the intervention of His Lordship's coal agent, Jeremiah Davies, had saved Alexander from his nomadic life and given him a home and education. Widowed and childless, the lonely businessman had offered to take on the troublesome boy as his own.

As Alexander walked on the soft drive, breathing in the scent of pine needles and freshly cut logs, he felt a stirring of the old resentment. Then he mocked himself for his self-pity. He might be lumbered with the names of Pringle and Davies – half wayward Scot, half upright man of business – but he felt in his bones he was an aristocrat.

'I am a Liddell!' he cried at the trees and waved his walking cane at a pheasant that flapped in alarm across his path. He laughed his quick, deep-throated laugh.

That was why he had the audacity to turn up at Ravensworth and expect Lord Ravensworth, his distant cousin, to offer him hospitality. He would not stay at the local inn like any ordinary commission agent or merchant. It was his birthright to stay in a place like Ravensworth. The earl was an amiable, generous man who had shown him kindness as a boy.

Yet once he was in the care of Davies, relations with the Liddells had cooled, for it was socially awkward to have the adopted son of an employee holidaying at Ravensworth. Once more he had been rebuffed. Then the earl's wife had died and to family surprise, Lord Ravensworth, at the age of seventy-one, had got remarried to a vivacious widow, who had breathed new life into the mournful estate and set little store by social convention.

Alexander smiled at the thought of the handsome middle-aged widow Emma Sophia, who so relished life. She loved

43

entertaining, lavish dinners, dances, picnics, hunts and a houseful of guests. She loved her new husband and his magnificent Gothic castle and she loved to fill it with lively young women and attractive young men who shared her appetite for society.

When Alexander had first come on business on behalf of his adoptive father, Lady Ravensworth had insisted he stay on for a few days' riding. The few days had turned into a fortnight, until Jeremiah had called him home to the south of the county and reprimanded him for outstaying his welcome. But Jeremiah was ageing and Alexander was quick to take up offers of travel on his behalf. On several occasions he had done business on behalf of the estate and the Liddells' extensive coal interests. Usually his visits had coincided with a summer carnival or a winter ball to which he had been pressed to stay.

It was too bad if Lady Ravensworth was away from home, Alexander thought ruefully. But he would beg a night or two with His Lordship and maybe there would be news of her return before he had to take ship from Newcastle. He was bound for Scandinavia and the Baltic States to secure contracts for selling coal and arranging return cargoes of timber for use in British mines.

Travelling suited his restless nature and he spent more time roaming the art galleries and museums, and playing cards at the gaming tables of the richer hotels than he ever did haggling over the price of coal with the managers of Swedish iron ore mines. But he dressed and talked like an English gentleman and his mixture of charm and knowledge of the host country brought more success than Jeremiah's honest but dour business talk.

Alexander walked briskly up the steep track, whistling as he went. A group of low-lying stone cottages came into view around the corner, their lintels obscured by honeysuckle. The sweet scent permeated the warm air. A be-capped gardener was helping a young woman out of a cart. Alexander caught a brief glimpse of a fair curved cheek under a large straw hat and a flash of stockinged ankle as she dismounted.

'Afternoon!' he called, touching the brim of his hat with his cane, thinking that the ruddy-faced man looked familiar.

The man pulled at his cap in reply, then a red-haired boy bounded out of the cottage and took his attention.

'Look, look! I've got a duck's egg. Look, Cousin Kate!'

'Let the lass down first, Alfred,' said his father.

Alexander grinned at the boy, whose exuberance reminded him of himself at that age, and walked on.

Kate, holding on to her Uncle Peter's earth-ingrained hand, jumped down from the small cart. She glanced at the walker's retreating back. He was tall and broad-shouldered, in a smart coat and hat, with thick, wavy hair that touched the back of his collar. Strangely, for a gentleman, he was carrying his own suitcase and seemed to have emerged from out of the woods. But in a few long strides he was gone, with a flash of silver-topped cane and a lusty tuneful whistling, and Kate wondered about him no more.

She turned to hug her young cousin.

'Hello, Alfred. Let's see this egg, then.'

The boy dragged her into the cottage, his boots clattering on the stone flags. The kitchen floor was covered in unwashed clothes and the table with dirty dishes. There were trails of dried mud across the rag mats and the range was dull and soot-encrusted. Kate looked around in dismay. Suddenly a pheasant came darting and squawking through the kitchen, making her start in fright. The bird fled out of the open door.

'That's Edward – he's called after the new king,' Alfred explained. 'He comes here for his dinner.'

A ginger cat yawned and stretched on a pile of straw near the hearth and fixed an interested gaze on the retreating bird.

'That's King Rufus,' said Alfred, running over to grab the cat. 'Our George learnt about him in school – said he had ginger hair.'

'What a lot of royalty!' Kate laughed. 'Didn't know I'd be living with all these kings.'

'I'll have to be gettin' back to work,' Peter said, his look harassed. 'George'll be back soon to help. Your aunt's in there.' He nodded towards a closed door. 'Make yourself at home.'

He raced out of the cottage like the pheasant, leaving her basket by the door.

'Ta for the lift, Uncle Peter,' Kate called after him, but he was gone.

Alfred was quite absorbed stroking the cat, but the creature objected to being grappled in his small arms and leapt down, padding quickly after the others.

Kate untied her hat and then wondered in all the mess where to put it. Holding on to it she said, 'Well, shall we go and tell your mam I'm here?'

'Yes!' Alfred cried, having already forgotten about the duck's egg. He ran to the closed door, jumped at the latch and flung it open. 'Mammy! Kate's here. Wake up, Mam!'

Kate stepped into the bedroom and peered into the gloom. 'Aunt Lizzie?'

A sneeze erupted from the depths of the high bed next to the tiny casement window. 'Kate? Is that you, hinny? Come closer.' Her voice was laden with cold.

Alfred had already scrambled on to the bed. 'Aye, it's Cousin Kate.'

'Ow, mind me leg!' Lizzie cried in pain.

Kate went quickly to her aunt's side, taking hold of her hand. 'How are you, Aunt Lizzie? We've all been worried – Mam especially.'

'Mammy's leg looks like a tree trunk, that's what me da says,' Alfred chirped.

Lizzie groaned in frustration. 'I cannot move out of bed without Peter's help. And now I've caught a cold. I was that worried about what to do until we got your note.' She gave a weak squeeze of her clammy hand.

'You don't have to worry,' Kate assured. 'I can stay as long as you need me.'

'This place is like a pigsty since I took to me bed.'

'Don't fret. I'll get it put right,' Kate smiled.

'You're a good lass,' Lizzie coughed.

'Haway, Alfred,' Kate said, pulling her young cousin off his mother, 'you said you'd show me that duck's egg.'

At the sudden reminder Alfred scrambled to the edge of the bed and slid off. He dashed out ahead of Kate.

'I'll bring you a cup of tea in a minute.' Her aunt sneezed in reply and Kate closed the door.

She moved around the unfamiliar kitchen, trying to bring a measure of order to the chaos, tidying and sweeping and trying not to step on Alfred's collection of eggs and berries and feathers. She cleared the grimy clothes into a pile by the back door and searched the pantry for something to make for tea. At least that seemed well stocked, with baskets of carrots, beans and eggs, a wooden platter of butter, earthenware jars of sugar and flour and a china pail half full of milk. Tomorrow she would tackle the washing and scrub the stone floors.

George, a stocky boy of twelve, returned, eyeing her cautiously from the open front door. He was bashful and sandy-haired like his father, and replied to her questions with grunts. Alfred interpreted for his older brother.

'He walks the long way back from school looking for birds' eggs. He got me this,' the small boy said, cradling the duck egg in his warm, dirty hands. 'George won't eat them, but he likes pigeon pie. And he's got a sweet tooth. Likes Mam's fruit pies best.'

'Shurr-up,' George growled in embarrassment and aimed a boot at his brother's leg.

Alfred squealed and kicked back. George shoved him, knocking the duck egg from his hands. It splattered over the stone floor. Alfred howled and flew at his older brother, kicking and punching.

Kate intervened, grabbing Alfred round the waist and pushing George away. She was strong-armed and used to separating Jack and Mary from fighting. She stood between them.

'Stop it! I'll have no such carry-on while I'm in charge.'

George scowled. 'You're not me mam.'

'No I'm not.' Kate was sharp. 'Your poor mam is lying in there trying to sleep. And while she's laid up, you've got me. So you can like it or lump it. Now start clearing up that mess you've made.' She turned to Alfred, who was crying. 'George'll find you another one, kiddar. You get a cloth and help an' all.'

They set about it in sullen silence while Kate got on with tea. By the time Peter came home, they were sat at a cleared table, their hands scrubbed and ready to eat. George had not uttered another word to her, but Alfred could not remain silent for more than a minute and was chattering about frogs and dung beetles.

'See you're settling in just grand.' Peter's sunburnt face smiled in relief. He wolfed down his tea, grabbed his cap and headed out the door once more. George licked his fingers, pushed back his chair and followed without a word.

She looked at Alfred. 'Where have they gone?'

'To put the garden to bed,' he said simply.

'Oh. How do they do that?'

Alfred considered this a moment. 'They water the plants and shut the hothouse windows.'

'Does that take long?'

'Till it's dark. Sometimes I'm asleep. Can I gan out now?'

'Aye, but not far else I won't know where to find you.'

Kate cleared the table and heated up water to wash the dishes. She found a tin tub and scrubbed them in front of the fire, leaving them to drain on the hearth. For a while she went into the bedroom and sat with her aunt, giving her news from the family and Jarrow. But Lizzie tired quickly and she made her comfortable for the night.

Taking out the chamber pot to empty in the midden, Kate had a yearning to explore her new surroundings in the mellow evening light. But she knew it would be foolish to wander off not knowing her way. Besides, she had Alfred and Lizzie to look after. That was why she was here.

Reluctantly she went in search of the young boy, calling him in for the night. She found him swinging from a low branch of a sycamore tree, his dirty impish face glowing in the twilight. For a moment she was reminded of Jack and had a brief pang of homesickness. But it did not last.

Tonight she would be bedding down on a borrowed truckle bed by the kitchen fire with a cat and a pheasant for company. There would be no Mary digging her in the back with her elbows, or the fear of Father's volatile moods. She would fall asleep knowing she was safe from sudden drunken shouting in the night or being roused from bed to sing for her drink-maddened stepfather.

'Haway, it's time for bed.' She smiled up at Alfred and held out her arms. 'Tomorrow you can show me all your hiding places.'

The small boy allowed himself to be lifted down.

'Are you going to stay for ever, Cousin Kate?'

'Not for ever.'

'More than a week?'

'Aye, more than a week.'

'Good,' he said, then yawned, his breath warm on her neck. 'I like you.'

She kissed his unkempt mop of curls. 'I like you an' all,' she smiled and carried him home.

Chapter 5

To Alexander's delight, Lady Ravensworth returned from the South of France the following week.

'It's far too hot there now and I didn't want to miss the Coronation celebrations,' she told her dinner guests.

'They say that won't be until August,' Alexander said.

'We'll have a grand ball and invite the whole county,' she enthused. 'You will stay, won't you?' She put a bejewelled hand on his arm.

'I have business abroad.' Alexander gave a shrug of apology.

'Oh, you must stay! Henry, tell him he must,' she called down the long gleaming table to her husband.

'What was that?'

She raised her voice almost to a shout. 'Tell Alex that he can't leave till after the Coronation ball.'

'What ball?'

'The one we're going to have for the King.'

'Kin?'

'Oh, never mind.' Emma waved her hand with a laugh and turned back to Alexander. 'You'll just have to delay your boring old business trip. It's your patriotic duty to stay. You simply can't leave the country at a time like this.'

'Not even for the Riviera?' Alexander teased.

'I came back, didn't I?' She pouted in mock offence.

'To everyone's delight,' he smiled.

She laughed and patted his hand. 'You are a terrible charmer. It's time I put my mind to finding you a wife.'

Alexander rolled his eyes. 'My father thinks of nothing else. He's scouring the North of England for someone suitable.'

'Oh, how depressing. You don't want suitable. You want someone to match your good looks and your tastes in life. Otherwise you'll be bored in a year.' She raised her voice again. 'Isn't that right, Henry? Alex must marry for love.'

'Alexander's getting married? Do we know her?'

'No, we have to find her first!' Emma laughed. She rose. It was the signal for the other women to retire to the drawing room and leave the men to their port.

Alexander gave a wistful look at the departing group, wishing he could carry on his flirtatious conversation with Lady Ravensworth and her friends rather than talk business or hunting with his aged cousin. But he was content to while away the evening drinking the dark port out of crystal glass in the glittering candlelight of the large dining room with its gilt-edged portraits of his ancestors.

He could string out his business at the estate and the surrounding mines for a couple more weeks and delay his voyage until mid-August. There was a weekly steamer from Newcastle to Gothenburg and he could accomplish his business in Sweden and elsewhere long before the Baltic ports became ice-bound.

In the meantime he would enjoy riding out among the Durham hills and roaming the estate and beyond with his sketch book and pencils. It amused Lady Ravensworth to see his cartoons of her neighbours and his drawings of life around the area. Men supping beer in a tap room, children playing with hoops, girls in summer bonnets. That was what intrigued and entertained her. A memory of a young woman stepping out of a cart with a flash of stockinged leg flitted through his mind. Lady Ravensworth would approve of that.

At home, his widowed father thought nothing of his artistic efforts, believing them a waste of productive time.

'You're a man of business,' he would protest. 'You'll never make a living from paper and paints. Leave that to artists and those leisured folk with nothing better to do.'

But Alexander yearned to be among the leisured; it was in his blood. He daydreamt of being an artist, pictured himself as a highborn aristocrat doing the Grand Tour through Europe and the Levant, painting as he went. Or maybe he would sail to some exotic paradise like Gauguin, live by the warm seas and paint the native people in vivid colours.

After an hour, the men rejoined the women at the far end of the vast drawing room. They were gathered around an elaborately carved fireplace in which a log fire blazed even on this warm summer's evening. Alexander strolled to one of the long windows and gazed out on to the wide terrace and the sweep of lawns beyond. The last blush of dying sun lit the high tops of the beech trees, which cast bulky shadows across the ornamental gardens.

How he loved being here! In his boyhood it had been a place of enchantment. He had distant memories of being brought here as a small child from smoky, dirty Tyneside, where he was living with Liddell cousins after his mother had died. He had kicked and screamed and run away at the end of the visit rather than be taken back to the dingy, damp rectory that was his temporary home.

'Would you like a breath of air?' Lady Ravensworth broke into his reverie.

'If you would come with me,' he smiled.

She took his arm. 'We shall inspect the gardens. Anyone else want to come?'

But the other guests, elderly friends of Sir Henry, took this as their cue to say farewells and call for their carriages, after which their host retired to bed.

Out in the twilight, the air was still warm and heavy with the scent of roses and mown grass. Alexander and his hostess strolled to the end of the terrace and took the steps down towards the walled garden and the path that meandered all the way to the boating lake. Emma kept him entertained with witty descriptions of her French travels and gossip about her fellow travellers.

'And what's been happening here in my absence?' she asked.

'I haven't been to Ravensworth since the turn of the year. Father has kept me busy in the south of the county. Now I'm to journey on to Sweden. So I'm quite useless in providing you with the local gossip, I'm afraid.'

'Poor boy. I think your father is trying to keep you away from us.'

Alexander grunted. 'He'd certainly rather see me chained to his office desk.'

They stopped by the lake and gazed into its purple depths.

'And what is it about Ravensworth that so concerns Mr Davies?' she asked with a note of laughter in her voice.

He looked down at her delicate face, the hair just beginning to grey at the temples, the lines around her blue eyes softened by shadow. If she had been twenty years younger . . .

'Too many temptations,' he answered in a low voice. 'He's jealous that I prefer to be here than anywhere else.'

She reached out and touched his face with a gloved hand. Such a strong face, without an old man's soft jowls, she thought. And those restless tawny eyes. She suspected a deep passion lay behind his guarded look. He had been a tempestuous small boy, by all accounts.

Alexander slipped his hand up to hers. He gripped it in his warm hold and kissed her scented gloved palm.

Quickly Emma withdrew her hand. What was she thinking of? She must not be tempted.

'You are a sweet boy,' she laughed, and drew away. 'But it just wouldn't do, would it?'

Alexander flushed. 'I didn't mean to—'

'No, no,' she hushed him, 'we'll blame it on too much wine at dinner and the smell of a summer's night.' She linked arms and led him back up the path. 'Did you know that we're growing oranges in the hothouses now? And the peaches this year are delicious – just like French ones. Come, let me show you.'

Alexander cursed himself for his impetuous kiss. The last thing he wanted was to endanger his position with his relations. But she seemed to think it of no account, as if it were the act of some foolish youth. This rankled too.

They mounted the steps once more and rounded the walled garden to the sheltered glasshouses. It was almost dark and Alexander held her arm to stop her tripping on the uneven flagstones. As they approached, a light became visible from inside. A youth was holding aloft a lantern while a thick-set gardener worked a pulley to close the high windows. They were illuminated behind the glass like players on a stage.

Then a young woman carrying a small boy in her arms stepped into the light. Her cheeks were flushed from the heat of the glasshouse and her mass of brown hair was escaping its pins. She was smiling at the others, saying something then laughing, kissing the top of the sleepy boy's head. It was a charming domestic picture, Alexander thought with a stab of envy. Once again he felt the outsider, put in his place by the unreachable woman at his side and just as much excluded from the simple family scene in front. He belonged to neither, had never been part of such a family.

'We've come just in time,' Lady Ravensworth said, quite unaware of his resentment, steering him forward through the open door.

A blanket of warm air hit them and a delicious heady scent of fruit: spicy orange mingled with the soft fragrance of peach. The gardener turned to them and pulled off his cap, flustered by their arrival.

'Ma'am,' he mumbled. Alexander suddenly remembered him, or rather he was struck by the likeness to his son.

'It's Peter Bain, isn't it?' he exclaimed. 'You used to chase after me for climbing the apple trees!'

The man gawped at him a moment, then realisation dawned. 'It's Master Alex! How do you do, sir?'

Alexander stepped forward and wrung him by the hand. 'Very well. And you?'

'Champion, sir,' he blushed.

'I can tell this is your son, Peter; he's your double.' Alexander grinned at the older boy. 'Hope you don't give your father as much trouble as I did when I was your age. Threatened to make a scarecrow out of me if I didn't stop trampling over his flowerbeds.'

'No, sir!' Peter protested. 'You were no trouble.'

'I can just imagine what a naughty boy he was,' Lady Ravensworth intervened with a laugh. 'You don't have to worry. Now I just wanted to let Mr Pringle-Davies pick one of your wonderful peaches.'

'Please, allow me to show you, ma'am.' Peter took the lantern from George and held it aloft. 'Follow me, Master – er – Mr Pringle-Davies.'

He led them to the far end of the hothouse, to a row of trees planted in huge wooden barrels, where the scent of sweet fruit was overpowering. Peter plucked a ripe peach and handed it to Alexander.

Alexander at once bit into the soft furry skin. Juice dribbled down his chin as he ate.

'Well, what do you think?' Lady Ravensworth demanded. 'Aren't they the best peaches outside of France?'

'Umm,' Alexander agreed, wiping his chin and licking his fingers, 'and as heavenly as their owner.'

She laughed. 'You are incorrigible!'

They thanked the gardener and turned to leave. Peter led them back with the lantern held high.

'George will see you back to the house with the lamp, ma'am,' he insisted.

'Thank you,' Lady Ravensworth accepted, slipping her arm once more through Alexander's.

'What about you, Peter?' Alexander turned to ask, aware of the shadowed figure of the girl and her young bundle standing behind the gardener. The young boy was stirring and fretting about the dark. The girl hushed him in a soft voice, but Alexander could not make out her face.

'We know these paths blindfolded, sir, and George will catch us up with the lamp.'

So Alexander nodded at them and bade good night.

Kate watched the handsome couple disappear arm in arm into the dark towards the black towering bulk of the castle.

'Was that Her Ladyship?' she gasped.

'Aye,' Peter nodded. 'Lady Ravensworth likes her fancy fruits.'

'And the man?' Kate asked. 'Was he one of the family?'

'Distantly.' Peter pulled the door shut behind them as if that was all there was to say. But Kate wanted to hear more.

'But you knew him?'

'Aye. Used to stay here as a boy now and then – troublesome as a wild pony, but a canny lad with it.'

'He seemed very friendly with Lady Ravensworth,' she ventured.

'Aye,' Peter grunted, 'she has many admirers.'

Alfred started whimpering that he wanted his bed. He was growing too heavy for Kate to hold.

'Can you walk, kiddar? It's not far.'

'I'll take the lad,' Peter said, holding out stout arms.

They walked home in silence, George catching them up where the path joined the back drive.

'Did they say anything else to you?' Kate asked.

George shook his head. 'But the man gave me sixpence,' he said with a note of glee.

'Did he? That's canny!' Kate exclaimed. But the others simply nodded and said no more.

That night, Kate lay on her narrow truckle bed, gazing through the casement window at a dusting of stars above the black woods and thought about how close she had stood to Lady Ravensworth in her shimmering evening dress. And the tall gentleman with the mane of hair that glinted like bronze in the lamplight. His deep voice had sent a thrill through her as she stood mute and overawed. She could have listened to him speak all night. If only she had managed to see his face more clearly. But it had been largely in shadow as he stood taller than George's lantern. Still, it was this face, half-shadowed and mysterious, that filled her thoughts as she drifted off to sleep in the quiet cottage.

Alexander stood at the open mullioned window of his bedroom, high in the east tower, and gazed out at the blackness. The night was warm and muggy, with few stars glinting above the solid mass of trees. He heard the haunting cry of foxes from far off and saw an owl flap out of the woods and swoop out of sight. It was too stuffy in this small high room to sleep. He had a mad notion to rush to the stables, saddle up and ride out on to the moors where the air would be cooler. But he curbed the desire. He must not cause his cousin Henry any embarrassment.

Alexander flushed to think of how close he had come to losing his head and kissing Lady Ravensworth by the tranquil lake. She was old enough to be his mother, yet she dazzled him with her looks and wit and experience. He felt restless, the taste of sweet peach still on his lips. Leaning his head on the cool glass pane, he tried to rid himself of thoughts of her.

That was when the memory of the silent young woman in the hothouse came back to him. She had been chatting and laughing before their arrival, then fallen into the shadows at their approach. He had the impression of rounded pink cheeks, soft as peaches, and tumbling hair, but nothing more.

Quickly, he turned and strode across the room to the table by his bedside and pulled a piece of paper under the pool of lamplight. He sketched swiftly, a girl's oval face bending over a small boy's. Something about the drawing, the curve of the cheek, reminded him of something else. Suddenly it came back to him. A young woman with a large straw hat stepping down from a cart. It had been Peter holding the pony. And the small boy had rushed from the cottage in greeting. A visitor, not his mother or sister, then, Alexander mused. He wished he had taken a closer look at the girl this evening. He tried to conjure up her face but it eluded him.

He turned over the paper and started again. A half-hidden face under a rim of hat, the hint of a smile. A boy running towards a cart. And a black woollen stocking showing beneath a hitched skirt, a shapely ankle. Underneath he gave it the title *The Mystery Girl*.

He smiled and lay down on the bed. Tomorrow he would go sketching, capturing the folk of Ravensworth going about their work. The place where he felt most at ease, among the people with whom he felt most at home.

Chapter 6

At the beginning of August, Kate was taken on at Farnacre Hall, the dower house on the estate, as a laundry maid. With Kate's help around the house and fussing attention, Aunt Lizzie was recovering swiftly and was now able to sit in the doorway of the cottage, mending clothes or peeling vegetables. Peter had made his wife a pair of walking sticks to help her move around, and she was no longer so dependent on Kate to nurse her or tend to the household chores.

But none of the family wanted the lively girl to return home to Jarrow so soon. Lizzie enjoyed her company, Alfred doted on his cousin and even George now answered her teasing questions with bashful mumbles. It was he who came home with the news that the housekeeper at Farnacre Hall was looking for extra help in the laundry. The earl's ancient mother, Horatia, Lady Ravensworth, who lived there, was increasingly frail and recently bed-bound. The chores in the laundry were increasing.

'Two lasses have up and left for the town,' George said. 'Say the pay's better.'

'Aye, and the dirt's thicker,' Lizzie snorted. 'Good luck to them. I wouldn't gan back for all the tea in China.'

'Have they taken on anyone else yet?' Kate asked eagerly. 'I'm used to that sort of work. Mam had me scrubbing butcher's aprons when I was still too small to see over the side of the poss tub!'

'You get yourself down there the morrow, hinny,' her aunt encouraged.

Kate went and had little trouble persuading the housekeeper of her willingness to work hard. Miss Peters, who had worked for the dowager all her life, was herself old and deaf and at a loss as to how to keep her young staff. Kate held herself erect and told her she had worked for the best in South Shields. She gave her name as Fawcett, her father's name, rather than her stepfather's Irish name of McMullen. Kate determined to start a new life here, well away from John McMullen's influence. Pleased with the look of her, Miss Peters started the Tyneside girl the next day at the rambling, ivy-covered manor house that nestled in a hollow in the woods, halfway up the castle drive.

The laundry room was cramped and hot. It was little bigger than the wash houses she'd worked in back in South Shields, and had none of the labour-saving devices that they used in the castle, Suky, the other laundry maid, was quick to tell her.

'Up at the big house they've got all these mangles and rollers all in one,' the young girl said as she and Kate hand-wrung a linen sheet between them over a stone trough. 'Me cousin Olive works there – head housemaid's a real dragon, but the place is spotless.'

They carried the sheets out to the moss-covered courtyard and threw them on to the washing lines.

'And they've got all these drying rooms – big wooden racks to put all the clothes on – warm as toast.' Suky pulled her black hair away from her damp forehead and blew out her cheeks.

Kate soon learnt that nothing at Farnacre Hall could compare with the standards at the castle. Every chore they did, Suky told her how much worse off they were working at the old manor house.

'None of this fiddling about with hot coals in these old box irons,' she grumbled. 'Always burning me fingers, I am. No, Olive says there's this great big iron stove they keep hot all the time – with eight irons on it all ready and waiting. And you know what they're talking of getting? Electric ones!'

Kate looked up over her mound of ironing. 'Electric irons? How do they work?'

'I don't know exactly, but Olive says they won't even need to stoke the stove. You stick a bit rope in the wall and they heat up, just like magic.'

Kate was dubious. 'Well, it's not going to happen here. Her Ladyship likes her oil lamps and her coal fires – she's not going to try anything fancy like electric.' She held up a piece of lace and grinned with satisfaction at the way she had mastered the crimping iron.

'Aye, we're lucky to have water in the house,' Suky grumbled, then mimicked the querulous voice of their ancient employer. 'In my day, young gels were happy to walk miles to draw water from the well.'

Kate snorted with laughter as Suky hobbled around the laundry room wagging her finger.

The cook, Mrs Benson, bellowed through the door from the kitchen, 'Stop larking on, or we'll have Miss Peters down here causing a riot!'

The girls stifled their sniggering. 'Aye,' Kate whispered, 'she'll give us a blast of her ear trumpet.'

'Boer War could break out down here and Miss P wouldn't hear it,' Suky muttered, and Kate burst out laughing again.

'Kate Fawcett, stop that noise!' Cook bellowed to no avail. She was a kind woman and Kate knew her reprimands were half-hearted. Besides, Kate was a hard worker and finished her jobs quicker than any of the other girls. Sometimes Cook would set her to small tasks in the kitchen, which she carried out willingly. The older woman quickly came to accept that Kate could not work in silence. If she wasn't chatting and laughing, she was singing songs. With sighs of resignation, Cook let her be.

Kate was happy. The work at Farnacre was hard and physical, but she felt full of energy since coming to Ravensworth, and relished her new life. She enjoyed Suky's droll company and Cook's fussing kindness, and she returned home to a friendly welcome at the gardener's cottage where she regaled them with the tales of the day.

Best of all, in the evening, she liked to walk around the vast gardens with Uncle Peter and the boys, helping him with fruit picking and watering, making the most of the dying daylight. Her uncle was only one of five gardeners, but he had a natural touch with fruit and salads, and his special concern was the orchards and hothouses. Kate touched and tasted fruits she had never seen before: redcurrants, gooseberries and apricots. The first crop of pears were ready, growing up the side of sheltered brick walls kept warm by coal stoves.

Peter showed her the dark heated forcing houses where chicory, asparagus and new potatoes were brought on quickly. Kate loved the warm earthy smell of the sheds and marvelled at the huge endless trenches of food: lettuce, radishes and fennel, rhubarb, sweet parsley and artichokes, exotic names and bitter-sweet tastes that made her tongue tingle.

Best of all she liked to breathe in the hot, honeyed air of the glasshouses where the peaches and melons grew. For it

64

was here that she had first seen the mysterious gentleman friend of Lady Ravensworth biting into the flesh of a peach, juice running down his strong jaw. His long hair had glinted in the lantern light and his deep voice had made her insides flutter. He reminded her of a lion, a picture in a scripture book from school that had fascinated her as a child.

She longed for another sight of the man that her uncle had called Master Alex and this was the unspoken reason for her keenness to help in the gardens each evening. But she had not seen him in his evening finery since that night. Once, when carrying a basket of cherries to Cook at the hall, she had glimpsed a man in the distance with a similar stance. He was watching some field workers bending to their task and recording something in a book. Kate had strained to see if it could be the same man, but decided it could not. What would a relation of the Liddells be doing showing such interest in the work of common labourers?

It was a disappointment not to see the man again; it had become almost like a game to go out in the evening hoping to spy him. Most likely he had long gone from the castle, important business having taken him elsewhere. She laughed at her own fanciful notion that he would even notice her should she happen upon him again.

Alexander tossed another fretful letter from his father on to the unlit fire in his garret room and strode to the door. It was the usual plea to finish his business at Ravensworth and set sail for Scandinavia. But this time Jeremiah Davies was threatening to come himself to the castle and prise him out. Making for the stables, Alexander knew his time here was running out. While Lord and Lady Ravensworth were happy to indulge him, his cousin would pack him off quickly if he thought the young man's continued presence was causing harm to his business interests. The earl seemed not to notice his cousin's adoration of Lady Ravensworth or if so, tolerated it as a young man's calf love.

Alexander took the saddled horse that the yawning stable boy had made ready for his usual early morning ride, almost curt in his annoyance. That was the best he could ever expect – to be tolerated by his elders and betters. He could never lay claim to the riches of Ravensworth, which he felt deeply should be his. Not that he wanted the trappings of wealth – he could live as simply as any man – but he yearned to belong. He felt a part of its wooded hills, its dark earth and seams of coal. He felt the pull of generations of northcountrymen who had tilled its soil and defended the ancient fortress whose medieval towers still stood behind the grand Victorian façade.

Alexander urged his horse into a trot. Outside the high protective walls he quickly left the road and made for the moors above the sheltering trees and swathes of mist. In the hazy Tyne valley, the early morning light bounced off the steel ribbon of river and the far away clusters of dockland and smoking chimney stacks.

As he cantered past small farms and pit villages clinging to the edge of the escarpment, he thought once more of his early days in this rugged land that had shaped the man he was. For a short, happy time he had lived with his cousin Edward, the rector of Jarrow, and his kind Scots wife, Christina. How he had adored his Uncle Edward! He had dogged his heels around the grimy streets of the riverside town, absorbing the smells of the docks and gasworks, in awe of the becapped gangs of dockers who streamed past the rector's cocoa stall at break of day.

His cousin Edward had been a highborn Liddell but had chosen to dedicate himself to improving conditions for the poorest in Jarrow. Alexander appreciated now the enormous sacrifice of the young couple, who could have taken an easy living in the south of England instead. Yet at the time Alexander thought nothing out of the ordinary about living in a blackened rectory beside foul-smelling effluent, and visiting houses without running water where children played barefoot in the dusty lanes.

'Oh, Uncle Edward!' Alexander cried aloud to the pearly sky. 'You were a fool!'

Alexander kicked his horse into a gallop across the heathery tracks. His cousin's task of making life better for the poor had been an impossible one. His health had broken down and they had all had to leave. With Edward no longer able to support him, Alexander had been passed on to yet another distant relation who had made it plain what a burden he was, so he had run away from the boarding school in which he had been dumped.

He had tried to find his way back north, to search for his beloved Uncle Edward, but in vain. Edward and Christina had gone abroad to seek a healthier climate, never to return to Jarrow. Their hinted promise of offering him a permanent home had been destroyed along with their health. Childless themselves, they would have been the perfect parents. Instead they left him with nothing, except an abiding memory of being taken to Ravensworth on a hot summer's day. That, and a strong sense of belonging among the people here.

Alexander rode until he was exhausted and had rid his head of angry thoughts about his rootless childhood. He imagined what Jeremiah would have to say about such reckless riding. 'Careful, young man, or you'll bring on one of those nosebleeds! God gave you a brain for commerce, not a constitution for the saddle.'

Alexander laughed off such concerns and turned for home. He would grasp life and live it to the full. The day after tomorrow was the ball for King Edward VII's delayed coronation. He would stay for that and then travel on.

Down in the woods again, the early morning mist still hung damp among the lush leaves as he rode up the back drive. He slowed to a trot, breathing in the sweet clear air, his chest heaving hard from the exertion. Round the bend the first shaft of strong sunlight was breaking through the trees, dazzling the dew-soaked track ahead.

In the sudden glare, he did not see the girl on the path till the last moment. He saw a flash of pale blue skirt and a startled face as she jumped clear. A basket flew from her hands and raspberries splattered around them, blood-red. Alexander reined in his horse at once, wheeling it round.

Below him, a young woman stared up in astonishment. Her eyes looked huge and the same startling blue as her dress. Her thick brown hair was tied back but uncovered, her cheeks flushed and mouth open wide as if she would give him a piece of her mind. But she said nothing, just dropped to her knees and attempted to scrape the fallen berries back into her basket.

Alexander dismounted and went to help.

'I'm sorry,' he gasped, touching her shoulder. She looked up in alarm.

'No, sir, it was me,' she answered in a strong voice that belied her slight frame.

'Let me help.'

'No, you mustn't.'

But he ignored her and began scooping handfuls of raspberries back into the basket. Unable to resist, he popped one into his mouth.

'My favourite fruit. They grow the best raspberries at Ravensworth, don't you think?'

She glanced up and eyed him from under thick dark lashes. Was there a hint of merriment in that intent blue gaze? he wondered.

'So me Uncle Peter says. Not tried them meself – not straight from the bush. Me aunt says too much raw fruit can bring on summer fever. They're grand baked in a pie, mind.' She suddenly blushed as if she'd said too much.

Alexander was entranced. 'You mean to say you've never eaten a raspberry straight from the basket?' She shook her head. He laughed. 'Well, you must. Go on, try one.' He picked one out and offered it.

She regarded him with suspicion and shook her head again.

'I promise you it won't make you delirious,' he grinned, pushing it towards her lips.

She pulled away, then changed her mind and opened her mouth. Alexander placed the berry on the tip of her tongue and watched her eat. She frowned in concentration and licked her lips. She had a generous, full mouth, he noticed.

Suddenly she smiled and her slim oval face lit up like a cat's in the sun. Alexander felt a jolt in his guts.

'Aye, taste's canny,' she agreed. They exchanged a long look, each assessing the other, then she looked away. She picked up her basket, straightened and smoothed out her skirt.

'Thank you, sir.' She bobbed. 'Must be off.'

Alexander stood and watched her dart away up the track. She ran swiftly but with uneven steps like a young colt with a stone in its hoof. He smiled in amusement at finding a pretty country girl who had never tasted a fresh raspberry. Where had she come from and where was she going? As she disappeared into the morning mist, he felt a stab of frustration that she had eluded him without him finding out more. Ridiculous as it seemed, he was disappointed that she was gone.

Chapter 7

Kate arrived at Farnacre Hall breathless and heart still hammering. She skidded across the dewy cobbles into the kitchen and almost collided with Cook.

'Watch yourself! You would think His Lordship's hunting dogs were after you.'

'Sorry,' Kate panted, dumping down her basket. 'Berries from me uncle – picked them last night.'

Cook eyed the battered mound of raspberries. 'They're no good for serving up at table. Have to hide them in a crumble.' She saw Kate's dashed expression. 'Still, that's how the dowager likes them – mushy and easy to eat.'

Kate smiled in relief and skipped off to the laundry room where Suky joined her. Her friend soon noticed how she worked with only half a mind on the job.

'Penny for your thoughts.'

Kate stopped humming and looked up from the steaming copper cauldron where she was stirring boiling linen.

'What?'

'You haven't been listening to a word I've said half the morning,' Suky said in exasperation. 'Are you not interested in the dance then?'

'What dance?' Kate asked, forcing herself back to the present. Her mind still reeled from the encounter with the rider.

'The servants' dance up at the castle! The one I've been telling you about.'

'At the castle?'

'Aye! On Friday night – after the nobs have had their ball on Thursday. There's a dance in the servants' hall. Always plenty to eat and drink up there. And think of all those footmen!'

'Umm . . .' Kate mused, though it was no footman that preoccupied her. All she could think of was the tall stranger with the tousled flaming hair appearing out of the mist on the sweating horse. She had not heard the faint drumming of hoofs on the soft ground until the black horse had broken from the trees into the small clearing. Startled, she had sprung out of the way just in time, dropping her basket in alarm.

But far from just riding on with a nod of apology, the man had dismounted at once and come to her assistance. It was then she had seen his face in full – long and lean with a smooth jaw and a generous, sensual mouth. His keen eyes had looked on her with amusement as she scrambled for the fallen fruit. He had laughed at her for not tasting fresh raspberries. How simple and unsophisticated she must have seemed!

Yet how her heart had pounded as he reached forward and pressed a berry to her lips, his fingers stained red with the juice. She could still taste the tangy sweetness of the fruit on her tongue and it conjured up the man's bold dark-eyed look. She knew it must be Master Alex, friend of Lady Ravensworth. He had the same auburn glint in his unruly hair and deep amused tone in his voice that she had witnessed in the hothouse.

'What you staring at?' Suky demanded. 'You're acting all strange this morning. You got a secret or some'at?'

Kate tried to hide a smile. 'No, course not.' No use confiding in Suky – she would think it too fanciful to be true. What gentleman would stop his horse to help a serving girl and feed her raspberries? Such things only happened in fairy tales. She hugged the knowledge to herself. Besides, he would have forgotten her already and she was never likely to chance upon him again in such a way. But that didn't stop her hoping for a glimpse of him up at the castle.

'Can we gan to the dance?' Kate asked.

'Aye, that's what I've been telling you! Us lasses from the hall are invited an' all. So do you want to come?'

Kate smiled. 'Aye, course I do.'

Dear Papa, *Alexander wrote to Jeremiah*

I set sail on Saturday for Gothenburg. At Lady Ravensworth's insistence I must stay for the carnival ball on Thursday evening. She has set herself the task of finding me a wife among the genteel women of the county. As this is a cause so dear to your heart, I see it as my duty to stay.

Rest assured, your business is in good hands. I have met with numerous mine managers over the past month and everything is in hand to expand our commercial affairs in Scandinavia and the Baltic. I will write to you from Sweden.

Your obedient son.

Alexander smiled as he signed it. No need to tell his father that he had done all his visits on horseback or that he had spent far more time sketching the pit villagers than talking to their bosses. After the ball he would have one more day of riding up on the moor before the long sea journey. But his father would only fret if he knew, for he stubbornly believed that riding brought on bouts of nosebleeding. But Alexander had not had one of his violent, debilitating bleeds in over six months and felt vigorously healthy.

In defiance, he rode down to the village of Lamesley to post the letter before returning to the castle to prepare for the ball. On the way there and back he looked out for any sign of the young woman with the basket of berries who had almost fallen under his hoofs the day before.

He wondered if she was the same girl he had seen in the hothouse several weeks earlier, the laughing face behind the glass who had inspired a series of pencil drawings. A straw hat, a stockinged ankle, the edge of a smile. He was sure it must be her. She was some relation of the gardener Peter and had been hurrying from the direction of the gardeners' cottages that misty morning.

Alexander was intrigued by her and frustrated not to see her on his ride. His interest in her was that of an artist. He wanted to gaze again on her smooth oval face with the dark arching eyebrows and discover the blue of her eyes. Were they cobalt or Prussian blue? But all he could do was wonder, for there was no sign of her outside the row of cottages. It was as if he had imagined her: a wood sprite conjured up out of the mist, only to vanish as soon as he put out his hand to touch her.

The carnival ball was a spectacular affair. The lords and ladies of the county came in gleaming black carriages up the long drive, lit by flaming torches. One wealthy shipowner caused a stir by arriving noisily in an open-topped autocar and hooting at the peacocks. The children on the estate crept to the edges of the trees to gaze at such a wonder.

The guests came sumptuously dressed as Tudor kings and medieval queens, eighteenth-century nobles and eastern princes. Alexander borrowed a costume from his cousin and went as an Arabian knight in a golden turban and glittering cloak. The dining hall was a shimmer of polished mahogany laden with silver, crystal and patterned china. The long tables were heaped with displays of exotic fruit and towering sculptures of sugar and multicoloured jellies.

Alexander was annoyed to find himself seated far away from Lady Ravensworth, and glanced with envy at the powerful local coal and shipping magnates who were her most favoured guests. Yet he supposed he was lucky to be here at all. If it were not for the kindness of His Lordship and the indulgence of his younger wife he would not even be staying at the castle, let alone be invited to this glittering ball. He and his stepfather were 'trade' and would never fully be able to cross the social chasm between their kind and the aristocratic Liddells, however much Alexander felt he belonged.

So he turned his charm to his female partners at table. One was the wife of a freeman of Newcastle, the other the daughter of a County Durham squire who had farms up on the fells around the lead mines of the west. Polly seemed shy and overawed by the occasion, and Alexander found himself enjoying taking her under his wing, pointing out the various guests he knew and telling her about Ravensworth as if he were one of the family.

'It must have been wonderful to spend all your summer holidays here,' she gasped.

He smiled and shrugged. 'Well, not every summer. Sometimes we went south – stayed with other relations.'

'You're so well-travelled,' she said admiringly. 'The furthest I ever get is to shop in Darlington or Durham. I'd love to go abroad – Paris or somewhere – but Mama won't go on trains and Papa hates to leave the farm for a minute – except to go riding.' She lowered her voice. 'He didn't want to stay here, but Mama refused to travel back tonight.'

She had quite a striking face under the weight of a Marie Antoinette wig, Alexander thought. Open and handsome, rather than pretty, with a sweet trusting smile.

'And do you like to ride, Polly?'

'Oh, I love it!'

'Then we shall ride out tomorrow before breakfast and I'll show you all there is to see around Ravensworth.'

Polly flushed with delight and Alexander turned to pay some attention to the freeman's wife. Later, full of the earl's best claret and half a bottle of port, Alexander threw himself into the dancing in the ballroom. He danced with Polly and several other young women, but managed to book Lady Ravensworth for a waltz late into the evening.

'You've made a conquest, I see,' she teased him.

'You know I'm devoted only to you, Cousin Emma,' he grinned, sweeping her around the crowded floor.

She laughed. 'Polly De Winton hasn't taken her eyes off you all evening. It's no surprise – you look quite dashing and mysterious in these robes.'

'I'm glad you've noticed me.'

'Dear Alex, how could I not? But you must be attentive to young Polly. Her father makes a good living from the dues from lead mining. She's his only heir – and old De Winton keeps a fine stable, so I hear.'

Alexander laughed. 'You are a more incorrigible match-maker than my father.'

'The best,' Emma smiled as the dance ended. 'Now go and work your Pringle charm.'

Alexander felt light-headed from the dance and the attention of his charismatic hostess. Impulsively, he grabbed Polly by the hand and pulled her from the ballroom.

'Fresh air is what we need,' he declared, and led her out onto the cool terrace.

He slipped her arm through his and felt her shiver either from the chill air or excitement. He knew she found him attractive and it fed his desire to be wanted, to be special and loved. It was like a shot of brandy going straight to his head. This was the moment he enjoyed most, the quickening of interest in someone else that stirred his own.

He led her down the stone path away from the terrace and towards the hothouses, telling her she must try the peaches. Polly had never tasted fresh peaches before, only tinned. In the warmth of the darkened glasshouse they shared the fruit, the blaze of lights from the castle spilling down the terraces behind them.

Her angular features were softened in the pale light, her eyes large as they gazed back at him.

'We shouldn't miss the fireworks,' she said, a little unsure.

'No,' Alexander agreed. Then quite without thought, he stooped down and kissed her firmly on the lips. She tasted sweet and sticky and smelt pleasantly of musk. He imagined her hair under the wig to be blonde, long tresses that would cascade about her strong shoulders once released. He slipped an arm around her waist.

She stepped away, her fingers flying to her mouth.

'We shouldn't be here – not on our own,' she said.

He saw her alarm and was quick to apologise. 'Sorry, Polly. I've drunk too much.'

'I want to go back,' she said, avoiding his look.

'Of course.' He had misread the situation again. For an instant he had imagined himself in love. No one else seemed as susceptible as he. He felt foolish.

They retraced their steps in silence back into the blaze of light. Once back among the dancers, Polly brightened and relaxed. But Alexander felt suddenly tired and jaded by drink and romantic disappointment. He excused himself and went off to the smoking room. Hours later he woke in one of the leather chairs, the fire gone out. Stiff and cold he emerged into the corridor, empty save for the glimpse of a maid carrying a bucket of coal up the far stairs.

Early morning light shone through the leaded panes of the gallery. Below they were clearing up the debris of discarded drinks and late night suppers. He had slept through the fireworks and the rest of the ball. Alexander crept up to his bedroom and lay down, his head thumping from the previous night's drinking. But he could not sleep. Instead he stripped off his fancy dress, plunged his face into cold water in the china basin on the washstand and splashed his upper body.

He remembered kissing Polly in the hothouse, and groaned. He hoped she hadn't complained to the bullish-faced De Winton. At least tomorrow he would be gone and no more of an embarrassment to his cousins. Suddenly he yearned to be at sea, with the salt wind in his face and the rocky shore of Sweden on the horizon.

Alexander dressed in riding clothes and strode out to the stables. He would have his final canter out across the moor. To his astonishment, Polly was there, wearing a green riding habit and black hard hat.

'You promised to show me the estate,' she blushed. Her features were sharp in the daylight. He had been wrong about her hair; it was brown under the hat. But her eyes shone with amusement and her look was challenging. His interest quickened.

'Of course,' he smiled and nodded. 'I hoped you would be here.'

'Liar,' she murmured.

He gave her a startled look.

'Come on,' she said, leading her horse over the cobbles. 'Don't want to miss breakfast in an hour.'

Alexander followed, entranced. He had misjudged Polly. There was no sign of the retiring wallflower he had thought to so easily impress the night before. She was obviously far more at ease among horses than high society. They set off at a brisk trot.

Aunt Lizzie helped Kate make ready for the evening, combing out her hair and fixing it up with combs and pins. Lizzie and Peter could not be persuaded to go, her aunt unable to walk the distance and her uncle happier to smoke a pipe at his front door than be made to dance.

'You've lovely skin, our Kate,' Lizzie marvelled, stroking the softness of her cheek. 'You've your da's fair face.'

Kate felt a stab of affection for her aunt for mentioning her long-dead father. Her own mother never talked of him for fear of riling John McMullen's jealousy. It was as if William Fawcett had never been. But now, by insisting on taking his name, Kate had reinvented herself and thrown off the yoke of being branded one of those unruly, boastful McMullens who fought with their neighbours and had been evicted more times than she could remember.

'What was he like?' Kate asked softly. 'Me da.'

Lizzie spoke with a hairpin between her teeth. 'Gentle.

Hard-working. Good with you bairns. Real family man like my Peter. A gentleman, I'd say. But proud of being a skilled working man.' She took the pin from her teeth and slid it into Kate's hair. 'Never had good health, mind, poor lad.'

Kate mused. 'I remember he used to take us by the hand and we'd run down the lane. He'd say, "Come on, lasses, catch the moon." ' Her eyes shone at the memory. 'And I remember him singing and playing the piano. Don't recall his face clearly, but I can still hear him singing.'

'Aye, he had a grand voice – him and your mam – sang like birds.'

'Mam an' all?' Kate asked in surprise.

Lizzie exclaimed, 'Of course! Our Rose had a voice like an angel – just like yours.'

'I never hear her sing.'

Lizzie grunted. 'Aye, well, your mam hasn't had much to sing about these past years with old John.'

'No,' Kate sighed, feeling a nagging guilt at how willingly she'd left her mother to cope with her boorish stepfather.

'Now don't you go worrying your pretty head with thoughts of home,' Lizzie said, seeing her niece's worried look. 'Tonight you're ganin' to the castle to enjoy yourself for once.'

Kate sprang up. She was to meet Suky at the gate to Farnacre at eight o'clock. She glanced quickly in the cracked mirror above her aunt's washstand. A pale oval face with large dark-lashed eyes stared back.

'Ta for doing me hair,' she smiled, and smoothed down the pink and white calico dress that Lizzie had helped her make.

'Hurry now,' her aunt said, hobbling after her on a stick. 'I'll see to the lads.'

Kate found Suky waiting impatiently by the wrought-iron gate to the old hall.

'Haway! It'll all be over if we don't get a move on.'

Kate laughed and linked her arm through her friend's. If John McMullen could see her now, he'd go off like one of last night's fireworks! Kate and the boys had gone out late to look at the cascade of bright colours showering the sky over the castle and marvelled at the distant sight of guests in fancy dress, but had been warned off by an officious footman from coming too close. Well, tonight it was their turn to have some fun.

Kate was amazed at the size of the servants' hall, where tables had been laid out with trenchers of meat and boiled potatoes, mounds of lettuce and radishes and steaming pies of cheese and potato. For pudding there were baked apples stuffed with raisins and jugs of custard, and wobbling jellies that sparkled in the overhead lights.

Even Suky seemed overawed as they squeezed on to a bench at the bottom of a long trestle table, the noise of chatter deafening around them. Jugs of beer were passed up and down the table. Suky tried some, but Kate wrinkled up her nose at the bitter smell. It reminded her too much of home and a familiar knot of tension gripped her insides.

Soon they were enlivened by food and were chattering with some of the kitchen maids around them. Halfway through the meal, the door at the far end opened and a well-dressed couple entered. Immediately a hush fell on the hall and everyone sprang to their feet. Kate craned for a view. An elderly gentleman in evening dress leaning on a stick made his way slowly down the length of the room, nodding and talking to people as he went. At his side, holding his arm, was a beautiful woman in a damson-coloured gown and strings of heavy pearls at her throat.

'Lady Ravensworth,' Kate breathed, recognising the woman at once.

Suky looked at her in surprise.

'Seen her before in the gardens,' Kate explained. She looked beyond to see if Master Alex might be with them too, but saw with disappointment that they were alone.

They came all the way down the hall, talking with all the staff, until finally they arrived at the bottom where the girls from the hall were standing.

Lady Ravensworth looked at them quizzically.

'Are you new?' she asked them.

'F-from Farnacre, ma'am,' Suky stammered, going puce.

She smiled at them. 'Can you sing?'

'Sing, ma'am?' Suky asked in confusion.

'Yes. Her Ladyship loves to be sung to. It's all she understands now.'

'Kate here's got a lovely singing voice, ma'am.'

Kate flushed, nudging her friend in embarrassment.

Lady Ravensworth eyed her, thinking how translucent the girl's skin was compared to the mottled complexions around her.

'Sing me something, Kate,' she smiled in encouragement.

'Now, ma'am?' Kate gulped.

Her Ladyship nodded.

Kate was suddenly aware of the silence all about. Lord Ravensworth had stopped speaking loudly to Miss Peters and people were glancing at Kate in sly amusement. She could tell some of them were willing her to make a fool of herself, the lowly laundry maid from the hall, with the Tyneside accent.

Kate lifted her chin. She would show them she could sing! Taking a deep breath, she began a song about the Waters of Tyne and a girl waiting for her sweetheart to return safely.

82

Unsure at first, Kate's voice soon found its strength and lifted high into the barrelled ceiling of the hall. The tender words rang out clear and melodious, needing no accompaniment. At the finish, the hall remained in silence as if wrapped in a spell. Then Lady Ravensworth clapped her gloved hands in delight and others followed her lead.

'Well done, child,' she smiled. 'You shall sing for His Lordship's mother.'

The earl nodded with a benign smile, then turned to move on.

Kate flushed deeper, only remembering to bob in curtsy after they had turned away.

When they had gone, Kate and Suky burst into giggles of relief. Everyone around them began to show more interest. Where on Tyneside did she come from? Had she had singing lessons? Kate laughed and shook her head.

'Everyone from Jarrow sings!'

There were demands for more songs and Kate needed little encouragement. Soon there was a general sing-song up and down the hall. Only the Farnacre housekeeper, Miss Peters, pursed her mouth in tight disapproval.

'She's no proper lady, that one,' she muttered. 'Takes too much interest in the servants, if you ask me. I'll not have you bothering the dowager with your noise, whatever that one says.'

Suky pulled Kate away. 'Don't listen to her,' she whispered. 'She hates it when folk enjoy themselves. Never approved of Lord Ravensworth remarrying, so they say.'

Later they went out to the stable courtyard from where the carriages had been moved to make room for dancing. It was a fine night and music from a fiddler filled the air. Kate threw herself into the dancing. In the semi-dark and confusion she became separated from her friend. She danced with several of the stable boys and a gardener's son she recognised. Then the musicians struck up a polka and someone grabbed her hand in the dark.

She turned laughing to find herself staring up at Alexander. Before she could say anything he was sweeping her away in the lively dance, her feet almost flying off the uneven flagstones. Her heart pounded as they twirled so fast everyone else around them was a blur. All she was aware of for those brief minutes was the grip of his hand on hers and the feel of his strong arm supporting her back. Kate hardly dared look into his face, so amazed was she to find herself in his arms.

'I thought I'd imagined you,' he laughed, 'a nymph from the woods with her basket of berries.'

Kate stole a look at him. His eyes glinted with merriment.

'But you are real,' he grinned. 'I can feel you are quite real.'

Kate smiled but could think of nothing to say.

'And now I know you have the voice of a nightingale.'

She shot him a look.

'Yes, I heard you sing for Lady Ravensworth.'

'I never saw you!'

He scrutinised her blushing face. 'Were you looking for me?'

Kate bit her lip and laughed in confusion.

'I hope that's a yes.' He held her closer for a moment so that she could feel the warmth of his breath on her forehead, then the dance finished and he let her go.

Alexander bowed and then he was gone, melting through the throng of dancers and drinkers and disappearing under the arch of the clock tower. Kate stood with thumping heart, peering after him, wondering if she had imagined the magical dance. What was he doing at such a party? Why had he suddenly appeared at her side and swept her into a polka? Had he been dancing with others or had he singled her out? It was like being given a sip of water when parched; she yearned for more.

But he was nowhere to be seen. Maybe he had come on a whim, a diversion from a dull evening after the grandeur of last night's ball. It couldn't have meant anything to him, yet it left her feeling bereft.

Suky found her. 'Who was that you were dancing with?'

Kate looked longingly over the crowd. 'A lad from the castle.'

'Didn't look like a servant to me,' Suky snorted. 'One of the guests having a bit fun, more like.'

'Aye,' Kate admitted.

'Well, you watch out for that sort,' she warned. 'Fancy silks and common serge don't mix in the poss tub.'

Kate gave her a shove of annoyance. 'You and your washing! I was just having a dance.'

Suky gave her a knowing look. 'Aye, well, don't say I didn't warn you.' She saw Kate's wistful look and took her by the arm. 'Haway, it's not over yet. Let's find a couple of footmen and have another jig.'

Chapter 8

The summer flew by for Kate. The days were spent working at Farnacre and the evenings helping her aunt at the cottage, with trips to the gardens with her uncle. As autumn arrived, they were frantically busy harvesting vegetables and filling the store houses. Turnips and cabbages were laid in sand in the cellars, while apples and pears were carefully placed in airy lofts to keep right through to Easter.

Kate helped knit together pungent onions into garlands, which were hung in the sheds along with carrots and parsnips. Peter nurtured his stores of fruit like a nurse, inspecting them daily, rooting out rotten pieces, setting traps for rats and sweeping out cobwebs. When frosts came, he would cover his crop with blankets or moss. Cherries were layered in hay and sealed in air-tight boxes; grapes were stored in earthenware jars with dry oats and sealed with pitch and beeswax.

At the hall there was a busy making of jams, preserves and syrups, of pickling cucumbers and drying out apples, quinces and artichoke hearts for cooking in winter stews and pies.

Kate enjoyed the work and the changing seasons, though she was never asked to sing for the dowager. Lady Ravensworth appeared to have forgotten her request at the servants' ball. She had probably never given it a second thought. Kate did not mind, though for her that night was still crystal clear months later. She would never forget the brief dance with Master Alex or the feel of being held in a man's arms.

Her only sorrow was that she had not seen him since. After several weeks of vainly looking out for him, she realised he must have left the estate. She did not know what business had brought him to Ravensworth, nor where he had gone. Once she asked about him when she and Suky were needed to help in the castle laundry. It was a cold winter and an outbreak of influenza laid low half the castle staff.

'You must mean Mr Pringle-Davies,' Hannah, a housemaid, preened. 'I laid his fire and brought his hot water.'

'Aye, that's the one,' Kate said eagerly. 'Where's he gone?'

'What's it to you?' Hannah sniffed.

'Just asking,' Kate blushed.

'The Davieses live in the south of the county – least that's where his letters came from.' Hannah gave a satisfied look, as if pleased with her detective work.

'So he's not one of the family then?' Kate persisted.

'No. The Davieses are coal agents. But Mr Pringle-Davies seems to spend his time drawing – pictures all over his room. Once asked if he could draw me laying the fire! Doesn't act like a man of business, that one.'

An older parlour maid joined in. 'I've heard it said he's a fortune-hunter,' Lily whispered as they hurriedly finished their tea. 'Very close to Her Ladyship – too close, some say. Waiting for the old earl to pass on.'

Hannah pulled a scandalised face.

'Aye,' Lily nodded, 'bit of a one for the ladies.'

Hannah clucked. 'And to think I let him draw me!'

Kate and Suky exchanged looks but said nothing as they cleared their tea plates in the large kitchen. Later, Suky commented, 'Told you to put him out your mind. Whatever interest he might show in lasses like us it won't come to any good. Got his eyes set on Lady Ravensworth – fancy that!'

'That's just castle tittle-tattle,' Kate snorted, but said no more. Whether any of it was true was nothing to do with her. He was so far out of her reach that she was foolish even to give him a second thought, let alone the hours of daydreaming she had wasted. So she put the mysterious Alexander from her mind and determined to look for a suitor among the estate staff like her Aunt Lizzie had done.

There was tall, serious-faced Robert, the head gardener's son, who worked hard in all weathers, or Tommy, one of the friendly stable lads who was always cheerful and telling jokes. She had danced with them both in the summer and sat near them at the harvest festival service at Lamesley parish church, which the Liddells attended. Tommy would be more fun, but Robert a better catch, diligently learning his craft from his father. Kate determined to impress him by offering to sweep out the store houses and feed the gardeners' cats that kept down the threat of mice in the sheds.

Suky became her ally in romance and was happy to spend snatched moments of freedom walking by the stables or potting sheds and exchanging a few words with the lads. On their fortnightly day off the girls would dress in their best and go down to St Andrew's church in Lamesley for the morning service, then walk up the hill to the mining village of Kibblesworth where Suky's family lived.

Kate loved the cosy fug in the squat cottage and the smell of roasting meat and the steam puddings that Suky's mother made. Suky had two younger brothers just recently started down the pit and a younger sister who demanded they play hopscotch as soon as they arrived. Suky's parents were kind and welcoming, and Kate envied her friend such a haven to which to return.

She felt guilty that she had never been home to Jarrow once since leaving in July, but had written to her mother that it was too far to travel for a day off. She would not get back by nightfall on these short dark days, she told them. She would wait until she could arrange two days off and come and see them, maybe near Christmas.

Kate received no letters back, but did not expect them. Her mother could barely write and she imagined Mary refusing to on her behalf, just out of awkwardness. No news probably meant that everything was fine.

She shuddered to think what her stepfather would say if he knew how she spent her free time, attending an Anglican church and sitting down to eat in a pitman's house. He would curse her into next week! Even though he never darkened a church door, John would fight to defend his Catholic faith and take a belt to any of his family who dared do anything else. As for miners and their families, to John they were dirty and rebellious and not to be trusted. How often had Kate heard him blame all their ill fortune and the slumps in trade on the miners? Even bad weather seemed to be the fault of the miners or the Protestants, or more usually both. Kate felt a defiant thrill of rebellion that she could do as she wanted at Ravensworth and her ranting stepfather was none the wiser.

Christmas came, but Kate never went home. She and Suky helped decorate Farnacre with streamers and glittering baubles, and a large Christmas tree with candles and gaudy paste bells. There was a generous Christmas dinner in the week before the day itself for the estate staff up at the castle to which they went, and every one of them received a present from the Liddells – small bars of soap, combs, mittens, handkerchiefs or ribbon.

Lizzie was walking properly again, but Kate insisted on cooking their Christmas dinner and roasting chestnuts in the dying embers of the fire. On Boxing Day it snowed, so she did not venture to Kibblesworth with Suky, but stayed and sledged on sacks with George and Alfred. They ended up in a snowball fight with Robert, and Kate thought with a brief pang of guilt how Jack would have enjoyed such an afternoon. How was her young half-brother faring this Christmas? She would go home soon.

Then suddenly, in the middle of January, the dowager died in her sleep. The estate was plunged into mourning and Kate's happy world was shaken.

'What'll happen to us?' Suky asked.

Kate shrugged in despair. If the house was closed, she would have no option but to return to Jarrow. Lizzie was well again and without the job at the hall there would be no excuse to stay.

For a month they carried on working at Farnacre while lawyers and estate managers came and went, assessing the contents and itemising the furniture. Suky and Kate were set to scrubbing the place from the attics to the cellars and packing away china and linen, which was carried off to the castle or to auction. Eventually the dustsheets were drawn over the remaining furniture and the life seeped out of the hall like the bleak, chill dead days of January.

At the end of the month, Miss Peters, the housekeeper, told them with a note of satisfaction that they would only be employed for a further week. She and Cook would be staying on to keep an eye on the place, but the young women would not be needed.

Suky pulled a face behind the woman's back. 'Least we won't have to see her miserable face every morning,' she muttered out of earshot.

The next day Suky disappeared.

'Gone home,' Cook told Kate.

'She never said goodbye,' Kate said, feeling hurt.

'Doesn't stand still long enough for goodbyes,' Cook grunted. 'Heard of a job down at the Ravensworth Inn. Told me to tell you. Don't want to work in a place like that,' she added in disapproval.

Kate knew the place; they had passed it often on their way up to Kibblesworth. It was a lively coaching inn, busy with passing trade and miners supping in the bar on pay day. On high days and feast days, staff from Ravensworth were known to quench their thirst there too. Compared to the pubs around Jarrow in which her stepfather spent his evenings, the local inn looked a palace, but Kate said nothing to Cook.

Feeling down at heart, Kate rolled up her sleeves and got on with the meagre pile of washing – a tablecloth, aprons and a handful of towels. Later, as she pegged them out in the raw air, she comforted herself by singing. A fluffed-up thrush sat on the nearby water barrel and listened to her mournful song, 'Thora', of a lost land of stars and happiness. She would look back on these golden months at Ravensworth with the same deep longing as she felt in the bitter-sweet song.

Only when she had finished did she become aware of someone pausing in the shadow of the courtyard gateway. The figure moved forward and Kate saw the strained, pale features of Lady Ravensworth, a fur cape pulled about her black silk mourning dress. Kate bobbed in curtsy.

'What beautiful singing,' the countess smiled. 'I've heard you before, haven't I?'

'Yes, ma'am,' Kate nodded, 'at the summer ball – for the servants, ma'am.'

'Of course. You were going to sing for Her Ladyship!' Lady Ravensworth recalled. 'Did you ever sing for her?'

Kate shook her head.

'What a pity.' She stepped across the icy cobbles.

'Watch your step, Your Ladyship!' Kate cried in alarm, rushing forward to support her. 'It's slippy as fish round here.'

Emma laughed, then checked herself. 'Oh, dear. I know we're all supposed to be so sad and solemn, but it is nice to hear someone singing for a change. It's so depressing up at the castle, everyone draped in black like crows. It's not as if Her Ladyship didn't have a good and happy life.'

Kate stared, embarrassed. Fancy Lady Ravensworth talking so candidly to her, a laundry maid!

'Oh, I'm sorry, I'm making you feel awkward.' Emma smiled, and patted Kate's pink cheek. 'It's just I've done my fair share of dressing in black.' She did not elaborate, just sighed and pulled her cape about her.

'Aye, it's sad for us all,' Kate blurted out. 'I've been that happy working here.'

The older woman eyed her in surprise. 'Aren't you staying?'

'No, ma'am. Not needed now the house is being closed up.'

'What will you do?'

Kate's shoulders drooped. 'Gan back to Jarrow and look for work.'

'Is that where you're from?'

Kate nodded.

'Isn't that strange?' Emma declared. 'The earl's family had a connection with that town. His Lordship's cousin Edward was the rector of Jarrow for several years. Perhaps you've heard of him, Canon Liddell?'

Kate shook her head, then remembered. 'There's a dispensary named after a Liddell, mind.'

'No doubt that was for Edward – such a kind, dear man. He came to our wedding. Was very frail by then. They say Jarrow killed him – worked himself into an early grave. Such a nice wife too.'

'I'm sorry,' Kate said, feeling in some way implicated. 'Jarrow's a hard place. Me own father died young too.'

'Poor girl!' Emma exclaimed, her delicately boned face creased in concern. Suddenly she made up her mind. 'You can't go back to that town – I won't allow it! If they don't need you here, you'll come and work at the castle. Yes, you'll brighten up all the long faces with your singing! Promise me you'll sing while you work?'

Kate gawped in astonishment. Was she really being offered a lifeline at the last moment? Or was this just another of Her Ladyship's whims that she would forget by night-fall?

'I'll sing as much as you want, ma'am,' she said quickly.

Lady Ravensworth laughed. 'Splendid! I'll speak to Miss Peters now – she can arrange it all.' She waved her cloak in the direction of the hall. Kate followed, stuttering her thanks.

As an afterthought, Her Ladyship asked, 'What is your name, child?'

'Kate, ma'am,' she smiled proudly, 'Kate Fawcett.'

Two days later, to the resentment of some servants who thought her a brazen upstart, Kate began at the castle as a housemaid, cleaning out fires and carrying pails of water with Hannah. She ignored the callous comments about her lowly origins and smothered her Jarrow accent as best she could, aping the more refined speech of the parlour maids. And she hummed and sang as she worked.

The following month, she got word from Suky that she was working at the inn at Lamesley, as Cook had indicated. They met up on Kate's day off and swapped news. Suky was courting a lad from Kibblesworth. Kate was struck by how alike their friendship and conversation were to hers and Sarah's. It was months since she had last gossiped with her older sister and walked arm in arm sharing secrets.

Kate knew then that she could not put off going home any longer. Now that she was working at the grand castle, she was keen to see her mother and tell her the news in person. For the first time since leaving Jarrow she had a rush of homesickness. She longed to see her mother and Jack, and catch a glimpse of Sarah. She even missed Mary.

Next month was Mothering Sunday. She would go home for that. Kate wrote to Rose the following week. As the days grew longer and daffodils sprang from the hard earth around, Kate was filled with sunny optimism. Maybe even her stepfather would be pleased to see her.

Chapter 9

Alexander gazed out over the grey, choppy waters of the Gulf of Bothnia, breathing in the sharp air. The coast here was low-lying, a lacework of waterways and islands, dark fir trees growing right to the water's edge. Dotted among them were wooden houses and churches, the smoke from their stoves hanging over the trees like a blanket.

After three frantic months of travelling the countries of the Baltic, always keeping on the move, he had wintered in Upsala, north of Stockholm. Constant ferry journeys, cheap hotels and touting for business had left him jaded and it had been a relief to see the winter draw in and the lakes freeze over. The eastern Swedish ports had become ice-bound and the steamers marooned, the flotilla of foreign ships slipping away.

He had taken rooms close to the lofty-spired cathedral, among Upsala's students, and hibernated. The furthest he went each day was to cross one of the five bridges over the icy Fyriså river to spend the short afternoon in the public reading room, flicking through the foreign newspapers. In the evening he would keep warm in a café, drinking arrack and eating a smorgasbord of herring and relishes, discussing literature and art with students. They argued about politics and whether Sweden should break away from Norway; they talked of workers' rights.

Alexander was impressed with conditions he found in the mining towns of Sweden. He had stayed with Baron Tamm in the forests of Österby and been taken to view the mines and iron works of Uppland. Close to the baron's mansion and parks was a purpose-built town of streets and canals radiating out from a central square. The workers' dwellings were rows of one-storey houses, each with a garden, byre and stable, with plots of cultivated land behind.

'Every family has at least one cow,' the baron told him proudly. 'Everyone should be able to feed their children.'

Alexander had nodded, reminded of dim childhood memories of Jarrow, a town of shipbuilding and iron works. How closely the baron's words echoed those of his beloved cousin Edward, the local rector. He remembered the damp and filth of the houses they had visited. He would cling to his cousin in fright on entering the dark cottages with the stench of excrement from the open middens making him gag. He could not remember anything growing in Jarrow, let alone gardens and smallholdings for the workers.

How Edward would have wept to see the comparative paradise of these Swedish labourers. All he had been able to give the people of Jarrow was cocoa in the cold of dawn and the comfort of companionship and sharing their plight. Alexander felt angry every time he thought of Jarrow – the town that had stolen his cousin's health and so robbed him of a loving family home. Not that Jeremiah had been unkind. But he was widowed and childless and had taken on Alexander as a commercial transaction as much as an act of charity. He was helping out his powerful employer at Ravensworth and training up a 'son' to carry on his business.

But Alexander was practised at banishing unhappy memories and had soon put thoughts of Jarrow from his mind. Instead he had enjoyed his stay with the baron and his family, especially the company of their daughter, Anna, who was lively and keen to practise her English. Alexander had spent a month hunting elk and shooting duck with the baron, and falling in love with fair-haired Anna.

Then letters had begun to arrive from Jeremiah, ordering him back to England, and Alexander had disappeared to Stockholm. There he had sent a message from the telegraph office of the Grand Hotel that he was ice-bound for the rest of the winter. He followed it up with a longer letter telling how he had secured a lucrative contract with Baron Tamm. The Swedish iron magnate needed a plentiful supply of British coal. While here he would seek out a ready supply of cheap timber for their North-East pits.

Alexander slipped north to Upsala. But his money was spent (Jeremiah had stopped his allowance until his return) and he could no longer barter for food in the cafés with his sketches, or cover his rent by giving drawing lessons to students. Besides, spring was stirring in the deep black forests and the groaning sound of ice cracking broke the quiet.

Now here he was in the port of Gefle watching the newly arrived ships queuing at the quayside to load with timber. This rapidly growing manufacturing town, with its large shipbuilding wharfs, reminded him of Newcastle. Like Newcastle, the whole of the quarter on the north bank had been destroyed by fire a generation ago and its quayside was now laid out with broad streets and solid buildings lapped by the dirty waters of a bustling harbour.

Alexander felt a sudden rush of desire to be home. He wanted to smell the oily, fishy mouth of the Tyne, to step on

97

the crowded quayside and hear the harsh cries of the brightly skirted fishwives. He thirsted for the taste of dark beer in the snug of a Newcastle pub, and yearned to ride out on the dun-coloured moors as the snows melted and the rivers roared with spring torrents.

He thought longingly of Ravensworth and the final ride he had taken with Polly De Winton. He'd hardly thought of the squire's daughter in months, but he recalled how nimbly she had mounted her horse and ridden for hours without tiring. He would pay her a call on his return.

Ravensworth! He conjured up the bare trees sticky with new buds and the carpets of daffodils dancing in the March wind. Lady Ravensworth would be pleased to see him and demand to be told of his adventures. He would bask in her interest like the welcome spring sunshine.

Two days later, Alexander took the train back to Stockholm and then the long trail to Gothenburg in the west. He was too impatient to wait for the steamer that would edge its way across the massive central lakes, but all he could afford was third class on the local goods trains (which his worn copy of Baedeker warned him to avoid). The journey seemed endless as they rattled over viaducts spanning foaming waterfalls, constantly lurching to a stop at small villages and weaving towns.

For once he did not want to linger in the pleasant, elegant city of Gothenburg with its canals and wide avenues. He had no money for the harbour restaurants, and the pleasure gardens and open-air swimming baths were still firmly closed.

Alexander went straight to the Stora Bommens Hamn where the large sea-going steamers moored, and booked a passage home. He telegraphed his father, who grumblingly pledged to cover his fare. Five days later, after a stormy crossing that left him sick and cabin-bound, Alexander stepped shakily but thankfully back on to Newcastle's quayside.

Chapter 10

When Kate rose on the morning of her journey home it was still dark, but Peter gave her a lift on his cart down to the station at Lamesley and young Alfred insisted on coming too. The small boy missed having Kate living at the cottage since she had moved into the castle to work. But all the household staff lived in, for their hours were long and the housekeeper and head butler wanted them under their rule.

Kate had packed jars of jam and pickled onions from Lizzie and had kept her Christmas soap from the Liddells for Mary, remembering her sister's plea to bring something back for her.

'We'll pick you up tonight,' Peter offered.

'No, I can walk up the hill no bother,' Kate insisted. 'Don't know which train I'll catch.'

Her uncle nodded, but Alfred cried in alarm, 'You will come back, won't you?'

'Course I will.' Kate ruffled his hair in affection. 'I love it here.'

All the way to Tyneside, her excitement at seeing her family mounted. She craned for a view of the river as the draughty train clattered along downriver from Gateshead. Was Jack stoking up the fire to heat the oven? Was her mother preparing a piece of brisket in thick gravy, knowing it was her favourite?

Her heart hammered as she stepped out on to the platform at Tyne Dock. It seemed an age since she had left last summer, shedding tears at leaving Jack and Mary at the last moment. Kate scanned the crowds at the barrier, family members waiting to welcome home girls in service like herself for Mothering Sunday. She clutched her parcel of presents and the posy of flowers she had picked fresh that morning.

Through the barrier, the crowds quickly melted and she was left alone. No one had thought to come to meet her. Kate swallowed her disappointment. They would all be busy doing jobs. She must get home as quickly as possible to help out.

Outside the station, Kate was overwhelmed by the cram of buildings and the milling of traffic, even on a Sunday morning. There were horse-drawn carts and bicycles to dodge. She stood on the kerb, suddenly paralysed. Kate had forgotten how noisy the town was. It clattered and hissed and roared like a beast. Everything seemed so large, so soot-blackened, so hemmed in.

She had grown used to wide open skies, the smell of cut grass or wet autumn leaves. The busiest place she had been to in the past eight months was the village of Kibblesworth – a few tight-knit streets and a pithead tucked in below the fell with a handful of shops. She felt like a country girl, frightened by the size and noise of the town, not knowing how to cross the road.

Kate stood there feeling foolish, finally galvanising herself to move one foot in front of the other. What was wrong with her? She knew these streets blindfold, had begged around them as a child, knew every hard inch of them. But she was no underfed girl with sores on her bare legs now, she told herself proudly. She was healthy and well-dressed, and worked in mighty Ravensworth Castle. Fortified with the thought,

101

she made her way swiftly out of Tyne Dock and up the hill towards Simonside and Cleveland Place.

To her right she could see Jarrow's thicket of housing and church spires peeping through the haze of chimney smoke. Below lay the gantries and cranes of Palmer's shipyards and the tidal mud flats of Jarrow Slake. The tide was in and the sludge-grey water bobbed with planks of seasoning timber. As a small child her father had told her how the pitch-smeared body of a martyred pitman had been hanged there in a gibbet, a grisly sight swaying in the wind to strike fear into rebellious miners. But his friends had conjured away Jobling's body and lived to fight on for workers' rights.

Her mother hated that story and had forbidden Kate and her sisters to play near the treacherous Slake when they were young. Kate had shivered in frightened delight at the telling, but the mention of Jobling or the Slake had always earned her a sharp slap from Rose or John, though Kate never knew why.

She hurried on up the bank away from the clutter of housing until the road turned to squelching mud. Ahead she could see the signal box and the uneven roofs of Cleveland Place. Wisps of smoke were wafting from the cottage chimneys. Kate broke into her loping run, not minding that the mud splattered her boots or the hem of her skirt.

She banged in through the wooden gate and up the uneven brick path, one of Jack's hens flapping out of the way in alarm.

'I'm home!' she cried, flinging open the door and rushing inside.

For a moment she could see nothing in the gloom. The light that trickled through the tiny windows was sepia, the fire smouldered and spat with dross. The place was empty.

'Mam?' Kate called in concern. 'Mam!'

Just then the back door swung open and a bulky figure came panting through. It was Rose, struggling with a bucket of potatoes. She looked up and caught sight of her daughter. The bucket clattered to the floor as Rose held out her arms.

'Mary, Mother of God! What a fright you gave me!'

'Mam!' Kate rushed forward, dumping her parcels on the table and throwing her arms about her mother. They hugged fiercely. 'I've missed you, Mam.'

For a moment Rose could not speak. Then she pushed her gently away. 'Here, you take these.' Rose thrust the bucket of potatoes at her.

'You shouldn't be carrying them!' Kate remonstrated. 'Where is everybody? Where's our Jack?'

'The Devil knows,' Rose panted. 'I've given them a scrub – you peel them for me, hinny.'

'Aye,' Kate said, feeling a niggle of disappointment. It was as if she had never been away and there was nothing special about the day. 'I brought you a bunch of flowers, Mam,' she brightened, nodding at the splash of yellow daffodils on the table. 'You should see them at Ravensworth – growing everywhere!'

Rose smiled at her daughter. 'Let's have a proper look at you. Are they feeding you enough?' She turned Kate's face to the light. 'You're looking bonny,' she conceded in a rare compliment. 'How's our Lizzie and her lads?'

'Grand, Mam.' Kate blushed with pleasure. 'And I've some'at special to tell you. I'm not working at Farnacre Hall any more – the old lady died. But Lady Ravensworth's started me on at the castle – saw to it in person! I'm a housemaid now, Mam, not in the laundry.'

Rose gasped. 'You're working for Lord Ravensworth himself?'

Kate nodded. 'And once I was laying the fire in Lady Ravensworth's bedroom and he came in and spoke to me! Lady Ravensworth told him I came from Jarrow and he said his cousin, Edward Liddell, was rector there at one time.'

'Canon Liddell?' Rose said hoarsely, gripping Kate's arm.

'Aye, did you know of him?'

Rose nodded, her breath catching in her throat. 'Used to work for him and Mrs Liddell when I was young. A real gentleman and a true Christian. Did His Lordship say how he was?'

'He died, Mam – few years back, I think he said.'

'Dead?' Rose's thick legs buckled beneath her. Kate grabbed her and pushed her into a chair. 'Mam, are you all right? I'll fetch a glass of water.'

'No,' Rose gasped for breath, a hand clamped to her chest, 'it was just the shock . . . that poor man . . . tried his best for Jarrow.' She sighed deeply and whispered half to herself, 'Took us to Ravensworth one summer – me and the bairns – your two dear sisters.'

Kate tensed. She knew when her mother spoke in that wistful tone she was talking about Margaret and Elizabeth, those shadowy elder sisters who had died when Kate was small. She half-remembered them as bossy and loving, with strong arms always picking her up and cuddling her, warm hands clutching and pulling her along. She had a bitter-sweet memory of racing down the street after Elizabeth, waving goodbye until she was long out of sight. It was the last time she saw her alive.

'Elizabeth was just a babe in arms,' Rose continued, 'but Margaret ran about like she'd found her legs for the first

104

time! A day in paradise, it was. And thanks to Mrs Liddell our Lizzie went to place at the castle and met Peter.' She glanced at Kate, her look briefly tender. 'So it's thanks to the Liddells that you're there an' all, I suppose.'

Kate looked at her mother in wonder, amazed that she could have known such important people. 'Were they like friends to you, Mam?' she asked quietly.

Rose nodded slowly. 'I suppose they were, in a way. It didn't bother them that we were Catholic. They were kind to everyone they met.' Her dark-ringed eyes looked sorrowful. 'The Reverend Mr Liddell was full of principles – just like your father. They were very alike.'

Kate's heart missed a beat. 'You mean me real da?'

'Aye,' Rose whispered, her eyes brimming, 'William.'

Kate's pulse quickened. She had not heard Rose utter her father's name for years. It seemed to conjure him up, as if he stood in the shadows of the dark cottage, watching them.

'Me da,' Kate murmured dreamily, 'he was a friend of Canon Liddell's?'

Rose turned from her abruptly. 'Well, maybe friend is too strong a word – they were two of a kind.'

'But they knew each other?' Kate pressed.

'Aye,' Rose admitted, pushing herself to her feet. 'Now hurry up with those tatties, or there'll be nowt to eat for dinner.'

The spell was broken, but the warm thrill Kate got from thinking that her father had been acquainted with some of the Liddells stayed with her. It made her feel even prouder to bear the name of Fawcett and not McMullen.

Kate unbuttoned her jacket and pulled off her mittens.

'Is Sarah coming over from Hebburn?' she asked, following her mother into the scullery.

'No, she can't get away.'

Kate felt dashed. 'She's doing canny, though?'

Rose shot her a look. 'She hasn't been home much either.'

Kate flushed. 'Sorry, Mam. I know I should've tried to get home sooner.'

Rose held up a finger. 'You don't have to apologise. You stick in with your job at the castle and make some'at of yourself, hinny. That's all that matters.' They began to prepare the meal together, a rabbit stew and boiled potatoes and turnip. Bit by bit they told each other their news.

'I think Sarah's courting. She hasn't said much, but I think that's why she's staying away. Doesn't want Father to find her out.'

Kate remembered the way she had encouraged Sarah to hurry back to Hebburn for the Coronation bonfire to see the lad who called round with vegetables. Maybe something had come of it.

'And you?' Rose asked abruptly. 'Are you courting yet?'

Kate blushed and laughed. 'No!'

'With all those lads around the estate?' Rose teased. 'Or does our Lizzie keep you that busy?'

'Aunt Lizzie's been grand,' Kate smiled. 'And there are some canny lads at Ravensworth – but no one in particular.'

For an instant, the image of the laughing Alexander swinging her round in the polka flashed through her mind. But he was the stuff of daydreams.

'Well, there's no hurry,' Rose said. 'Not like our Mary – she may be only fifteen but she wants to be wed and kept in luxury for evermore.'

'Where is she?'

Rose let out a long sigh. 'Down at Maggie's. Spends more time there than here these days.'

Kate felt annoyance rise. 'She should be here helping you!'

'Aye, but it's the only way I get a minute's peace. If she's here she's ranting on about how badly she's tret, how it's not fair her sisters get to live away, how Jack's spoilt rotten. Oh!' Rose exclaimed in exasperation. 'Nothing suits our Mary – she gets more difficult by the day. And don't expect her to welcome you with open arms. Ever since we heard you were coming home she's been crying and wailing about how you get everything you want and she gets nowt. Your father's at his wits' end!'

It was the first time either of them had mentioned John. If Mary had lost her ally in her stepfather then the situation must be bad.

'Can't she get a job?' Kate suggested.

'Your father wants her here giving me a hand around the house. He doesn't know she spends most of the day down at Maggie's. He'd knock her into next week if he knew.' Rose shook her head. 'It worries me that much.' She gave a pleading look. 'Do you think you could find her some'at over at Ravensworth? It might be the best thing for all of us if she gets away.'

Kate's heart sank at the thought of the disruptive Mary barging her way into her new happy life.

'Father would never agree, would he?'

'He wouldn't need much persuading.'

Kate saw the bleak look on her mother's lined face. She was worn out with worry. Kate chided herself for being mean-spirited and put a hand on her mother's. 'I'll ask about,' she promised.

Kate lit a lamp to make the room more welcoming and set the table with the cheerful daffodils in the centre. At midday, without warning, Jack appeared like a ghost at the back door.

107

He had grown six inches, his arms dangling from a too-short jacket. She grinned at her brother and held out her hands.

'By heck, you've grown! You're as tall as me.'

'Taller,' he said with a shy smile, but did not go to greet her. Instead he busied himself unlacing his muddy boots and placing them carefully by the fender.

Kate dropped her arms. 'Where you been? Playing up the tree?'

He glanced at her in disdain. 'I don't play any more. Been down Bonham's farm – catching rats.' His dark eyes challenged her. 'Shoot crows an' all.'

'Shoot! You mean with a gun?' Kate exclaimed.

'Aye,' he gave a grin of satisfaction, 'he's teaching me to use a real gun.'

Rose shushed him. 'Don't go telling your father. He'll just take against old man Bonham and stop you going.'

'I don't care,' Jack said scornfully. 'He'll not stop us.'

Rose rolled her eyes as if she had heard it all before. But Kate was surprised at Jack's defiance. It was not like him to speak his mind or talk of defying John. Of all of them, she suspected he had changed the most in the months of her absence.

An hour later, Mary sauntered in, just ahead of her stepfather.

'Father's on his way up the hill,' she announced. 'Well, look who's here! Have you brought me anything?'

'Here,' Kate smiled in greeting and held out the small parcel of soap, 'I kept this for you specially.'

Mary tore it open at once and pressed the cake of soap to her nose.

'It's rosewater,' Kate grinned. 'Lady Ravensworth gave some to all us lasses.'

Mary pulled a face. 'Ooh, Lady Ravensworth!' she mimicked. 'So how come you didn't want it?'

'I did, but I thought you'd like it.'

'Well, I don't want it if you've used it already.'

'I haven't touched it,' Kate protested. 'And I'll have it back if it doesn't suit you.'

'No,' Mary said, pocketing it swiftly, 'I'll have it.' Catching Rose's warning look she added with an effort, 'Ta very much.'

Kate turned to Jack, who was whittling a stick with a penknife by the fire. He'd hardly spoken a word in an hour. 'Sorry I didn't bring you a present – I didn't know what you'd want. But I knew you'd like Aunt Lizzie's plum jam.'

Jack said nothing, just went on methodically carving.

'It's like talking to a block of wood,' Mary complained. 'Don't expect it to speak back.'

She missed the resentful glance Jack gave her, but Kate didn't. She stepped between them quickly.

'Haway, Mary, help me serve up the dinner. I can hear Father at the gate.'

'Serve it up yourself,' Mary muttered. 'I've done it every week you've been away.'

Rose's scolding was interrupted by loud whistling at the door and John pushed his way in. He at least looked just the same, Kate thought drily. As smartly dressed as possible in his slightly threadbare suit, his white hair and moustache neatly combed. His face was as gaunt as ever, but he moved quickly, exuding a brutish strength in his long limbs and powerful shoulders. The beery-tobacco smell of the bar wafted in with him.

'My chickens home to roost, eh!' he cried on seeing the sudden bustle around the table. 'And how's our Kate? Putting on weight, I'd say.'

109

'No she's not,' Rose protested on her behalf.

'Hello, Father.' Kate went over and gave him a peck on the cheek, then quickly retreated. She hated the smell on his breath.

'Come and tell me all about it.' He sat down at the head of the table and Mary made a sudden fuss of serving him, vying for his attention as Kate described life at Ravensworth.

'Tell him about the new position,' Rose urged.

'What new position?' Mary demanded. 'You never told me.'

'I'm working up at the castle now,' Kate said proudly. 'I'm a housemaid for Lord and Lady Ravensworth.'

'Isn't that grand, John?' Rose beamed.

'Well, I never!' John slapped his knee, already thinking of how he would boast around the dockyard pubs. 'Working for Lord Ravensworth himself, eh?'

'Aye,' Kate went on excitedly, 'I lay the fires and fetch hot water for their baths and polish the stairs – you wouldn't believe how many steps there are!'

Suddenly Mary flung back her chair. 'It's not fair!' she cried. 'You never said anything about being a housemaid. Said you were working in the laundry.'

'Sit down,' Rose ordered. 'You should be pleased for your sister.'

'Well, I'm not!' Mary pouted. 'I'd make a better housemaid than her. She can't even walk properly with her gammy foot.'

'That's enough,' John growled. 'Sit down, lass.'

'No I won't! Why can't I be a housemaid? You should have thought of me!' she yelled at Kate.

'Sit down and shurr-up,' John snapped.

But Mary was too riled to stop. She was puce in the face, her eyes welling with resentful tears.

'Kate always gets everything! I'm sick of hearing what a grand life she's having at Ravensworth while I'm stuck here in this dirty old cottage with you lot.'

'I'll take me belt to yer!' John half rose.

Mary turned on him in defiance. 'You'll not whip me like you did our Sarah. I'm not your dog!'

'Mary!' Rose gasped in shock.

'Nobody cares for me!' Mary screamed. 'None of you do – only Aunt Maggie. And you can have this back.' She pulled out the bar of soap and threw it across the table at Kate. It bounced into her plate and splashed her with gravy.

There was a moment of stunned silence. Mary stared at Kate wiping the brown flecks from her starched white blouse, the look on her face as surprised as Kate's. Then the kitchen erupted.

John sprang from his chair, grabbed the soap from out of the stew with one hand and seized Mary with the other.

'I'll give you Aunt-bloody-Maggie!' he roared. 'I'll wash your dirty little mouth out!'

Mary screamed as he hauled her across the kitchen. Rose hobbled over to intervene but was not quick enough. She tried to catch John's arm but he threw her off.

'Get in there!' he bawled, shoving the young girl into the scullery. He saw the bucket of cold muddy water still full of potato peelings and plunged her head in.

'John, stop it!' Rose shouted, thumping him on the back.

He yanked Mary up by the hair. She spluttered and spat. John rammed the bar of soap into her mouth. Mary gagged and tried to scream. He thrust her head back in the bucket.

'Help her!' Rose pleaded to Kate and Jack, who were hovering in the doorway, too stunned to act. The anger

111

and violence had flared out of nothing in an instant. Kate remembered with a sick churning inside how quickly storms brewed and erupted in this household.

Kate was finally stung into action by her mother's entreaties. She barged into the narrow scullery and threw herself at John's stooped back, grabbing at his short hair. Momentarily he lost his grip and Rose took the chance to seize Mary and pull her out from under him. They tussled and the pail of water crashed over, flooding the stone floor and soaking Kate's skirt. John pushed her out of the way and barged out of the narrow scullery. But Kate's intervention had given Rose just enough time to shove Mary through the kitchen and up the ladder to the loft.

Rose stood at the bottom, guarding it.

John shouted up, 'You can stay up there! That soap's the last food you'll taste till the morrow! I don't want to see your twisty face again, do you hear?'

All they could hear in return was Mary's loud sobbing. Kate wanted to rush upstairs to make sure she was all right, but did not dare rile John further.

'Come and eat, John,' Rose coaxed. 'Mary's learnt her lesson.'

'She never learns,' he snarled. 'You're too soft on her – on all of them – always have been.'

Rose swallowed her pride. 'Aye, you're right. It might be best if she was sent away – into place. Somewhere they'll keep her in order better than I can.'

John gave her a wary look, then nodded. 'And curb that tongue of hers.'

'Aye, that's what she needs,' Rose encouraged. 'She takes no heed of what I say any more.'

'Never has done,' John grumbled.

'Kate will ask around Ravensworth way, won't you?' Rose looked for her daughter's support.

'Soon as I get back,' Kate promised, thinking how she couldn't get back to the haven of Ravensworth quick enough.

'So come and eat, John,' Rose said, steering him away from the ladder and back to the table.

He allowed himself to be led and was soon munching hungrily on the stew. Kate had no appetite any more and went to dry off her skirt by the fire. It was then that she noticed Jack had disappeared. He must have fled during the brawl in the scullery. But neither Rose nor John made any comment and she wondered how often he took flight from the wrangling at Cleveland Place.

After the meal, John lay down on the bed in the corner and slept off his Sunday dinner. Kate helped her mother clear up and then quietly mounted the ladder with a piece of bread dipped in gravy for Mary.

'Here, eat this,' she whispered across the dark room in the eaves. 'I've got to go for me train now. But I'm ganin' to look out for you – find you a job if I can, get you away from here.'

Mary did not stir from under the bundle of covers on the mattress, so Kate put the plate down beside her and turned to go. As she climbed on to the ladder, a muffled voice spoke from the lump of blankets.

'Kate?'

'Aye?'

'I'm sorry . . . sorry about spoiling the soap. I wanted it really.'

'Doesn't matter. You can still use it.'

'Never!' Mary said in defiance. 'Not after he's touched it.'

'Ta-ra then.' Kate began to descend.

'Write to us, won't you?' Mary called after her. 'Don't forget me.'

Kate paused and whispered back, 'I'll write.'

She took a swift farewell of Rose, hugging her briefly, but eager to be gone before John awoke.

'Go and find our Jack,' Rose told her. 'He'll be that upset if you go without saying goodbye. He misses you.'

'Didn't seem that pleased to see me,' Kate pointed out.

'Doesn't show it. But he moped around here like a lost dog for weeks after you went in the summer.'

Kate went outside and called for her brother. When no answer came she set off for the station with a shrug of resignation. But at the end of the row she found him huddled next to Harry Burn's rain barrel, waiting for her.

'Come and see me off?' she asked. He nodded and allowed her to slip an arm through his.

'I wish Mary would gan and live with Aunt Maggie,' he muttered as they walked down the bank.

'We'll sort Mary out,' Kate assured him, 'then you'll have some peace. Does Father tret you fairly?'

Jack hunched his shoulders. 'Stay out his way mostly. Prefer me own company, any road.'

Kate glanced at her shy, gawky brother with a pang of pity. He would be quite on his own if Mary was sent into service, and Cleveland Place was too solitary for a boy of twelve. But Jack did not appear to be lonely; he preferred the company of crows and farm animals to that of his warring family.

She squeezed his arm. 'By the end of next year you'll be starting work – you'll be earning a wage like Father. One day soon you'll be a man and able to stand up to him – stand up for Mam. Your turn will come, kiddar.'

114

Jack said nothing to this, but his face looked thoughtful. He let Kate hold on to his arm all the way into town, only breaking free when they neared the station. This time he saw her on to the train and waved her away with a bashful smile, and Kate was gladdened to see a glimpse of the old affectionate Jack.

Soon her thoughts were racing ahead to Ravensworth, and she sat impatiently in the chilly, gas-lit carriage as the train clanked south. She would not be going home again in a hurry.

To her delight, Peter and Alfred were waiting at the station for her.

'The lad made me come,' her uncle said wryly, 'and Lizzie says to drop by for a cup of tea before you gan back to the castle. She wants all the news from home.'

Kate swung Alfred into her arms and kissed the top of his head in greeting. It came to her in a rush. After the disappointments and upsets of the day, she felt more than ever that Ravensworth was now her home.

Chapter 11

Blossom was falling from the cherry trees when Alexander next found a chance to visit Ravensworth. Jeremiah had kept him busy with visits to mines in South Yorkshire and had demanded his company at home for several weeks after his return. It struck Alexander that his father was lonely and increasingly fretful about his adopted son's future.

'It's time you found yourself a wife,' he lectured. 'I'd like to see you settle down – start your own family. They could live here and keep me company when you travel. This house is too big and empty for an old man like me.'

'You're not old,' Alexander insisted, trying to laugh it off. 'You'll probably outlive me!'

'Don't say such a thing!' Jeremiah snapped. 'No, no. You must think seriously about marriage. What about this De Winton girl you talked about? I've made enquiries about the family – good farming stock and quite a bit of land up Weardale. It could be just the match. You liked her, didn't you?'

'She was pleasant enough,' Alexander conceded.

'Then you must call on her – or invite her here so I can meet her. We could arrange a concert party or go to the theatre.'

'If you like,' Alexander said, only half listening. He was looking at the changing light on the slate rooftops of the

116

solid mansions opposite and wondering if he could capture it in paint.

'It's what you would like, not me,' Jeremiah said querulously.

'Yes, yes.'

'Are you listening?' his father demanded. 'What are you staring at?'

'It's like molten gold,' Alexander said dreamily. 'The way the sun shines on a wet roof after the rain.'

Jeremiah huffed with impatience. 'You haven't listened to a word, have you?'

Alexander turned from the window and smiled. 'Yes I have. You want me to marry Polly De Winton.'

'Well, I – er . . .' Jeremiah began to bluster with embarrassment at his son's sudden forthrightness.

Alexander laughed. 'I shall call on her sometime, if it makes you happy. Though whether she'll want to see me is another matter.'

Jeremiah caught his arm as he passed. 'It's you I want to see happy, boy. Happy and settled. And why shouldn't she want to see you? You're a handsome young gentleman with a good business to inherit from me when the time comes.'

Alexander was not going to tell his father about his inebriated attempt to kiss Polly in the hothouse. He smiled ruefully. 'I wish everyone had as good an opinion of me as you do, Papa.'

So far he had avoided making a trip up to Weardale, though to keep his father from badgering him further he had sent a brief letter to Polly, saying he was returned from Scandinavia and that perhaps they might meet over the summer season.

Now as he approached Ravensworth, he felt free of his father's fussing control or any obligation to go courting Polly.

He breathed in the scented air as he strode over a carpet of fallen petals and felt the May sun warm his back. The woods were noisy with birdsong and the sound of woodcutting. Ahead, gardeners were busy planting out flowerbeds in front of the castle terrace and the newly cut lawns were the emerald green of early summer.

James, the affable young head footman, greeted him cheerfully and took his bags. Alexander followed him up the stairs and along corridors till they reached the small tower bedroom that he had come to think of as his own. He had slept there as a child and declined to stay in any of the grander guest rooms on the lower floors.

'His Lordship's resting,' James explained, 'and Lady Ravensworth's gone to Newcastle for the day. Says to tell you she'll be back in time for afternoon tea.'

The quiet of the house was broken on Emma's arrival with her friend Hester Bellamy, with whom she'd been shopping. 'We'll take tea on the terrace,' she ordered. 'It's too gloomy inside.'

She slipped an arm through Alexander's and steered him outside. 'It's been so dull here all winter since Henry's mother died. I'm supposed to be in full mourning still, but I just refuse to wear black in May. It's an offence to nature.' She rustled her purple dress. 'Come July I shall throw a party to celebrate the end of mourning. You will come, won't you?'

Alexander laughed. 'If you order it, ma'am.'

'Of course I do,' she smiled as they took seats in the shade of a portico.

Around them servants bustled with tea trays and table-cloths. A large silver teapot was carried out, and plates of buttered scones and thinly cut sandwiches. Emma presided over the cutting of a large chocolate cake while Alexander told the women of his adventures in Sweden.

'So you fell in love with the baron's daughter. How romantic! But it's very bad of you, Alex, to go losing your heart without consulting me. And here I've been fretting over finding you a suitable wife.'

'My heart isn't free to give while you still possess it, Cousin Emma,' he declared.

She laughed in delight. 'Oh, dear boy, how I've missed you. You've stayed away far too long – and it's been so dreary here. You must promise me and Hester to be around all summer to keep us company and stop Henry from moping about his health. He's feeling very mortal since his mother passed away.'

'Nothing would give me more pleasure,' Alexander grinned.

'Ah, here he comes at last,' Emma said, waving at her husband as he walked towards them with the aid of a stick.

Alexander jumped up and went to greet his relation.

The first time Kate realised he had returned was when the head housemaid told her to take up extra coal to the bedroom in the east tower for a newly arrived guest. She passed him on the back stairs as she was going up and he coming down. He must have been making for the stables to have been using the servants' staircase, and he barely glanced at her in his rush to be gone. But she recognised his tall athletic frame and wolfish lean face in an instant. Alexander Pringle-Davies. He gave her a quick smile as she stopped with her load to let him past, but said nothing to indicate he remembered her.

She stared after him as he leapt down the steps in threes, a flash of dark coppery hair, and then he was out of sight. A door slammed far below.

119

Kate stood there with heart hammering at the sudden encounter. She had thought about him often over the winter months, every detail of their two brief encounters etched in her mind. The way he had held a raspberry to her lips with long fingers, the feel of his hand in the small of her back as they danced, the swift sensuous smile.

But it was painfully obvious that he had not recognised her under her maid's cap, struggling up with a scuttleful of coal. She had just been a faceless servant. She felt dashed as she continued up the stairs with her load. By the time she reached his room, Kate was chiding herself for being so foolish. Why should a gentleman like Pringle-Davies care two pins for the likes of her? He had danced with her that night on a whim, nothing more, and had forgotten her months ago.

Still, she could not help being curious on seeing his room. It was starkly furnished for a guest's bedroom, with nowhere to sit at ease, just a hard chair by a small desk table in the window. There was a marble washstand next to a high narrow bed, and a wardrobe in the corner. It was hardly more luxurious than the servants' quarters. The walls were bare apart from a solitary print. Kate peered. It was of a sailing ship leaving the Tyne. In the foreground she was amazed to see the dark outline of St Paul's church and the ruined monastery at Jarrow.

The ruins always made her think of her long-dead father telling her the story of St Bede and the early monks. Or perhaps she only remembered it because Sarah had told her their father had spoken of such things. Either way, she felt strangely comforted to find the monastery on the picture and wondered why it should hang in this room. Did it mean anything to its occupant or did he not even glance at it? There was very little else in the room to indicate the man's interests. A silver-topped walking stick was propped by the door and sheaves of paper and an ink pen lay on the table in the window. A pile of clothes lay heaped carelessly on a clothes basket, and a shaving blade and brush stood next to the wash jug and basin. It spoke of a man who travelled lightly or held little store by material things.

She quickly emptied the coals from the scuttle into the brass hod on the small tiled hearth. With a last glance round she hurried from the room.

All that week Kate humped coal up to the high bedroom, offering to do so for Hannah in return for her polishing the brass stair rods. But Alexander was never in his room. Before breakfast, she left jugs of hot water outside for shaving, but never saw him. Nevertheless, the thought of encountering him spurred her to spring out of bed in the morning and made her eager to do her chores. She sang as she worked, unable to suppress her excitement. She craved another look at his handsome face, yet mocked herself for her skittishness.

It would be something to laugh about with Suky when they met up on their days off and talked about lads. Though she would have to be careful Mary did not overhear her confidences. Thanks to Suky, Mary was now working at the Ravensworth Arms too, serving tables at the inn. Kate was pleased she had been able to get Mary away from home and give her mother some peace. And Mary appeared happier. She revelled in the gossip that blew in with the travellers and drinkers at the busy coaching inn. She and Suky had made friends too, sharing an attic bedroom.

One warm day at the end of May, Kate was dispatched to sweep the bedrooms and lead the grates. Fires were still needed until into June. By the time she got to the one in the east tower, she was hot with exhaustion. Finding the room

121

empty as usual, she plonked herself down on the chair in the sunshine, stretched her aching legs and arched her back. On the table lay a drawing of a woman with head bent over a book. Kate leant forward. It looked like Lady Ravensworth. She lifted it carefully and underneath was another sketch of the same woman, stretched out on a sofa, eyes closed.

Kate flushed with embarrassment; the sketch seemed to capture an intimate moment that she should not have seen. Hurrying to the fireplace she got down on her knees and began to sweep up the fallen soot.

As Alexander strode to his bedroom he heard a voice beyond the open door singing lustily. He paused for a moment, entranced by the cheerful sound, and then entered. The maid was crouched over the fender, brushing the grate, unaware of his presence. She carried on singing about the Waters of Tyne, a song that took him back to his boyhood. He stood there quite still, not wanting to interrupt her. Then when she sang the last refrain he joined in.

Kate whipped round, startled. She gasped in shock, her face going crimson to see him suddenly standing there. If he only knew she had been thinking about him as she sang the love song!

'Sorry, I didn't mean to frighten you,' Alexander grinned. 'I was enjoying your singing and didn't want you to stop.'

Kate felt her face going even hotter as she stared up at him. 'I always sing – can't help meself, sir.'

She turned away quickly, but something about her pink-cheeked face and the tendrils of brown hair escaping under her cap was familiar. Alexander looked at her more closely.

'What's your name?' he asked.

She half turned round. 'Kate, sir.'

The slim oval face, the glimpse of blue eyes under the dark lashes, the song . . . It came to him abruptly.

'You're the wood sprite with the berries!' he cried in recognition. 'You sang that song to Her Ladyship at the servants' ball, didn't you?'

Kate laughed to cover her embarrassment, inwardly thrilled he had remembered her after all.

'Aye, I did.' She stole a look at him and dared to add, 'And you danced a polka with me.'

He laughed too. 'So I did,' he admitted, though he had forgotten the moment until now. He crossed the room, discarding his riding jacket on the bed, and splashed water into the wash bowl. Unselfconsciously, he plunged his face in the water and reached for a towel.

Kate went back to scrubbing the grate, acutely aware of his movements from the corner of her eye.

Alexander rubbed his face and studied the girl. 'So you work at the castle – you're not a nymph from the woods after all.'

'Been here since old Lady Ravensworth died, sir,' Kate answered while still vigorously leading the grate. 'Her Ladyship took me in when Farnacre was closed up. She's been that good to me.'

'She is a very generous lady,' Alexander said, leaning against the bed.

Kate thought of the casual sketches on the table and couldn't help wondering about his relationship with Her Ladyship. Lily had called him a fortune-hunter. Kate hurried to finish and gather up her brushes.

Alexander watched her. She looked hot and flustered and keen to be gone. A smut of soot was smeared across her cheek and he had a sudden desire to wipe it clean. He half moved towards her, but her blue eyes widened in alarm so he stopped.

'I'll be off, sir,' she said with a quick bob, and rushed for the door.

'Goodbye, Kate. Come and sing to me again,' he called after her.

She did not reply. Alexander gave a rueful smile. Beauty could be found in unexpected places. He went to the table and pulled a folder out of the drawer. Leafing through the sketches he found the old pencil drawings he sought – a girl stepping down from a cart with a flash of ankle and a smooth oval cheek under a straw hat.

Sitting down at once, all thought of lunch forgotten, he reached for a blank piece of paper and picked up the ink pen. If he focused on her eyes he could conjure up the rest of her fair face and the wisps of escaping hair on her pale brow. Alexander began to draw.

Chapter 12

The next day, Kate went hurrying up to the east tower with hot water and left it outside Alexander's room. She thrilled to think of him lying just feet away in the small bedroom, imagining him waking and stretching in the bright morning light. Other guests brought valets with them to attend to their needs and put out their clothes, but not this man. He seemed different from other well-to-do visitors, not quite family and not quite a guest.

The casual gossip of other staff only increased Alexander's mysteriousness in Kate's eyes. Was Pringle-Davies a man of business or an artist? A long-lost family member or a chancer who took advantage of His Lordship's good nature?

Later in the day, she returned with coal. To her disappointment the room was empty and the fire needed no tending as he had not lit it the night before. She left the extra coals and retreated. All that week she hoped to glimpse him when polishing the stairs or sweeping the corridors, but there was never any sign. Picnics were ordered daily from the kitchen and she assumed he went out riding or on outings with Lady Ravensworth in the fine weather.

The days were now long, and Kate enjoyed walking out in the evening after her duties were finished to visit Aunt Lizzie and the family. The quickest way was to pass the stables, go down the back drive and cut along a bridlepath through the woods to the back of the gardeners' cottages. Alfred always ran out to greet her and talked nonstop about what he had been doing that day. Lizzie would give her a cup of elderflower juice and Alfred would drag her off to the gardens to find Peter and George.

On one particularly warm evening at the beginning of June, she took the long way back to the castle around the fishing lake. It was tranquil in the fading light, flies hovering above the still surface, an empty boat moored on the far side. Somewhere in the encircling trees a fox called soulfully to its mate. She loved the peaceful quiet of this place, an antidote to the bustle of the castle. It was so far removed from the cramped, noisy, teeming life on Tyneside that she was used to that she never tired of walking its woodland paths.

She did not find its solitariness frightening, for she liked to think of her mother visiting here as a young woman with her two small daughters. A day in paradise, Rose had called the Sunday School outing. And that was what it looked like that evening, Kate mused.

She might be a child of Jarrow too, but there was something about this place that tugged at her very soul and made her feel she belonged. Perhaps it was due to stories of Ravensworth that Rose had passed down from her own mother, who had worked here long ago, before Queen Victoria had come to the throne. Perhaps she was a country girl at heart. Or maybe it was the first time since she was a small girl that she was truly happy again.

A rustle in the trees and a snap of twig behind her made Kate swing round, startled out of her reverie. A figure loomed out of the twilight clutching a stick. Kate stepped back, preparing for flight.

'Don't go!' the man pleaded and strode up to her. The dying sun caught the auburn light in his hair.

'Mr Pringle-Davies!' she gasped.

'I saw you from across the lake,' he smiled, 'my wood nymph. You looked quite alone.'

'I've been visiting my aunt at the cottages,' Kate managed to say despite the hammering in her chest. 'I left my Uncle Peter at the walled garden and came this way.'

'Are you meeting someone, Kate?' he asked. 'This seems a fine trysting place.'

'No, sir,' she gulped, 'no one.'

He studied her a moment. 'Then will you allow me to walk you home?'

She smiled at him at last and his heart missed a beat.

'If you please, sir,' she blushed.

'It would please me greatly,' he said. 'Let's walk around the lake first and enjoy the sunset.'

They set off side by side on the wide path, each heady with their daring. Kate knew she should have declined and hurried home; Alexander knew he should not be encouraging the girl, for it could come to nothing. But neither of them wanted to obey sensible thoughts on such a magical evening.

He asked about her uncle and joked at how mischievous he had been towards him as a boy.

'Peter was very long suffering – I must've been the bane of his life. I was wild in those days,' he said. 'Did you live here then, Kate?'

'No, sir, I come from near Shields.'

'Whereabouts?'

'Born in Jarrow, sir.'

Alexander stopped and exclaimed, 'Jarrow? Well, well!'

Kate looked at him quizzically.

127

'I knew Jarrow too as a boy – briefly. Stayed there with relations of mine. My cousin Edward was rector of St Paul's.'

Kate said without thinking, 'So that's why you've got that picture on your wall?'

He raised an eyebrow. 'You're very observant.'

'It just caught me eye,' she said bashfully.

He smiled. 'It's hung there since I was a boy. I always used that room when Cousin Edward – Canon Liddell – brought me to stay.'

Kate gaped. 'Canon Liddell was your relation?'

'Yes.' Alexander smiled in surprise. 'Did you know him?'

Kate shook her head. 'But me father did – Mam said so, said they were friends,' Kate said proudly. Something made her omit that they only knew each other because her mother had cleaned for the Liddells.

Alexander looked pleased. 'What's your father's name?'

'Fawcett. William Fawcett.'

He frowned as he tried to remember. The name sounded familiar. There had been a William, a kind man with a handsome wife who had once taken him to the circus. When his beloved cousin Edward had fallen ill, Alexander had wanted to go to live with them rather than be sent away to strangers. Could it be possible that this was the same man's daughter?

'Perhaps I met him then,' he smiled. 'Visitors were always coming to the rectory. Kate Fawcett, I feel as if I know you!'

She grinned back at him and they continued to walk.

'I was very fond of my cousin Edward,' he told her. 'He was a father to me for a while – when my own father wanted nothing to do with me. My mother was a Liddell, you see – caused a scandal by eloping with a coachman and died before I got to know her. I'm a bit of a black sheep. Then along came

128

Jeremiah Davies and adopted me – saved me from the house of correction!'

His speech was flippant, but his tone was bitter. Kate was astonished he was telling her any of it. Perhaps he was drunk.

'How unhappy you must've been,' she murmured.

Alexander gave her a sharp look, then realised it was true. He had been deeply unhappy and lonely as a boy, latching on desperately to anyone who showed him an ounce of affection. How strange that this ordinary girl from Jarrow should understand that so plainly when he had denied it for years. Except Kate Fawcett did not strike him as ordinary. She had more than surface prettiness. A simple dignity and inner grace shone through her that made him forget she was a mere housemaid.

'It's like a ship losing its anchor,' Kate continued quietly, 'when a bairn loses a mother or father. My father died when I was barely six years old.'

Alexander felt a sudden closeness to her. He put a hand on her shoulder. 'So that's how you came on hard times?'

Kate flinched at the touch as if she had been scalded. 'Aye, we've had hard times,' she flushed. 'Mam lost two of her bairns an' all. But she's brought up another four and lived to tell the tale.'

'She must be a remarkable woman. Just like her daughter.' Alexander searched her face in the half-dark.

Kate's heart thumped. 'You don't know me, sir.'

He leant closer. 'I'd like to get to know you, Kate.'

She dropped her gaze, suddenly unsure of the situation. Suky's words of warning rang in her head. *Watch out for that sort. Fancy silks and common serge don't mix . . .*

'I must be gettin' back, sir,' she said hastily, stepping away, 'else I'll be locked out.'

129

Alexander said sardonically, 'I know where to climb in when the back door's bolted – did it as a lad.'

'Well, I'm no lad and I'll be in a heap of bother from the housekeeper if I start climbing in windows!'

They both looked at each other and laughed, the seriousness of moments before broken.

'Come on then, Kate,' he said, ushering her in front of him.

They said little else on their brisk walk back, Kate keeping ahead of him. At the foot of the terrace, by the hothouses, they parted. Kate took the path round to the back of the castle and Alexander the steps leading up to the front.

'Good night, Kate,' he called with a wave of his walking cane.

'Sir,' she answered, picking up her skirt and running into the dark shadows.

That fiery sunset marked the end of the spell of good weather and when Kate rose early the next day it was grey and wet. Gazing out at the rain drumming on the courtyard cobbles, she wondered if she had dreamt the previous evening. The head housemaid had been suspicious of her late return and started asking questions. Kate decided not to venture out that evening in the wet, though she longed to come across Alexander in the grounds again.

Two days later she and Hannah were told to clean out the bedroom in the east tower. Rushing there, Kate found to her dismay that it was empty. All trace of Alexander was gone. She tried to hide her disappointment and helped Hannah strip the bed and bundle the linen into a basket. They swept out the room and carried away the ashes from the dead fire.

What did she expect? she berated herself. For all his chequered childhood, he was a gentleman far out of her reach with business to take him elsewhere. He had more in common with Lady Ravensworth than he ever would with her. That night by the lake he had merely been kind in offering to see her safely home. It was just talk of Jarrow and the mention of the Liddells that had made her feel closer to him than she should have dared.

She had given him the impression that she was from a social class not far removed from the rector's. He had assumed she had fallen on hard times because her father had died, little guessing that being housemaid to Lord Ravensworth was a dream come true for a girl who had begged round the streets of Tyneside. She had kept from him that her mother had remarried a boorish drunk who could not even write his own name.

He may have talked to her, but it had not meant the same for him. He was gone as he had before, without warning, and it might be months before she set eyes on him again. She must bury her foolish feelings for him, she told herself harshly.

Chapter 13

A week after returning home to Darlington, Alexander felt restless once more. There had been no excuse to stay on at Ravensworth, though he had promised Cousin Emma he would return for the summer ball in July. The fine weather had broken and he had left abruptly, desiring a taste of town life. But a few days of his father's company and social calls were enough.

He arranged to go to Newcastle to check on timber imports and visit their shipping agents, ignoring Davies's complaints that it could be done by letter. He booked into a boarding house near the Central Station that he used before voyages, run by tight-lipped widow Timmins, who kept the narrow house spotless for her travellers.

Alexander made a cursory call to the agents on the quayside and spent the rest of the week wandering the anonymous city with his notebook and pen. When the sun shone through the billowing chimney smoke that hung over the town he sat on walls and quaysides, drawing the life of the streets: dockers and draymen, pedlars and hawkers, children crouched over games of marbles in the dust. When it rained he retreated to a bar and sat in the corner nursing a pint of beer and sketching his fellow drinkers.

He felt compelled to draw people, recreating the faces of

his childhood as he listened to their sharp, lilting voices and quick laughter. But every time he caught sight of a young woman with a basket on her arm or a face shaded by a bonnet, his thoughts turned to Kate. She was in every sketch he made. He tried to draw what he saw, but the curve of her jaw or her slim waist, the line of her neat ankle or the edge of her smile came out on the paper.

He could not rid his mind of her. What was it about her that made him unable to settle to anything but this frenzied drawing? She was pretty, but he had seen prettier young women in Gothenburg. She sang well, but with an untrained voice. As he drank his fill and became morose he realised it was something to do with her uncomplicated naturalness, her simplicity of speech, the way she had sympathised with him. He detected a generosity of spirit and a loving nature.

And she came from Jarrow and her family had known his. It did not concern him that she was beneath him socially; such barriers had never held the importance that they did for others, people like Davies. After all, his mother had run off with a coachman. Barriers were there to be broken, in Alexander's view.

He could not work or sleep in this state of preoccupation. He must get back to Ravensworth. Alexander returned to his boarding house and penned a letter to the earl, inviting himself to stay.

By return of post, a note came from Lady Ravensworth, telling him he must come at once. With the house still in mourning there was a dearth of visitors, so it was his duty to cheer them up. Two weeks after leaving the castle, Alexander was hurrying back.

*

133

Kate and Hannah were sent to prepare the bedroom. Kate knew at once that Alexander must be returning, for no one else used the room. She found it hard to contain her excitement or from blurting out to the other maid that she had met and walked with this gentleman in the woods.

'Wonder why he always sleeps in this room?' Hannah asked. 'Bit poky, if you ask me.'

'He used it when he was a boy, that's why,' Kate answered without thinking.

'How would you know?' Hannah looked at her sharply.

Kate flushed. 'So I've heard – from me Uncle Peter – he knew him as a lad.' She turned and busied herself polishing the leather-topped table.

'What would a gardener know?' Hannah said sniffily.

Kate said nothing, not wanting to get into an argument or be questioned further.

Hannah continued, 'I think he must be sweet on Her Ladyship, else why does he keep coming back?'

'It's only the second time this year,' Kate said, annoyed by the suggestion.

'Second time in a month,' Hannah snorted. 'Lily thinks so too. Overheard them talking – 'bout affairs of the heart and that.'

'Lily just likes to gossip. Shouldn't say such things about Her Ladyship.'

'Oh, I was forgetting you were one of her strays brought in from Farnacre,' Hannah teased. 'I won't say another word!'

Kate threw her duster at Hannah and meowed like a cat, turning their argument into a joke.

The following day Kate glimpsed Alexander in the distance, riding out in the early morning, and the day after that, climbing into an open carriage beside Lady Ravensworth. She began to suspect that Hannah's gossip might be true. She could not understand why it should upset her so much, but it did. Better to smother her feelings for him now and to avoid setting eyes on Alexander at all.

So when orders came to take hot water or an extra lamp or a cake of soap up to the east tower, she asked Hannah to go. A week went by and she did not see him. Then Hannah began to tire of traipsing up and down the many stairs and told Kate it was her turn.

The following morning, as Kate was leaving a jug of steaming water outside Alexander's room, she heard a groan from inside. She stopped and listened and heard it again. She hesitated, then heard his muffled voice calling for help.

Kate knocked. 'Are you all right, sir?'

Another groan. Kate tried the door. It was unlocked, so she went in. The curtains were drawn back and Alexander was lying on the floor half dressed. There was blood all over his face and hair. He clutched a linen towel, which was blood-soaked too.

'Sir!' Kate cried and rushed to him. 'What's happened to you?'

He stared at her with vacant eyes, then buried his face in the towel again. She reached forward and pulled it gently away from his face to see where the cut was. Perhaps he had fallen and hit his head. He moaned in pain. Blood poured from his nose. Quickly Kate seized a fresh towel from the stand and gave it to him.

'Can you sit up, sir?' she asked. 'Here, put an arm round me shoulder.'

Kate coaxed him with comforting words, though her heart

hammered in fright at the sight of so much blood. She managed to haul him into a sitting position, propped against the bed.

'Keep your head forward so you don't choke on your blood. I'll get help.'

She bolted from the room and ran down the stairs, shouting for help. She ran into a footman in the gallery.

'Mr Wadsworth, we need a doctor quickly! It's Mr Pringle-Davies. I found him bleedin' on the floor!'

James told her to alert the housekeeper while he rang for the doctor. 'Then go back and stay with him until someone comes,' he ordered.

Kate flew to the housekeeper's room behind the kitchens and gabbled her story. The housekeeper sent her back upstairs while she broke the news to Lady Ravensworth. Kate returned with a pile of extra towels to the tower room and found Alexander still slumped against the bed. She poured water into a bowl and carried it over to the bedside.

Dipping a fresh towel in the water, she tentatively pulled away the bloodied one.

'Hold this,' she said gently. Wringing out another one, she began to wash his brow, pushing the matted hair away from his temples and talking to him calmly.

He watched her with glazed eyes that did not seem to recognise her, but she went on washing him and talking softly as if dealing with a frightened child, while inside, it was she who was terrified.

Minutes later, James appeared to tell them the doctor was on his way. Between them, they managed to pull Alexander on to the bed.

'What should I do now, Mr Wadsworth?' she asked.

'Better get back downstairs,' he said.

Alexander spoke for the first time. 'No, let her stay,' he mumbled. 'Please.'

The footman looked surprised, but nodded. 'I'll go and show the doctor the way,' he said, and disappeared.

Kate sat down on the bed and carried on bathing Alexander's face. His look was glazed.

'Thank you, Kate,' he croaked.

Her heart thumped. He had recognised her.

'Don't speak,' she whispered. 'Save your strength, sir.'

He reached up and covered the hand that was wiping his brow, so that she had to stop. He pulled it to his lips and brushed her fingers with a kiss. She looked into his tawny eyes and began to shake. What did he mean by such a kiss?

Moments later, she heard voices on the stairs beyond and the housekeeper swept in with Lady Ravensworth. Kate sprang up nervously and curtsied. Lady Ravensworth went straight to Alexander and kissed the top of his head.

'My poor, dear Alexander! How dreadful!'

'I'll be fine,' he answered weakly, 'I just need to rest. It'll pass – it always does.' He lay back on the pillow, drained and exhausted by the loss of blood.

'It's happened before?' Her Ladyship cried.

Alexander nodded.

'We must send word to your father at once.'

'No,' Alexander protested, 'he just fusses.'

'Well, I won't hear of you going anywhere until you're quite better. Dr Lawson is just the man to take care of you. Henry's valet will stay with you too.'

'There's no need,' Alexander said. 'Kate here can nurse me. She has a gentle touch.'

Lady Emma looked at Kate with interest. 'My singing maid,' she smiled in recognition. 'Very well.'

Kate was astounded at the bold request and caught the look of disapproval on the housekeeper's face. She did not want to be the cause of tongues wagging around the castle staff, however much she wanted to stay with Alexander. But the housekeeper made no protest and soon after Dr Lawson arrived and they were all sent out of the room.

Complete bed rest was ordered and no more energetic trips on horseback. For the next few days Alexander slept for hours on end, often fretful in his sleep. Kate would steal in and watch him toss restlessly and cry out. At other times he lay pale and peaceful, his brow smoothed of worry like a small boy's.

On one occasion while he slept, she was drawn to the table in the window where pieces of paper spilt out of a leather folder. Making sure he still slept, Kate opened the folder and looked through the drawings. She was curious for some proof that Lady Ravensworth meant more to him than being a kind hostess and patron. But there were no more pictures of Lady Ravensworth. Instead there were dozens of drawings of ordinary people at work and rest. Kate gasped in shock. One of the sketches looked like her holding Alfred in her arms. But flicking quickly through the others, the same young woman appeared again and again in different poses and settings – places to which she had never been.

Perhaps she was an artist's model or his lover? With a stab of jealousy, she pushed the pictures quickly back into the folder. She should not have looked. Lady Ravensworth might not be the target for his affections, but some other woman clearly was.

Kate tried to be more distant. After three days Alexander was taking an interest in the meals of liver and beer that she brought up for him to build up his strength. He would smile,

138

thank her and try to engage her in conversation, but she would say little and withdraw quickly.

The next day the calm was shattered by the unexpected arrival of Jeremiah Davies to see his son. Having heard Alexander had left Newcastle the week before, he guessed where he had gone.

'You should have told me sooner that you were ill,' Davies scolded. 'Lady Ravensworth's letter arrived yesterday. Were you ever going to tell me yourself?'

'Don't fret, Papa,' Alexander replied. 'I didn't want you worrying.'

'Of course I'm worried! We must get you home at once. You shall see our own physician.'

'I'm perfectly well looked after here. Dr Lawson has called every day – and I have Kate here to tend me.'

Davies looked round and noticed the maid for the first time. 'Are you a nurse?' he demanded.

'No, sir,' Kate admitted.

Davies turned back to Alexander. 'I will arrange a proper nurse to care for you until you are quite fit again. And you shall go to see a specialist – in London if needs be. These attacks are getting worse.'

'No, Papa, I'm staying here. Lady Ravensworth's orders. Can't be disobeyed.' He sank back on the pillow and closed his eyes.

Kate tried not to laugh at his cheeky defiance or Davies's blustering. She could see that the elderly white-haired man was concerned for his son, yet angry not to get his own way. She imagined the plain-talking coal agent was not used to being thwarted by people saying no to him. But short of hauling Alexander down the stairs himself, there was little he could do.

139

Davies cried, 'Have it your own way! But I want you home as soon as you can travel. I can't imagine why His Lordship allows you to spend so much time here,' he added peevishly.

He threw a disparaging look at Kate on his way out. She showed him to the door and curtsied. When he had gone she heard Alexander call her back.

'Did I look suitably near death's door?' he asked.

'Yes, sir,' she smirked.

'Good,' he smiled, closing his eyes again. 'It could be days before I'm able to travel, don't you think?'

'Maybes weeks, sir,' Kate agreed.

As she closed the door to let him rest she heard him chuckling to himself.

As if Davies's visit had spurred him to defiance, Alexander was abruptly better again. Kate came in with breakfast one day to find him up and dressed. He took the tray from her.

'Think I'll eat this downstairs today,' he told her.

She nodded, suddenly disappointed. 'You look much better, sir. Colour in your cheeks.'

'I feel it. Thank you for looking after me. I'm sorry for causing such a fuss. It can't have been very pleasant for you.'

She had the impression he was embarrassed. Perhaps he regretted asking for her help and being seen in such a weakened state.

'Was no bother, sir,' she told him. 'Shall I carry the tray for you?'

'No, I can do that.'

'Do you need anything else, sir?'

He shook his head. 'I'll attempt some fresh air later.' He hesitated. 'I hear the lake can look very beautiful in the evening.'

She shot him a look. 'Aye, sir, it can.'

'Think I might take a stroll down there after dinner,' he said, holding her gaze.

Her heart lurched.

'Then I might see you on me way home from Aunt Lizzie's,' she dared to say.

'I'd like that,' he smiled.

Kate hurried out ahead of him, barely able to believe that they had made a tentative assignation for the evening. She could hardly wait, yet part of her told her not to be such a fool.

Chapter 14

When Kate strolled down the woodland path from the walled garden, Alexander was already waiting by the lakeside. The sky was streaked with dark purple clouds and a chill breeze stirred the water and rustled the reeds, making a sound like the sea.

'You came!' he said, relief on his face.

Kate was surprised that he should have been worrying too. Her heart was pounding with excitement and nerves.

'Let's walk, Kate,' he said, offering his arm. She slipped her arm through his, unable to speak, and they began to follow the path that skirted the lake. With the trees in full leaf and the grass high, they were hidden from view from the castle and any of the surrounding cottages. The lake was set apart and no one came here after dark, except to poach.

'Tell me about yourself, Kate. I want to know all about you.'

'Nothing to tell, sir. I'm just a lass like any other.'

She had no intention of telling him what her life had been like in Jarrow. It was a different world and she would be ashamed for him to know of her past poverty or her life with her ignorant stepfather.

'You're not like any other,' Alexander protested. 'You are as charming and beautiful as this place.'

'Sir!' Kate laughed.

'And as mysterious.'

'That makes two of us then.'

'Me, Kate? I'm just a simple man of business.'

'And a good horseman – and an artist.'

He looked pleased. 'Is that what they say about me in the servants' hall?'

'That's what I've noticed. They say all sorts of nonsense among the staff.'

'Such as?'

'That you're a fortune-seeker – and close to Her Ladyship.'

Alexander flushed. 'Then they are impudent!'

'That's not my belief, sir,' Kate said hastily.

He stopped and looked at her intently. There was something dangerous in that look. 'But I am close to Lady Ravensworth. She is a remarkable woman.'

Kate felt uncomfortable. 'Yes, sir.'

'Perhaps the gossips speak the truth. Maybe I am a seeker after fortune – the Liddell fortune. Why shouldn't I be? Don't I have a right to some of it? I'm a Liddell too!'

He leant over her, eyes glittering with anger, and Kate felt fear.

'It's not for me to say, sir,' she gulped. 'But you don't strike me as a man who sets any great store by wealth – or silly gossip.'

For a moment they stared at each other. Alexander had a sudden desire to kiss her, but something held him back. He had ruined too many friendships by his impulsiveness and he did not want to spoil this moment with Kate. Deep inside he knew there was something special about this girl, something that he craved more than quick satisfaction. He stepped back and laughed.

'You're right, Kate. Let the gossips go to the Devil!'

He took her arm and they walked on, Kate relieved that his anger had gone as quickly as it had come. She would keep castle tittle-tattle to herself in future. Instead she listened to him talk of his travels abroad and marvelled at the places he described: dark endless forests frozen in snow and dazzling stars over ice-bound seas. They had the magical ring of folk songs.

'I once went to the Lake District with the Patersons – folk I worked for in Shields. Apart from that, this is as far as I've ever been,' Kate mused.

They stopped and gazed at the shadowed lake, the light almost gone.

'You don't need to go any further. This is as beautiful as anything in the world,' Alexander murmured. 'Sometimes it's the things right under your nose that bring you the greatest happiness – but you have to go away before you can appreciate them.'

'Yes,' Kate whispered, thinking of her unhappy trip home in March and how it had made her love Ravensworth all the more. 'I'd be sad to have to leave here.'

He took her hand and pressed it lightly to his lips. 'And I would be sad too.'

Kate's heart hammered. Could he really mean it?

'You're very kind.'

'It's the truth,' he smiled. 'You are my Florence Nightingale. You saved my life.'

'Hardly that, sir!'

'And you must stop calling me sir – at least when we are walking alone by the lake. In future you will call me Alex.'

'Will there be another time, sir?'

'I hope so, Kate. If you would like it?'

144

'Oh yes, sir, I would.'

'There you go again. My name is Alex,' he laughed. 'Next time, can I draw you sitting by the lakeside?'

'What you want to do that for?'

'Because you are my pretty wood nymph and I will have the excuse to gaze on you for as long as I like.'

Kate spluttered with laughter. 'I never heard such talk!'

'It's true. I've been trying to draw other people for weeks, but you keep appearing on the page.'

'Me!'

'Yes, you've bewitched me and the only way to break the spell is to draw you. So for the good of my health you must say yes.'

'Well, just for your health's sake – Master Alex.'

'Not "Master Alex" – that makes me feel like a schoolboy in britches!'

They laughed and continued their way round the lake, parting at the walled garden and agreeing to meet the next evening if the weather was fine. Kate thrilled at the thought, going over in her mind all the amazing things he had said to her. She imagined Suky's worried fussings. *He'll just be after one thing! Stop now – you can't shut the stable door once the horse has bolted.*

But Kate knew she would go – couldn't stop herself. She wanted nothing more than to be in his company. She didn't care if he sought her out merely to paint her picture. She knew he couldn't possibly care for her the way she did for him, but it was enough just to sit close to him and gaze at his handsome face while he drew her own.

So she met him the following evening and they sat behind the boathouse in the twilight of midsummer while he sketched. They met several times over the next couple of weeks, secret

145

trysts among the trees like pastoral lovers, though they did nothing more than talk and laugh and briefly touch hands in between his bouts of drawing.

When they parted, Alexander would raise her work-roughened hands to his lips and gently brush them with a kiss. Then her heart would pound and she would feel almost sick with longing. At night she lay sleepless in the stuffy attic bedroom, thinking of him lying in the east tower and wondering if he lay awake too.

By July, Hannah was giving her suspicious looks when she came in late, as if she did not believe she stayed so long at her aunt's cottage. Kate knew she must not start any rumours that would get her into trouble, for the housekeeper made no secret of her resentment that Kate had been brought from Farnacre without her approval and she would relish an excuse to be rid of one of Lady Ravensworth's favourites.

Alexander did not think beyond the day. He dwelt on little else but his meetings with Kate; she entranced him with her fresh looks and good humour. She was friendly and open and eager to please him. He liked to think that she might be the daughter of the kind Jarrow woman who had taken him to the circus and visited Ravensworth with her babies on that distant golden summer. He had long forgotten her name, but Kate reminded him of the pretty, generous lady who had shown him friendship.

Alexander thought of Kate as he rode the Durham hills and each evening was impatient for dinner to end so he could walk to the lake. The secrecy of their meetings only heightened his impatience and excitement. Perhaps Lady Ravensworth suspected there was a purpose to his late evening walks for she did not insist on coming with him.

'Henry's looking tired – we'll retire early,' she would say, and wave him off.

He had filled a whole sketchbook with drawings of Kate. He knew her features so well he could draw her from memory, but still used it as an excuse to meet. He had no idea where the liaison would lead, he just wanted the summer to continue like this for ever and not to have to think of the future.

One evening an impulse struck him.

'Kate, I'd like to go back to Jarrow – see where I used to live. In all these years I've never been back – never wanted to. But now, knowing you, it's something we share. Would you come with me and show me? I could meet your mother – see if she's the woman I remember.'

Kate looked at him appalled. 'No! I mean – what for? There's nothing much to see – just the new town hall – and the old vicarage is gone. You wouldn't recognise the place. And Mam doesn't live in Jarrow any longer. Moved out to the country a couple of years back with our Jack.'

'That sounds more pleasant.' Alexander was astonished by her agitation.

'Aye, but she doesn't take to visitors. Health's not good.'

'How does she manage on her own?'

Kate winced. 'Our Jack's still at home.' Why had she not mentioned John McMullen before? It seemed too late now.

'Well, we could still pay a visit to the town – look round the old monastery.'

'Why bother when you've got all this bonny countryside round here?' Her look was pleading. 'Any road, I wouldn't get the time off. Best if you went on your own.'

Alexander was dashed by her refusal, but he could see by the stubborn set of her mouth that she would not be persuaded. Perhaps the notion was a foolish one, to want to see the place

147

of fleeting happiness with his Cousin Edward. He thought it might have pleased Kate to be taken to see her mother, show off her acquaintance with a Liddell. But she was more practical than he. It was fanciful to think they could go about in public as equals or friends. People would rush to the wrong conclusion and condemn such a liaison.

'You're right,' he said with a rueful smile. 'Let us drop the subject.'

He saw how Kate at once regained her cheerfulness. He must remember to keep their relationship simple – and secret.

'But maybe we could spend your day off in another way?' he suggested. 'A walk in the hills, perhaps?'

Kate eyed him. She would like nothing more, but could not see how it could be achieved without discovery. She had promised to meet up with Mary the following Sunday.

'I can't,' she said reluctantly. 'I'm meeting someone.'

Alexander looked away in disappointment. 'I'm sorry. I've no right to stand in the way. A girl like you must have no end of suitors wishing to court you.'

Kate gawped. 'It's not that—'

'No, don't apologise.'

'It's not a lad I'm meeting!' Kate burst out, then blushed furiously.

'It's not?' Alexander brightened.

'No,' she laughed, 'it's a lass – me sister Mary. She's working at the Ravensworth Arms.'

'I see. That's good,' Alexander grinned.

They gazed at each other. Kate wondered whether he was courting but would never dare ask. He might already be married, for all she knew. She could be endangering her mortal soul by continuing to see him. But at that moment, the flames of Hell seemed a distant punishment.

148

'Have you ever ridden, Kate?' he suddenly asked.

'A donkey on the beach once,' she laughed.

'I'll take you riding then.'

'I couldn't!' she spluttered.

'I'll arrange it.'

'When?'

'After you've met your sister. Get away early – I'll meet you beyond the church at Lamesley. Say yes, Kate.'

Her heart jolted at such daring, but when he looked at her with those intent eyes, she would risk anything.

'Aye, I will,' she smiled.

He leant forward as if he would kiss her, then hesitated.

'Splendid! Sunday it is – about three o'clock?'

The next three days it rained continuously and Kate was kept indoors in the evenings, frustrated at the weather and wondering if it would prevent their ride on Sunday. She glimpsed Alexander twice with Lady Ravensworth, but he made no show of recognising her. They looked preoccupied. A ball was being planned for the middle of the month, but the earl was confined to bed with a cold, and rumours came back from the parlourmaids that Her Ladyship was fretting the event might have to be postponed.

'Typical!' muttered the housekeeper. 'Just thinks of her own pleasure, and there's the poor old earl a-lying in his bed.'

'Watch what you say,' James, the head footman, warned.

'I'll say what I like,' she declared. 'It's nothing but the truth. The house should still be in mourning for old Lady Ravensworth.'

'That's for Her Ladyship to decide,' James said loyally.

'And you'll be the first to know what she wants,' the housekeeper said waspishly.

149

'She wants His Lordship to be better before filling the house with guests,' James said levelly.

'Is he very ill?' Kate asked Lily in concern. She had taken up soup to Lord Ravensworth's room earlier.

Lily shrugged. 'Doctor's been in every day this week, but he was sat up in bed chatting when I went in. Always got a nice word to say, has His Lordship.'

'Aye,' Kate agreed, remembering how he had once made her feel at home by talking about Jarrow and his Cousin Edward. But she fretted that Alexander might not be able to get away on Sunday. Perhaps he would feel he had to keep Lady Ravensworth company or, worse, leave the castle and return home if there was to be no ball.

Sunday came and to Kate's joy the sun broke through the canvas of grey clouds that had brought such rain for the best part of a week. She worked quickly that morning to finish her chores and then set out on the downhill mile walk to the Ravensworth Arms. She had seen the Liddells' carriage return from the service at Lamesley church, but knew from Lily that Lord Ravensworth was still confined to bed. No doubt Alexander would have accompanied Her Ladyship, but would he be able to get away later?

Mary wanted to walk up to Kibblesworth and look in the shop windows.

'I can't – have to get back soon,' Kate said.

'Why? You've got a couple of hours still!'

'There's that much to do – all these guests arriving over the next week. Lady Ravensworth's planning dinners and a big dance and a day at the races.'

Mary brightened. 'You could take me back with you. You promised you'd show me round.'

'Not today.'

'Why not? You're such a spoilsport!'

'You could call on Aunt Lizzie – see the cousins.'

Mary pulled a face. 'I'll end up having to spread muck on the roses or touch Alfred's pet rat. Ugh!'

'Next day off we'll gan up to Kibblesworth, I promise – do something with Suky and her lad.'

Mary gave her a sulky look as they rounded the side of the inn. Kate glanced nervously in the direction of the distant church.

'I'll be off then.'

'Maybes I'll gan to Aunt Lizzie's after all. I'll walk up with you,' Mary announced.

Kate's heart sank. They would have to pass right by the church. What if Alexander said something? She would have to walk straight on, pretending she did not know him. Mary must never suspect she was meeting a man, especially a man so far above their class. How frustrating! She might not have time to come back and meet him.

Kate tried to hide her annoyance as they set off together, down the lane towards Lamesley village. Her heart began to pound as they neared the church. The tower clock struck three.

While Mary gossiped about people at the inn, Kate glanced nervously about her. There was no sign of Alexander or a horse anywhere near the church. As they passed the open gate, she glimpsed someone picking flowers in the graveyard. A young couple strolled by and nodded to them.

A wave of relief came over Kate that Alexander was nowhere to be seen. How foolhardy to have made such an arrangement with all these villagers about – and so close to Mary and the inn. It had been the madness of a magical summer's evening.

151

Still her heart hammered as they left the village and climbed the road to the castle, hidden among dense woods. What if he should come riding out of the trees? What would she say? But they walked on and no rider came.

'You're not listening, are you?' Mary demanded.

'Sorry?'

'Just 'cos I'm not working with the nobs up at the castle. Still think you're better than me, don't you?'

'No, don't be daft.' Kate paused on the brow of the hill and looked back at the village. There was no sign of Alexander. The distant St Andrew's clock struck half-past three. Despite the situation, she felt a stab of disappointment. He was not going to come after all, perhaps had never intended to. In the cold light of day he had changed his mind and thought nothing more of it.

'What's that for?' Mary asked, interrupting her thoughts.

'What?' Kate asked.

'The bells. Why they ringing the bells?'

Kate hadn't noticed, but the Lamesley bells had begun to toll. Their ring was slow and ponderous. Her insides jolted.

'Oh, no!'

'What?'

'Something's happened.' Kate seized Mary by the arm. Her sister looked mystified. 'They rang like that when old Lady Ravensworth died. Come on, quick! I must get back to the castle.'

She picked up her skirts and ran, Mary shouting after her to slow down. They raced through the side gate in the South Lodge. The gatekeeper's wife was standing in her doorway, listening.

'What's happened?' Kate called to her.

152

'Don't rightly know,' said the stooped old woman. 'But I fear it's bad news.'

They raced on, Mary complaining of a stitch in her side and the mud sticking to her shoes. But Kate did not stop till they reached the gardeners' cottages.

Peter was standing outside, talking quietly with a neighbour. He turned at the sound of the girls racing round the corner. His face was sombre.

'The bells,' Kate gasped, 'down Lamesley – w-what do they mean?'

Peter stood twisting his cap. 'They called all the staff in the hall half an hour ago.'

'It's Lord Ravensworth?' Kate braced herself for the answer.

Peter nodded. 'Passed away in his sleep.'

Kate felt winded.

'And Her Ladyship?'

'Came and told us herself. Full o' dignity, she was.'

Kate felt tears sting her eyes. She was suddenly more upset than she could have imagined. She turned to Mary and flung her arms around her for comfort.

'Poor Lady Ravensworth!'

Peter looked on in pity. 'Aye, it's the end of an era, old Lord Ravensworth going. Who knows what changes it'll bring?'

Kate burst into tears.

153

Chapter 15

Lord Ravensworth's funeral was a grand affair, the cortège of gleaming black carriages and plumed horses drawing large crowds along the route from Ravensworth Castle to Lamesley. The old earl had been popular and lived among his people for years.

'What's the new earl like?' Kate asked Hannah as they sheltered from rain under the trees. They had not been allowed to attend the service; there was too much work to be done preparing for the funeral tea. The castle was packed with visiting family and political friends come to pay their respects.

'Captain Charles? He's a brother of Lord Henry, that's all I know. No spring chicken himself.'

Lily nudged them both as an open carriage of mourners went by.

'That's him there – with the new Lady Ravensworth. Live down south.'

Lily could be relied upon to relay gossip from the drawing rooms.

'So they might not want to come and live here?' Kate asked in hope. She wanted the Dowager Lady Ravensworth to stay on.

'Course they will! They'd be soft in the head not to come and live at the castle. Anyways, I've heard things.'

'What things?'

'Talk of lawyers and dividing up the furniture – Lady Ravensworth taking what's hers and the new Lady Ravensworth – Caroline – moving hers in.'

'What'll happen to us?' Kate asked anxiously.

But even Lily did not seem to have the answer to that. The last of the carriages squelched past, flicking mud at their skirts. Kate had craned for a view of Alexander sitting next to Lady Ravensworth, but they were gone so quickly she did not see his expression. He had not looked out at the crowds or searched for her. Neither had he looked for her all week. She had been to the lake twice but he had not appeared. During the day she had been kept busy cleaning rooms in the west wing for visitors, or helping in the kitchens, and had seen no sign of him. She was cheered only by the thought that there would be much to sort out of the old earl's business affairs that might keep him at Ravensworth. Surely she would be able to speak to him soon.

Kate was kept busy washing up during the vast funeral tea and saw nothing of the ranks of county gentry and wealthy Tyneside merchants milling around the dining hall and galleries. All she knew was that every piece of china that the Liddells possessed seemed to have been used that day. Lily came with tales of the guests' outfits and the magnificent black silk dress worn by Lady Ravensworth.

'Still the prettiest woman in the county, for all she's pale and tired-looking.'

'Is Mr Pringle-Davies in attendance?' Kate asked cautiously.

Lily nodded vigorously. 'Never leaves her side. Told you he was after her and the Liddell money. Now there's nothing to stop him.'

'Shush!' Hannah said. 'Don't let Mr Wadsworth hear you.'

'Well, there's higher up than him have said as much,' Lily pouted. They all knew she meant the housekeeper, who made no secret of her disapproval of the fun-loving Lady Ravensworth and the upstart Pringle-Davies.

Kate felt wretched at the thought that Alexander might be biding his time for Lady Ravensworth's hand. Had he not told her how much he admired Her Ladyship? Her own thoughts of romance with him were the wild dreams of her over-imaginative mind. She was of fleeting interest, the subject of his artistic whim.

Over the next uncertain weeks, Kate buried her disappointment and waited to see what would happen. There was much coming and going of lawyers, and rumours flew around the castle. The Dowager Lady Ravensworth was refusing to move out. There was dispute with her brother-in-law, the third Earl of Ravensworth, about what belonged to whom. Lady Caroline did not want to move north.

Then suddenly, at the end of August, it was announced that Lady Ravensworth would move into Farnacre Hall and the new earl and his wife would be moving into Ravensworth Castle by the end of September. There was consternation among the staff. Who would stay to serve the new earl? How many of their own staff would they bring from the south?

It was left to the housekeeper and butler to make the arrangements. The head footman, James Wadsworth, went with the Dowager Lady Ravensworth, along with her lady's maid and two favourite parlourmaids. Lily preened.

'I'm to stay at the castle and work for the new Lady Ravensworth.'

Hannah too was being kept on. Kate was called into the housekeeper's room to face her sour-faced employer.

'You're not needed here any longer,' she said with satisfaction. 'You can go back to Farnacre and work for the dowager in the laundry – work you're more suited to.'

Kate flushed at the slight. She knew the woman had never forgiven her for daring to sing in front of the old earl and speak to her social superiors as if she wasn't some common girl from Jarrow.

'I'd be pleased to serve Her Ladyship,' she said proudly.

She hid her sadness at leaving the castle and her friends Hannah and Lily, but at least she could remain on the estate, working for Her Ladyship. And there was always the chance that Alexander might stay at Farnacre rather than the castle now that Lady Ravensworth was there. Kate could at least gaze on him from afar.

Alexander was plagued by conflicting thoughts. He lamented the passing of his kind Cousin Henry and the turmoil it had thrown his life into. On the point of venturing out to meet Kate, he had been called to his cousin's bedside and watched by him as his breathing became ragged and shallow. He had wished for some dying words, some parting permission to take care of Emma or some final wisdom about what to do with his life. But none came. Henry's life had ebbed away in the gloomy bedchamber while outside Alexander imagined Kate waiting for him in the sunshine, thinking him a man of broken promise.

The next days had been chaotic. He found himself caught halfway between comforter to the bereaved Emma and agent of business, locked in meetings with lawyers and land agents.

On only one evening did he manage to slip away to the lakeside in search of Kate, but found the place desolate and empty. The lake was choppy and the long reeds sighed in the

157

night wind. Only restless bats flitted around the deserted boathouse. He cursed his ill luck and his romantic notion that she would be waiting for him after a week. Kate was too sensible and down-to-earth to take his words seriously. She had probably put all thought of him firmly out of her mind.

Still he strung out his business in the hope that he might have the chance to see her once more, explain that he had wanted to take her for an afternoon's riding through the Durham hills. But he saw no sign of her and had no excuse to go looking for her in the servants' quarters.

Then matters were taken firmly out of his hands. The new earl had business contacts in South America. Jeremiah Davies recommended Alexander as the ideal envoy. There were rich contracts to be made selling coal to Argentina.

'You'll be gone all winter,' Jeremiah told his son, having called him home.

'Why now? There's so much to sort out at the estate,' Alexander protested.

'I can take care of business locally.' His father eyed him. 'You're causing tongues to wag by staying on at Ravensworth. It would cause a scandal if—'

'If what?' Alexander demanded angrily.

'Things are different now. The new earl is your employer. You cannot expect the same latitude as with Lord Henry. To the new Lord Ravensworth you are just another of his servants taking care of his interests.'

Alexander spun round impatiently. 'That's not what this is about, is it? It's about Lady Ravensworth – Emma.'

'As you raise the subject then, yes, that is partly my concern. It is no longer appropriate for you to stay like a guest at Ravensworth – especially not at Farnacre. Your duty is to the new earl – not the dowager.'

Alexander laughed bleakly at this description of Cousin Emma. It made her sound so old and dull. But he could not help a guilty flush. It was true that he had half entertained thoughts of courting his cousin's widow, but had dismissed them quickly. Half of her attraction was that her friendship had enabled him to come and go freely at Ravensworth and feel a part of the family. She had made him feel wanted – made him feel like a Liddell.

At Farnacre it would not be the same. The ancient house would be a place of mourning, a twilight existence far removed from the social bustle of the castle. Summer picnics, long rides and languorous meals in the panelled dining hall were a thing of the past for him. Never again would he be able to lay claim to his boyhood room in the east tower. Only Henry and Emma could indulge him in that. The new earl he hardly knew.

Yet it was ironic that Davies should seek to send him abroad now, when his boyish crush on Emma was extinguished. His father would be far more scandalised if he knew that Alexander's desire to stay at Ravensworth was caused by a simple housemaid. The thought of drawing Kate's broad smile or touching her fair cheek was what set his pulse racing and the colour rising to his face.

'I can see that I am right,' Davies grunted. 'A spell of travel will do you the world of good. Rid yourself of such feelings.'

Alexander sighed in exasperation.

'And when you return, I expect you to pay some attention to Polly De Winton. She would be an excellent match for you. De Winton and I are in agreement.'

Alexander exclaimed. 'You've been talking to Polly's father behind my back?'

159

'Oh, don't be so sensitive! You like the girl and she, by all accounts, finds you to her liking too. It's natural that De Winton and I should discuss such matters. Write to her while you are away,' Jeremiah urged.

Alexander knew argument was pointless. It was easier to go along with his father's wishes than fight him. Besides, the thought of travel to South America excited him. Perhaps it was best if he put distance between himself and Ravensworth. He might be able to rid his mind of his obsession with Kate Fawcett.

In September he set sail from Liverpool, intending to put the past behind him.

Chapter 16

Kate was not surprised when Lady Ravensworth declared she was shutting up the hall for the winter. Dismayed but not taken unawares. Her Ladyship had been restless and subdued all autumn.

'It's so depressing here,' Kate overheard her say to the footman James Wadsworth. 'I can't be invited anywhere and no one comes to call. It's too much to bear. To be widowed twice . . .'

In early November, when the drabness of winter and the long dark evenings began, Her Ladyship ordered the packing up of her personal possessions. Kate helped the lady's maid fill three trunks full of dresses and shoes.

'She must be going for a long time,' Kate said anxiously.

'Aye, she likes the South of France. Be there till she can come out of mourning, I wouldn't wonder.'

'What will the rest of us do?'

The maid shrugged. 'Some'll have to stay to keep an eye on things. It's up to Miss Peters.'

The day came when Lady Ravensworth and her few chosen servants made ready to leave. They were going by train to London and then on to France by steamer. Her Ladyship called the remaining staff in one by one and gave them each a small gift. Kate's turn came.

'Ah, my singing girl from Jarrow,' Her Ladyship smiled. 'You at least have helped brighten up this dull place these past months.'

Kate blushed. 'Thank you, ma'am.' She curtsied and took the parcel offered. She hesitated, then dared to ask, 'Will you be coming back, Your Ladyship?'

'Of course! Why ever not?'

'I just hoped you would be – you've been that kind to me, ma'am.'

Emma smiled and touched her cheek. 'You are a sweet child. And I hope you'll still be here when I get back.'

'Ma'am.' Kate curtsied again. As she turned to go, Emma spoke as an afterthought.

'My nightingale,' she mused. 'That's what he called you.'

Kate started. 'Ma'am?'

'A friend of mine – that was his pet name for you, ever since he heard you sing at the servants' dance. My nightingale. It used to amuse me.'

'Who said, Ma'am?' Kate had to ask.

'Mr Pringle-Davies.'

Kate's heart thumped in shock at hearing his name. He had spoken of her with Her Ladyship! They had laughed about her together. Had he told her of their secret trysts by the lakeside and amused her with that too? She flushed red at the thought.

Kate rushed from the room quickly before Her Ladyship could see the tears of humiliation flood her eyes. Well, she wouldn't be the butt of their little jokes any longer, now that the house was being closed up and only the favoured few were travelling with the dowager.

Later, she opened her gift and found a piece of lace wrapped around a small metal brooch with a painted bird of paradise in china blue. It was beautiful and Kate felt guilty at her resentful thoughts and wished she had waved harder at the departing carriage. Lady Ravensworth would have meant no slight by the comment. What if they had discussed her? She was a lowly servant, nothing more, remarkable only in her ability to sing with an untrained voice.

Miss Peters lost no time in shutting up the hall. Kate was called in the next day.

'You can stay on till the end of the week, then you're no longer needed.'

'B-but Her Ladyship said she'd be coming back,' Kate stuttered.

'That's no business of yours. We don't need a full staff all winter. A strong girl like you will find work back where you come from.'

Kate felt winded. Go back? She had no intention of doing that!

'There must be some'at I can do here?'

'Not at Farnacre.' Miss Peters was abrupt. 'Nor at the castle.'

Kate felt quick annoyance. They were all the same, these jumped-up housekeepers and parlour maids who thought themselves better than the likes of her just because of a bit of extra frill on their uniform! She was a Fawcett – the daughter of a skilled steelman and friend of highborn Liddells – not some peasant's offspring!

'I'll give you a good reference,' Miss Peters said as if bestowing a great favour. 'I'm sure some public laundry or local merchant would be happy to employ you.'

'There's no need,' Kate said proudly. 'I'll not be looking for laundry work. I'll find me own position, ta very much.' She stormed from the room, livid with anger. She would show them all!

But as the week wore on and Kate's temper subsided, she began to fret about what to do. Aunt Lizzie was sympathetic but fatalistic.

'You've had a grand time of it, but all good things come to an end. Maybe it's time for you to go home and help your mam again, eh? Maggie says our Rose is struggling to manage at the cottage, with her legs so bad.'

'But I want to stay!'

Alfred joined in. 'I want Kate to stay an' all. Kate can stay and Mary can go and help Aunt Rose.'

Kate and Lizzie exchanged amused looks.

'Why don't you go and see Mary?' Lizzie suggested.

'She'll never agree to gan back home.'

'No, but she hears all the comings and goings at the inn. If there's work to be had you'll hear about it there.'

Doubtful, Kate decided to pay Mary a visit, even if it was just to say goodbye before returning heavy-hearted to Jarrow. It was her last chance. But her sister was out running an errand for the landlord when Kate called. Bram Taylor was a large, red-cheeked man who puffed and wheezed like bellows as he walked.

'Is Suky in then?' Kate asked, disappointed to miss her sister.

'No, she's up and left,' he grumbled. 'Gone to marry her pit lad.'

Kate felt dashed. Then a thought suddenly struck her. 'So you'll be needing a bit help?' she said with a quick smile.

Bram Taylor eyed the smart young woman before him. 'Aye, reckon we do. Do you know of someone?'

'Aye, I'm looking for a job.'

'You? I thought you worked up at the castle?'

'Worked for the dowager Lady Ravensworth,' Kate said in

164

her most ladylike manner, 'but she's gone abroad for the winter. I'm looking for something to see me over.'

Taylor's eyes lit with interest, yet he was cautious. Why was someone with Kate's good looks and manners looking for work in a public house?

'You're not in any trouble, are you?'

'Course not.' Kate was offended. 'I'm a hard worker and I want to stay in the country.'

That seemed good enough for Taylor. 'When can you start?'

'Day after the morra, if you like.'

'Done. Mary can gan up and help bring your bags down.'

Kate said quickly, 'I can manage on me own.' She wasn't sure how Mary would take to the idea of her working there, let alone being told to fetch and carry for her. But she could tell by the pleased look on the landlord's face that he thought he had just employed a lass of quality who would be good for business.

Two days later, Kate was working at the inn and sharing a cramped attic bedroom with Mary once more. Her sister did not seem too dismayed at the situation, for Kate brought all the inside gossip from Farnacre and the castle.

'Just like old times, sharing a bed again, eh?' Kate teased.

'Aye, and we're sharing all the chores an' all,' Mary reminded her.

For a few weeks it went well and the two sisters spent their half-days off together, going up to Kibblesworth to see Suky and her young husband in their own two-roomed house. Bill was a hewer, a skilled pitman on good wages, whom Suky had chosen with her head as much as her heart. Still, they both seemed content enough.

'Glad you're getting on grand at the inn,' Suky said.

165

'It's thanks to me she got the job,' Mary boasted. 'Told Mr Taylor she was a hard grafter.'

Kate said nothing to spoil Mary's story, for she did not mind her taking the credit. But just before Christmas, their old wrangling started again.

'How come you get to serve at table instead of me?' Mary demanded tearfully after a hectic night. 'I should have that job.'

'It's that busy,' Kate said, flopping down in exhaustion on the icy bed. 'He just asked me, that's all.'

'Just 'cos you put on airs and graces – pretend you're better than the rest of us.'

'No I don't – I just work harder than some.'

'Meaning me, I suppose? Well, just look at me hands – red raw with washing up in cold water! While you get to serve at table and behind the bar. Gabbing on with all the lads – I've heard you.'

'I'm just being civil to the customers like Mr Taylor wants.'

'Hark at her! "Civil to the customers." Stop talking all posh.'

Kate lost patience. 'Maybe he doesn't want your twisty face putting them off.'

Mary kicked her under the covers. 'I hate you! You always get what you want – just 'cos butter wouldn't melt in your mouth.' Then she burst into floods of tears.

Kate remembered what it had been like at home and her heart sank. The only difference was that there wasn't John McMullen to fuel the criticism of her. She'd put up with Taylor's demands for hard work any day. Turning over, she put out her arms and tried to comfort her resentful sister.

They went home briefly for Boxing Day and swapped news with Sarah and their mother, who insisted she could still manage at the cottage without them. Mary went off to visit

Aunt Maggie but they caught the same train together back to Lamesley.

'Glad I'm not stopping at home any longer,' Mary said. 'One day back's enough for me.'

Kate silently agreed. After that, Mary was less complaining and Kate did her best to share the serving in the parlour. But Taylor preferred her behind the bar where she was cheerful and obliging and popular with the customers. She could deal swiftly and firmly with drunks without causing a scene. Taylor was impressed with the way she could humour them and steer them out. Kate kept quiet about the years of practice she had had with her stepfather.

On New Year's Eve, the inn was full of revellers and it took little persuasion for Kate to sing to the crowds. Taylor was delighted with the amount of beer drunk that night. As 1904 progressed, he encouraged her to sing whenever custom was slow and word spread of the barmaid's lusty voice.

Then, abruptly in February, the third earl died and the estate was plunged into mourning again.

'His Lordship has no heirs,' Hannah told her when they met up one Sunday. 'There's no one to carry on the line.'

'So what will happen?' Kate asked.

Hannah shrugged. 'There's talk of a cousin coming to live here. But nothing's certain. And there's poor Lady Caroline just moved up here and left all alone. Two dowagers and only one Farnacre!'

'Is there any news of Lady Emma?'

'Not a dicky bird. But she'll have to come back for the funeral, I wouldn't wonder. Unless she's found herself a French count.'

'She's not like that!' Kate protested. 'She just likes company.'

'Well, they'll have to sort out who goes where and who gets what. The place'll be full of lawyers and land agents again.'

Kate's heart leapt. Perhaps Alexander would return.

'Has that Mr Pringle-Davies been back at all?' She held her breath.

Hannah shook her head. 'Not since the summer. I think Lily was right – he must've been sweet on the dowager. Maybe he's out in France with her. It's the old man Davies who's been seeing to His Lordship's business, according to Lily. Mark my words, the young 'un will turn up like a bad penny once Lady Emma comes home.'

'You shouldn't speak about them like that,' Kate reproved.

'And who's going to hear? Anyway, why you so loyal to Lady Emma when you lost your job at Farnacre?'

'Still hoping if she comes back I might be started on again,' Kate said quietly, not wanting to be overheard by Mary or the cook.

'Well, who can say?' Hannah sighed. 'It's all a mess.'

A week later, Kate stood on the hard, frosty ground outside Lamesley church and watched the funeral procession. She peered at the mourners as they descended from their carriages and her heart skipped a beat to see a figure like Lady Ravensworth wrapped in a black velvet cloak step forward. Her face was veiled, but when she saw James Wadsworth help her down, Kate knew it was her. She had come back! Perhaps there would be a chance of returning to Farnacre Hall after all.

There was no sign of Alexander, and Kate's feelings were mixed. She had longed to catch sight of him, yet if he was not in attendance then the rumours about him and Lady Ravensworth might not be true. She could not wait to discuss it all with Hannah.

But to her disappointment, her friend came with the news that Lady Emma had gone away again as soon as the funeral was over.

'Where? Back to France?' Kate asked in dismay.

'Don't know – not even Lily can find out.'

There was much talk at the inn about the dealings at the castle. Agents and lawyers for the two dowagers stayed or called in for refreshment. Their coaches stopped at the inn to water and stable the horses. The earldom was now extinct, but a cousin, Arthur Thomas, and his wife, Sophia, were to inherit the barony of Ravensworth and would be moving into the castle. Lady Caroline was moving into Farnacre, but it was rumoured she wished to retire south.

Surely Lady Emma would return and claim her home? Kate thought in concern.

Spring came. Kate took a walk up to Ravensworth to visit her aunt and uncle, and to see the swaying blanket of daffodils lining the drive.

Passing the gates and ivy-clad walls of Farnacre Hall, she slowed and peered through the iron railings. The shutters were bolted at the downstairs windows and no smoke wafted from the many chimneypots. It looked quite deserted.

She found Lizzie at her door, in deep conversation with a neighbour. Alfred bounded forward to greet her.

'I've got a new mouse – come and see!'

Kate hugged him and took his hand, greeting the women. As Alfred pulled her past them she asked about Farnacre.

'It looks all closed up. Has Lady Caroline gone?'

'Aye,' Lizzie nodded.

'So Lady Emma's coming back then?' She brightened.

The two women exchanged glances.

169

'She'll not come back now,' the neighbour said with a disapproving frown.

'I thought you would have heard down at the inn by now.'

'Heard what?'

Her aunt looked uncomfortable. 'Not in front of the bairn.'

'Come on, Kate!' Alfred was impatient.

'You go and fetch the mouse,' Kate encouraged, 'while I have a word with your mam.' He sped off inside. 'What's happened?' she asked nervously.

'Gone and got herself wed, that's what!' the neighbour snorted. 'And her still in mourning for His Lordship. It's a disgrace.'

Kate's heart thudded in alarm. 'Wed? Never so soon.'

'Aye – and to that upstart,' the woman complained. 'The shame of it!'

Kate felt sick. 'Who – who's she married?'

Her aunt looked agitated as if she could not bring herself to say the name.

'Is it Mr Pringle-Davies?' Kate asked hoarsely.

They both gave her a strange look. For a moment no one spoke. Finally the neighbour said, 'It was no gentleman. 'Twas that footman James Wadsworth.'

Kate gawped at them in disbelief. 'Mr Wadsworth? Never in the world!'

'It's as true as I'm standing here.'

Lizzie nodded in agreement.

Kate threw back her head and laughed in relief. They stared at her as if she'd gone mad.

'It's nowt to laugh about, hinny,' Lizzie reproved. 'It's a scandal, that's what it is.'

Chapter 17

Alexander returned in the early summer to the uproar of Emma's swift marriage.

'And to her footman!' Jeremiah said with scorn. 'She should still be in widow's weeds, not taking another husband – and what a husband! What's the world coming to when the ruling class start marrying their servants? Nobody knows where they stand!'

Alexander tried to hide his amusement at his father's rantings, though it came as a shock to him too. Emma married to James Wadsworth, her handsome footman, and he half her age! Like himself, James must be about twenty-eight, no more. He felt a mixture of pique and admiration.

'Where are they living?'

'Not at Ravensworth, that's for certain,' Jeremiah spluttered. 'No, no. They've taken some mansion in Newcastle – near Jesmond Dene, I'm told.' He looked at his tall son in alarm. 'You're not to go there.'

Alexander just smiled. 'It'll blow over. The gossips will tire of them and find someone else to prey on.'

'Maybe.' Jeremiah cleared his throat and returned to the more certain ground of business.

Alexander spent the first couple of weeks contentedly at home. The long voyage back from South America had left him weak. Stormy weather and bouts of bleeding had confined him to his cabin and sapped him of strength. He had returned leaner, his face gaunt and weather-beaten. Travel had changed him. He had fallen in love with the open pampas of Argentina, a country of strong sunlight and baked hills, where he could ride for days without interruption.

He had attempted to fall in love with a woman, but his heart had not been in it. Kate Fawcett's blushing features and easy laughter plagued him, though he knew he was being absurd. Perhaps he had fallen in love with his own drawings and not the real woman at all. For how could he love a simple maid whom he hardly knew? Yet, from the distance of thousands of miles, the rigid class barriers of England did not seem such an obstacle.

A month went by and he regained his strength. When his father suggested he accompany him on a trip to Ravensworth to meet Lord Thomas, Alexander jumped at the chance.

The castle seemed to bustle with as much life as ever, he was pleased to see. Lord and Lady Thomas were genial company and entertained them to lunch. But there was no question of him resuming the close family friendship of old. Alexander excused himself and said he needed fresh air.

'His constitution's not as robust since he's been away,' Jeremiah explained. 'But he's well enough. Quite able to take up the reins when I retire.'

Alexander groaned inwardly as he escaped on to the terrace. His father had been talking of retirement ever since his return. And he was pressing him about a betrothal to Polly De Winton once more. He could not evade it for ever.

It felt so good to be back at Ravensworth. The rhododendrons that Emma loved were in full bloom. He plucked a blossom as he passed, but it fell in a shower at his feet.

Alexander strolled through the gardens and around the lake, feeling a pang of longing for the previous summer when he had walked in the setting sun with Kate. Someone was fishing out on the water and birdsong filled the warm air, but it felt empty.

He had no way of knowing if Kate still worked at the castle. There had been so much upheaval in the past months. Perhaps she had gone with Emma and was working for her in Newcastle? Suddenly Alexander was filled with a desire to find out.

He made excuses not to return with his father to Darlington, insisting he visit their shipping agents on Tyneside.

'I'll return in a few days,' he promised.

'You better had,' Jeremiah warned. 'We have that theatre and supper party arranged for the De Wintons, remember. You miss that at your peril.'

It did not take long to find the modern red-brick mansion that Emma and her new husband had taken overlooking the wooded gorge of Jesmond Dene. The couple were out walking when he called, so Alexander waited impatiently in the upstairs drawing room.

'Tell me,' he asked the maid, who showed him into the light, well-furnished room, 'does a girl called Kate Fawcett work here?'

She shook her head. 'No, sir.'

Alexander felt a stab of disappointment. 'Never mind, thank you.' She curtsied and left.

Minutes later he heard voices below and went out to greet Emma.

'Alex? This is wonderful!' She threw out her arms to him as she mounted the stairs.

'Mrs Wadsworth!' he teased.

173

She laughed and they embraced like mother and son.

'How are you?' She steered him back to the drawing room. 'You look thinner. Tell me every detail of your South American journey,' she ordered, 'right from the beginning. James and I want to hear everything.'

Alexander glanced behind them and saw her young husband stride in and hold out a hand in greeting. Alexander hesitated a fraction then shook it.

'James – it's good to see you.'

'Sir,' James grinned.

'You can call him Alexander now, dear,' Emma said. 'Remember your position.'

The men laughed and sat down either side of her. Tea was brought in while Alexander enthused about Argentina and the riding.

'Have you been back to Ravensworth?' Emma asked abruptly.

'Yes.' His look was cautious. 'It's not the same without you there. Why did you not return to Farnacre?'

She gave a smile of regret and reached out to hold James's hand. 'It would have been too awkward. You know how unkind gossip can be. Better to start afresh somewhere new. We're thinking of doing some travelling for a while. Perhaps Argentina, if it's so wonderful. What do you think, dearest?'

James flushed. 'Anywhere you choose.'

Alexander could see his host found the situation awkward and so he declined an invitation to stay for dinner.

'No, I return to Darlington tonight,' he said, kissing Emma's hand. 'Papa is matchmaking for me this week.'

'Polly De Winton, I hope?'

'Why do you hope?'

'Because she'd make you happy. She's in love with you.'

'How could you possibly know?' Alexander laughed.

'She was one of the few county friends who dared to send us a message of goodwill on our marriage. Polly's been a visitor here – she talked about you a lot.'

Alexander laughed it off. 'You must have been stuck for conversation!'

As he left, he asked as casually as possible, 'By the way, whatever happened to that singing maid of yours?'

Emma looked blank.

'Your nightingale?' he prompted. 'Kate, I think she was called.'

'Oh, the housemaid.' Emma remembered. 'She came with me to Farnacre. I suppose she must still be there.'

'The hall is closed up,' he told her. 'Caroline returned south.'

'Then I don't know.'

James spoke behind them. 'Do you mean Kate Fawcett?'

Alexander's heart jumped. 'Yes – that could be her name.'

'She has an uncle in the gardens. Spoke to him at the late earl's funeral. Said Miss Peters sent her and the other maids packing after we left.'

Why hadn't he thought of seeking out her Uncle Peter? Although how could he explain his interest in Kate without causing suspicion?

'So she left the estate?'

'Yes. Said something about her working in a public house. Bit of a comedown for a girl like her.'

She must have gone back to Jarrow, Alexander thought in disappointment. The place was full of drinking houses, as far as he could remember. He hated to think of her there. Was she reduced to serving dockers in some dingy bar, shut away from the fresh air and sunlight? He had an urge to rush to the

175

town and search until he found her, rescue her and take her into his own household.

'Is it important?' Emma asked.

'No,' he said quickly. 'She just crossed my mind – with all this talk of Ravensworth.'

She gave him a curious look as he went.

How stupid of him even to mention her. He had been harbouring a ridiculous dream all these months. Nothing could ever come of it. Kate was gone and he was never likely to see her again.

All the way back on the train he felt wretched, but by the time he reached home he had convinced himself that he must put her from his mind. He would do something to please his father for once, and begin to court Polly in earnest.

Chapter 18

Late October 1904

The snow came down so suddenly that drinkers at the Ravensworth Arms were caught unawares. The light went quickly from the short afternoon and they left the fug of the taproom for the thick, silent white world of a snowstorm. Some struggled home, cursing the lack of moon, while others returned to the haven of the warm inn.

Kate was kept extra busy behind the bar and serving food, while Mary helped prepare rooms for stranded travellers. There was a commotion at the door.

'Carriage gone in the ditch up the hill.' Bram Taylor shouted the news. 'I'll take a couple of lads and see if we can pull them out.'

Kate nodded for Robert to go and help. The gardener's son had been calling in to see her regularly since the summer. He drank little but made it last all evening in the hope of exchanging a few words with her. She found him likeable but tongue-tied and was growing impatient that he would ever ask her to walk out.

'Tell them there's mutton broth to warm them before they travel on.'

Half an hour later, the men stamped back in with a blast of icy air and swirls of snow.

'Two more for the night,' Bram called cheerfully, ushering in two becloaked figures. 'Mary, show them to our best bedchamber.'

Kate glanced through the door to see her sister bobbing at the behatted gentlemen and leading them to the stairs.

'Someone grand?' Kate asked Robert in amusement.

'Aye,' he blew on his numb hands, 'been at the castle – left too late. Coach is stuck fast. We've stabled the horses.'

Kate grinned to hear him so garrulous. 'Two more for supper then.'

But Mary came back saying the old man was staying in the room.

'Wants a bowl of broth taken up to him – too grand for sitting in a public parlour,' she said, pulling a face. 'Other one's coming down. Now he looks a real gentleman – posh voice and clothes. Handsome too.'

Kate rolled her eyes. 'Suppose you'd like me to take the soup up to the old man while you serve down here?'

'Aye,' said Mary with a quick smile. 'Ta, our Kate.'

Kate knocked at the door to the large bedroom and went in. She found a thin man with sparse grey hair sitting huddled by the coal fire, wrapped in a blanket.

'Soup, sir.' Kate put it on the table next to him. 'Are you warm enough?'

He fixed her with red-rimmed, watery eyes. 'Thank you, yes.'

'Is there anything else you'd like? Mug of beer? I could warm it with the poker.'

178

He shook his head. 'Don't touch the evil liquid.'

Kate felt the reproof. 'I'll bring a jug of hot water for washing, then. Nothing devilish in that.'

'Wait. Have I seen you before?' he asked suspiciously.

'Don't know, sir. I used to work at the castle,' she said with a lift of her chin.

'That must be it,' he said, and turned to his soup. 'You may go.'

Kate descended the stairs wondering who this man with the well-cut clothes and superior air could be. There was something familiar about him too. But the bar was busy and she had no chance to question Mary on his companion.

The night wore on and the snow stopped, but nobody seemed in a hurry to go home.

'Give us a song, Kate!' a miner from Kibblesworth called. 'Then we'll gan home.'

Taylor encouraged her with a wink, so she went and stood by the fire and began to sing popular songs.

Pushing back his chair, Alexander thanked the pretty, thin-faced maid and headed for the stairs. Behind, the door to the taproom opened and a blast of noisy singing spilt out. He hesitated. Jeremiah was upstairs waiting to talk over their latest business at the castle and a possible trade mission to Germany. The bar looked warm and welcoming. A swift whisky to warm him before bed would do no harm. His father could wait.

Alexander turned back. As he stepped through the door, a woman's voice came strong and clear. 'The Waters of Tyne', he thought in recognition. In an instant he was reminded of a summer's evening at Ravensworth.

His insides clenched. That voice. It wasn't just the song that was familiar. His heart started to thud. Alexander pushed

179

his way into the room, past the drinkers at the bar. The singer was staring into the flames, her soft cheeks flushed in the firelight, hair glinting.

Kate!

He did not think he had spoken aloud, but she chose that moment to turn and look across the room. Her eyes widened in astonishment and she faltered in her song. They gazed at each other in shock.

Kate, seeing how others turned to stare, recovered herself and ploughed on with the song. Seeing how flustered she was, Taylor called a halt to the singsong and told his customers to drink up and get off home before the snow started again.

Kate dashed for the safety of the kitchen. Her heart drummed so much she felt sick and breathless. After all this time! She had not set eyes on him for over a year and had given up any hope of seeing him again. Yet here he was, conjured out of the storm, and instantly he had the effect of making her legs useless and her words trapped in her throat.

'What's wrong with you?' Mary demanded.

'Just catching me breath,' Kate gasped, clutching the table.

Taylor called, 'There's glasses to clear!'

'I'll go,' Mary offered, alarmed by Kate's look.

Kate nodded and sank into a chair. This was ridiculous! How could he affect her so? He probably hardly remembered her or his once-rash promise to take her riding. Though his aghast look suggested he had recognised her. Was it embarrassment that coloured his lean face?

She stood up and splashed water on her cheeks. No one was going to make her cower in the kitchen. She had nothing of which to be ashamed. Kate emerged and set about clearing the bar. Alexander was sitting at a table by the fire being served by Mary. She was laughing at something he said.

Kate's insides somersaulted to see his sensuous smile and tawny eyes, and she felt a stab of jealousy. She busied herself with clearing the glasses and saying good night to the last of the drinkers. As she wiped a table close to Alexander, she heard him speak her name.

'Kate,' he said in a low voice, 'do you not remember me?'

She looked up and felt her face burn under his reproachful look. Remember him? How could she not!

'Aye, sir,' she managed to say, continuing a vigorous mopping of the table.

Alexander felt dashed. He had found her again after all this time, having forced her from his mind, yet she hardly gave him a passing glance! Their summer walks must have meant nothing to her. Or was she wary of him after he broke their tryst?

'Kate, come and sit with me.'

She glanced at the landlord, who was ushering people out of the door. 'I can't stop, sir.'

'Then just a word,' he insisted. 'You could bring me another whisky.'

She nodded and went to pour the drink. Mary shot her a suspicious look.

'How does he know you?' she hissed.

'From the castle,' Kate whispered. 'I used to clean his room.'

'Fancy him remembering that,' she said in surprise.

'Aye,' Kate said, and hurried back. As she put the glass on the table, Alexander stopped her with a hand on hers. She jolted.

'I'm sorry that I never got the chance to see you again,' he said softly. He watched her intently. 'Everything changed when Lord Ravensworth died.'

181

She nodded.

'How have you been, Kate? I thought you'd returned to Jarrow.'

She eyed him. Had he asked about her? 'I thought I'd have to when Lady Ravensworth left, but I found work here with Mary – she's me sister.' Kate nodded towards Mary, who was watching them with interest.

'Two pretty Fawcett daughters – no wonder the inn is so popular.'

She smiled, unable to resist his charm. 'It's more to do with the snow than a couple of lasses.'

Taylor called over as he bustled Mary from the room. 'Kate, don't be bothering Mr Davies. You're needed in the back.'

Alexander's grip tightened for an instant. 'I want to see you again – talk to you.'

'It's not possible here,' she said, looking around nervously.

'When is your next day off?'

'Sunday week.'

'I'll come back then. Meet me, Kate,' he urged.

She nodded quickly and pulled her hand free. Hurrying from the room, she did not dare look back for fear he would see the longing in her face.

The next day, the men left early after bowls of porridge in their room, which Mary took up to them. Kate wondered if she had dreamt the previous night's conversation and was sure Alexander would not return on her day off. Still, as the day drew near her hopes and nervousness grew. If he came at all, would he call boldly at the inn and ask for her? Should she walk into the village and look out for him?

Mary, who was working that Sunday, was suspicious of her evasiveness.

'Are you ganin' to meet Robert?'

'No, but I might walk up to Ravensworth – call on Aunt Lizzie.' Kate avoided her sister's look. She did not dare tell her in case it came to nothing. Mary would ridicule her for being a romantic fool with ideas far above herself.

The afternoon came, bright and blustery, and Kate set out, unable to contain her restlessness any longer. Even if he never came, she could not be confined to the inn. She would walk all afternoon until it grew dark and her yearning was spent.

As she picked her way along the muddy verge, where lumps of snow still lingered under hedges, she heard the hooting of a train as it pulled into Lamesley station. It was coming from Newcastle on its way south and Kate thought nothing of it. She knew if Alexander came it would be from the other direction.

She stopped under the sheltering wall of St Andrew's church. Her mother had once described sitting on the church wall as a small girl, long, long ago, watching a Liddell wedding. As beautiful as an angel, she said of the young bride, in a voice of rare softness. Kate looked up at the stone wall and tried to imagine Rose as an excited child perched up there, clutching the hand of her old grandmother, who had been a servant at Ravensworth.

How different life would have been for them all if Rose's mother had not left the village to marry an Irishman on Tyneside. Kate touched the cold stone and felt a strange bond with the place, deep roots that went back through the generations. She was connected to these ancient stone walls, dun-coloured fields and rounded Durham hills that seemed changeless under the cold open sky. They were her inheritance as much as anybody else's.

Footsteps approaching made her glance round, her mind still half in the past. The familiar figure striding towards her with a glint of silver-topped cane made her heart jump. He had come as promised!

Alexander grinned in delight to see her waiting at the church gate for him. It quelled his nervousness at the thought she might have gone out for the day, not believing his words. But here she was, looking pink-cheeked and dreamy under the last copper leaves of autumn.

He stopped short, curbing his urge to reach out and seize her hands.

'You came to meet me!'

'Sir,' she blushed, 'I was on me way up to see me aunt. I wasn't sure . . .'

'That I'd keep my promise? I don't blame you, Kate, after the last time. I intended to meet you, but I couldn't get away. There was no way of letting you know. I thought you would understand.'

'I did.'

'And I tried to find you at the lake – but you never came.' His voice was reproachful.

'I did go!' she protested. 'Twice that following week. But you weren't there.' She stopped, going hot under his gaze.

He smiled in delight. 'So you did think of me! I've thought of you often, Kate.' He stepped towards her. 'You still appear in my drawings. Even in South America you haunted me.'

'South America!' she gasped.

'That's where I went after Lord Ravensworth died. Then I came back to find Her Ladyship married to James, the next earl dead, and a new baron installed at Ravensworth – and my wood sprite vanished from the estate.' His look was teasing.

'Do you see Her Ladyship?' she asked warily.

'Yes. That's where I've come from today – Newcastle.'

'Is she well?'

Alexander nodded. 'She seems very happy.'

'The marriage caused a right fuss round here!'

This made him laugh. 'I'm sure it did. But good luck to them, I say. And let the killjoys go to the Devil!'

She looked shocked, then burst out laughing too.

'Who would have thought? James Wadsworth!'

Alexander held out his arm. 'Come, Kate, it's too cold to linger. I want to hear of everything that's happened to you this last year and more.'

She took his arm and smiled. 'I'd sooner hear about South America.'

'Then you shall. It might take until dusk. Can you walk that long?'

'Till the cows come home,' she grinned.

He squeezed her arm and led her out of the village and down the valley, skirting the wooded estate. Neither said so, but both thought it better to avoid coming across people they might know.

Kate could have carried on for ever, walking and listening to his tales of foreign travel.

'There's something about going to sea, Kate,' he said eagerly, 'the adventure, the freedom – that empty horizon beckoning. There's no feeling like it.'

'I prefer me feet on dry land,' she mused. As they walked on she made him laugh with her pithy comments on life at the inn. But the short afternoon sped by too quickly and the light was already fading as they turned back for Lamesley.

'Can we do this again?' he asked as they approached the inn. 'On your next day off.'

'I'd like that, sir.'

185

He took her hands in his gloved ones. They were numb with cold but she did not mind.

'Please call me Alex,' he insisted. 'When we're together like this, it doesn't seem like master and servant – not to me. Is that how you still see me?'

'No, Alex,' she murmured, her pulse hammering at their daring.

'Good!' he cried, pressing her fingers to his warm lips and kissing them. 'I'll call for you in two Sundays' time. Meet me by the church again.'

'I will.' She smiled broadly, reluctantly pulling her hands away. She hurried towards the lights of the inn, thrilled at the thought of their next meeting. Two weeks seemed an eternity to wait!

Turning at the gate, she could still make out his tall figure, a shadow in the dark, watching her. She waved and he raised his stick in farewell. Kate rushed inside, unable to keep the grin of happiness from her face. She had to tell someone about this afternoon. Even Mary would do. She could not keep such a secret to herself or she would burst with the excitement and joy that bubbled inside her.

'Mary!' she gabbled to her sister, finding her in their attic room. 'I've got something to tell you . . .!'

Alexander strode back to the station, warmed by the thought of Kate's eagerness to see him again. What rashness had seized him? He felt light-headed, as if his actions weren't his own, but those of a bolder man. His father would take a fit if he knew of the association. But what harm did it do? He enjoyed Kate's company and she his. There was nothing more to it than that. He would choose his own friends.

Yet as he waited for the train in the frosty dark, he felt a pang of misgiving. In all the long conversations this afternoon, he had made no mention of Polly De Winton or the promise he had made to Jeremiah that he would propose to Polly come the new year. It had just been to keep him from the constant nagging about settling his future.

Alexander had been happy to court Polly that autumn; she was pleasant company. But to him, their marriage would be little more than a business arrangement to please his father and hers. It was nothing to do with love. And he needed love. He would take it where he found it.

Only after he had climbed on board and was passing the lights of the Ravensworth Arms did it strike Alexander. The sweet pain in his chest that he felt when he thought of Kate, the longing inside. It was love. He was in love with the blue-eyed maid from Ravensworth.

Chapter 19

The next time they met, Alexander drove a small pony trap. 'I'm taking you into Gateshead,' he declared. 'We'll walk around Saltwell Park and take tea. I want to treat you!'

Kate grinned with delight as he helped her up and was glad she had put on her best dress – one that Suky had given her in a flush of generosity after becoming pregnant and too big to button it up. It was deep blue and matched a hat Kate had bought at a village bazaar that had belonged to the stylish Mrs Fairish, wife of a master baker.

She felt like a lady, riding into town beside her handsome companion. They walked around the public gardens, arm in arm, stopping to listen to a brass band playing Christmas carols under the gilded bandstand. Afterwards, they warmed themselves by a roaring fire in a nearby tea room and ate hungrily through a plate of currant bread and cherry cake.

'My favourite cake,' Kate mused. 'Reminds me of being happy as a bairn – before my father died.'

'I like to think your father was the William I remember – the kind man who took me to the circus with his pretty wife.'

'So do I,' Kate smiled wistfully. 'I'm sure he must've been to a circus, 'cos he made a lion and cage out of old wood for my older sisters. It's the only toy that didn't get sold—' She stopped herself quickly. 'I mean, it's the only toy I remember my mam keeping. Our Jack used to play with it.'

'Is your mother pretty, Kate? With daughters like you and Mary, she must be,' he flattered.

Kate thought of her mother's tired, dark-ringed eyes and sallow square face, her once full mouth permanently set in a thin grim line. She hobbled and wheezed like an old woman. Only the treasured faded photograph of Kate's parents and their young family showed that her mother had once been beautiful. She kept the photograph wrapped in brown paper and hidden under her mattress, for fear of inciting Mary's jealousy. It had been taken on a rare trip to the seaside, before her youngest sister had been born. It depicted a happy family of which she had never had the chance to be a part.

'My mother was bonny once,' Kate answered. 'But life's been hard for her these past years. Likely you wouldn't recognise her, even if she was the woman you met as a lad.'

'Maybe one day I'll drive you over to see her – give her a surprise.'

Kate felt alarm. She could not imagine taking Alexander to the squat little railway cottage above the cutting. Yet her mother kept it tidy and the front garden neat and he seemed to find something charming in the way working people lived: he was forever drawing them outside pit cottages or in the fields. Kate could not understand it. Perhaps it would be possible to take him there and show him off to her mother, she daydreamt. As long as she could be sure John McMullen would not be there to cause a scene or give offence.

She smiled and said nothing. It excited her that Alexander spoke about future meetings. Could it be possible he intended courting her? Kate dared not hope. He might enjoy spending the day with her once in a while, but he lived in a different

189

world that she could not hope to enter. She would have to content herself with these delicious snatched moments together when they could play at being equals.

December came and Alexander grew bolder. He called at the inn and had meals there whenever business took him to Ravensworth or Newcastle. He made no secret of knowing Kate and kept her in conversation when she served him in the taproom. The landlord was wary at first, but seeing how it pleased his free-spending customer, did not scold her. Still, Kate could tell Bram Taylor was uneasy when Alexander stopped by at the inn on her next Sunday off.

'I'm on my way to the castle,' he said breezily. 'Would you like a lift in my carriage, Kate? I know your aunt would be pleased to see you.'

Kate flushed at the brazenness, but, avoiding Mary's scandalised look and the landlord's frown, went with him.

Once down the lane, he turned to her and grinned. 'A fine day for walking in the hills. You can visit your aunt another day, can't you?'

She nodded and he set the pony to a brisk trot. Up on the moors they walked along an old wagon way in the sharp frost, knocking at an ale house he knew for a mug of warmed beer when the low afternoon sun began to dip.

They sat by the innkeeper's fire, sharing the drink. Kate had never tasted beer before – the smell reminding her of her drunken stepfather – but sitting next to Alexander in the isolated cottage decorated with holly for Christmas, she found the drink warming and intoxicating. She felt so happy she started to sing, songs pouring out of her in a torrent. The family of the house stopped their chores to listen and join in.

'She's my nightingale,' Alexander boasted in merriment.

The wife gave Kate a knowing look, which made her blush.

The woman thought she was Alexander's fancy woman! Kate decided it was time to leave. She was uncertain when he suggested meeting her in a fortnight, frightened of the feelings he stirred in her.

'It's too near to Christmas. You'll be busy at home, won't you? Christmas dances and that, with your own kind?' she tried to joke.

Alexander tipped her chin so she had to look into his face. His eyes blazed.

'My kind? I don't give two pennies for the dull gentry of the county, if that's what you mean. It's your company I want, Kate!'

Kate's heart thudded. They were so close she could feel the warmth of his breath on her face.

'Why?' she whispered. 'I'm not good enough for you.'

He grabbed her hands and held on, his look fierce. 'By God, you are! You're the kindest, prettiest, most loving girl I've ever met, with the sweetest singing voice in the world. It's me who isn't good enough for you, Kate. Say you'll see me again!'

She trembled at his touch and the passionate words he spoke just for her. Or were they just for her? an inner voice cautioned. Did he act like this with other girls, other women in different towns? She did not know. But the words made her heady and she wanted to believe them.

'Don't leave me broken-hearted,' he protested. 'You do want to see me again, don't you, Kate?'

'Aye, I do,' she confessed, 'more than anything.'

He gave her the warm smile that made her insides somersault. Then briefly he leant forward and kissed her on the cheek for the first time.

'Till we meet again, sweet Kate,' he said tenderly.

Chapter 20

Rose prepared excitedly for the girls coming home for Christmas, or to be exact, Boxing Day. With the luxury of Jack's new wages from the docks, she had bought a leg of pork from a local farmer and a bagful of vegetables from Harry Burn. She had to be careful when she spoke to him, for ever since Mrs Burn had died the previous winter, John was suspicious of her conversing with the widower.

It amazed Rose that John could still be jealous over her. She had long ago stopped looking in the stained mirror that hung in the scullery where Mary used to preen every morning and apply her Ponds cold cream. At forty-six, Rose knew her looks and figure were gone. She had the slow painful gait of a much older woman and had long given up trying to mount the stairs to the loft.

Rose felt her stomach lurch in anticipation of the visit. It was over a year since the family had all been together. She had decorated the room with streamers of coloured paper and holly that Jack had helped her pick from along the railway cutting. She glanced at the clock yet again.

Sarah would be here first from Hebburn, with the mince pies that she had promised and to help her cook the festive dinner. Rose had not seen her eldest since she had turned twenty-four. Sarah was courting and happy; everyone knew except John.

'When can I meet the lad?' Rose had asked in the summer.

'I'm not bringing him back here!' Sarah had declared. 'Father would kill me – or him.'

Rose had no answer. Sarah's sweetheart was a miner and John thought them the lowest form of life. He was suspicious of men who chose to crawl underground for a living and never see daylight. He cursed them for their readiness to strike for better conditions, calling them lazy, whereas William would have blamed the pit owners. John only cared that the disruption in the coal supply could bring the mills and yards grinding to a standstill and make men like himself idle.

' 'Tis the fault of the pitmen we have no work on the river,' she had often heard him rail, whether there had been a strike or not. 'They can't be trusted with owt.'

Once she might also have disapproved of Sarah being courted by a miner, thinking the match too lowly. They were a breed apart, rough and dirty, and kept closely to themselves. Rose had grown up with such views. But Sarah's stories of her pitman and his family were quite different. She spoke of kind, generous folk and a spotless kitchen despite the grime that the men tramped in. Besides, Rose had learnt from experience that you could not judge a man by his outward appearance. Her head had been turned by the sight of an army coat and a strong handsome face and look where it had got her. She did not object but worried for Sarah if John should find out.

Rose had to accept that she could not offer hospitality to Sarah's young man. Anyway, the romance might come to nothing, so it was not worth riling John's temper over the matter. For her husband's ill humour had got no better over the three

193

and a half years they had lived at Cleveland Place. His attempts at sobriety had not lasted long and when in work he would often get no further than the pubs on Leam Lane, a stone's throw from the dock gates, forgetting about his long walk home. Many was the time she had had to send Jack searching for him late in the evening, for she was too lame and would not have suffered the indignity of entering a public house.

Jack, a tall, wiry youth, was often repaid with a 'smack in the gob' for his efforts in trying to prise his belligerent father from the cosiness of some bar.

Rose would try to comfort her son after such bouts of violence. 'Your day will come,' she promised him. 'He'll not be the stronger one for ever.' The saints forgive her, but she almost willed the moment to come when Jack would stand up to his father and gave him a taste of his own medicine.

Sometimes Rose worried about Jack. He had become increasingly moody and withdrawn since his sisters had left home, especially Kate, who had always been openly affectionate with her half-brother. He had moped for months after she left, long after he had stopped asking when his sister was coming home. But faced with John's constant criticism at his lack of hardness or teasing about girls, Jack kept to himself, disappearing on his own to trap rabbits or fish the streams.

He would shadow the local farmer when he went out to shoot crows, and once or twice the man had let Jack have a go with the gun. Jack seemed to gain more pleasure from this than any amount of socialising. The boy had a good aim and had once returned from a fair with four coconuts with which Rose had not known what to do.

Rose often wondered if she had been right to bring them out of the overcrowded town to their semi-rural retreat. She had been in despair at the evictions and flits forced on them by John's boorish behaviour and frightened at the yellow fog of chemical fumes permeating their last home, which had been slowly suffocating young Jack. Perhaps now Jack needed more company; he was turning into a loner. But better that than a fighting, cussed drunk like his father. Not one day did Rose regret the move for her own sake. Even in the depths of winter, when she had to break the ice on the pail to get water for the kettle and struggle through the snow to search for tinder, she thanked the saints for her primitive cottage.

Like an animal in hibernation she had rested her bruised spirit, slowly reawakening to the world with a new inner strength. She delighted in spring rain, summer birdsong and autumn sun as if she was experiencing them for the first time. While she tended her garden, the earth seemed to nurture her in return. During these years when she had often been on her own for long hours at the cottage, Rose had rediscovered a sense of worth after years of degradation. She kept hens and grew giant rhubarb and strong onions. She exchanged these with her neighbours for jams, relish or firewood. She bartered produce with itinerant pedlars for buttons, hairpins, or Emerson's Bromo Seltzer, which she forced on John when he complained of sore head, stomach or bowels.

Rose would take Jack with her blackberry picking along the railway line and gather elderflowers and wild mint for cordials. Her son would return from his wanderings with crab apples and nuts, the occasional rabbit or wood pigeon for the pot. On rare occasions, John would return early and in good mood, and they would eat together and walk out along the embankment to view the trains, and Rose wished life could always be that tranquil.

Certainly, it had been easier this last year without Mary in the house. Kate had saved the day by finding her work at the Ravensworth Arms. When Mary heard that this was no common hostelry but the hub of social life for the staff at the castle, she lost no time in boarding the train for Lamesley.

Rose glanced at the clock again. Kate and Mary might be at Lamesley station at this very moment, waiting for the train to take them to Gateshead and then on to South Shields. They would get off at Tyne Dock station and walk up the hill. Jack had gone down to meet them and carry their bags . . .

It had been one of the best decisions of her life to send Kate to Lizzie's, Rose felt sure of it. She noticed how Kate held herself with a new dignity and spoke with assurance in a voice that had subdued the rough edges of her speech. Rose was secretly proud of her daughter's ability to improve herself, despite John's teasing and Mary's mimicry. Even though Kate no longer worked at the castle and was only a barmaid at the inn, Rose still felt a sense of triumph.

She had stubbornly resisted John's decrees that Kate should come home and be of more help to her mother. Rose might be finding it harder to manage on her own, but she refused to let Kate be bullied back by her stepfather. She would rather struggle on uncomplaining, knowing that her daughters were happy in their new lives.

It was worth it on her rare days off to see Kate blooming and full of life, her hair loosely gathered on the nape of her neck and swept back from her forehead in the latest style. She had not been back since harvest time and Rose was impatient to see her again.

All was quiet in the house now as Rose waited for her family to gather. John had disappeared to buy a newspaper,

196

which probably meant she would not see him until dinner was on the table. But by half-past ten, Sarah had arrived and was bustling around the dark kitchen, shoving the meat into the oven and heaving the chopped vegetables into a large pot to simmer on top of the range.

If Rose could have run, she would have done so when she heard Jack's whistling and footsteps approaching up the garden path. She hobbled to the door and flung it open. Kate and Mary were there, pink-cheeked and chattering, their breath billowing in frozen clouds. Jack was behind them, almost hidden by a mound of Christmas parcels.

'It's Kate's fault,' Mary said, by way of a greeting, 'she spent every penny of her Christmas wages at the village bazaar. You wouldn't believe the rubbish she's got!'

'Happy Christmas, Mam!' Kate cried, ambling towards her with her quick limp and nearly knocking her over in an exuberant hug. Rose was sometimes embarrassed by these shows of affection, but today she did not mind.

'Haway inside, hinnies,' she said. 'Sarah's got the dinner on. Jack, you open that bottle of ginger wine – I've been keeping it hid from your father. Take your coats off and let's have a good look at you!'

She surveyed her daughters in their neat dresses and boots, their hair well groomed and Kate in a fetching blue hat. What a picture they looked! But she could not help fussing.

'Mary, are they feedin' you enough? I've seen better-fed scarecrows!'

'I'm run off me feet all day long, that's why,' Mary complained.

'They feed us plenty, Mam,' Kate assured her.

'Well, you look well enough on it, our Kate,' Rose remarked. 'Mind you, you've rings around your eyes. Are

197

you gettin' enough sleep? They don't keep you up all hours, do they?'

'I don't mind the hours, Mam, I like me job,' Kate smiled.

'She's lovesick, that's what,' Mary said drily.

Kate blushed. 'Give over, our Mary!'

Rose eyed her more closely. 'So that's it. I could tell there was some'at. Who is he, then?'

'Nobody!'

Sarah joined in. 'Mr Nobody?'

'Are you courting?' Rose asked excitedly.

'No!'

'Yes you are,' Mary contradicted. 'He's a gentleman an' all. Our Kate's quite turned his head.'

'A gentleman!' Rose gasped. 'What sort of gentleman?'

Kate hid her face in her hands in consternation. 'He's just an acquaintance.'

'Hark at her – "he's just an acquaintance"!' Mary mimicked.

'He's friendly, that's all – it's in his nature,' Kate blustered. 'He's like that to all the staff.'

'Just happens to call round on your day off,' Mary smirked.

'So you are courtin'!' Sarah cried.

'Not properly—'

'But this lad – he's special to you?' Rose asked.

Kate looked at her with shining eyes and Rose knew that it was true without her having to speak. There was an expectation in her flushed expression, a quickening of the voice as she talked about him.

Before she could answer, they heard a shout on the path outside. John was back.

'Quick, get the table set!' Rose ordered. 'Jack, more coal on the fire.'

Kate said in alarm, 'Don't say anything to Father, will you?'

'I thought there was nowt to tell?' Mary baited.

'You say a word and I'll pull your hair out!' Kate threatened.

'She'll not,' Rose warned. 'We'll not have today spoilt with silly tittle-tattle or give your father the excuse to lose his temper.'

But by the sound of John's singing, she gauged he was in a good mood. He came banging through the door, clutching two bottles of beer, to find them all bustling round industriously.

'Now isn't that a grand sight!' he crowed. 'A family making ready for the master! Is me dinner ready, Rose Ann?'

'We've all the presents to open first,' Kate said, pointing at the pile on the hearth. She loved the present-giving more than anything. The more she gave the more it made up for those barren Christmases after Jack had been born when there had been no treats and no gifts.

'We'll eat first.' John was firm. 'Jack, pour me a beer, son.'

With a look from Rose, Kate did not argue further. They gathered around the oval table, John in his high-backed fireside chair, the others on an assortment of chairs and stools. Once it was all served up and John was digging into his food, Rose sat down with satisfaction. The table was laden with good things to eat and the smell of roast pork and steaming potatoes filled the warm kitchen. Her family tucked in eagerly, their faces flushed, their chatter light-hearted. She wished she could savour this moment for ever.

After the mince pies and custard, John pushed back his chair and eased his belt.

'By, that was a good dinner, lass,' he said with satisfaction, and Rose thought how that was praise indeed from her taciturn husband.

199

'Please, Father, let's open the presents now!' Kate pleaded. She was almost bursting with the effort not to tear open the parcels at once.

John gave a grunt of agreement. 'What've you got us then?'

Kate scrabbled among the pile. 'This is for you, Mam. It's a hat so you don't have to keep wearing that old bonnet.'

'You're not supposed to tell her till she's opened it,' Sarah laughed.

'I like me old bonnet,' Rose said, looking doubtfully at the brown paper package.

'Put it on, woman, and let's have a look at you,' John said indulgently.

Rose unwrapped the parcel and found a neat, flattish green hat like a stunted boater with a large bow of pale green ribbon tied at the front.

'It's not quite the latest fashion – Mrs Fairish in the village wore it a few years,' Kate explained. 'But no one round here will know that. I remember you having a green hat when I was a bairn,' she smiled.

'You remember that?' Rose said in amazement. 'You were a baby.' A green hat and a green dress that had been her pride and joy when married to William. She had never worn anything as elegant since. Rose put it on.

'Suits you,' Sarah said.

'It'll blow off in the wind,' John snorted.

'You can use one of me hatpins,' Mary offered.

'It's bonny,' Rose said, her voice suddenly wavering. She took it off quickly and busied herself wrapping it up again, in case anyone saw the glint of tears in her eyes. It would not do to get sentimental about the past, and all over a silly hat.

'I'll find a hatbox for it next time,' Kate promised.

'Haway, what else've you brought?' John asked impatiently.

Kate handed out the other present: stockings for Sarah, a clothes brush for Mary and a book for Jack.

'What's that?' John asked suspiciously, eyeing the second-hand book.

'It's all about the Boer War,' Kate said, unable to keep the surprise.

Jack read out the title slowly: '*With Roberts to Pretoria* by G. A. Henty.' He looked up at Kate and gave one of his rare smiles. 'Ta, our Kate. That's champion.'

'What use is a book?' John scoffed. 'And about that bugger Roberts an' all.'

'I thought Lord Roberts was your hero?' Kate asked in dismay.

John snorted. 'He might be a good commander,' he conceded, 'but when I was in Afghanistan he treated us lads like muck – drove us till we dropped. It's us soldiers should get the glory, not the generals on horseback. It's easy to shout orders.'

'You should know,' Mary murmured, and Rose tried not to smile.

But John's hearing was not what it used to be and he missed the remark.

Kate heaved her final present from the floor. 'You'll not be wanting this then.'

'What is it?' John eyed the flat parcel, the largest of them all.

'It's a picture of—'

'Don't tell me!' he shouted. 'Give it here!'

Kate helped him untie the string. Everyone crowded round. It was a painting in a heavy wood frame. A British general on a horse with an African servant holding the reins.

'By, that's grand!' Jack exclaimed in admiration.

'Who is it?' Sarah asked.

'That's what I said when Kate bought it at the bazaar,' Mary smirked.

'Lord Roberts, of course,' Jack said impatiently.

'Which one?' Mary laughed. 'The soldier or the servant?'

'Don't be cheeky,' John said, flicking a hand at her. He sat back and looked at it. 'Stand over there and hold it up.' Jack and Kate did so, Kate holding her breath for some sign of approval.

'Well, John?' Rose grew impatient. She could see how much it mattered to Kate that he liked it. She must have spent a small fortune on it.

John sucked in his cheeks, then nodded. His face broke into a smile. 'Fancy me having a grand picture like that.'

'You like it then?' Kate asked.

'Aye, it's a canny picture.'

Kate gushed in relief, 'It used to hang in the big hall – but the new mistress didn't like it and gave it to the butler. His missus didn't like it either – so she gave it to the bazaar. Think of that: it once hung in Ravensworth Castle!'

Rose could see John swelling with pride before her very eyes. Kate had played cleverly to his vanity.

'Pity there's not enough room to hang it above the fireplace,' Mary said cattily. 'I told Kate that but she wouldn't listen.'

'We can move the dresser and hang it over there,' Rose said quickly, not wanting Kate's moment spoilt.

'Dresser be damned!' John cried. 'We won't need to. I nearly forgot.' He slapped his knee, looking pleased with himself.

'Forgot what?' Rose asked.

'My Christmas present to you,' John grinned. 'I heard about it this morning.'

'Heard what?' Rose was nonplussed. He had not bought her a present at Christmas for years.

'Where is it?' Kate asked in excitement.

'Down in the town,' John chuckled. 'We've got the chance of a place – Leam Lane – right next door to the Twenty-Seven. No more tramping up here in the pouring rain for me and the lad. And it'll be much easier for you to manage, Rose. We'll hang Lord Roberts over the mantelpiece in Leam Lane! What d'you say?'

There was complete silence. Rose was appalled. But she could not say that she was completely taken by surprise. John had been itching to get them back to the town where he felt more at home. Jack was just an excuse. So was her health.

'We're canny here,' Rose answered. 'I can manage.'

'No you can't!' John snapped, displeased with all the long faces around him. 'I thought you'd be happy at the idea. Close to the shops, no stairs, a tap in the back yard. Better than living like peasants up here.' He glared round the room. 'Tell your mother it's the best thing for her. Unless one of you wants to come home and run this place for her?' he challenged them.

Rose saw them all look away, one by one. She would not ask it of them and John knew that. She knew that she had no choice. He was right, she struggled to manage as it was. Leam Lane would be far more practical for all of them, especially for John and Jack working at the docks.

'Well, it's all arranged,' John said brusquely. 'We'll move come the new year.' He glanced around. 'Look at your twisty faces – you'd think we were headed for Botany Bay! Jack, open that other bottle and let's drink to better times – to living in Shields. We'll hang the old dog Roberts over the fireplace, eh, our Kate?'

Rose caught the look of horror on her daughter's face. She looked on the point of tears.

Kate sprang up. 'Hang it where you bloody well like! I don't care!' Then she fled to the door and rushed outside into the dusk, slamming it behind her.

'Kate? *Kate!*' John shouted after her. He looked at Rose quite baffled. 'What's got into her?'

Rose was surprised too by the girl's response to the news. It would hardly affect her away in Lamesley. Rose had spared her the need to come back.

'Sarah, put the kettle on,' she sighed. 'I'll go after her.'

Chapter 21

Rose found Kate at the bottom of the garden, shivering by the fence. The last glimmer of silvery light in the west touched her downcast face. Her cheeks were wet with tears. Rose was puzzled by why she should be so upset; Kate hardly let anything get her down.

'You shouldn't worry what he says about Lord Roberts,' Rose chided. 'He was pleased with the picture, I could tell.'

Kate shook her head. 'It wasn't the picture.'

'Us moving then?' Rose questioned. 'You're upset at us moving.'

Kate sniffed. 'Aye.'

Rose sighed. 'It had to come sometime – I knew we couldn't stay on here for ever. Your father's right: I can't manage and it'll be easier for Jack—'

'Jack!' Kate cried. 'It's always what's best for Jack.'

Rose was taken aback. 'He's just turned fourteen. He's still a young lad, and he still lives at home – you don't,' Rose said pointedly. 'It's not like you to be jealous of our Jack.'

Kate looked at her with soulful eyes. 'Oh, Mam, I'm sorry. It's not our Jack either.'

'Then what?' Rose pressed. 'What's bothering you, hinny?'

'It's Leam Lane – Tyne Dock – we don't belong there! And next to the Twenty-Seven – that terrible place!'

Kate could not begin to explain to her mother how much she was afraid of it. It was part of the nightmare of her childhood, begging on the streets for food. When the doors of the well-off had been shut in her face, Tyne Dock was where she had stood outside the pubs begging the men for the remains in their bait tins. Grubby bread and treacle wrapped in newspaper, that was what Leam Lane and the Twenty-Seven meant to her.

'We've managed in worse places,' Rose said defensively. 'There're still decent folk live round there, don't you forget that. Don't judge a book by its cover!'

'That's as maybe,' Kate cried in desperation, 'but I could never bring *him* home to such a place!' It was out before she could stop herself.

Rose stared at her, first in disbelief, then with shock as realisation dawned. 'Your gentleman,' Rose whispered. 'You're talking about him, aren't you?'

Kate bit her lip, furious with herself for speaking her thoughts. They were wild thoughts, dreams that might come to nothing. And because of her impetuous words she had hurt her mother, she could tell by the wounded look on the older woman's face.

'You're ashamed of us,' Rose said, feeling numb inside. 'You're ashamed of your own mother!'

'No, Mam!' Kate cried, grabbing her mother's arm. 'Not of you!' Her pretty face was pleading. 'Please believe, I'd never be ashamed of you! It's just Leam Lane and . . .'

Rose felt tears sting her eyes. 'I know – your father,' she finished for her.

'He's not me father!' Kate said in a voice full of rancour.

Rose pulled away. 'He's kept a roof over our heads all these years – including yours. He at least deserves your respect for that.'

Kate shook her head. 'You did that, not him,' she cried.

Rose looked at her daughter and felt overwhelming sadness. A huge gulf separated them and it was of her own making. She had encouraged Kate to go away and better herself, yearned for the day she would return with a ring on her finger, having won the heart of a respectable, prosperous man. How could she blame her for wanting to distance herself from the grubby, noisy poverty of Tyne Dock? Wherever they lived, Rose realised too late, Kate would probably shun them. That must be why she had been so coy about telling them she was courting. She wanted to keep her admirer and her new life quite separate from them.

'Is he so very grand?' Rose asked quietly, searching her daughter's face.

Kate hardly dared meet her mother's look. 'Yes,' she whispered.

Suddenly Rose was filled with foreboding. Had Kate set her sights too high? Was she involved with someone too far above her station for safety? On impulse she stepped towards Kate and pulled her close, gathering her arms about the girl's slender shoulders.

'Oh, lass! I fear for you!'

'Oh, Mam, don't!'

Kate clung to her mother as she had not done since childhood, and wept. She had thought never to feel her strong hug again. Her mother seemed to have forgotten how to touch them these past years. But it felt so good now! She felt strength flow from the older woman to her and give her courage.

'I know you'd like him. He's kind and funny and so handsome. I don't know what he sees in me.'

'Don't you do yourself down,' Rose declared. 'You were meant for better things than skivvying. You hold your head up

207

high when you walk out with this Mr – what d'you call him?'

'Pringle-Davies.' Kate blushed.

'Aye, Pringle . . .' What was it about the name that was familiar? Rose struggled to remember. It did not matter now. Having Kate hold on so affectionately was weakening her resolve to let her daughter go.

With difficulty, Rose pulled away. She would not break down in front of her daughter. She had not stayed strong for her all these years to betray herself as weak now. Rose gulped back the tears in her throat. How she wanted to protect Kate!

'You're right,' Rose said hoarsely, 'don't let him come here. If you've a chance of happiness, lass, take it. By God, you take it!'

They looked at each other, both shaking with the cold and the emotion that clawed at their insides. Kate reached forward to touch her again, but Rose drew back. She did not trust herself to embrace the girl again; she would not have the strength to let her go.

'But whatever you do and wherever you go,' Rose added stoutly, 'don't you *ever* be ashamed of who you are! You've had good parents – God-fearing parents who've brought you up to do right, however poor we've been.' She raised her hand and lightly touched Kate's cheek as if in farewell. 'Remember you were born a Fawcett – you were your da's favourite. I've given you that, so be proud of it. Make me proud of you, lass!'

She withdrew her hand swiftly and turned away.

'Mam,' Kate rasped, 'don't go!'

But Rose kept on walking towards the cottage. They both knew that in that moment of truth when Rose had laid bare her feelings, she was also letting go. Rose did not look back;

she could not in case her resolve wavered. She would rather her daughter went back to Lamesley and never saw her again, disowned her family, if it meant a chance at happiness with a man above her station who could give her security. Although the pain of separation would be raw, she would give up her daughter for William's sake – for her beloved William's memory!

As she reached the door, Rose heard Kate sob, 'I will, Mam – I'll make you proud!'

Rose glanced round and gasped to see Kate's face caught in the golden light of the winter sunset. Her tear-stained face looked beatific. There was no other way to describe it. At that moment she had the face of an angel.

The long ago words of a gypsy whom John had riled at a fair rang in her ears. The woman had predicted the sorrows and upheavals of the past years, but also a ray of hope, that at the end of her life Rose would be blessed with an angel child. Kate would give her that angel child, Rose was certain of it. Kate was her chosen one. She would carry on where Rose could not. In time she would bring her greater joy. Rose smiled at her daughter, then opened the door and went inside.

Kate was left trembling in the dark, weeping at the weight of responsibility she felt pressing upon her. She had seen it in her mother's eyes, heard it in the way she spoke of Kate's real father. Her mother had freed her from her stepfather's dominance, but in return there was a price to pay. Rose expected the world from her.

Kate looked up into the late afternoon sky, already dark. There was just a glimpse of a new moon hanging over the copse, lifting like the sail of a ship. A new beginning. Kate took heart from the omen. She turned and looked behind her, to the south where Ravensworth and her other existence lay.

'Oh, Mam,' she whispered in the frosty stillness, 'I wish I had as much faith in myself as you do – and as stout a heart.'

Then she thought of the man she loved, the man with auburn hair and glinting eyes that danced with dangerous merriment. The man with the deep voice that flattered and teased and told her she was beautiful. The man of a hundred tales, who claimed his mother had been a Liddell who had eloped with the coachman Pringle. The man who tempted her to recklessness too.

'Alexander.' She whispered his name tentatively, blushing at her daring. A wave of tender longing swept over her.

'Alexander!' she called out more boldly, as if she could conjure him to her. 'Soon we'll be together again!'

Then, before facing the others and putting on a cheerful façade, she blew a kiss in the direction of Ravensworth. For after today, Kate knew more than ever that was where her heart and her destiny lay.

Chapter 22

1905

Throughout the spring, Alexander came to court Kate. Appearing on her fortnightly day off, he would take her out for walks or trips to town. Sometimes she would manage to change her day to a Wednesday or Saturday so that they could go to a music-hall show. He bought her chocolates and flowers and small gifts on a whim – a pair of lace gloves to match her hat and a brooch of lapis lazuli to wear at her throat.

'It matches the blue of your eyes today,' he smiled, 'the blue-green of a tropical sea.'

Kate laughed with embarrassment and delight and let him pin it to her high-necked blouse. She wore it when Alexander took her to have her photograph taken in a Newcastle studio. She was bashful and did not look the camera in the eye, but Alexander seemed delighted with the results and kept one for himself.

'To remind me of my wood nymph,' he teased. 'I'll carry it at all times.'

The mood at the inn was disapproving. Bram Taylor was nervous at the attention his barmaid was attracting, but hid it from his well-to-do visitor, for he spent generously at the bar. It did not stop him issuing warnings to Kate.

'You watch yourself, lass. Men like Pringle-Davies don't go marrying their maids. It can't come to anything.' On another occasion when Kate returned late, he said angrily, 'You're getting above yourself, lass. Old man Davies would never have you in his family in a month of Sundays. I've heard Pringle-Davies is as good as betrothed to some squire's daughter.'

'I've done nothing to be ashamed of,' Kate said indignantly. 'He's a real gentleman.'

'Don't say I didn't warn you,' Taylor grumbled.

Mary was even more scornful. 'You're making a spectacle of yoursel', our Kate! Everyone's laughing at you behind your back – being all hoity-toity with that man. You don't fool the regulars. They all know you're just a common lass from Jarrow.'

Kate was hurt by her harsh words, but dismissed them as jealousy. They did not know Alexander like she did or understand that social differences meant nothing to him. He was a free spirit. Besides, it was not unknown for people to marry across the social class. Look at Lady Ravensworth and James Wadsworth – the gulf between them had been even greater. And hadn't her mother told her to hold her head high and be proud she was a Fawcett?

The truth was Kate was so deeply in love with Alexander now she could not pull back. She was content with the occasional days together, however brief, just so long as she could carry on seeing him. She pushed aside Taylor's warning about some squire's daughter; he was just trying to put her off.

With early summer and longer days came the chance to go further afield. Kate and Alexander took the train to the seaside

212

and strolled along the promenade to watch a troupe of travelling players and buy ice cream from a barrow. It was Kate's first taste and she enjoyed it so much that Alexander insisted on buying another.

'You can have as much as you want,' he decreed, enchanted by her childish delight.

As the day cooled they caught the train inland, the smell of the sea lingering on her skin and clothes long after he departed.

Another time they took the pony trap deep into the hills and Alexander untethered the horse from its shaft.

'I'm going to teach you to ride,' he declared.

'How do I get up there?' Kate stifled a laugh.

He showed her how to grab the horse's mane while he made a stirrup with his hands.

'You'll have to ride it like a man, not side-saddle,' he said, heaving her on to its back.

'It's very high up,' she said in alarm, gripping on tight, and self-conscious at her show of leg. He laughed and swung up behind her, encircling her body as he held the reins.

'I'll keep you safe,' he murmured into her hair and snapped at the reins. Her heart hammered as much from the closeness to Alexander as from fright. The horse began to trot forward.

Kate clung on half laughing, half crying in excitement and fear as they headed up a bracken-covered track. The breeze was stiff, buffeting clouds above them. They passed a deserted shepherd's hut and a small copse of wind-blasted trees. She was exhilarated. The view from the top of the hill was breathtaking, the world dropping away from them into a pearly blue haze. It made her feel weightless and dizzy, like a bird in flight.

'It's beautiful up here,' she gasped, and felt Alexander's arms tighten around her.

'I knew you'd like it. It's one of my favourite places. Not a soul about. Just north country earth and heaven.'

Then quite suddenly he bowed his head and began kissing her neck. Kate's pulse throbbed in her throat, she could not speak.

'You're shaking,' he said in surprise. 'Are you cold?'

'Y-yes.'

Without another word, he steered the horse south, dropping down from the top along an overgrown sheep path. Kate noticed a straggle of bushes and could hear running water though could see no stream. They rounded a flank of hillside and abruptly were on a sheltered plateau surrounded by a ring of fallen stone.

'It's an old iron-age fort,' Alexander explained. 'Lord Ravensworth brought me here as a boy. Used to pretend it was my castle.'

They halted and Alexander swung down. He looked up at Kate, eyes narrowed against the glare, and held out his arms.

'Come, we'll rest here for a bit.'

She leaned down and let him lift her clear of the horse. Alexander held on to her a moment, then led her over to one of the large slabs of fallen stone. She sat down as he secured the reins to a gorse bush. Leaning against a mottled stone, Kate found it warmed by the sun. Alexander flopped down close beside her.

'Kate,' he said, slipping an arm round her waist, 'I'm in love with you.'

Before she had time to respond, he pulled her gently to him and kissed her on the lips. Her heart thudded. Drawing back slightly, he stroked loosened strands of hair away from

214

her face and ran a finger down her cheek and neck, making her pulse race. 'Do you love me, Kate?'

She looked into his vital eyes and saw his uncertainty.

'How can you doubt it?' she whispered, shaking with emotion. All she craved was another taste of his warm mouth.

But he dropped his hand from her face and looked away. 'Oh, Kate,' he said in a despairing voice, 'what are we to do?'

'What do you mean?'

He pulled distractedly at the mossy grass at his feet.

'There's nothing wrong, is there?' she asked nervously. He avoided her look, so she forced herself to ask, 'Is there someone else? Are you promised to someone else?'

He shot her a suspicious look. 'What makes you say that?'

'N-nothing. It's just – silly gossip. I don't take any notice.'

Suddenly he leant back over her, clutching her arm, his look intense. 'What do they know? It's you I love, Kate! You do believe me, don't you?'

'Aye, I do,' she gasped. He searched her face as if he did not quite trust her. She reached up and touched his strong jaw. 'I love you an' all, Alexander.'

She trembled at her own daring, uttering such intimate words to anyone.

In an instant his arms were around her and his lips on hers. His kisses were generous and passionate. Kate was intoxicated by them. Gently he pushed her back and began to loosen her jacket, caressing her and kissing her all the while. She thrilled at his touch. Then he tried to unbutton the bodice of her dress and she felt sudden alarm. No man had ever touched her body. She knew little of how babies came about but knew it was something to do with intimacy between a man and a woman. Her mother's bitter allusions to the marital bed, her stepfather's crude teasing were hints of how it was done. The

215

thought of John's leering face was enough to break the spell.

She grabbed Alexander's exploring fingers and pushed them away.

'No, please, not that,' she panted and sat up.

He was breathing fast, his look perplexed. 'But you love me, Kate?'

'Of course I do.'

'Then show me!'

'But we mustn't—' She broke off, flushing with embarrassment.

He rolled away from her with a sigh of impatience.

Kate's eyes stung with sudden tears. She had spoilt the moment, made him angry. It was all so confusing. She wanted his love, yet feared it. What should she do? Kate bowed her head, trying to hide her distress.

Alexander stood up. What had possessed him? He was heady from the scent of her skin, the touch of her soft cheek, the adoration in her blue eyes with their long dark lashes. Here in this haven of moss and old stone, ringed with bright gorse, he had thoughts for no one but her. He wanted her with a sick yearning, wanted to make love to her and be loved back.

Why had he brought her here? He had intended to be honest this time, tell her of his father's insistence he propose to Polly at the June county ball. Jeremiah's patience had run out. There was no future in his romance with Kate. In his head he knew that, yet his heart cried out for the freedom to love her.

He looked down at her bowed head of thick luxurious hair and felt a pang of guilt. He knew she loved him, would probably give in to his pleadings in time. Men of his class treated women of hers with such casual thoughtlessness all

216

the time. Enjoy them, then cast them aside. How could he do that to Kate?

Alexander stooped down and caressed her hair. 'I'm sorry. I shouldn't have taken advantage like that. Will you forgive me?'

She looked up and he saw her tears.

'Oh Kate!' he groaned, bending quickly to pull her into his arms. 'I never meant to upset you like this. Forgive me, my love!'

Kate clung to him, too overcome to speak. She longed for him to kiss her again, but all he did was hold her and stroke her hair in comfort. After a while he broke off and stood up.

'It's time we went,' he said with a quiet finality, and turned to untie the horse.

They said little on the journey home. The sun disappeared and the wind increased, chilling Kate to the bone by the time they reached the inn. She tried to hide her shaking as they said goodbye.

Avoiding her look Alexander said, 'I sail for Hamburg in July – I'll be gone a month or so.'

Kate's heart sank. 'Will you call before you leave?'

'I'll try, of course.'

'It's still only early June.' She tried to smile.

'Yes.' He gave her a look of regret.

'Will you come in for a drink before you go?'

He shook his head. 'Not tonight.'

Kate swallowed hard, her insides leaden. 'Goodbye then,' she said, climbing down from the trap.

Suddenly he was jumping down and helping her to the ground. His hands were warm on her shaking ones. His look was desperate.

'I will come before I sail for Germany, I promise. I couldn't go so long without seeing you!' He kissed her quick and hard on the lips. Then he dropped his hold on her and swung up into the carriage again.

A moment later he was gone down the lane at a brisk trot and Kate was left numb and baffled by his erratic behaviour. One moment he was covering her in kisses, the next he was brooding and aloof as if something troubled him deeply. Was it because she had pushed him away and stopped their lovemaking? Or was there something else that he had not told her? All through the afternoon she had the impression he was about to tell her some confidence, but could not bring himself to do so.

Kate traipsed wearily into the inn, too exhausted with the emotions of the day to ponder any further. She felt wretched that she might have angered him in some way, but clung on to the promise that he would come and see her before June was out. With that thought to comfort her, Kate returned to the humdrum life of the inn.

June wore on and her next day off came. Kate made ready, although no word had come from Alexander. She paced up and down the lane, pretending to pick flowers from the hedgerows, but he did not appear. In the end, Mary came out to fetch her in.

'Haway, he's not coming.'

'Maybes he's sick,' Kate fretted. 'He gets these bad nosebleeds. Or maybes he's had an accident on the way.'

'Or maybe he's never set off,' Mary said flatly.

Kate swallowed tears of disappointment. 'He said he loved me,' she whispered. 'No one else – just me.'

Mary's scornful look softened. 'Likely he does, but he's got another life in another place.'

'But he promised he'd come before July.'

'Maybes he still will.' Mary put an arm around her in comfort. 'But you can't expect a gentleman like that to be at your beck and call. Haway, let's gan up to Aunt Lizzie's for a cup of tea,' she cajoled.

Kate sniffed and tried to smile. 'Aye, let's.'

Mary linked her arm through her sister's as they walked. 'I told you nowt good would come of courtin' a nob – Suky said the same. Fancy silks and common serge don't mix in the poss tub.' Mary did not seem to notice the way Kate winced at her bald words. 'No, he'll not be back. Best you forget all about him, I say.'

Chapter 23

Alexander lay in the gloomy room with its blinds drawn for an eternity. The bleeding had come on a few days after his last visit to Tyneside, sudden and heavy and debilitating. For a week or more he drifted in and out of consciousness, unaware of what went on beyond the limpid light of his bedroom. His head throbbed and his limbs ached, all energy drained from his body.

He knew of the doctor coming and going and his father watching anxiously at the end of the bed, but he was too weak to summon up speech. Finally, the bleeding stopped and his head cleared, yet he was gripped by a strange lassitude. He took no interest in the newspapers Jeremiah brought for him to read, or the post that lay unopened by his bedside. There were three letters in Polly's handwriting.

'She wishes to come and see you; you have matters to resolve,' his father told him pointedly.

'Not yet,' Alexander said wearily. How long had he lain here?

'You're not fit enough to attend the county ball, but the doctor said you were well enough to receive visitors. I've sent word to Miss De Winton that she may call tomorrow.'

'You've no right!' Alexander protested, struggling to sit up.

'I've every right!' Jeremiah snapped back. He paced the room. 'I've been worried sick about you these past two weeks, wondering if this time you might not pull through!' He stopped and glared. 'You've been overdoing it – all this constant toing and froing to Newcastle. And what for, eh? That's what I've been asking myself. Not business, as I thought. Going up to town on a Saturday – I should have known! And not staying where you said you were – not at Mrs Timmins's lodging house, nor even at Mrs Wadsworth's.'

'You checked with Cousin Emma?' Alexander croaked incredulously. 'You've been spying on me!'

'You gave me cause to,' Davies rounded on him. '*This* gave me cause to.' He strode across the room, yanked open the top drawer of the leather-topped desk and pulled out a mounted picture. He held it aloft, glaring.

It was the photograph of Kate. Alexander's head pounded.

'And not just this,' he shook the print, 'but it's the same girl in all these drawings.' He jabbed a finger at the scatter of sketches on the desk. 'Is this who's been keeping you away from home so much?' his father demanded. 'Who is she?'

Alexander coloured furiously. 'That's my affair. You had no right to go prying into my possessions.'

'She looks familiar. Pretty enough – but obviously socially inferior. A daughter of some publican, knowing you.'

'Her father was a skilled steelman,' he defended Kate. 'Only his early death meant Kate has to work for a living. She has the manners of a lady, and her father was a friend of Cousin Edward's in Jarrow.'

'She's from Jarrow? You've been back there?' his father asked in astonishment.

'No. I met her at Ravensworth. She worked for Cousin Emma.'

'And now?'

'Didn't your spies tell you? She's at the Ravensworth Arms.'

'That servant! Now I remember. I thought at the time I knew her.' He looked hard at his son as realisation dawned. 'You've known her since Lord Ravensworth's time! She was that maid who nursed you, wasn't she? How long have you been seeing her? Months? Years!'

'I'm in love with her,' he announced boldly.

'Oh, don't be ridiculous!'

Suddenly Jeremiah sighed and sat down on the end of the bed. 'Oh, I can see why. You are cursed with a romantic's heart, this I know.' His face clouded. 'But it can't go on – not once you are betrothed to Polly. I'll not have this girl spoiling your chances of a good match. We'll have no scandals in this family like the Wadsworths. You must give her up.'

'I'll not be told what to do.' Alexander was indignant. 'I'm a grown man, for God's sake!'

Jeremiah stood up, his stooped body trembling. 'Then start acting like one!' He paced again in agitation. 'I'm doing this for your own good, Alexander. You've had your fun, now it's high time you settled down. When you are well enough you will go to De Winton and ask for Polly's hand in marriage. I have put off your trip to the Continent until you are fully recovered and in the meantime the question of marriage will be resolved.'

He made it sound so cut and dried, like a business transaction, dismissing his son's love for Kate as something so trivial it could be dispensed with in a moment.

'And what if I decide to marry Kate Fawcett?' Alexander challenged.

His father did not hesitate. 'Then I will disown you! You won't have a penny to live on.' His face was thunderous.

Alexander glared back, but he felt too weak to argue. In his wilder moments he imagined himself travelling the world living as an artist, but he knew that he was not good enough. He was dependent on his father's goodwill. Besides, had Jeremiah not always been fair and generous to him? He was the one person who had given him a home and education and stuck by him all these years. He could not have done more for him had he been his own son.

Lying there, drained of the will to fight, Alexander saw his love for Kate was futile. He had no right to lead her on in the expectation that anything could come of their friendship. He thought with longing of the last time they had been together, lying in the sheltered circle of the ancient dun. She had curbed his reckless desire, knowing the dangers of an affair. Kate had seen only sorrow would come of it.

He looked at his father and saw how frail he was, despite his forceful words. He was an old and anxious man. All Jeremiah asked of him was that he do his duty as a respectful son and heir. He bowed his head in submission.

'I'll talk to Polly tomorrow,' he said with resignation.

By the end of July Alexander and Polly were engaged to be married. The wedding was set for the following spring. His strength regained, Alexander enjoyed some riding up on the moors around the De Wintons' farm. It was a bleak landscape even in high summer, scarred by lead mines, but it suited his frame of mind.

Try as he might, he could not rid his thoughts of Kate. Every hilltop and rickle of stones reminded him of their time together. Polly's angular fair looks and amiable company left

223

him empty. He did not love her, could never love her while Kate existed somewhere else. He was guilty at his lack of feeling, but the thought of years ahead with this woman made him desolate. Alexander rode hard and fast to rid himself of his unhappiness.

He was relentless in his activity, so he had no time to dwell. He worked, he rode, he filled his evenings with entertainment and fell into bed in the early hours of the morning for a few hours of exhausted sleep. Maybe if he drove himself enough he would not live to see a barren loveless marriage. He lived under the threat of a blood disorder that no one knew how to cure. It spurred him on to be more reckless. Better to live for the moment and die young than live a long and dull life. But, oh, to see Kate one more time!

Jeremiah worried at his frenzied pace and the dark shadows under his eyes. He knew that his son had not been near Ravensworth in weeks, for he had paid the landlord of the inn to send word if he did. Any business to be done at the estate, Jeremiah had seen to himself. Yet he did not trust Alexander not to do something rash, so he kept ever watchful.

August came and went and the time drew near for Alexander's postponed trip to Germany. He told his father with some defiance that he was going to stay a few days with Emma before he sailed.

'She is thinking of going abroad to live. I wish to see her before she goes.'

'Very well,' Jeremiah agreed. He did not speak of the possibility of his son seeing Kate on his way to Newcastle. Even if he did, little damage could be done at this stage. The marriage to Polly was all arranged and Alexander would sail for Germany by late September and be out of the country for a couple of months.

Alexander felt his spirits lighten as he travelled north to Tyneside. As the train passed Lamesley he peered for a view of the inn, desperate for a glimpse of Kate. What a fool he was! He had not been near the place in nearly three months; she would have long given up hope that he would keep his promise to come and see her. What must she think of him? He had no right to go seeking her out and expecting her still to be waiting for him.

He resisted the strong urge to jump off the train there and then. At Newcastle station he hailed a cab and went directly to the Wadsworths' town house. That evening they went to the theatre, but afterwards, over a nightcap, he poured out his troubles to his old patron.

'Go and see her,' Emma encouraged, 'if only to explain your new circumstances to the girl. She deserves that at least. It would be better that she knows of your betrothal, rather than to wonder for years what happened to you.'

Alexander flushed in shame. He had thought too little of how Kate must have been hurt by his disappearance. Or was she just angry? He would never know unless he faced her and told her the truth.

'Sometimes, I have these mad thoughts,' he confessed with a bleak laugh, 'of eloping with Kate. Running away together and saying to hell with propriety! Like you and James—'

He stopped abruptly at the look of displeasure on her face.

'There was nothing improper in our marriage. I was widowed, remember, not betrothed to another.'

'I'm sorry, I didn't mean . . . It's just you didn't let social convention stand in your way.'

'I could afford to do so.' Emma was frank. 'I'm a rich woman. I didn't need to bow to petty-minded snobbery.' She reached out and patted his arm. 'It's different for you, dear

Alex. You are not rich. If you turn your back on your father and insult the De Wintons you will be an outcast. Are you prepared to live a life of uncertainty, maybe poverty? Is Kate?' She gazed at him searchingly. 'I thought after your childhood that what you would crave most would be security, stability. Polly will give you that.'

Alexander swallowed the bitter bile that rose in his throat. He could not tell her that what he craved above all was to love and be loved. Kate was the only woman he had ever known who loved him deeply and completely for who he was. But even Emma, who had followed her heart, did not think he should throw away everything for the sake of love.

'Then I will go and say goodbye,' he said quietly, feeling the weight of resignation press down on him once more.

Chapter 24

Kate was busy serving in the taproom when he strode in. He looked straight at her as if she should be expecting him, yet his smile was unsure. She gasped as if someone had winded her, her fair face flooding with colour.

Bram Taylor bowled across the room and cut him off from the bar. 'Good day to you, sir. Is it a meal you're after? It's quiet in the parlour. I'll have Mary lay a table for you.'

'I'm quite happy in here, thank you. It's Kate I came to see.'

The landlord appeared flustered and Kate looked away in consternation. Others were glancing round with interest.

What was he doing here after all this time? How could he waltz in and demand to speak to her after he'd put her through weeks of anxiety, then disappointment? Anger bubbled up inside. Yet she could not help but look at him. His face was so gaunt, his eyes dark-ringed – that face she had yearned to see these past desolate weeks, that had prompted her to wake in the dead of night!

'Then perhaps you'd like to take a seat outside in the courtyard, sir. I'll get the lass to bring you out a glass of beer.' Taylor did not want a scene in his bar. Whatever the young gentleman had to say could be said in private, dismayed though he was to see him back again.

'Thank you, I'd like that.' Alexander smiled, and followed him through the bar out into the sheltered yard where a couple of weather-beaten trestle tables and benches stood. It smelt strongly of the stables, but that made him feel more at ease.

He sat waiting for Kate, his heart pounding and his nerve beginning to fail.

Then she was there, with her quick loping walk and her scent of violets. He looked up into her smooth oval face, the large enquiring blue eyes, and knew in an instant he was still hopelessly in love.

'Kate!' He stood up and reached out. But she stood her distance, clutching the glass of ale.

'Sir,' she murmured. The word made his heart heavy. He had destroyed her trust.

'I'm sorry. I should've sent word. I don't blame you for hating me.'

'I don't hate you,' she said quietly, 'surely you know that?'

'But I've disappointed you. Please, Kate, sit with me a moment. I need to explain.'

She hesitated, glancing over her shoulder.

'Just for a minute,' he pleaded. 'Taylor won't mind.'

He took the beer from her, gestured at the bench and they both sat down. Kate thrust her hands in her lap to stop them shaking.

'I've been ill again,' he began.

She looked at him in alarm. 'The bleeding?'

He nodded. 'I was bed-bound for a couple of weeks or more.'

Her face broke into a smile of relief. 'I knew it! I knew there was a reason. I said as much to Mary – he's ill and has no way of telling me. But now you're better! You are better, aren't you?'

Alexander wanted to kiss her there and then for her concern. He had expected scorn. But, oh, this made it so much harder to tell her why he had come!

'I am better,' he admitted, glancing away. 'But that's not the only reason I have not been to see you.'

'Oh? Not more bad news, is it? Your father's not sick?'

His heart twisted to hear her worry. If only she knew how much Jeremiah was against her. He did not deserve her concern.

'No.' He turned to look at her, steeling himself for what he must say.

'Then what?' She put out a hand and touched his arm. 'Tell me, Alexander.'

He swallowed hard. 'I – I've come to say goodbye. I am engaged to another woman. It's an arranged match – not of my choosing – but I am bound by it now.'

Kate felt punched in the stomach. For a moment she thought she had him back again, but it was all an illusion.

'I see,' she whispered, drawing back.

Alexander felt wretched at her crest-fallen look. 'No you don't!' He seized her hands. 'It's been forced on me – a business arrangement of my father's. I don't love this woman – it's you I love, Kate! But my father knows about you. He'll never allow us to marry, never.'

'Marry?' Kate said the word so softly he hardly heard it. 'No, of course he wouldn't.'

'What can I do, Kate?' he asked in despair.

She pulled her hands away. 'Do?' Her voice shook. 'You know what you've got to do! Marry your lady friend, that's what. I was daft to think it could be otherwise!' She sprang up.

'Kate, I'm sorry.' He tried to stop her, but she brushed past him and fled into the inn.

She forced back tears as she stumbled into the gloom of the passageway. Mary was there. She must have been watching from one of the windows.

'Trouble back again?'

'Not for much longer,' Kate said bitterly. 'He's gettin' wed.'

The next moment she was sobbing into Mary's shoulder.

'Forget about him,' her sister said brusquely. 'It was never meant to be more than a bit o' fun.'

'It was to me!'

'You're too soft,' Mary said, pulling away and thrusting a handkerchief at her sister. 'Too romantic for your own good. You'll be better off without him calling round and putting fancy ideas in your head.'

Kate blew her nose and wiped her eyes. She must not make a spectacle of herself in front of the landlord and his customers.

Somehow she forced herself to smile and carry on working for the rest of the day. Thankfully, Alexander left without reappearing in the taproom, his beer untouched on the table.

But she could not stop thinking about him and what he had said. He loved her still. He had even talked of marriage, as if it might have been a possibility. If this other woman did not exist; if his father had not disapproved of her so much. How dare he judge her when he did not know her? Yet it was no surprise. She had been foolish even to dream of marrying so far above her.

Kate tossed in her attic bed, plagued by her thoughts, hot and sticky in the muggy air. The next day she was tired and listless, struggling through her chores, her mind elsewhere. Mary tried to chivvy her up and Taylor complained at her slapdash work, but neither could shake her out of her misery.

Three days later, after Kate and Mary had gone last to bed, she was woken from shallow sleep by a noise. She sat up in the dark. It came again: a pebble thrown up against the skylight. Slipping out of bed, Kate stood on a stool and peered out of the high window. She could see nothing below. Just about to close it again, she heard a man's voice.

'Kate? Kate! Come down,' he hissed.

As her eyes grew accustomed to the dark, a figure detached itself from the shadows and stood in the moonlight. It was Alexander!

She did not stop to think. In an instant she was pulling on her work dress over the petticoat she slept in and, grabbing her boots in her hands, tiptoed out of the room. As quietly as she could, she climbed down the creaking stairs, unbolted the kitchen door and ran barefoot across the stable yard to where he waited beyond.

'Kate!' he cried in relief as she fell into his arms.

'You came back!' she whispered in exultation. 'I thought I'd never see you again.'

'I've been in hell,' he groaned, clutching her to him. 'Come away with me, Kate.'

He steered her out of the yard.

'But where can we go?'

'Anywhere – just so we can be alone together.'

Kate thrust on her boots and they began to walk in the moonlight, arms linked around each other. Somehow, in the quiet magic of the night, the differences between them melted into the dark, the opposition to their love seemed trivial. At first their walk seemed aimless as they made their way out of Lamesley, but both seemed drawn towards the wooded secrecy of the path into the Ravensworth estate.

Skirting the massed walls and turrets of the castle, they followed the silvery path around the walled garden and the orchards to the lake. It lay still and deep in the moonlight. An owl hooted and flew further into the black canopy of trees.

'This is our place, Kate,' Alexander murmured. 'This is where I fell in love with you.'

She felt a deep wave of tenderness for him. 'Aye, it's where I think of us too.'

His arm gripped tighter around her. 'You do love me, don't you?'

'More than me own life,' she whispered.

He smiled and kissed her forehead. 'Come, we'll shelter in the boathouse.'

They hurried around the lake to the solitary wooden hut jutting out on its promontory into the tranquil water. Alexander pushed at the door and it opened with a sigh.

'Came here with my Cousin Edward – hid when it was time for us to go – didn't want to go back to Jarrow,' he laughed ruefully.

Kate thought of the small boy, happy in these blissful surroundings, being dragged back kicking and screaming to the confines of the smoke-blackened town. Her heart went out to him.

'Poor little lad,' she said, reaching up to touch his face.

Alexander grasped her hand and kissed the palm. 'Lie with me, Kate,' he urged.

Her heart began to hammer. 'I don't know . . .'

'I do!' he cried. 'I know that you're the only woman I'll ever love. I need you, Kate. This might be our only chance. In two days I set sail for Germany.'

Still she hesitated. She yearned for his kisses, yet feared what might happen.

He dropped her hand in disappointment. 'You don't love me the way I love you.'

'I do,' she insisted. 'But everything's against us. Think of your father – you're promised to another lass.'

'Forget my father!' Alexander cried rashly. 'I'll do what I please. I'll break off the engagement! Just show me that you love me – we have so little time together.'

Even in the darkness she could see the agony of his expression. He desired her like no man ever had, was prepared to throw away everything for her. She loved him for his recklessness and passion, and at that moment would do anything to make him happy.

Trembling, she touched his arm. 'Kiss me,' she whispered.

In an instant, his arms were about her and he was covering her face with urgent kisses. Breaking off, he threw his coat on to the wooden floor and pulled her down beside him. Shards of soft light pierced the darkness as he began to undress her, opening the half-buttoned dress she had thrown on in haste an hour ago. He caressed her body with eager kisses and Kate's heart pounded in excitement, her insides melting at his touch.

They made love on the hard floor without a thought beyond the moment, heady in their mutual desire. She tasted his skin and dug her fingers into his tousled hair, crying out with delight. Never had she imagined such joy existed.

When the moment of union came, Alexander nearly wept with exultation. She was his, and he loved her with every inch of his being.

They lay in each other's arms, breathless and happy, touching and stroking in the darkness.

'We'll run away,' he planned dreamily. 'Go abroad. I'll make a living as a painter. You'll be my model, my inspiration.'

He kissed her again and she let him talk on about fantastical plans for a future together. In the musty intimacy of the

233

deserted boathouse, lapped by the unseen lake, anything seemed possible. They fell into a contented, sleepy silence, dozing in each other's arms. Later, she woke to his sensual caressing and they made love again, slow and languorous as the lake outside.

Maybe it was the sound of a fox barking in the early dawn, but something woke Kate. Grey light was filtering through the crack in the door. She sat up in alarm, her limbs stiff and cold.

'Alexander!' She shook him awake. 'We must go. It's morning already.'

He stirred and yawned, giving her a sleepy smile. 'Stay a little longer, nightingale. It's the moonlight.'

But Kate was on her feet, dressing hurriedly. 'It's no moon, it's the dawn – and they'll have me guts for garters if they find me gone!'

She peered out. The lake was shrouded in grey mist, a fine drizzle spattering the surface. Gone was the clear starlit sky of before.

'I have to go,' she said, nervous at the thought of being caught.

'I'll come too,' Alexander declared, getting to his feet.

'No, best go back on me own. You mustn't be seen with me.'

'Wait,' he ordered, reaching forward to grab her arm. 'Give me a last kiss.' She saw the longing in his unshaven face and relented.

They held each other tight and kissed one last time.

'I'll be back long before Christmas,' he promised. 'You'll wait for me, won't you?'

She searched his face for reassurance, suddenly over-whelmed by the rashness of last night's act.

234

'I can do nothing but wait,' she said, with a feeling of desperation.

He hugged her close. 'I'll find a way for us to be together. I'll convince my father.'

But something in his voice told her that he was trying to convince himself more than her. How could they stand up to the forces that ranged against them? What love was strong enough?

She let go. 'Take care of yoursel', Alexander,' she smiled sadly. 'Maybes send word that you're well – I worry that much about you with your bleeding.'

'Sweet Kate!' He held out his arms again, miserable at the thought of their parting. But she stepped out of his reach and hurried through the door.

'Goodbye,' she croaked, her heart leaden.

Kate almost ran from the boathouse, half blinded with sudden tears. Leaving him was such pain! How could she bear not seeing him, not touching him for so long? He would be away for months. As she made her way back down to Lamesley, numb and soaked in the early morning rain, she wondered if she would ever see him again. For all his passionate words, would his desire cool in the long months apart? Would he be made to see sense by his strict father and avoid the scandal of a broken betrothal and an illicit affair with a common maid?

By the time Kate reached the muddy cobbles of the yard and let herself in at the kitchen door, she was tortured by dark thoughts that she could never be more to Alexander than a brief love affair. Only time would tell, she thought miserably.

Miraculously, the household was not yet stirring. As she stripped off her soaking clothes, Mary woke.

'Look at the state of you! Where've you been?'

235

'Couldn't sleep,' Kate mumbled, avoiding her sister's curious gaze.

'Your side of the bed's cold,' she said suspiciously. 'Have you stopped out all night?'

Kate said nothing.

'You have, haven't you?' Mary gasped in disapproval. She clambered out of bed and confronted her. 'Who you been with? Have you been seeing that Pringle-Davies?'

Kate reddened.

'Our Kate! How could you?'

'We love each other,' she defended, stung by her sister's look.

'He's promised to another.'

'He said he'll come back for me,' Kate said proudly.

Mary laughed in derision. 'Bet he says that to all the maids he gans with. You're daft in the head to believe him. Fancy you doing such a thing.'

Kate was filled with sudden alarm. She seized her sister by the arm. 'You mustn't tell a soul. Promise me, Mary!'

'Ow! Gerr off us.' Mary shook off her hold. They stared at each other as the enormity of what Kate had done sunk in.

'You and him,' she said, almost in awe. 'You really went with him?'

Kate flushed a deeper crimson. She knew she could not lie. 'Please don't tell Taylor – or I'll be out on me ear.'

'Taylor?' Mary said in surprise. 'I wasn't thinking of him.'

Kate's pulse began to hammer, she felt hot and cold all at once. 'What you mean?'

'I was thinking what Father would do to you if he ever found out.'

Chapter 25

Kate felt strangely detached from the world in the weeks that followed Alexander's departure. She went about her work mechanically, with only half a thought for what she did. Her mind dwelled too long on her absent lover. Whenever she stopped for water from the tap in the yard, her gaze would lift to the far tree-lined hills of Ravensworth. She would think of the lake and the boathouse and sigh with longing.

The trees were copper-coloured now, the fields harvested and the days chill, but she clung to the memory of late summer and her one night of love with the man who held her heart. She was desolate without him, dreaming of him at night and sick with yearning for him during the day.

She put up with ribald comments from some of the drinkers.

'Lady Kate's not looking well the day!'

'Missing her knight in shining armour, aren't you, pet?'

'Don't expect her to speak to the likes of ye! She likes them with fancy walking sticks and plums in their throats.'

Kate ignored them, but Mary grew anxious.

'You'll make yoursel' ill,' she scolded, alarmed by her sister's pale preoccupied look. 'You hardly touch your food.'

'I've no appetite for eatin',' Kate replied.

'You've got to keep your strength up,' Mary said. 'Taylor's startin' to complain about you shirkin' the chores. Says you're too off-hand with the customers an' all. They're laughing at you.'

Kate sighed. 'I can't be bothered. Why should I sing for them, any road? I'm too tired.'

'That's 'cos you're not eatin' proper,' Mary said impatiently. 'Forget about your fancy man – he's gone! And if you ask my opinion, that's the last you'll see of him.'

Kate was stung. 'Well, I'm not askin'! He loves me and he says he's coming back – before Christmas most likely.'

Mary's look was incredulous. 'Don't be daft! He'll never marry the likes of you. Not in a month o' Sundays. Can't you see that?' Mary looked at her with a mixture of pity and scorn. 'You gave him what he wanted. He's not ganin' to turn his back on a rich marriage for a barmaid, is he?'

Kate flinched at her brutal candidness.

'You don't know him like I do!' she cried.

'I know his type,' Mary said with disdain. 'Nothing but a lady's man.'

Kate turned her back, refusing to speak any more. But for a long time after, she pondered on what Mary had said. She wanted to dismiss their argument as jealousy on her sister's part. Alexander had chosen her, not Mary. Mary resented the thought that Kate might better herself and, with Alexander, escape a life of low-paid work.

Yet deep inside she harboured unspoken fears that Mary was right. Alexander was charming and impetuous, with no thought for the morrow. He had no real plan of how they might be together. She had given in to his flattery and soft caresses too easily. She would not be so hasty another time.

As October waned, Kate determined to shake herself out of her lethargy. She would stop pining for him and get on with her job, put a stop to the half-whispered comments. And when Alexander returned at Christmas time, she would prove the gossips wrong.

November came, but there was no word from Alexander. Even in the dark hours of the night when her doubts about him surfaced, she had clung to the belief he would get a message to her. Just a word that he was well, that he still loved her and intended to return, was all she craved.

The last of the autumn leaves were ripped from the trees in a gale, and on clear, frosty days she could see the drab grey battlements of the castle jutting through the web of black branches. They seemed to mock her, aloof and unattainable, like her absent lover.

Kate, who was never ill, caught a fever. She lay in the icy attic bed, shivering and hot with a streaming cold that made her head pound. At times she felt so nauseous, she retched rank-smelling sputum into a china basin Mary had left for her. She could not keep down the thin soup her sister brought; only dry biscuits quelled the retching and sickness.

After three days, Mary said, 'Taylor's talking of gettin' out the doctor.'

Kate closed her eyes in fatigue. She had never felt so wretched. 'Thinks I'm skiving, does he?' she groaned.

'No,' said Mary shortly. 'Doesn't want us all coming down with fever, that's all. He'll take it off your wages, mind.'

Kate felt too ill to care. 'If he wants.'

The following day, a stout, bewhiskered doctor came wheezing into the room behind Mary, out of breath from the steep climb to the attic. He plonked down his leather bag and sat on the bed regaining his breath, wrinkling his nose at the smell of sick in the low room. Mary hovered by the door.

'Let's take a look at you, young lady,' he ordered. He placed a cold hand on her forehead and took her pulse. He stuck a glass tube under her tongue.

'Well, your temperature's normal,' he declared.

Kate felt light-headed as he bombarded her with questions. He kept looking at the basin and then back at her. Finally, he coughed and said he needed to examine her stomach. He prodded her vigorously as if kneading dough.

'Any pain?' Kate shook her head. 'Any tenderness in the breasts?'

She blushed and stammered, 'N-no. Well, maybes a bit.'

His look made her uncomfortable. He pulled the covers back over her and stood up.

'It seems plain to me.' He glared down at her as if her ailments were her fault. 'I take it you're not married?'

Kate looked at him, baffled. 'N-no.'

'Well, you sharp better be,' he grunted. 'You're with child. Two – three months gone, I'd say.'

Kate gasped as a wave of nausea engulfed her. She lurched to the side of the bed and vomited into the basin. With child? Impossible! She retched again. Her head throbbed. Of course not impossible! She heard the doctor's footsteps retreat, but was too ashamed to look up.

Mary stopped him. 'Please, sir, you don't have to tell Mr Taylor, do you?'

He snorted. 'He'll soon see for himself, girl.' Then he left.

Kate sat up, shaking from shock. Mary stood staring at her. Kate's face crumpled like a small girl's as she held out her arms. Mary rushed to her and put her arms around in comfort.

'Oh, Mary!' Kate sobbed. 'What am I ganin' to do?'

Mary patted her back but for once was lost for words.

They clung to each other in the chill gloomy room, each afraid to speak. She was carrying Alexander's child. She was fallen, disgraced, outcast. Unless he came back to save her. But she had no idea where he was or whether he ever intended to return. His father would never allow them to marry now! She was shameful, a fornicator! Kate could hear the venomous words on John McMullen's tongue already.

Oh, dear God! What if her stepfather were to find out? Then she had a sudden image of her mother's face smiling in expectation. *Make me proud.*

Kate let out a moan of terror. 'What'll Mam say?' she whispered.

Mary squeezed her tighter in panic. 'Maybes the doctor's got it wrong,' she tried to reassure. 'You might not be expectin' at all.'

But the truth of it hit Kate with a cold clammy crawling of her skin.

'I am,' she said numbly. 'I've had no bleedin' since August. Isn't it supposed to stop when you're . . .?'

Mary drew back in alarm. 'Oh, our Kate, you've done it now!'

Fearful, the sisters tried to keep the news from Taylor, but within a couple of weeks rumours filtered back to the inn. A drinker from Kibblesworth had heard from a neighbour who'd heard it from a friend who'd bumped into someone from Lamesley who'd been told by the housemaid at the doctor's. 'You know that lass behind the bar who was courting the posh gentleman with the astrakhan coat and the silver walking cane . . .'

It was early December when Taylor confronted Kate about it. By then her bodice was tight across her breasts and the

241

buttons at the waist of her skirt would not do up. She had tried to laugh off the smutty remarks, but her fair face was too quick to colour and her red-rimmed eyes betrayed her frequent tearfulness.

'Aye, it's true,' she whispered in reply to the landlord's curt question.

'Oh, lass!' he cried in disappointment. 'I never would've expected this of you. How could you be so daft?'

Kate hung her head in humiliation. 'He'll come back—'

'Don't talk so stupid!' He grew angry. 'The best you can do is gan home and face the music – hope your mam'll take pity on you.'

'Home?' Kate gasped. 'Please, Mr Taylor, don't send me away.'

'You cannot stop here, lass, not in your condition. You've been a canny worker, but you're no use to me with a bairn on the way. Bad for business. I work hard to give this place a good reputation – somewhere decent for the business classes as well as ordinary folk. Not a rough bar for women of easy virtue.'

Kate went crimson. One night of weakness and her reputation was in shreds.

'I'm s-sorry,' she stammered. 'Please let me stay on till Christmas. Me stepfather – he'll kill us!' Kate began to weep and shake in fear.

Taylor relented. 'Another couple of weeks then. But you swap duties with Mary and keep out of the way. I'll not have you the laughing stock of my pub.'

Kate's one hope was that Alexander would return in December as promised and save her from this living hell. But the days dragged by, the frost killing off the last of the briars and turning the water to ice in the pails. She thought of her mother making ready for their return on Boxing Day and her courage failed. How happy and carefree she had been this time last year, how exciting the future.

Now she carried her dread at the future around with her like a stone in the pit of her stomach. Alexander had forgotten her, or decided not to bother with her further. Mary had been right all along. He had taken what he wanted and now he had no more need. No doubt he would be horrified to discover her pregnant. Perhaps he would deny it was his. He had lain with her only once, after all. Kate despaired. She had to admit she did not really know Alexander at all. She had built him into a romantic hero like a character out of one of the novels Aunt Maggie read so avidly. He was a figment of her foolish imagination. And yet she loved him so much!

In all her nights and days of torment, Kate hardly spared a thought for the child she carried in her womb. If she thought of it at all, it was with a sense of repulsion. It was an ever more visible sign of her plight and shame. She wished she could tear it out of her body with her own hands and be done with it! Then she shrank with guilt at such unchristian thoughts and believed herself evil.

On the morning of their departure, Mary helped her pack up her few possessions. She had bought a few small gifts of soap and lavender water for her mother and Sarah, a penknife for Jack and a pouch of tobacco for John. Taylor gave them a lift in his cart to the station. Kate felt sick as they jostled in silence out of the gate and down the lane. She looked back at the inn and the small high window where Alexander had woken her from sleep with a fateful tap of a pebble. If only she had slept on and never got up to answer its call.

She strained for one last look at the wooded hills and castle towers of Ravensworth, but a cold mist hid them from view. Even at this final hour she half expected, half hoped to see Alexander riding out of the gloom to meet her. But the road leading to the estate was deserted. Mary had agreed to tell Aunt Lizzie on her return, for Kate did not have the courage to face her aunt and uncle or say goodbye to her boisterous cousin Alfred. She could not bear the thought of his puzzled look and questions at her going.

'Look after yourself,' Taylor said with an awkward nod, and left them standing on the platform.

'Ta, Mr Taylor.' Kate smiled bravely. 'Ta for everything you've done for me.'

She looked deathly pale as she climbed on board the train, but she held herself erect and did not look back.

Later, perhaps pricked by Kate's quiet dignity and word of thanks, Taylor sat down and wrote a message to Davies. He told him of the girl's departure and that she was with child. Perhaps it would spark some sympathy in the old man for the trouble his son had caused. Maybe it would prompt him to provide a bit of money to help Kate out in her need. Taylor wasn't sure, but that was the reasoning behind his letter. He still felt guilty for intercepting Alexander's letters and sending them to Davies, though he believed it was in Kate's best interests to end the affair. His fear that it would end in disaster had been proved right. At least now, Davies would stop pestering him to spy on his wayward son.

All the way back to Jarrow, Kate was in turmoil. How could she bring herself to tell her parents of what she had done? Perhaps she should get off at Gateshead and disappear. But where? She had no savings and no one would employ her now. The only possessions of any worth were her two brooches, one from Lady Ravensworth and one from

Alexander. As the train picked up speed, she contemplated rushing to the door and throwing herself on to the tracks. Anything but face the wrath of John McMullen! She buried her face in her hands.

Why had she ever believed the honeyed words of Pringle-Davies? What a fool she had been.

As they approached the hazy outline of Tyneside and its mass of smoking chimneys, Kate's dread increased. At Gateshead, they boarded the train for South Shields and the familiar landmarks rushed to encircle them – the spire of St Bede's in Jarrow where they had gone as girls, the forest of cranes and chimney stacks and tenements piled up on the river bank, the sludge-grey water of Jarrow Slake where timber bobbed on the tide.

She felt this old half-forgotten world close around her, hemming her in. The throb of the train was like the pounding of her heart. They surged through the cutting below the cottages of Cleveland Place, leaving the last patches of countryside, and down into the blackened clutter of buildings that was Tyne Dock.

Chapter 26

Only twice had Kate been home since her family had moved to the dingy flat in Leam Lane. It stank of the docks and shook each time a goods train thundered down to the staithes. As the sisters alighted on the smoky platform of Tyne Dock station, panic gripped Kate's chest and squeezed the air in her throat. She couldn't breathe.

'I c-cannot . . .' Kate gasped, frozen to the station platform. At the barrier she could see Jack and Sarah waiting to greet them. '. . . cannot . . . move . . .' She clutched Mary's arm, feeling faint.

'Haway,' Mary chivvied, 'there's nowt you can do about it now.'

'They'll kill me,' Kate whispered.

'No they won't. I'll not let 'em,' Mary said with spirit. 'Your family's all you've got now, our Kate, so don't be so soft.'

Somehow she made it through the barrier and was enveloped in a generous hug from her older sister.

'By, you've put on a bit o' beef! Feedin' you well, I see.'

Kate promptly burst into tears.

'I didn't mean owt by it,' Sarah said in consternation.

Jack, hovering a few feet away, stared in embarrassment at the commotion. Through her tears, Kate noticed how he had thickened out and grown another few inches. There was a shadow of hair on his upper lip that had not been there before and she felt suddenly shy of him.

'You might as well tell her,' Mary hissed.

'Not here,' Kate sobbed, glancing around in fear at being recognised. 'Not in front of the lad.'

Mary threw Jack a dismissive look. 'He's ganin' to hear about it soon enough.'

'Hear what?' Sarah demanded. She held Kate away and scrutinised her. But Kate turned in embarrassment and began to hurry away from the hubbub at the station entrance.

Mary was about to explain, but Kate swung round. 'Don't you dare say a thing! Not till Mam's been told.' Her stormy look was enough to silence Mary's gossip.

From somewhere deep inside, Kate found a steely courage. She was Rose Fawcett's daughter and she would not cringe in fear from facing her parents. Her mother had lived through worse than this and survived. She had made a terrible mistake and no doubt would be made to pay for it. But she would walk down these streets with her head held high and brazen it out.

Kate's courage lasted until she stepped through the door of the downstairs dwelling and saw her mother's flushed expectant face. Behind, her anxious siblings shuffled through the door.

'Haway in, hinnies!' Rose wheezed. 'What's all the long faces? Not been scrappin' already, have you?'

'No, Mam,' Kate said, squeezing past the wooden settle and throwing her arms about her in a desperate hug.

'Kate's got some'at to tell you,' Mary said at once. Kate glared, prompting her sister to protest, 'Haway and get it over with!'

'Where's Father?' Kate asked nervously.

247

Rose nodded next door with disapproval. 'In the Twenty-Seven.' She pushed Kate away, alerted by her look. 'What's wrong? You been sacked?'

Kate swallowed and nodded.

'Oh, lass! What you gone and done?'

Kate started to shake. 'I – I cannot tell you . . .'

Rose looked over at the others, but Sarah shrugged in bewilderment and Jack stared at the floor. Only Mary, fierce-eyed, seemed fit to burst with the news.

'Spit it out, lass,' Rose said grimly, 'before you choke on it.'

Kate's knees buckled. She sat down abruptly on the hard settle that dominated the cramped room. The one piece of furniture that had survived countless flits and trips to the pawnshop; bought with Father's army bounty and his pride and joy. Father! Fear engulfed her.

'I've done a terrible thing,' Kate whispered. 'You'll never forgive us.'

'That's for me to decide,' Rose said. Then added more gently, 'Haway, hinny, you can tell your mam.' She squeezed her shoulder in encouragement.

Kate looked into her mother's florid, square face, puckered in concern, deep lines of suffering scored into her brow and around her once full mouth. In that moment, she hated herself for the pain she was about to inflict, the shame she was visiting on her mother's name and family. Kate gazed into Rose's worried brown eyes. The compassion she saw there gave her the courage to speak.

'That man I told you about,' Kate gulped, 'the one I was courtin'?'

Rose nodded.

'He's . . . I . . . I'm carrying . . . his . . .' Kate floundered.

'She's expectin'!' Mary burst out, unable to contain herself.

Rose looked nonplussed. She gazed between the two of them. Sarah's hand flew to her mouth to stifle a cry.

'She's having his bairn,' Mary cried.

Rose whipped round suddenly. 'I know what expectin' means! Hold your tongue.'

She stared down at Kate in disbelief, her mouth creasing into a hard tight line. Kate's stomach clenched at the look of raw hurt in her mother's eyes.

'Is it true?' Rose demanded.

Kate nodded.

'And is he ganin' to stand by you – this *gentleman* of yours?' She almost spat out the word.

Kate flinched. 'He doesn't know,' she said hoarsely.

Mary butted in. 'Hasn't been back since September. And he's ganin' to marry some posh squire's daughter, any road.'

Rose gave out a shudder. Her eyes glittered with anger as the enormity of Kate's disgrace sank in. She raised a large roughened hand and slapped her daughter hard across the face.

Kate gasped and fell sideways from the force of the blow.

'How could you?' Rose yelled and, grabbing hold of her, yanked her upright. 'How *dare* you?'

'No, Mam!' Sarah jumped forward and held on to Rose's arm. 'No more hittin'.'

'I'll box her bloody ears!' Rose cried in fury.

But Sarah was strong and thrust herself between the women, then Mary waded in too. 'Leave off her, Mam. Fightin' doesn't change owt. What's done's done.' Both daughters pulled their mother away.

Rose's chest heaved as she panted, glaring at Kate all the while as if she were a serpent coiled on the seat. There was fear and contempt in that look that turned Kate's blood cold.

'I'm sorry, Mam,' she choked, and began to weep.

Suddenly Rose was gulping for air, her breathing as noisy as bellows. The colour was draining from her sweating face.

'Mam, you're having a turn!' Sarah cried, steering her into a chair. She pulled at the buttons of her high-necked blouse and loosened the constricting collar. 'Take it steady, that's it, get your breath back,' she soothed.

As Rose wheezed and fought for breath, Kate rushed over in concern.

'Mam, I'm sorry, I never meant—'

But Sarah gave her a warning look and she stood back, not knowing what to do, while Mary fetched water and Sarah fanned her mother's face. Rose refused to look at her. Kate turned away, utterly wretched. It was then she remembered Jack. He was standing by the door as if on the point of flight, glowering at them all.

He flicked Kate a look from under his dark brows, his blue eyes sharp and appraising. For the first time it struck her how alike he looked to John – a handsome younger version of his father. They held each other's look for a long moment, though Kate could read nothing of his thoughts from his set expression. Did he despise her too? Or was he too young to understand? No, there was something knowing in that look that told her otherwise. He was half man himself already. Yet there was still a young boy's awkwardness in the way he hesitated by the doorway, alone and unsure.

All at once, his body stiffened and he whipped round like an animal sensing danger.

'Me da's comin',' he said in a low mumble.

'Oh, Mary Mother!' Kate moaned.

Rose pushed away her fussing daughters and, clutching the table, heaved herself to her feet.

'Let me deal wi' him,' she ordered, breathing hard, but her face set in determination. 'Lasses, get the food out the oven. No one breathe a word of this till I say, you an' all, Mary,' she warned. She gave Kate a contemptuous glance. 'And you gan and wash your face. Don't let him see you've been blubbin'.'

Kate edged round the table and escaped to the scullery just as she heard her stepfather's heavy tread at the front door. He was whistling 'Sweet Molly Malone'. There was a flurry of activity as Sarah and Mary competed to busy themselves with a clatter of plates and steaming pots of vegetables.

'That's a grand sight!' she heard John exclaim as he tramped into the room, stamping his boots from the cold. 'Here, you useless beggar, get this beer poured – you can have one an' all.'

Kate splashed icy water on to her face with shaking hands, as Jack appeared searching for an extra cup, an earthen jug in his hands. She caught a whiff of the hoppy liquid and felt queasy. She gave him a desperate look. A memory came back to her with sickening clarity of the way her stepfather had once taken the belt to Sarah for failing to return home from a day out in Newcastle. He had whipped her almost to death for being a few hours late – and she had not even been with a man!

'Jack, I cannot face him,' she whispered, shivering with terror.

Her half-brother carried on pouring as if he had not heard. But Kate saw from the flush creeping into his cheeks that he had. He was embarrassed and ashamed of her. Somehow she had disappointed him too. Kate took a deep breath. She was going to have to face this alone. She had no one to blame but herself. Why should Jack protect her when she was bringing dishonour to their family? As she made for the door to the

251

kitchen, she was aware of him glancing at her sideways, but still he said nothing.

John McMullen was sitting in his high-backed chair in its chosen spot by the fire. The room felt oppressively stuffy and Kate's head swam.

'So there you are, lass! What you got for me, eh?'

Kate forced a smile. Around the table the others shot her nervous looks as they brought food to the table, fiddled and rearranged plates and cutlery.

'It's not much this year, Father,' she said, avoiding his look and scrabbling for the parcel of tobacco. It seemed so meagre compared to last year's ostentatious present of the picture of Lord Roberts, which now hung above the fireplace.

He sniffed it and tore off the wrapper like a child. 'Baccy – that's grand. What you got me, our Mary?' He pocketed the tobacco swiftly.

'That's from both of us,' she told him with a defiant look. 'Mam, we got you some canny soap.' She took over from Kate, seizing the basket and handing out the other small gifts, seeing how her sister was paralysed with fear.

'Let's eat before the dinner gets cold,' Rose instructed. 'Jack, you carve.'

The memory of John threatening them with a kitchen knife the night he discovered Sarah gone leapt into Kate's mind. Perhaps her mother did not trust him with the carving knife. She sat down, feeling faint.

'What's wrong wi' you?' John snorted.

'She's a bit under the weather,' Rose said quickly. 'Food'll help.' She pushed a plate of pork and potatoes and cabbage across the table. Kate felt bile rise in her throat. 'Eat,' Rose told her.

'How about a drop of beer?' John chuckled. 'That'll perk you up.'

Kate shook her head.

'You know she doesn't touch it,' Rose said primly.

'She works in a pub, you silly bitch,' John said with derision. 'Bet she has it for breakfast. Fill it up again, Jack lad,' he ordered, banging his empty glass on the table.

He intercepted a look between Rose and her son.

'It's a holiday, woman! And don't you go all high and mighty on me, Rose Ann. I remember when you liked your fill o' beer – working in them puddling mills—'

'Stop it, John,' she remonstrated. 'That's ancient history.'

'Saved your mam from a fate worse than death, I did,' he continued. 'Not that she's thanked me from that day to this.'

Rose sighed with impatience but bit back a retort.

'By, she could sup with the best of us in those days.'

Kate felt the familiar dread at a row brewing. It always started with John needling Rose about some petty fault he saw in her or women in general. The more he belittled her the more puffed out he became with his own importance. According to him, he had saved them from the gutter and made them respectable. Their descent into debt and poverty over the years was blamed on Rose's bad housekeeping and slovenly ways, never his drinking or lack of work.

The family had all learnt it did not pay to answer back. Around the table they sat tensely, making half-hearted attempts to eat the food.

'Your mam was two steps from the gutter when I made an honest woman out of her,' he goaded.

Kate dropped her fork with a clatter. Rose glared at her in warning. The time was wrong. He was in one of his contrary moods – half joking, half vindictive.

Suddenly he was suspicious. 'What's ganin' on?'

'Nothing.' Rose kept calm.

'Some'at is,' he growled. 'All sitting there with red-hot pokers up your backsides.'

'John . . .' Rose tutted.

'Don't John me, woman,' he snarled. 'Look at them – faces as long as bloody puritans. I want to know what's been ganin' on behind me back. Been bad-mouthing me, have you? Settin' them against me as usual, eh?'

'Course not,' Rose protested. 'Nothing to do with you.'

He slammed his fist down on the table, making them all jump.

'Nothing to do with me? I'm the head of the house! I've a right to know what gans on here.' He seized Mary by the arm.

'Ah-ya!'

'You tell me what they've been saying – you've always got ten words when one will do.'

'Ow, Father, you're hurting me,' Mary whimpered.

'Let her be, John,' Rose pleaded. 'Eat your meal. It's gettin' cold.'

John's eyes narrowed in anger. 'Don't tell me what to do. What you keepin' from me?' He glared around the table. 'No other bugger's eating. It tastes of the midden!' With his free hand he up-ended his plate, splattering the old sheet Rose used as a tablecloth with meat and gravy.

Kate could bear it no longer. A sick fury churned inside her. How dare he treat them like worse than muck? Other men did not. Uncle Peter, Bram Taylor – they were respectful and loving. Even Alexander, for all he had abandoned her now, had treated her as someone special. How had her mother put up with such a boor for so long?

She got to her feet. She might have sinned, but it was nothing to the hell this man subjected his wife and family to. She would never be as bad as him.

'It's me,' she declared defiantly. 'I'm the reason for the long faces, not me mam, so leave off her.'

John gawped at her in surprise, loosening his grip on Mary. She pulled her arm away, nursing the bruises. Kate ignored her mother's look of alarm.

'I've got myself into trouble.'

'Trouble?'

'I – I cannot gan back to Ravensworth. Lost me job.'

'What you mean, lost your job?'

Kate swallowed hard. 'I met this man – this gentleman – thought he was ganin' to marry me. He's not.' She looked him straight in the eye. 'But I'm carrying his bairn.'

For a moment it was so quiet that the tick of the clock on the mantelpiece sounded as loud as the thumping in her chest. Someone's laughter in the lane came sharp and clear.

Then John barked, 'A *bairn*?'

Kate nodded.

He staggered to his feet, roaring, 'You've been whoring with a man? Who is he? I'll beat the living daylights out o' him! Out of you! Come here, you little bitch!'

Pushing the table aside and thrusting Mary out of the way, he grabbed at Kate. She dodged and he missed.

'Leave her, John,' Rose ordered to no avail.

Kate could see the blind fury in his bloodshot eyes. He lunged again. She was pushed up against the settle and could not escape. He seized a handful of her hair and pulled hard. Kate screamed. He yanked her out of the corner by her hair.

'You slut!' he thundered. 'Filthy little slut. Who is he?'

255

'A gentleman,' Kate cried, 'a businessman at the castle.'

'Gentleman!' He dragged her across the room. 'What sort of fool do you take me for?'

'He was, Father,' Mary cut in. 'Related to the Liddells.'

But this seemed to inflame him further. 'You stupid bitch! Taken in by fancy talk, were you? Think yourself Lady Muck? Or do you open your legs for any bugger?'

He punched her breast. Kate yelled at the shooting pain. 'John, stop it!'

'I only went with him the once, I promise,' she sobbed.

He laughed savagely. 'Liar! You're as bad as the rest of them. Pretend you're like the Virgin Mary – but you're all a pack of whores!'

He flung her to the floor. 'I'll teach you to shame me and the name of McMullen,' he panted, and began to unbuckle his thick leather belt.

Kate threw her arms over her head to protect herself from the beating she knew was to come. Rose and Sarah were screaming at him now to stop.

'You'll harm the bairn,' Rose wailed, 'think of the bairn.'

'The bastard in her belly!' John shouted. 'I'll whip it out of her.'

He was drawing the worn leather strap from his trousers as he ranted, filling the stifling air with obscenities and speaking aloud foul thoughts. Wrapping it once round his large fist, he raised the belt above his head, the heavy buckle dangling.

'You'll never go with another man as long as I live!' he cried.

At the point of whipping the weapon over his head, Jack leapt forward and caught the buckle.

'Don't touch her!' he growled. They struggled over the belt.

'Leave off,' John roared, kicking his son on the shins. 'It's nowt to do with you, you little runt.'

Jack winced at the pain but held on. Kate looked up to see them tussling and punching each other over the belt. John thrashed about in fury, while Jack stood his ground, clinging on and jabbing back.

Swiftly, Rose came round and pulled Kate up.

'Get out of here quick,' she ordered.

Kate almost vomited from the pain in her chest and head. It felt as if half her hair had been ripped out. She hesitated.

'I cannot leave the lad,' she sobbed.

Rose shoved her towards the door. 'Save yourself and the bairn.'

'Where, Mam?'

'Anywhere, just gan!'

Sarah grabbed her arm and pulled her away from the brawling men. 'I'll gan with you. Come on, Kate!'

She threw one last glance at Jack. His face was red with exertion, blood gushing from his mouth where his lip was split. But he was getting the better of his father. John was panting and swearing, his strength waning. The next moment Sarah was bundling Kate through the door into the dank lane. The sharp air stung her face and clamped on her chest so that she struggled for breath.

Sarah would not let her rest. She put a strong arm about her and hurried her down the street.

'Good on the lad,' Sarah said with savage triumph, 'standing up to the old devil at last.'

'Aye,' Kate agreed, feeling both awe and relief at what Jack had done. She would be in his debt for this for a long time.

'Wish he'd been old enough to stand up for me,' Sarah added. 'I've still got the scars on me back from that beatin'.'

'Aye,' Kate agreed, remembering how Jack had cowered and dirtied himself in fear at their father's violence. 'That lad's seen too much already.'

As Sarah helped her hobble away, Kate felt a fresh wave of guilt at the trouble she was bringing on her family.

Chapter 27

At the moment of flight, the sisters had no thought of where they were going, just the urgency to be gone. They took shelter from the misty drizzle under the vast echoing arches of the dock staithes. But it chilled them to the bone to stand under the slimy dripping walls. Light was fading from the short day and it was eerily dark in the tunnel.

Kate shook uncontrollably. 'What do you think's happening to Jack? I'm that scared. I should've stayed to help him.'

'The best help you can be is to stay out of Father's way,' Sarah declared, 'if you want to live till the morra.'

'But what about Mam – and Mary?'

'They can take care of themselves. Haway, we'll catch our death stopping out here. Let's gan to Aunt Maggie's. She'll take us in.'

Kate grabbed her arm. 'But what'll we tell her?'

Sarah sighed. 'She's ganin' to hear soon enough – you cannot keep it from family.' She saw Kate's harrowed look. 'We'll just say there's been fightin'. She's taken us in before, remember; she knows what Father's like.'

Kate did remember. As young girls, when Rose had been widowed, they had lived with Maggie and Danny at their smallholding up Simonside. And later, when their aunt and uncle had moved down to East Jarrow, they had taken shelter with their long-suffering aunt after John's attack on Sarah. Kate nodded in agreement and they hurried out of the tunnel.

They had to pass the end of Leam Lane again, crossing over to the far side and hurrying past the blacksmith's, heads down. Kate did not dare look across the street to the cluster of houses sandwiched between two shops and the notorious Twenty-Seven. The lane was deserted and no sounds came from Number Five, but they did not stop in their hurry up the bank towards Jarrow.

The road was potholed and muddy, and a raw wind hit them as they climbed above the river. Below lay the Slake, a stinking inlet of mud now the tide was going out. Rose had never let them play there as children, fearful of the ghost of the striking miner who had been hanged and gibbeted there long ago.

The isolated grid of streets known as the New Buildings hove into sight over the brow of the hill. During a brief prosperous spell they had lived there themselves, among this half-finished block of houses begun by a well-intentioned employer of a chemical works. They were solidly built workers' houses, upwind of the sulphurous factory and surrounded by open wasteland.

Their young cousin Margaret came to the door. 'It's our Kate!' she cried to her mother in delight. 'And Sarah.'

Aunt Maggie appeared behind her and squinted short-sightedly. 'Well, let them in, lass. This is a grand surprise. Our Mary not with you?'

'No, there's bother at home.' Sarah was blunt. 'Mam told us to make ourselves scarce.'

Maggie clucked in sympathy and bustled them into her cosy parlour. 'Your uncle's having a nap. Come by the fire and tell me how you're getting on.'

She poured them hot cups of stewed tea from the pot on the range and Sarah talked about Hebburn. Kate wondered if she was still seeing her young miner from Birtley but did not have the heart to ask. It might lead to awkward questions about courting. Oh, Alexander! If only he could see the trouble he had caused. Why had he not come back for her?

'And you, Kate? How's our Lizzie and the lads?'

'Haven't seen them for a bit,' Kate mumbled.

'Well, I'll send you back with a pair of Danny's breeks I've cut down for Alfred.'

'I'm not ganin' back,' she burst out, then, covering her face, succumbed to tears.

Sarah nodded at Margaret and Maggie swiftly sent the girl outside to play under the lamppost with her younger sister. In a hushed voice, Sarah explained Kate's predicament.

'Saint Teresa! This is terrible,' Maggie cried. 'My lasses mustn't hear of such carry-on. Our Rose must be beside herself. She had such high hopes for you, Kate. Oh, Mary Mother, what'll the priest say?'

'Never mind the priest,' Sarah exclaimed. 'It's Father's ganin' to give her a skelpin'!'

Maggie crossed herself and called to Our Lady again. 'He'll not set foot in this house,' she promised stoutly. 'You can sleep here the night. My Danny's a match for old John any day.'

Soon after, Sarah left for Hebburn. The sisters gripped hands in parting.

'Send word if you need me,' Sarah urged. Kate nodded, trying to be brave, feeling bereft at her going.

Maggie told Danny that Kate had argued with her step-father and nothing more was said that night. She spent sleepless hours curled up with her cousin Margaret in a narrow

261

bed, fretting about her family. With any luck, John would be down to the docks for work in the morning and she could sneak home. But what then?

Kate got up at dawn, stoked up the fire and made tea. Danny went off to the steel works after a breakfast of porridge, and the street came alive with the sounds of men going to work and children gathering to play. In the distance, the clang and din of the dockside told of the brief holiday over.

'I'll walk down with you,' Maggie offered, asking a neighbour to keep an eye on her daughters.

As they descended the long downhill stretch into Tyne Dock, Kate found her steps dragging. Ahead she could see the curve of Leam Lane. People were going in and out of Lawson's corner shop and the pounding of metal could be heard from the blacksmith's opposite. A horse tram splashed mud at them as it passed.

Suddenly Kate seized her aunt's arm in alarm.

'Don't worry, I'll stay with you,' Maggie reassured.

'No,' Kate gasped, 'it's not that.' She felt the spasm again. 'Some'at's wrong with me.' She clutched her belly in fear.

'What's it feel like?'

'Like – little hammers.'

A strange look came over her aunt's face. 'How far gone are you?' she whispered.

'Four months,' Kate flushed.

Maggie gave a pitying look. 'It's the bairn, hinny. He's started kickin'.'

Kate gaped at her in shock. 'The bairn?'

Maggie nodded. Kate put a tentative hand where the gentle drumming had been. All at once she was overwhelmed with a confusion of dread and wonder. It was real. She was carrying Alexander's child. Through all the sickness, tiredness and

262

anxiety, she had never thought of the weight inside her as anything but a curse and a source of shame. But now she felt the stirrings of another human being, a small life growing within her, her own child.

Her eyes stung with tears. Standing there in the drab lane by the blacksmith's with the scorched smell of hot metal on hoofs filling the raw air, she knew she could not give up her baby, whatever her stepfather might say. Her fight would not just be for herself, but for her unborn son or daughter. Illegitimate or not, it was hers.

Linking arms with her aunt, she walked the last few yards with a new determination. She would not go running away to save her own skin again.

They found the house deserted, but for Rose struggling in from the back lane with a full pail of water.

'Let me, Mam.' Kate was quick to relieve her.

'Mary left early,' Rose told them. 'Father and Jack are down the dock.'

'How's Jack?'

'Got an eye like a football, but he wouldn't stay off. John's got bruises to show for it an' all,' she added with a glint of satisfaction. 'You'd best stay up at Maggie's for a day or two.'

'I'm stopping here with you.' Kate was defiant. 'I'll not have others doing me fightin' for me.'

'You'll do as you're told,' Rose snapped.

'This is me home,' Kate said stubbornly.

'She's felt the bairn moving,' Maggie interjected. 'You cannot let John throw her out – it'd be a sin.'

'She's the one done the sinning!' Rose cried, jabbing a finger at her daughter. She felt so angry at Kate for what she had done. Yet as she glared into her soft pale face and large sorrowful eyes, she felt a stab of protectiveness. Had she not

263

encouraged her daughter to be courted by this gentleman? Instead of warning her to be cautious, she had fed Kate's vanity about their connection with the Liddells and allowed her to get above herself. She was as much to blame, Rose admitted bitterly.

All at once the fight went out of her and Rose sank on to a chair. Up till now, she had thought only of the disgrace to herself and John. Now, she feared for her daughter. She knew how harshly Kate would be judged by the priests, how cruel would be the wagging tongues of neighbours. The censure would be universal and relentless.

'Oh, lass, what's to become of you?'

They looked at each other in despair, not knowing the answer. Kate dashed forward and sank to her mother's feet, throwing her arms about her waist and burying her face in her lap.

'I'm sorry, Mam. I'll do anything you ask – just let me stay.'

In reply, Rose placed a callused hand on her daughter's silky hair and stroked it in reassurance.

It was dark when the men came banging in the door. Jack started to see Kate standing by the range, stirring a pot of broth. Even in the dim light she could see his left eye was half closed with bruising and his bottom lip badly swollen. He said nothing but gave a half-smile of encouragement. Behind came her stepfather. Her stomach jolted at the look of loathing he gave her.

'What's the harlot doing here?' John snarled at Rose.

'It's her home, John,' Rose said evenly. 'Get the broth served, lass.'

Jack went straight to the scullery to wash, but John stood glaring at Kate.

'This isn't your home,' he spat. 'You belong in the pigsty with that fancy man with the fancy name, Pringle-Davies.'

Kate flinched to hear his name spoken. How much had Mary told them about Alexander?

'You know she can't gan to him,' Rose said quietly. 'Now come and eat.'

'Well, I'll not have her in my house.' John was adamant. He strode towards Kate. 'You've brought shame on it. You're a bloody disgrace. Go on, get out!'

'Please, Father, let me stay,' Kate said, holding her ground. 'I've nowhere else to gan.'

'Should've thought of that before you opened your legs for your fancy man,' he said savagely, thrusting his face into hers.

Kate felt nauseous at his foul breath. 'Just till the bairn's born,' she whispered.

'And what do we tell the neighbours when your belly gets big with that man's bastard?' he taunted. 'What do we tell the priest?'

'When've you ever cared what the neighbours or the priest think of us?' Rose retorted.

'Shut your gob, woman.' He turned on her.

Rose put her hands on her hips. 'No I won't. She's already feeling the bairn, John. I'll not have her put out on the street like a dog.'

'That's what the slut deserves!'

'No it's not. She was daft enough to be taken in by some fancy-talking man – but she's not the first and she'll not be the last. If you hoy her out she'll have nowhere to gan but the workhouse. I can't believe you would ever want that to happen to any of yours, John McMullen. Don't you remember that terrible place?' she challenged.

265

'Aye, of course I do,' he said in agitation. 'Don't you lecture me about it – I was the one went breaking rocks for you and your pack of brats!'

'Then you know what they do to lasses like Kate.' Rose advanced on him. 'They hoy them in with the loonies and thems with filthy diseases. And they'll tak the bairn off her and she'll never see it again and they'll keep her locked up like a criminal for years. Is that what you want? 'Cos the John McMullen I married never would have!'

John looked stunned. 'Maybes I don't!' he cried. Turning from them, he smashed his fist into the wall, sending a shower of plaster to the floor.

Rose motioned for Kate to keep quiet. Jack came quietly out of the scullery, poised in the doorway ready to defend his sister again.

John spun round and stared at them all. 'And what are we to do with her, eh? Come on, Missus Big Gob, the one with all the answers.'

'Let her stay here and have the baby,' Rose reasoned. 'When it's born, the lass can gan back to work to pay for its keep.'

Kate felt a wave of gratitude. Not only was her mother standing by her, she was prepared to keep the child too.

'You mean have it livin' here? Someone else's bastard?' John railed.

'I've brought up plenty bairns,' Rose said with resignation. 'What's the harm in one more?'

'Mam!' Kate cried in relief and moved towards her. 'Thank you.'

But Rose held herself away. 'There's one condition,' she said, her look suddenly severe.

'Aye, anything,' Kate agreed.

266

'We bring the bairn up as our own – me and John.'

Kate was nonplussed. 'As yours? But – but what about me?' she gasped.

'You gan back to work like it didn't happen. As far as the neighbours are concerned, the bairn is ours. That way we can all hold our heads up round these streets.'

'And me baby?' Kate whispered, a strange pain sweeping through her.

'She's not to know. You'll be her big sister, that's all. We'll bring her up strict like I should've done with you – knowing what's right and wrong. You won't have to bother yourself with being a mam. You'll work hard and keep your nose clean.'

'Aye,' John joined in, warming to the idea of being a father again, 'we'll not spare the rod with this one. You'll have nowt to do with it – no spoiling like you got. And if I catch you looking at another man again,' he threatened, 'I'll kill ye.'

Kate swallowed the tearful angry words she wanted to shout. She had no intention of looking at any other man but Alexander. He was the only man she could love – still loved! And they would not stop her loving his child. She looked to her mother for a softening of her stepfather's words, but Rose's face was closed.

'If you do anything more to shame us, you're out. I'll not stand up for you a second time,' Rose warned. Her words turned Kate's insides to ice.

Chapter 28

As the dreary weeks of January and February dragged on, Kate existed in a strange limbo. To the prying world beyond the doorstep, she was home to help Rose, who was having a bad spell with her legs and chest. To her family she was an embarrassment, the source of which was never referred to. Her mother was distant, Jack was wary. As her belly grew, he would sneak her bashful sidelong glances, half fascinated, half appalled. Any lingering playfulness between them had vanished in the shock of her pregnancy and its aftermath. Where once he had looked up to Kate and followed her around like a loyal puppy, she now turned to him for protection.

At fifteen he was tall and brawny, already hardened by a year grafting on the dockside, and he had shown he could stand up to his father's bullying. He had not done so since, but this did not stop John punching him and ridiculing him for defending his 'fallen' sister. Jack would stand his ground and fend off John's fists, which only infuriated his father more.

But most of John's drunken goading was aimed at Kate. After a couple of hours in the pub, he would stagger in, filthy and sodden from labouring waist-deep in river water unloading iron ore, and begin his taunting.

'Fetch me some'at to eat, slut. Tak off me wet boots and

troosers – should be used to that,' he would laugh crudely. 'Did that for yer *gentleman*, did you?' When she ignored him, he would jab her belly and curse her for her shamelessness.

The foul-mouthed ridicule and threats to tell Father O'Neill, the local firebrand priest, were unremitting. Occasionally, Jack, fuelled with swigs from his father's jug of whisky, would spark back.

'Father O'Neill wouldn't know you if he passed you in the street,' he muttered on one occasion.

'What's that?' John demanded, not hearing the jibe.

'Nowt.'

'I'll give you nowt!' John bawled, slapping him round the head, and the fighting would start again.

Later Rose would scold Kate for these attacks. 'Look at the trouble you cause our Jack.' But Kate could do nothing to stop their sparring, or John's relentless criticism.

Ahead stretched a bleak future for Kate at Leam Lane, forever at the beck and call of her ageing parents, forever in their debt. In the quiet of the night, miserable and angry, trying to get comfortable on the hard wooden settle that had become her bed, she gave in to tears.

At twenty-three, her life was in ruins. Nothing could save her now, except Alexander. Alternately, she agonised about what might have happened to him and railed at his abandonment of her. What if something terrible had happened? He had been taken ill again, had bled to death? He had gone down at sea in a storm? But there had been no rumours of a tragedy circulating at the inn. Never in all these months had she had one word from him.

It pained her to remember, but the only reason he had returned to see her at the end of the summer was to say goodbye and tell her of his impending marriage. Passion had

269

overcome his better judgement for a brief moment, nothing more. His promises were empty, his words as profligate and reckless as his actions. She would never see him again.

She shrank back from the flickering firelight and covered her womb with anxious hands. 'You'll burn in the flames of hell for what you've done!' John had preached.

Stifling her sobs so no one in the next room would hear, she hissed to her unborn child, 'Hell can't be any worse than this!'

Chapter 29

The forests around Ravensworth were bursting with the vibrant green of late spring, when Alexander took the train north to Newcastle. He had not travelled through these parts since returning hurriedly in November. So much had happened these past months, it seemed another life he had led here. News had reached him in Cologne that his father was dangerously ill and it had taken an anxious week to get home and discover Jeremiah had almost died from septicaemia.

He had stayed with his father all through December and Polly had come to keep him company and help nurse her future father-in-law, despite being in mourning for her own father. De Winton had died in the October.

'I know the anguish you're feeling,' Polly had said sadly, and Alexander had felt guilty for not returning sooner, even though news of the squire's death had reached him only after the funeral.

All his carefully rehearsed speeches breaking off their engagement dried on his lips in the face of her kindness and grief. They played endless games of chess and she talked with tearful fondness of her father and bashfully of how he had looked forward to seeing them married. She was now a wealthy heiress and Alexander could not pretend the thought of being independent from his father did not excite him. Yet for all this, he did not love Polly.

While his father lay weak and feverish, darker thoughts occupied Alexander's mind. If Jeremiah died now, he would be free to marry whom he wished and have the financial independence to do so. He hated himself for wishing his father dead, but could not banish the thought. It meant he and Kate could be together.

Yet why had Kate never answered any of his letters? He had left a poste restante address in Germany and that of Mrs Timmins's lodging house in Newcastle. Just a brief word to tell him she still loved him would have helped to give him the courage to defy his father. But nothing awaited him on his return.

Still, he promised himself he would go to Ravensworth as soon as his father was out of danger and discover how Kate really felt. Perhaps the silence meant she had doubts about his foolhardy plan for them to run away together. Did she not believe him? Worse still, had she found another suitor – that hard-working gardener's son who could not hide his love for her? Someone more suited to her station, who could provide for her without causing a scandal and upsetting her family?

Such thoughts had plagued him while he waited to see if his father recovered. And all the time Polly had been a constant and thoughtful visitor, and he had been riddled with guilt at the humiliation he would bring her by breaking off their betrothal. Was he mad even to contemplate such a headstrong course of action? Yes, he admitted, mad with an obsessive passion for Kate.

His father began to recover before Christmas and they spent the festival quietly together. Jeremiah had been delighted at Polly's attentiveness.

'Nothing will bring me greater pleasure than to see you two married this coming year,' he told her as she departed home to her mother on Christmas Eve. 'I thank God I have been spared to see such happiness.'

He pressed Alexander to set the date as soon as possible and did not take kindly to his prevarication.

'There's no hurry.' He tried to laugh it off.

'There's every reason to hurry,' Jeremiah said querulously. 'I'm not long for this world – and I *will* see you married, Alexander!'

'But Polly is still in mourning, Papa. We cannot in all decency marry before the summer now.'

'May at the latest,' Jeremiah ordered. 'You've had your fun, now you will face up to your responsibilities.' Then his father had stunned him with a seemingly casual remark. 'By the way, I heard that the chambermaid you were seeing at Ravensworth has left.'

Alexander spun round. 'Left? How could you possibly know?'

His father gave him a satisfied look. 'I make it my business to know. You'll not find her there, so don't bother looking. Taylor says she's gone home to whatever slum it is she came from.'

Alexander went crimson. 'She's no slum girl! Her parents were friends of Uncle Edward's.'

'Well, be that as it may, she's returned to her own kind. And from what I gather, she should be married by now.'

The words came like a blow to the head. Married! His worst fears were confirmed. He had left it too long. Why should she wait for him all this time, when he had made promises to her before that he had not kept? He looked at his

273

father in fury. No doubt he would say anything to get him married off to the wealthy Polly.

'Why should I believe you?'

'Don't be such a fool, boy. Do you think I would let you throw away your future for the likes of a serving maid? She has shown more sense than you – gone back where she belongs. Now you can put her from your mind once and for all.'

His father's face was pale and drawn, but his words were iron hard. 'Don't defy me on this, Alexander. If you don't marry Polly, I'll cut you off without a penny. I've changed the terms of my will. If I die before you marry, my business and wealth will pass to my second cousin in Durham. I will not see you make a fool of either of us.'

Alexander was dumbstruck. To think his father would go to such lengths to keep him apart from Kate. It would not surprise him to learn Jeremiah had paid the landlord to get rid of her. He was furious that his father should treat him with such distrust, and slammed out of the room. Later, a morose calm settled over him and he admitted that the old man was right to be suspicious. For had he not been harbouring plans to defy his father and elope with Kate? He had not really thought beyond the thrill of escape, but assumed his father would come round to the idea in time – once he had got to know how genteel Kate was.

But he was in no doubt now that his father would carry out his threat. If he did not marry Polly, Alexander would be condemned to an uncertain, itinerant life living on his wits and his mediocre painting. At least with Polly he would have comfort and ease and a secure life of pleasure. Was he not a fool to throw it back in his father's face, all for the sake of a simple maid? Besides, his love had not been returned. Kate had gone without a word, disappeared back to Jarrow to marry someone else, if his father was to be believed.

In bitter disappointment, Alexander finally bowed to his father's pressure and went along with the wedding plans for May. When he thought of Kate, it was with jealousy that she was probably already married to some other man.

Alexander gazed out of the train window as it slowed into Lamesley station. Through the steam he caught a glimpse of the castle towers glinting in the April sunshine. He peered for a view of the inn and its blackened stone frontage. Now, seeing the familiar fields around the square-towered church at Lamesley from the train, he was filled with a wave of regret and longing for his lover, like a huge empty aching in the pit of his being. The whistle blew for the train to move on.

All at once, Alexander sprang from his seat and yanked open the carriage door. As the train lurched and clanked into motion, he jumped down on to the platform and slammed the door behind him. His trip to the shipping agents in Newcastle could wait another hour or two. He would catch the next train. All he could think of at that moment was to discover what had happened to Kate and hear for himself that she was finally beyond his reach. Almost at a run, he left the station and took the road to the Ravensworth Arms.

Bram Taylor seemed startled to see him.

'Good day, sir,' he said, ushering his customer into the parlour. 'Have you business at the castle?'

'I'm on my way to Newcastle on my father's behalf – he's been ill.'

'Sorry to hear it, sir.'

Alexander looked around. 'Thank you. And you, Bram, are you well?'

The landlord nodded, but seemed edgy. 'I'll get the lass to bring you in some refreshment,' he said quickly.

'Kate?' Alexander said with a pang of hope.

Taylor cleared his throat in discomfort. 'No, sir, she's been gone since Christmas.'

So it was true! Alexander felt a thump of disappointment. He watched the older man hurry from the room as if he did not want to linger in his presence. A few minutes later he recognised the dark-haired girl with the slim face and bold eyes who carried in a plate of ham sandwiches and glass of beer.

'It's Mary, isn't it?' he exclaimed. 'Kate's sister?'

'Aye, sir,' she said with a wary look. Plonking the meal down and turning away swiftly.

'Wait, Mary.' Alexander smiled at her. 'Please stay a moment. How is your sister?'

She gave him a surly look. 'Well as can be expected.'

He was baffled, but nodded. 'She's returned home, I'm told.'

Mary nodded. She was on the point of withdrawing, then decided to speak her mind. 'Had no choice, did she?'

Alexander felt uncomfortable at the girl's accusing tone. 'Why's that?'

Mary coloured. 'Being in her condition.'

Alexander frowned. 'You mean, now that she's married?'

'Married!' Mary exclaimed. 'Who's gan to marry her the way she is?'

'I don't understand. Has something happened to Kate?' he asked in alarm. 'Please, Mary, tell me.'

Mary began to retreat, flustered. 'Not for me to say, sir. She's that ashamed about it.'

Alexander rose and strode over to stop her going. 'What has she got to be ashamed about? I thought she had gone back to Jarrow to get married. Tell me, Mary!' He seized her arms.

'She's expectin'!' Mary blurted out, fearful of his look.

Alexander's heart jolted. 'She's with child?'

'Aye.'

He swallowed hard. 'And the father?' he rasped.

She just looked at him with frightened accusing eyes and the truth hit him. Kate was carrying his child!

'Why didn't she get word to me?' he cried angrily, shaking her.

'How could she?' Mary demanded. 'You never came back for her like you said.'

Alexander glared. 'But I wrote!'

'She waited till Christmas but you never came – so she had to gan home and face 'em. Never said owt about any letters.'

Alexander dropped his hold with a bitter exclamation. Mary stood clutching her arms.

'I'm sorry, I didn't mean to hurt you,' he apologised. 'I must go to her. Is she at your mother's?'

Mary nodded.

'Where can I find Mrs Fawcett?'

Mary looked confused.

'Your mother, Mary, where does she live?'

Realisation dawned. 'Mrs Fawcett! Is that what she told you? Aye, she would.' Mary gave a mirthless laugh. 'Me mam's not been Mrs Fawcett since I was a bairn. She's married to me stepda – John McMullen. But Kate's ashamed of him and me mam, since she took up with you.'

'She's no reason to be,' Alexander flushed.

Something like relish gleamed for a moment in the girl's eyes. 'You'll find them down Leam Lane in Tyne Dock – unless me stepda finds you first,' she muttered.

Alexander did not wait to hear any more. Throwing down a handful of coins on the table, he thanked her distractedly and rushed from the room. What terrible fate had he subjected Kate to? he accused himself savagely as he hurried back to the station. And why had she never mentioned her stepfather? Wherever she was, he would find her, before it was too late.

Chapter 30

Alexander was in a fever of agitation by the time the train drew into Jarrow station. He was tempted to jump off and explore the place of his childhood. But he could not put off facing Kate's parents. He must get to her as quickly as possible.

Staring out of the grimy window, streaked by heavy spring showers, he saw the solid buildings of the town hall and a large hotel dominate the streets of shops. The place bustled with people, delivery carts and trams, but none of it looked familiar. As the train pulled out, the prosperous heart of the town gave way to rows of soot-blackened terraces and the sprawl of steelworks, sheds and chimneys. He peered for a view of the ruined monastery and the old vicarage, but a blanket of smoke from the quickening train obscured all but a glimpse of crude fence and pale dead grass.

The train disappeared into a cutting, then curved around a bend and picked up speed. Suddenly the smoke cleared to reveal a mass of rooftops marching down to the grey river and a web of cranes, gantries, masts and funnels. Out of the opposite window rose the pit wheels of South Shields and a glimpse of larger, grander houses in the distance.

Then all about grew a network of railway sidings and slowly bumping coal trucks, as the train slowed and eased into Tyne Dock with a shriek of steam. Alexander was glad to be out of the stuffy, tightly packed carriage with its smell of bodies and damp clothing. The station rang with noise and shouts and the squeal of iron.

He hurried out into a busy street and headed uphill. The streets around were made up of solidly built terraces, a mixture of houses and shops. He had a vague notion from something Kate had said that her mother lived on the edge of the countryside, where she had a little land and a kitchen garden. Mary had said Leam Lane, which sounded like a country road.

After ten minutes of fruitless searching for a way out of the tightly packed streets, he asked a passer-by.

'Leam Lane? That's the other way, hinny. Doon there.' She jerked a thumb towards the docks.

'Are you sure?'

'Aye. See that gas tower? Well, it's right opposite.'

Alexander thanked her and with sinking heart retraced his steps. As he descended the hill, the noise of the docks grew louder and the noxious smell of coal smoke and sulphur became tinged with a strong whiff of the river. Dismayed, he saw the streets of houses give way to an industrial muddle of factories, cobbled lanes, railway arches and towering warehouses. Squeezed between them were older cottages and truncated streets, some half built into the bank as if for shelter.

To his disbelief, one such mean street clinging to the slope turned out to be Leam Lane. A public house with a filthy half-frosted window, grandly claiming the name of the Alexandria, was the only building of any note. He had a sudden strong recollection of standing outside similar tough bars in Jarrow, clutching the hand of his cousin Edward and gazing up in terror at the dirt-ingrained faces of the dockers who entered, shrugging off the rector's attempts to offer them hot cocoa.

Alexander felt his heart thudding as if he were that frightened boy once more. Surely Kate did not live among such squalor? He had imagined her living in genteel poverty in a picturesque cottage with her stoical widowed mother. But then her mother had remarried years ago – to an Irishman by the sound of it. How much else had Kate kept from him? Screwing up his courage, he went in to ask where the McMullens lived.

'Old John?' the barman grunted. 'In trouble, is he? Owes you money?'

'No,' Alexander said, with mounting disquiet.

The gaunt-faced man cleared his throat into a spittoon by the counter. 'When he's not in here, he's next door. Downstairs house. Unless he's found work the day. Likely still be down the docks – hooter's not gone yet.'

Alexander could feel the group of drinkers watching him as he quickly retreated. What sort of man was McMullen? A ne'er-do-well, by the sound of it. For several minutes he stood outside the door to Number Five and fought off a desire to turn and run. Its small door and worn step gave straight on to the street without a railing or patch of garden to relieve its grimy ugliness – not even a window box of flowers. He feared what he would find beyond.

But before he could move, the door banged open and a stout old woman appeared with a rag mat. She banged it hard on the brick wall below the window and black dust flew up in a cloud, choking her. She stood on the step coughing, her large chest heaving for breath, her face the colour of putty under a severe bun of greying hair. Rose Fawcett? This woman bore not the slightest resemblance to the handsome woman he had known as a child. With a surge

281

of relief he realised he must have got the wrong house, the wrong Leam Lane.

At that moment, she glanced up and caught him staring at her. For a brief second he saw a look in her wide-set eyes and the curve of her broad mouth that reminded him of Kate. He felt a pang of horror. This was Kate in thirty years' time. Then the woman frowned and the likeness was gone.

Before his courage failed him completely, Alexander forced himself to step forward with his cane and raise his hat.

'Mrs McMullen? Mrs Rose McMullen?'

She stared at him in suspicion. 'Who's wantin' to know?'

He hesitated. 'I'm Alexander Pringle-Davies – a friend of Kate Fawcett's.' Her eyes widened. 'Have I come to the right place?'

She gasped as if stung. 'Mr Pringle-Davies!' Rose buckled at the knees and grabbed the door post. Alexander reached forward to steady her. 'Oh, the saints!'

'I'm sorry, I know it's a shock. Is Kate here? Can I come in?'

She clutched her throat and nodded, speechless. Then with a darting look into the lane, she pulled him through the door and shut it behind them.

At first he could make out nothing in the gloom, only aware of a musty smell and brownish light. Groping through a short passage, they came into a kitchen crowded with furniture that seemed to serve as bedroom and dining room too. Rose dumped down the clippy mat by the hearth and cleared a pile of mending from a chair.

'Please, sit yourself down,' she wheezed, hobbling towards the far door. 'Kate. Kate, get up! There's a man to see you.'

Alexander's pulse surged to think Kate was just beyond the door. Only the thought of her stopped him bolting from this terrible place. He sat down, stood up, unable to sit still. It seemed an age that he waited, wondering if his own sweet Kate would appear through the door. Half of him longed for her and half was repelled by this hovel, hoping it was all some hideous mistake.

The door opened and a large figure lumbered through into the dingy light of the fire. At first he could not believe it was her. Kate's once slender body was swollen like a balloon, lumpen and shapeless in a dirty brown dress. She moved with her hands pressed to her back, her belly huge before her. Lank strands of hair, indifferently pinned, stuck to her pasty cheeks. Her face was puffy, the once vital eyes dulled and dark-ringed.

Alexander stood paralysed in shock, unable to match this pregnant woman with the spirited girl he had lain with last summer. She gawped at him and mouthed his name, but no words came. Kate pitched forward, grabbing the table to stop herself falling. Rose steered her on to the hard wooden settle.

'Sit, hinny, I'll fetch a cup of water.' She escaped into the scullery and left them alone for a few moments.

'Alexander,' Kate whispered in wonder, tears blurring her vision of him. 'How did you find me?'

'Mary told me – I came straight here. I had no idea. The baby – it's – is it . . .?' His voice trailed off.

'Aye, it's yours,' she nodded, her look hurt.

He glanced away in agitation. Those eyes made him feel so guilty! The room stank of sour clothes drying over the fender and something rancid that had been thrown on to the fire. Suddenly anger pricked him. She had lied to him about her circumstances! Her mother was no gentlewoman fallen on hard times. She was the wife of a common docker. The woman in the scullery could not possibly have been the friend or equal of his cousins. Kate had tricked him into loving her!

'I waited for you,' Kate whispered reproachfully. 'You said you'd come back.'

'I wrote to you,' Alexander defended, 'but not a word in reply. All I knew was that you'd left the inn. They said you'd got married.'

'Who did?'

'That's what I heard,' Alexander blustered, not wanting to say it was his father who had misled him.

Kate pushed away tears and stood up. 'Well, I'm not. Wouldn't look at any other lad but you.' She came towards him, arms outstretched, trying to smile. 'It doesn't matter, you're here now, Alexander. You've come to fetch me – I told them you would. The things they've said to me – nearly sent me mental! Specially me step—' She broke off.

'Your stepfather, McMullen?' Alexander accused crossly, holding himself away. 'Never told me about him, did you? No, you made out you were a Fawcett – respectable – as good as my Liddell cousins.'

'I *am* a Fawcett,' Kate said in agitation, clutching her belly.

Suddenly Rose was back in the room, banging a cup of water on the table. 'Don't you go upsetting her! My lass was respectable till you got your hands on her.'

'Don't, Mam—'

'Well, what have you come here for?' Rose was blunt. 'Are you ganin' to see her right and wed the lass or not? 'Cos if you're not, God help you when my man gets back.'

Alexander was stung by her forthright words. What right had she to speak to him like that? He looked from her hostile face to Kate's anxious one and felt panic overwhelming him.

'I can't marry her. I'm betrothed to another – Kate knew that.' He gulped and looked away. 'We marry next month.'

The words hung in the dark, oppressive room. For a long moment no one spoke. Then Rose said, 'Get out me house.'

'No, Mam!' Kate suddenly found her voice and stepped between them. She rounded on Alexander. 'I want to know why you came here. Why did you raise me hopes like this?' she demanded, her eyes regaining their spark. 'You cannot imagine what it's been like for me these past months – not knowing what's become of you or if I'll ever set eyes on you again. Having to come back here and face them all with *this*.' She jabbed a thumb at her distended womb. 'Months of waitin' and frettin' and gettin' so big I cannot gan out for fear of what the neighbours'll say.' Her look was beseeching. 'And all the time watching the door to see you step through it – praying for a miracle – just to see your bonny face . . .!' She covered her mouth with trembling hands, swallowing her tears.

'Answer the lass,' Rose ordered. 'Why have you come?'

Alexander felt a cold sweat breaking out over his whole body. He knew it was to do with guilt, but he tried to stifle it. Better to feel hurt indignation, else he could not look Kate in the face.

'I came to help financially,' he lied, 'for when your – for when the time comes.' He could not bear the look of desolation in her eyes. 'I wanted to know that you were all right – that you were properly cared for,' he floundered.

'She's cared for as well as we can manage,' Rose bristled. 'There's them that would put a lass in trouble out on the street, but I'm not one of them. I'll not desert her – nor the bairn she carries.'

Alexander flushed at the implied criticism. 'No, of course not.' Hastily, he pulled out his wallet and emptied it out on the table. There was five pounds and ten shillings in notes. He scrabbled in his coat pocket and produced another six shillings and sixpence half-penny. 'It's not much, but I'll send more. If you ever want for money, send a message to Mrs Timmins in Stair Leap, by the High Level Bridge. It's a boarding house I use when in Newcastle.'

Kate just stared at him in misery while Rose eagerly gathered up the money and pocketed it in the fold of her vast apron. It was worth a month's wages.

'I'm sorry, Kate,' he spoke to her at last, 'I never meant to cause you such trouble. I wish it had been otherwise. But you do see I can't marry you?'

He wanted her to say she understood, make him feel less terrible about what he was doing, but she said nothing. Her eyes looked huge and accusing in her pale face.

'Aye, she knows that,' Rose said, mollified by the money. 'I blame mesel' for letting her think she could get above her own class.' She looked at him squarely, a thought coming back to her. 'What was that you were saying before about the Liddells?'

Alexander raised his chin. 'I'm related to the Ravensworths. My mother was a Liddell.'

'So you knew Canon Liddell here in Jarrow?' Rose eyed him keenly.

'Yes, my cousin Edward. I lived with him for a while when I was a small boy. It's what Kate and I shared in common – a link with Jarrow. She claimed you and Mr Fawcett were friends of my cousins.'

'Friends! Well, they were very kind to me when I worked for them,' Rose blustered.

'*Worked* for them?'

'Aye, I did a bit cleaning at the old rectory.'

Kate burst out, 'But you said me da was a friend of the rector's, Mam.'

'Oh, hinny, maybes I let you think that 'cos you had your heart set on the idea—' Rose suddenly stopped and gazed at Alexander. 'You lived at the rectory when you were a lad?'

'Yes – after my mother died.'

'Little Alexander Pringle!' Rose gasped. 'That was you?' Her hands flew to her mouth as he nodded.

'Mam, what's wrong?'

Rose shook her head, tears welling in her deep brown eyes. 'Always wondered what became of you,' she whispered. 'Such a bright little lad – always wantin' attention. My William was that taken with you.'

Alexander started at the name.

'Don't you remember us? We took you to the circus.'

He felt winded. 'So that *was* you?'

Rose nodded.

They stared at each other, Alexander not wanting it to be true. He was repulsed by the thought that this rough woman could be the pretty, friendly young mother of his memory with the kind husband whom he had once wished to live with. Yet guilt swept over him for thinking so badly of her and bringing such trouble to her door.

'Poor bairn,' Rose said pityingly, 'you went around like a lamb that'd lost its sheep. Nobody wanted to keep you.'

Alexander could cope with her anger, but he could not bear to be pitied. He *had* been wanted! The Liddells had loved him and Jeremiah had adopted him. He didn't need her to be sorry for him – she was the one to be pitied!

'I don't see how you could possibly know,' he said hotly, 'being just the daily maid.'

Rose coloured. 'Aye, you did all right for yoursel' in the end,' she said, her tone hardening. 'For a coachman's son.'

'I must go,' he said curtly, grabbing up his hat and cane from the table.

Rose came after him as he made for the door. 'Just remember I knew you when you were a nipper – when your posh relations washed their hands of you. We showed you more kindness than half of them.'

'You don't know what you're talking about,' Alexander said in disdain. 'Good day to you, Mrs McMullen.'

'I know this much,' Rose retorted. 'The rector would turn in his grave if he knew what you'd done to one of my daughters! Not so high and mighty after all, are you? Scratch the surface and you're a common Pringle underneath, for all your airs and graces.'

She pursued him out of the house. Kate tried to hold her back.

'Stop, Mam. Let him go!'

'It's not just our Kate who's made up a fancy story about her family, is it?' Rose couldn't stem her anger. 'And you dare to judge her for saying her da was as good as the likes of a Liddell? Well, he was! My William was worth ten of your kind – a hundred! Do you hear?'

Alexander strode away with Rose's furious words echoing against the brick walls around him. He could not look back nor get away quickly enough. His heart pounded with anger and fear. To think he had come here to save Kate. He had so nearly made the most foolish mistake of his life. He ran up Leam Lane, away from the docks, not caring where he went as long as it put distance between him and that harridan of a mother.

Ten minutes later he found himself on high ground overlooking Jarrow. In the distance sat the hunched black outline of the old monastery, marooned by the greenish sludge

288

of the River Don, which spewed into the choppy Tyne. Jarrow Slake. He remembered it now, the tidal backwash of filthy water where he had watched enviously as other children played on the floating timbers. Cousin Christina had forbidden him to go near it.

A sudden wave of regret and longing for those far-off days engulfed him. For a moment he remembered the intense excitement of being taken to the circus, of grasping a hand either side of him and being lifted into the air like a bird. William's hand, Rose's hand. Alexander gave out a deep cry of anguish. How could he have been so cruel to Kate and her mother? He was beyond contempt!

He turned and looked back on the grey huddle of Tyne Dock. Should he go back? But what would he say? What could he possibly do to make amends apart from marry Kate? And deep in the pit of his stomach he knew the answer. He had loved her recklessly – loved her still. But he did not have the courage to give up everything for her. The poverty that clung to her frightened him. He had been cast adrift too often in life not to hanker for the security and fussing love that Jeremiah and Polly could give him. Unlike Lady Ravensworth, he was not rich enough to defy society and follow his heart.

He was a romantic, but a coward. Kate knew that now; it had shown in her look of bitter betrayal as he fled. He could do nothing to change the way he was. Alexander cursed himself for having tried to find her. He had been in love with an illusion, a romantic link back to his briefly happy time at the rectory. But he had left and lost Jarrow a long time ago and there was no going back.

Striding down towards the town and the station, Alexander knew he would never come here again.

Chapter 31

Kate watched Alexander's retreating figure through a blur of hot tears. He was deserting her! Rose's screaming abuse made her cower against the wall in shame. Blood raced in her ears, making her sick and dizzy. All her being wanted to race after him and beg to be taken with him, but her legs were shaking and useless.

'He's gone!' she moaned in disbelief, sinking on to the worn step, a huge sob building up inside like a tidal wave.

For one brief, glorious moment she believed he had come to rescue her from this purgatory, from the whispers and looks and avoidance of neighbours, from the daily castigation of her stepfather, from pretending to be ill every time Father O'Neill called. But he had only come out of curiosity, a twinge of guilt that he hoped to ease by throwing his pocket change at her. How dare he? How wrong she had been about him. Where was the generous, passionate man who had told her how much he loved her and promised they would find a way to be together? Kate buried her face in her hands and wept.

'Haway inside, lass,' Rose urged, pulling her up, her anger abating at the sight of her distraught daughter.

Kate clung to her, sobbing and shaking in shock. Inside again, she collapsed on the settle, weeping uncontrollably.

'Stop that,' Rose commanded, alarmed by her hysteria. 'He's gone and there's nowt we can do.'

'B-but I want him, Mam,' Kate cried. 'He's the father of me bairn. How can he do this to us? I wish he'd never come!'

'And I wish you'd had more sense! Fancy you thinking such a man would marry you,' Rose scolded in her misery. 'You can tell by looking he's a bad 'un. Was wild as a bairn and he hasn't got better with age.'

Kate was reproachful. 'You wanted me to court him. You told me to make some'at of myself.'

'Don't blame this mess on me.' Rose was sharp. 'I never told you to commit a mortal sin.'

Suddenly Kate was seized by a sharp pain and screamed.

'Whatever's the matter?' Rose cried.

Kate clutched her belly. 'Oh, Mam, the bairn,' she whimpered in fear.

Quickly Rose was at her side, feeling her brow. 'You're hot as a furnace. Lie down.' She loosened Kate's clothing and, fetching a basin of water, began to wipe her burning face and neck.

'Will the baby be all right?' Kate asked in agitation.

'Lie still and don't fuss. The bairn's had a shock an' all with all this carry-on. We'll say no more about it.'

'What about Father? What will we tell him?' Kate panted.

Rose frowned. 'Nowt. It'll just give him some'at else to shout and rant about.'

'We can't pretend he never came. The neighbours – he'll hear it from them.'

'They're too frightened round here to tell him owt,' Rose snorted. 'And if they do, we'll say it was the tickman I chased away.'

'What about the money?' Kate worried.

291

'He'll not get his hands on that.' Rose was adamant. 'I'll not have him pouring it down his neck before the bairn's born. So don't you say a word about the money – or any of this.'

Kate closed her eyes in despair. If she thought she was in torment before, it was nothing to what she felt now. Until today, she had clung to a thread of hope that Alexander would come and save her. She had been able to endure her situation with thoughts of him, comforted by the belief that he still loved her wherever he might be.

But that hope had been torn to pieces by his sudden brutal visit. She would never forget the look of horror on his face when she entered the room, the way he recoiled to see her pregnant state. All she had longed to do was rush to him and throw her arms about him in joy. But he had not even tried to touch her. He had been repulsed by her lowly situation and the dismal surroundings of Leam Lane – just as she knew he would be.

How did she ever think she could cross the huge social chasm between them? Only in the magical surroundings of Ravensworth had they been able to create the illusion that the differences between them did not matter. If they had met in a tavern in Jarrow, he might never have given her a second glance. Oh, how bitterly she regretted their meeting now! Kate wished she had never set eyes on Alexander Pringle-Davies.

The weeks of late pregnancy dragged on interminably. Kate retreated into herself, tormented by inner thoughts and hardly speaking a word. Her family watched her warily and even John noticed how subdued and miserable she seemed. He put it down to a guilty conscience and continued to badger her to stay indoors and not give the neighbours an excuse to gossip.

Kate needed no lecturing. She went nowhere and spoke to no one outside her immediate family. She felt unwell most of the time. In the warmer weather she could not settle at night or find a comfortable way to lie. Her heart pounded erratically and tears came unbidden at any time of the day or night. The baby twisted and turned restlessly within, then lay for long hours like a leaden weight, frightening her with its stillness.

Kate yearned to be rid of it. It was a constant reminder of her weakness and foolish love for Alexander. No other man would want her now and she never wanted to look at another man again.

The bitterness over her predicament increased when Sarah came home towards the end of May. Kate lay in the gloom of the back bedroom with the blinds pulled down as if she were in mourning. Sarah sat whispering on the end of the bed.

'Michael wants me to marry him,' she told her.

Kate felt a sharp pang of envy. 'That's grand,' she murmured.

'Aye – well – I've not said yes.'

'What?' Kate leant up. 'Are you daft?'

Sarah pulled a face. 'He's smaller than me.'

Kate gave a snort of disbelief.

'And with him working doon the pit,' Sarah added quickly. 'It's champion now, but what'll it be like as a pitman's missus? His mam skivvies like a slave – up all hours of the day and night feedin' and washin' and gettin' them off to work. And living by the pit, never rid of the dirt . . .' Sarah agonised. 'What d'you think I should do?'

Kate seized her sister, shaking her hard. 'Don't be so bloody daft!' she said fiercely. 'You've the chance of gettin' wed, so take it. Any sort of marriage is better than nowt.

You're not shy of a bit o' hard work. The lad cares for you – you should thank your lucky stars. Marry him, Sarah,' she cried, ' 'cos you don't want to end up like me!'

Sarah looked shocked by her sister's outburst. Kate had said so little of late, she wondered if she had gone a bit mad in the head. But this was a flash of the old Kate, bossy and forthright and caring. Sarah saw the pain in the younger woman's face and wrapped strong arms around her.

'Oh, Kate!' she whispered. 'I'm sorry for what's happened to you. Maybes he'll come for you. You mustn't give up hope.'

Kate pushed her away. She could not bring herself to tell Sarah of Alexander's visit – Sarah whom she had told everything to until now. But it was too painful, and Rose had forbidden his name to be mentioned.

'He'll not be back,' she said dully. 'He's wed another lass.' She lay back and turned her face to the yellow-stained wall. 'Don't ask me about him again.'

Alexander and Polly were married in the old parish church at St John's Chapel up Weardale, amid the late blossom and the lush green of May. Alexander looked gaunt and pale, after a bout of haemorrhaging that had kept him in bed most of the month. But he put on a cheerful face and drank deeply at the wedding feast, keeping the demons in his mind at bay. His father looked frail but happy and Alexander convinced himself he had done the right thing.

When ill and feverish he had been plagued by images of Kate that were so real he sometimes cried out her name as if she were there in the room with him. She would bathe his face and body and sing to him. But when the fever left him, so did the delusions and he felt lonelier than he'd ever done in his life.

So when her fair face came to mind during his wedding day, Alexander forced himself to think of her among the squalor of Tyne Dock and how revolted he had felt on that terrible day in April. But when he finally lay with Polly that night, he could not summon up the eager passion he had felt so intensely for Kate. It was then that the crushing weight of guilt he had tried so hard to shirk nearly suffocated him.

Kate was carrying his child and he had cast her aside with cowardly callousness. She might be giving birth at the very time he was marrying another. He had hardly thought about the baby, only how he did not want to be trapped in a life of poverty by it. Now he wondered if it was a girl or a boy. Did it have his hazel eyes or Kate's vivid blue?

'Perhaps we should postpone our trip to Scandinavia?' Polly suggested, concerned at his tense, preoccupied look. 'You don't look at all well.'

'No, we shall go,' Alexander insisted. 'It will do us good to get away from here.'

So at the beginning of June they travelled to Newcastle and boarded a ship for Gothenburg. Despite a heavy summer shower, Alexander stood gripping the rail, staring out along the banks of the Tyne as they edged downriver. He ground his teeth to stop himself crying out as they passed Jarrow Slake and the half-hidden monastery, then the massive thrusting staithes of Tyne Dock.

'I'm sorry,' he whispered, his mind in turmoil. 'Please forgive me, Kate!'

He had made the wrong choice. He should be with her now. It should be Kate sailing with him. Only his cowardly fear of being cut off without an income and his childish revulsion of Kate's origins had stopped them being together.

He would leave Polly! On their return he would go to Kate and ask her forgiveness. He could make a living at something. He would plead for Baron Tamm to give him a job at his ironworks in Sweden. He and Kate would live in one of the neat cottages with its own garden. She would milk the cow . . .

Alexander squeezed his eyes closed to force back the stinging tears. Always full of such plans and boasts! he mocked himself. Never having the guts to carry them out. Well, he would send Kate money, he sobbed quietly. At least he could do that. When he returned home . . .

Averting his face from the sight of the docks and the bustling outcrop of South Shields, Alexander turned his face towards the open sea. He filled his lungs with the salty smell and felt the familiar easing of his worries at the thought of escaping across the blank, empty horizon.

Chapter 32

Kate was standing at the kitchen table, sweating over the ironing, when the pain seized her. She yelped in agony and dropped the iron. Doubling up, she almost vomited.

'Mam,' she gasped, 'Mam, help us!'

But her mother was down the street buying suet and potatoes for tea. She would take ages to walk the few hundred yards from the shop, putting down her load every couple of paces. Kate felt faint in the stifling heat of the kitchen. Outside, the hot June sun bounced off the brick walls and no air stirred in the baking streets. She sank to her knees, struggling for breath, panting on all fours like a dog.

After a moment the stabbing pain eased, leaving her light-headed with relief. Was this how a baby came, bursting out of the belly? Was she going into labour or was there something wrong with her?

'Mam, come back quick,' she whimpered in fear.

She stood up and saw with horror that she had singed the sleeve of her stepfather's shirt. Kate knew she'd be in deep trouble for that. She lumbered over to the scullery for a cup of water. If she scrubbed it quickly, the stain might lessen. Halfway back, the shooting pain gripped her again and she dropped the cup. It bounced on the hard floor and broke.

Kate began to cry in panic, scrabbling on the floor to pick up the shards of pottery and shove them under the chest of drawers in the corner. The pain went, then minutes later it was back again. What should she do? Call a neighbour? But Rose did not want to bring in local help; they would deal with it themselves, she had decreed.

If she could drag herself through to the bedroom, it would be cooler. She would lie down until her mother came. Kate moved as swiftly as her lumbering body would allow. She was about to haul herself on to her parents' high iron-framed bed, then thought of John's disgust and flopped on to Jack's narrow desk bed instead. Lying gave her little relief. The pain was shooting down between her legs now, then to her horror, there was a sudden gush of water.

In seconds her petticoats and skirt were soaked. She wept in shame as the bed below her grew damp. It seemed an age before she heard Rose wheezing in the kitchen door.

'Mam,' she croaked, 'Mam, I'm in here!'

Her mother filled the doorway with her stout frame as she peered into the gloom of the back room.

'What you doing on Jack's bed?'

'Mam, I've wet meself,' Kate confessed. Then she doubled up in another spasm.

Rose struggled out of her coat and bonnet, discarding them on the big bed.

'Let's have a look at you.' In a trice she could see what was happening. 'Your waters have broken. Tak your dress off.'

'What d'you mean?' Kate asked in fright.

'You've started. The bairn's on her way.'

Kate clutched at her mother. 'Stay, Mam. You'll not leave us, will you? I'm that scared.'

Rose thought how terrified she had been as a young wife facing the birth of her first daughter.

'Don't fuss, hinny, I'm not ganin' anywhere.'

She helped Kate out of her wet skirts and fetched rags and brown paper to lay under her.

'What's that for?'

'There'll be blood.' Rose was matter-of-fact.

Kate began to shake. For the thousandth time she cursed Alexander and what he had done to her. Why should she suffer the agony and shame while he walked away without a backward glance? Bile rose in her throat. Sudden anger tempered her fear and gave her a spark of courage. Her mother kept referring to the baby as a girl, as if she knew, but Kate prayed it would be a boy. A lass had too many crosses to bear in this life! She'll be tarred with the same brush as me, Kate thought bitterly. Please, God, be a lad!

The heat of afternoon subsided and shadows cooled the backyard, but nothing changed. Just the relentless cycle of contractions, that neither increased in frequency nor eased off a fraction. Rose sat puffing beside her, exhausted with waiting and cooling her daughter's body with wet rags.

'I'll have to get the tea on,' she said at last. 'Your father won't tak kindly to his tea being late 'cos a bairn's on its way.'

Kate lay squirming on the creaking bed, listening to her mother panting around the kitchen, wishing she could get up and help. She would much rather be peeling and cooking than pinned in this damp-smelling room awaiting childbirth. How she wanted rid of it, this leaden disgrace in her belly! Kate had thought little beyond the interminable hell of her pregnancy. Months ago they had talked of how she would go back to work and the baby would be given over to her parents. Good riddance! Her mother was welcome to Alexander's brat.

299

Quietly, they had accumulated a small drawerful of second-hand baby clothes with some of Alexander's money, but they never spoke of a time after the baby would be born. The rest of the money had been frittered away on paying off little debts to the grocer and the coalman, and retrieving items of clothing from the pawnshop. No more had been sent and Kate could not remember the name of the lodging house in Newcastle that Alexander had mentioned. Even if she had, they could not have afforded the tram fare, and John would have had to be told.

Kate dozed off under a blanket of pain. A clatter of boots and men's voices woke her with a start. She heard Rose's hushed explanation beyond the half-open door.

'Don't you go bothering her,' she ordered. 'You can both make yourself scarce after tea till it's all over.'

Later, when John had disappeared to the pub next door, Rose came in with a slice of meat pie and a cup of tea. Kate felt nauseous at the smell, but her mother told her to drink. The tea was strong and sweet, and Kate felt a flicker of energy return. She pulled herself up to get comfortable and caught Jack peering in at the door. He stared at her strangely and she was suddenly aware of her undressed state and hot bare legs straddling the bed. She quickly pulled the sheet back over her.

Rose noticed Kate's bashful gesture and turned.

'Jack! Get out or I'll skelp ye! This is no place for a lad,' she ordered.

Jack scowled with embarrassment and disappeared. The front door slammed.

The sounds of evening came muffled from beyond the room: boys playing football in the dusty lane, a mother banging two pan lids to bring her children indoors, the squawk of a hen flapping on to a neighbour's wall. The glow of the

300

long June evening faded from the kitchen and Rose went to light the lamp.

Maybe it was the agitation at her stepfather banging in from the pub, but Kate's contractions sharpened and Rose came bustling to her side, closing the door firmly behind. When Kate cried out, Rose tore off a piece of rag and twisted it into rope.

'Bite on that, hinny. Can't have you screaming the house down – Father'll sharp complain.'

Kate looked at her in disbelief. She didn't care if the whole of Shields heard her, so long as the agony stopped. But she said nothing and when the pain tore through her again she clamped her teeth on the gag and retched. She clung to her mother as her body convulsed in a mad rhythm of its own.

'Don't push yet,' Rose commanded, peering anxiously between her legs. 'It's not time. Save your breath for the hard part.'

Kate sank back on the bed in despair. What could be worse than this? She was burning all over, streams of sweat running down her back and breasts. She could barely breath in the fetid, stinking room. She was vaguely aware of John knocking into furniture in the kitchen, exchanging sharp words with Jack. The candle in the room burnt down slowly.

A while later, Rose roused her from semi-consciousness.

'Can you still feel the pains?' she asked anxiously.

Kate nodded. Her whole body felt wrapped in a red-hot blanket of pain.

'When you feel it come again, give a push, hinny.'

Kate hardly knew what she meant, or cared. She had no energy to push anything anywhere.

'Haway!' Rose ordered, shaking her out of her stupor. 'You've got to shove the bairn out!'

301

Kate tried to rally. She felt the next wave grip her body and gritted her teeth in a stifled roar as she jerked in response.

'Again!' Rose ordered. Kate sweated and panted and heaved.

'I cannot, Mam!' she sobbed, falling back again in defeat. The baby would not come.

Rose went to the door and hissed for Jack. 'Gan and fetch Dr Dyer!'

John stirred from his reverie by the fire. 'The doctor? We cannot afford him. You stop where you are, lad.'

Rose lost her patience. 'He'll gan for him this minute – unless you want a corpse on your hands by mornin'! The lass is all done in.' She pushed Jack towards the door. 'Gan and fetch him – Sutton Street – tell him he'll get paid after. Run!'

'Paid with what?' John slurred.

But Jack did not wait for further argument. He clattered out of the house and ran down the lane as fast as he could.

Kate did not know whether he was gone five minutes or fifty. She seemed trapped in a dark, timeless world of neverending pain. No amount of repentance could save her now. She was surely dying.

'Kate?' A deep soft voice was calling her through the red mists. 'Kate, can you hear me? It's Dr Dyer.'

Kate mouthed in reply, too parched to form words.

'Fetch a cup of water, please, Mrs McMullen,' he ordered. 'Put sugar in it and a pinch of salt.' Then he was dabbing her cracked lips with a wet rag and speaking to her in a low calm voice.

'I'm going to give you something to ease the pain, Kate. Then together we'll bring this baby into the world. It's taking its time, that's all.'

'Must know what it's coming to,' Kate whispered, tears welling in her eyes. 'I wouldn't want to be born to this.'

'It's a lucky baby having such a pretty and kind-hearted mother,' Dr Dyer said gallantly. 'It'll all be over soon. Now drink this and stop worrying.'

Kate felt a surge of gratitude to the young Scots doctor. No one had spoken to her so kindly for a long time. She drank the medicine he proffered and felt herself relaxing, the waves of pain subsiding a fraction. With Rose's help, he hauled her into a sitting position.

'Hold on to your mother when the pain comes. We'll not need this,' he said, discarding the gag. 'You shout your head off if you feel like it.'

Kate roared and pushed with each contraction. This time she felt swept along instead of buffeted by the waves of pain.

'Good girl, again!' Dr Dyer encouraged.

'I can't, she sobbed.

'Yes you can. The head's almost through. We're nearly there!'

Kate cried in anguish and excitement, 'Nearly there?'

'Yes. Now come on, Kate, push!'

Using up her last ounce of energy, Kate yelled and thrust in a final effort. She felt as if a dam were bursting. There was pressure and searing pain and then she could feel the baby slithering out of her. Almost at once there was a numb relief, before the throbbing pain returned.

'That's it!' the doctor cried. 'Well done, Kate.' He was wiping the sticky, purple creature she had just ejected and clearing its mouth. A sharp tremulous noise, half cough, half cry of indignation, rose out of the baby.

'What is it?' Kate rasped.

'A bonny wee girl,' Dr Dyer smiled, holding her up for Kate to see.

'I knew it was,' Rose murmured.

Kate sank back in disappointment and closed her eyes. The throbbing pain returned. All she wanted to do was fall asleep and never wake up.

Rose and the doctor exchanged looks.

'You should get her cleaned up,' he said quietly, 'both of them.'

'Leave her be,' Rose answered, holding out her arms for the baby. 'Let me see the lass.'

Dr Dyer handed her over. 'She should try and feed her as soon as she wakes.'

Rose nodded, peering at the crinkled face. The warmth of the baby in her arms gave her an unexpected surge of delight. Her eyes were open wide, dark and soulful, as if they already held knowledge and experience. They gazed at each other for a long moment and Rose felt a stirring of possessiveness for her granddaughter that she had not anticipated.

'She's been here before, this 'un,' she murmured, cuddling her closer.

Dr Dyer went out to the scullery to wash his hands and tell the men that Kate had a daughter.

John struggled to his feet and said belligerently, 'It's my lass now – mine and the missus's. That whore's having nowt to do with it from now on. So don't you breathe a word about Kate having a bairn, d'you hear?'

Dr Dyer looked at him in dislike, but said nothing. He turned to Rose, who was standing in the doorway, clasping the small mewling bundle.

'Remember what I said about feeding. And keep an eye on Kate – she's very weak and possibly feverish. Give her boiled water to drink – and maybe a touch of whisky and sugar in it.'

'Whisky? Can't afford that!' John growled.

304

Dr Dyer ignored him. 'Call me if she gets worse, Mrs McMullen.' He dropped his voice. 'I won't charge for it.'

'Ta, Dr Dyer,' Rose said gratefully.

With a tired smile, he said good night and left.

'Call him back? Over my dead body!' John snarled. 'You'll see to her from now on, Rose. We'll not waste a penny more on that slut.'

'He didn't charge owt,' Rose said tiredly.

John looked at her blearily and snorted. 'I'll not be beholden to that Protestant Scotchman. Comes in here lording it over us.' He kicked a stool in bad temper.

Rose gave Jack a quick nod. 'You sleep on the settle the night,' she murmured. 'Haway, John, let's to bed with the bairn.'

Within ten minutes of coaxing John into bed, he was snoring loudly. Rose stared in the guttering candlelight at Kate's shadowed, exhausted face. The stench of childbirth still hung about her, but Rose was too tired to do anything more. Instead she lay down with the baby and made a nest in the crook of her arm, her back protecting her from John's bulk. The troubles of tomorrow would come soon enough; tonight she would think no further than falling asleep with her new granddaughter – her new *daughter*.

She was certain that here, at last, was the angel child that the gypsy had promised her so long ago. The consolation for the years of struggle and heartache and disappointment. She and John would bring this one up right. She would not be allowed to make the mistake Kate had. This child would bring her joy in her old age.

Comforted, Rose fell asleep.

Chapter 33

Kate was woken by a strange sound. She lay for a moment in the pearly dawn light, wondering where she was. She ached badly. Then she heard the snuffling, whimpering sound again and remembered. The baby. The noise was coming from the large bed, muffled by her stepfather's heavy snoring.

Kate pulled herself up, wincing at the effort, and gingerly got to her feet. For a moment all the blood seemed to drain from her and she nearly passed out. Gripping the top of the desk bed, she steadied herself, then inched forward.

Peering in the half-dark, Kate could make out the blanketed creature, half smothered by her mother's thick arm. Her tiny face was creased and whimpering. At the same moment Kate became aware of a strange sensation, her breasts beginning to tingle. She hesitated, then leant forward and lifted the baby from her mother's hold. Although she was tiny, Kate feared she would drop her, she felt so weak. Moving back to her bed, she lay down with the infant nuzzling and grizzling at her bodice.

Kate did what she had seen her aunts do with their young. She untied her bodice and held the baby close to her breast. She pecked at her like a young bird, mouth open and searching. Kate shifted more on to her side and guided the snuffling creature to her nipple. Suddenly there was a sharp nipping sensation as the baby latched on, then she was sucking.

Kate was exhilarated. She had managed to feed her own child without any help from her mother. It was easy. She held herself as still as possible, gazing at her new daughter. She had a small, sweet nose and a covering of brown hair that was as soft as down to the touch. She stroked her pink face, still creased and sticky from birth, and determined she would bathe her and put her in a cotton gown as soon as it was light.

Kate closed her eyes in sudden contentment. She had dreaded the baby's coming, had thought she would die of the pain of giving birth. But now it was over and she had a suckling baby in her arms. It felt good and natural to be lying there with her daughter. Snuggled together, she felt the first stirrings of love towards her new-born.

When Kate woke again, the baby was gone. It was broad daylight and the big brass bed next to her was empty. Judging by the sun hitting the back wall of the yard, it must already be midday. She could hear her mother moving breathlessly around the kitchen, humming. Rose had not sung in years. Kate struggled up, feeling instantly sick and faint.

'Mam,' she croaked, 'Mam! Where's the bairn?'

She shuffled to the bedroom door and peered beyond. The baby was lying in an orange box on the kitchen table, washed and swaddled in a clean sheet, sleeping. Rose hobbled in with an armful of washing.

'I wanted to bath her,' Kate said hoarsely.

'Well, you can wash yoursel' down instead,' Rose said brusquely. 'And clean up Jack's bed.'

Kate gripped the back of the settle. 'I fed her, Mam,' she said proudly.

'Aye, that's grand,' Rose said, ' 'cos we cannot afford to buy milk.'

'Shall I feed her now?'

'No, she's sleeping, leave her be. You get those under-clothes off before they walk out the room on their own.'

Kate flushed. With a great effort she inched her way towards the scullery where her mother helped peel off her soiled clothing. Rose doused her in cold water from a jug. Kate gasped as it splashed on her clammy limbs. Congealed blood washed on to the brick floor. She began to shake at the enormity of what had happened.

She, Kate Fawcett, fallen woman, had given birth to Alexander's bastard. The smell of her disgrace filled her nostrils, the shameful blood washed around her feet. They would have to scrub all trace of it away before her stepfather returned. Kate clutched her body self-consciously and started to shiver uncontrollably.

She was an unmarried mother, passing on her shame to her small innocent daughter. She could give her no father, no name, no cause to hold her head high among the pious and the gossips. Her eyes filled with tears to think of the kind, overworked Dr Dyer, who had not judged her. She could not expect such treatment from her own kind; they would shrink from her as if her sin could taint them.

'What you ganin' to call the bairn?' Rose asked suddenly.

Kate hung her head in resignation. 'I don't care. You can call her what you like.'

They did not speak again while they stripped Jack's bed and threw the soiled newspaper on to the fire. Kate felt unsteady on her feet and was thankful when her mother packed her off to bed.

'I'll bring the bairn to you when it's time for a feed,' Rose said, closing the door on her.

Later Rose woke her with hot sweet tea and a slice

of bread and jam. But the food made her sick. She heard the men return and John's voice grunt with interest at the new member of the family. Kate felt jealous anger at the thought of her boorish stepfather prodding her baby with his dirty shovel-like hands. It made her nauseous to think he would be playing the role of father to her sweet girl, when her real father was so much more handsome and loving . . .

What stupid thoughts! Kate mocked herself. The lass had no father – or not one that wished to acknowledge her. John McMullen, coarse though he was, would be better than no father at all. He stood between her and the workhouse and an upbringing of orphaned shame for her daughter. What right had she to judge him?

For the next three days, Rose brought the unnamed baby into Kate to be fed. But as soon as she finished suckling and had dropped off to sleep, Rose came and took her away again and placed her by the hearth in the orange box that was her crib. She seemed contented and sleepy during the day, but at night became fretful and plucked at her mother's breasts until they were raw.

John complained that he could not sleep with the noise, so Kate would get up and sit in the kitchen, half-dozing and exhausted. Jack lay still in the shadows and she did not know if he saw her attempting to feed and placate the demanding baby, but he never complained.

After five days, Kate could bear it no longer.

'She's always crying to be fed,' she said weepily to Rose when John and Jack had left for work. 'I can't give her any more.'

'You can't be feeding her right,' Rose scolded. 'Let's have a look at you.'

309

Kate blushed as her mother opened her blouse and peered at her. Rose clucked, 'Well, they're full o' milk. You'll get used to it.' Then she went to hang out the washing.

Kate determined to leave her bed and not be shut away all day where she could not see her baby. But increasingly she felt unwell as she struggled to help around the house. Sweat poured off her and she had to keep sitting down to stop herself fainting. Her breasts were swollen and aching and she could hardly bear the baby to touch them. That evening, as she was pulling a potato pie out of the oven, stabbing pains shot through her and she collapsed on the hearth.

There was consternation at the kitchen table and John cursed her for being clumsy, but Rose soon realised there was something very wrong.

'Help me carry her to the settle,' she ordered Jack. She felt Kate's head. 'She's hot as a furnace. Fetch some water, lad.'

'Stop bossin' him about like a girl,' John snapped.

Rose ignored him while she peered into Kate's glazed unfocused eyes.

'Can you hear me, lass?' she asked anxiously, but Kate just moaned and shook. Rose undid her blouse and gasped at the swollen, engorged breasts. She knew just how much pain her daughter suffered; the same thing had happened to her when Jack had been a babe. But Kate was far more ill than she had been. She was shaking with fever and whimpering incoherently. In the corner, the baby began to wail.

She turned to John. 'We'll have to send for Dr Dyer. The lass has milk fever.'

'No!' John growled, all the time staring at Kate's prone body.

'Please, John, I'm frightened,' Rose pleaded. 'We cannot leave the lass like this – and the bairn needs feedin'. The doctor will give her some'at to bring out the fever.'

The baby's fractious crying filled the room.

'We don't need the doctor,' John said in a low rumble. 'I can do it.'

Rose and John stared at each other. Jack looked between them, puzzled. He was disturbed by the sight of Kate's half-undressed body on the settle. He glanced away.

Rose swallowed. John was proposing to do for Kate what he had done so eagerly for her all those years ago – suck the milk from her breasts to relieve the swelling and allow the baby to latch on again. The thought of it made her stomach heave.

'No,' she said stubbornly.

John glared at her. 'Well, I'll not have that doctor touching her again.' He was just as adamant. He sat down and carried on eating his tea as if nothing was wrong.

Rose turned to Kate, her heart pounding with anger, and tried to get her to take sips of water. The baby's crying grew more distressed. The noise was relentless. Kate whimpered something that Rose could not catch.

John scraped back his chair and stood up, unable to bear the wailing. 'I'm ganin' next door,' he snapped and strode out.

'Jack, fetch me the flannel and a clean teaspoon,' his mother ordered, reaching over for her untouched cup of tea. When he came back she shovelled in extra sugar and stirred. 'Now lift the bairn out its box and come and sit here.'

'Me?' Jack asked in astonishment.

'Aye, she won't bite ye,' Rose said impatiently.

She watched him pick up his tiny niece like a piece of rare china and was reminded of John holding his new-born son with the same mixture of fear and wonder. What had happened to that fiercely caring man who had stayed up all night saving the life of his precious Jack, defying them all? Too sodden in drink and his own self-pity to care about any of them any more. Rose swallowed her bitterness.

She showed Jack how to cradle the bawling baby in the crook of his arm and give her drops of tea on the end of his finger. His frowning face broke into a smile of amazement as the baby began to suck hungrily at his little finger.

'She'll not be fooled for long,' Rose warned him.

She turned to Kate and began mopping her face and neck with the damp flannel. Her daughter shivered and flinched away from the touch. Rose tried to soothe her, but Kate grew more agitated, tossing her head from side to side, babbling incoherently. Rose watched in mounting alarm, paralysed with indecision. Time, on the mantelpiece clock, ticked on. The baby dropped off into a fretful sleep.

Jack glanced anxiously at his half-delirious sister.

Kate stirred restlessly under the blanket, attempting to throw it off. Rose got up. 'I'm ganin' for Dr Dyer.'

'Let me,' Jack offered, springing up. 'I'll be quicker and – you know . . .' he blushed, 'you're supposed to have just had a bairn.'

'Aye, you're right.' Rose nodded in embarrassment. 'Haway and tell him it's urgent.'

She sat for what felt like an eternity, waiting for Jack to return with the doctor. When the door banged open she leapt up, only to see John swaying in the doorway. Rose could smell the reek of whisky from across the room.

'How's the lass?' he slurred.

'I've sent Jack for the doctor,' she said defiantly.

John barged across the room. 'I told you no doctor,' he snarled. 'Let me at the lass,' he ordered.

Rose stood in his way, turning her face from his foul breath. 'No, John, please, let the doctor see to her.'

'We can't afford him,' John barked. 'Out me way.'

He shoved her aside roughly. Rose's unsteady legs buckled and she fell heavily to the floor. She was filled with disgust at the relish with which John knelt to his task.

She heaved herself up and limped to the hearth, her eyes averted. She could not fight her husband. Neither could she block out the sound of John's smacking lips and noisy sucking as his mouth filled with Kate's milk. Rose felt sick to the core. Why had she not done the deed herself while John was out? She was disgusted at her own inaction. Rose bent and picked up the baby, rocking her in her arms for comfort, gulping back tears of anger that things should come to this. Her lascivious husband sating his thirst on her daughter – and she was responsible.

Rose tried to block out Kate's small cries of anguish. Were they of pain or relief? She was suddenly filled with angry disgust for her daughter too. It was all her fault that they were reduced to such measures! She would not be made to feel guilty. It was to save Kate's life – and that of her baby.

Rose sat, gulping back tears, until she heard John grunt in satisfaction and get up. He came and stood over her, wiping flecks of milk from his moustache.

'It's done,' he announced proudly. 'The bairn can suck now.'

She could not look into his eyes for fear at what she would see there. Rose nodded. She waited for John to make his way unsteadily to the bedroom door and stumble to bed. For a

313

long moment she sat still, clutching the baby, unable to move. Then she gritted her teeth and got up, hobbling over to Kate with her grizzling bundle.

'Are you all right, lass?' she whispered. There was no reply from the shadows. At the smell of milk and sweat, the baby began to wail. Rose thrust her at the figure on the settle. 'Here, she needs feedin'.'

Kate stirred and the purplish light of the June night caught her face. Her cheeks were wet with tears. Rose's heart felt leaden. She sat down heavily and reached out a hand in the dark. Finding Kate's, she gently nestled the baby into her hold. 'She needs you now, hinny.'

For a moment, she wanted to gather Kate into her arms and cradle her like a child, hush her fears. But at that moment Jack rushed in, followed by the doctor. She stood aside.

'The milk's coming now,' she mumbled. 'I'm sorry you were bothered.'

'No bother at all,' Dr Dyer said kindly, and bent to examine Kate, speaking to her softly.

Rose turned away, heavy-hearted. 'Go to bed,' she ordered Jack.

He hesitated. 'Will she be all right?'

She nodded and he went without another word, though his look was perplexed. She watched while the doctor gave Kate a draught to ease the pain and help her sleep.

'I'll call again tomorrow,' he promised.

'There's no need,' Rose said firmly. 'We can manage now.'

'Still, I'd like to—'

'Better if you didn't.' They exchanged looks and she knew the young doctor understood. He nodded and left. Rose sat on the end of the settle, watching Kate feed her baby, wanting to say something but not finding the words. Her feelings for her

314

daughter were so confused now. She smothered her pity. No point showing her weakness when one of them had to stay strong. Rose heaved herself up and turned away before Kate could see the anguish that glittered in her eyes.

Chapter 34

Afterwards, Kate could not bring herself to look at her stepfather. She retreated to the bedroom with the baby whenever he came home. She was sapped by the fever and weak from suckling her demanding infant. For weeks she never left the house, imprisoning herself in its two musty rooms, unable to face the world.

She could not rid her mind of that terrible night, when John had bent over her with his rank breath and drunken lustful look. Sometimes she convinced herself it had only been a nightmare, a trick of her fevered brain. She had been shaking and delirious, hearing voices come and go, faces distorting and dissolving before her eyes.

She had thought young Dr Dyer had lifted her on to the settle, but the face that loomed over her had been Jack's. Later she had been roused by someone's touch and for a brief heady moment thought Alexander had come to claim her. Perhaps she had whimpered his name. Kate burnt with shame to think of it now, for the hands and lips on her skin had not been her lover's, but those of her hateful stepfather.

Her skin crawled to think of the way he had touched her. She could not wash herself enough to rid her of the shame. Now, every time her baby suckled, it reminded her of the brutal way John had bitten her breasts and squeezed hard until the milk came. Even after it poured from her, he did not stop sucking until he was sated.

Worse still, she had to endure his boasting about it.

'I saved her life, you kna,' he told Dr Dyer in triumph when he called round to check on Kate and the baby a few days later. Kate blushed furiously to hear him describe his heroics and could hardly look at their visitor.

But when Father O'Neill got to hear of a birth in the house, he came round to demand when the infant would be christened. They had kept other visitors away with stories of sickness in the house, but Rose suspected the priest was not fooled. He eyed Kate with suspicion.

'The lass's been ill,' Rose excused her.

'The child must be christened,' the priest declared, 'to save her mortal soul from everlasting hell.'

When he had gone, Rose turned to her and said, 'He knows, I'm sure of it. You cannot hide away for ever. It just makes it look suspicious. I'm the one supposed to be keeping to the house.'

'Aye,' John agreed, 'I don't want that bugger on me doorstep every day.'

'And the bairn needs a name,' Rose persisted. 'We need to register the birth, else we'll have the coppers round here an' all.'

'I'll gan,' John grunted, 'if you fetch me suit from the in-and-out.'

Kate was shocked out of her silence. 'No!' She looked at them both with a glint of defiance. 'I'll go – she's my bairn.'

'She should be called Rose Ann,' John continued as if she had not spoken, 'after the mam who's ganin' to bring her up.'

Kate's heart hammered. She would be called Catherine after her! It was the only thing she could give – her name. But

317

she kept quiet, knowing that to argue would only rile her stepfather. She could not rely on her mother to support her over this either. Since the incident of the milk fever, Rose had been more distant, as if she somehow blamed her for what John had done. But to her surprise her mother said, 'Let Kate go. It's me that's pretending to be in confinement. She can make herself useful.'

It was August already. Kate knew she could not delay facing the world outside any longer. Dr Dyer had told her weeks ago that she must go to the registrar or else incur a fine for late registration. None of them could afford to pay that.

The next day, Kate squeezed into her best blue dress – the one she had worn during those carefree days at Ravensworth – and pulling on the lace gloves Alexander had given her, set out with the baby wrapped in a blanket for the registry office. Nodding at the people she passed in the lane, Kate hid her feeling of lack of self-worth beneath a cheery smile and a breezy, 'Afternoon!'

By the time she reached the town hall, she was perspiring with the exertion of walking so far and nervousness at what she had to do. She wanted no one to be there to witness her shame at registering an illegitimate child. Kate hovered on the steps, regaining her breath. Her arms ached from holding the baby. Damn you, Alexander! Damn you for bringing me to this!

For a snatched moment, she contemplated dumping the infant on the steps and running away. No one would know it was hers. She was nameless, unregistered, unclaimed. In a few short minutes she could be out of the town and walking to Gateshead, or Newcastle – somewhere she could start a new life, unknown to anyone. Kate's heart hammered at the

318

thought. Then the baby stirred in her arms and bleated, her tiny lips smacking in anticipation of the next feed.

What would become of her? Would Rose come looking for her? She would be given up to the workhouse orphanage, more likely. Kate felt a wave of guilt for even thinking it. She had brought this babe into the world; she could not abandon her as easily as Alexander had done. Then a thought struck her. A daring one, a reckless one. It would take all her courage to carry it out. Lifting her chin in defiance, Kate clutched the baby tighter and entered the office.

While she waited for her turn, she almost changed her mind. But when she was called through, she gave her answers boldly and without betraying the fear that pummelled her insides.

'The child's name?'

'Catherine Ann Davies.'

'Father's name and occupation?'

'Alexander Davies – he's a man of business.'

The clerk gave her a querying look. She thought quickly of the term used by visitors to the Ravensworth Arms.

'Commission Agent,' she smiled.

'And your name, please?'

'Catherine Davies, born Fawcett,' Kate announced, her hands clammy inside the gloves that hid her lack of a wedding ring. She watched in amazement as he carefully wrote in her details. It had been so easy. But what would they do to her if they discovered the lie? Throw her in prison? Kate felt faint.

'And date of birth?'

'The twentieth of June.'

The clerk looked up at her and frowned. He had guessed. It must be obvious she was a woman in disgrace with a bastard child. Fear rose in her throat.

'You must be mistaken,' he said quietly. 'That is over seven weeks ago. And you wouldn't be registering late, would you?' He held her look.

'No,' Kate gulped. 'Daft of me. I've been poorly with the fever – I'm not thinkin' right.' She stared at him in panic. What should she say? She was going to be found out after all.

The clerk cleared his throat and studied the certificate. 'Perhaps it was a week later,' he prompted, 'the twenty-seventh?'

'Aye,' Kate gasped, 'that was it.' She held her breath while he wrote in the date.

'Now, if you could sign here.'

Kate was careful to sign her imaginary married name. A moment later it was all over and he was handing her the certificate. She felt light-headed.

'Thank you,' she said, smiling at him in gratitude. Then she was hurrying out of the office into the hot blustery street, before anyone should call her back.

She had done it! Given her little girl a father and herself a fictitious respectability. Not Pringle-Davies – such an unusual name would have drawn too much attention – but a name none the less. It would count for nothing round where she lived and God help her if the authorities discovered her deceit! But it was worth the risk to give Catherine a legitimate name. Some day in the future she might turn round and thank her for that. Deep down, Kate still kept alive a flicker of hope that Alexander might return some day, if not for her sake, then for their child's.

As Kate set off back to Leam Lane, with her newly named daughter cradled on her shoulder, she thought in defiance: at least she'll not be a common McMullen! She'll be better than that, much better!

Chapter 35

By autumn, both John and Rose were nagging Kate to go back to work. Their meagre funds were dwindling. Sarah had been quietly married to her pitman, Michael. John had cursed her for a fool, but Sarah moved thankfully to Birtley and beyond his control.

'Your father's on short time,' her mother fretted, 'and our Jack'll be next. We need the money.'

'Aye,' John snarled, 'it's time you paid for your sinning. We're slaving away all day to feed your brat – and what are you doing? Lying around the house like Lady Muck.'

'I do more than me fair share around here!' Kate protested. 'Don't I, Mam?'

But Rose said nothing. Kate could see by her worried look that money was more important than help around the house. Her time with Catherine was running out.

'I'll gan into Shields the morrow and ask around,' Kate acquiesced.

'Not Shields,' Rose said quickly. 'Not round here. You can't sneeze but everyone knows about it.'

Kate looked at her in surprise.

'You'll have to gan to place,' her mother said sternly. 'We can't afford to keep you here. You can send your wages home.'

'But, the bairn?' Kate stuttered. 'I'm still feedin''—'

321

'It's time she was weaned.'

'Don't send me away, Mam!'

But Rose was adamant. 'We'll ask our Mary if there's anything over Gateshead way.'

John barked. 'She's not ganin' back to Ravensworth!' He seemed as taken aback by Rose's suggestion as Kate was.

'Sarah, then,' Rose said stubbornly. 'She'll find some'at for our Kate.'

'I'll not trust her out me sight, woman!' John blustered.

Rose gave him a withering look as if his opinion did not matter, and it suddenly dawned on Kate why her mother was so set on sending her away. She wanted her gone from home, not only for the money but to stifle scandal. Only with her gone could they hope to carry out the pretence that Catherine was their child. Kate felt wretched at the thought. She was a constant source of shame under their roof. For the sake of saving face she had to go.

During the following two weeks, while word was put about the family that Kate was looking for a position, she began to wean Catherine. Rose helped her bind up her breasts tightly when they filled with milk. She had to watch her mother bottle-feed the baby on her knee while she got on with cooking and scrubbing.

'She'll smell the milk on you and not take to the bottle,' Rose said bluntly, when Kate asked to feed her.

For several days she suffered agony with tender breasts, huge and bruised with undrunk milk. She could not lie comfortably at night, nor fit into her dress by day, having to wear a voluminous old-fashioned blouse of her mother's. Yet at night, Kate would rise from the settle and gaze into the cot that Jack had made for Catherine, that was squeezed into the corner behind John's large chair.

She would pick her up and cradle her, crooning softly in the flickering firelight. She was allowed to give her a bottle in the early hours, to save Rose getting up. But often in those final days before leaving, she would pick her up just for comfort. There was nothing in her life that matched the joy of seeing her daughter open her large solemn eyes and look trustingly up at her. Catherine responded to Kate's generous smiles and they made soft gurgling sounds at each other. Softly, she sang the bitter-sweet song of a lost child in a winter world, and thought tearfully how this winter they would be parted.

> Child of my dreams, love of my life,
> Hope of my world to be . . .

Then word came from Sarah. A general maid was needed at a bakery in Chester-le-Street, down the train line from Birtley. A cousin of Michael's worked in the shop. On a raw, windy day at the end of October, Kate packed a basket of clothes and a jam sandwich wrapped in newspaper for the journey. When her mother was not looking, she snipped a small auburn curl from Catherine's warm head and hid it in a screw of brown paper in her pocket.

Clasping the baby fiercely to her, she kissed her soft cheek.

'I'll be back for Christmas,' she promised. Her heart squeezed to see Catherine's answering smile. She was going away when her daughter was just beginning to smile!

'Don't miss your train,' Rose warned.

Kate handed the baby to her, tears stinging her eyes.

'Look after her for me, Mam,' she whispered.

'I'll not spoil her,' Rose answered. 'She'll be brought up right.'

Kate blushed, feeling rebuked. There was a hardness in her mother's look that made her shrivel inside. This time there would be no fond words and loving hugs at her going. She was being sent away – punished for her mistake – and no one was more bitterly disappointed in the way things had turned out than her mother.

Kate looked away, picking up her small basket of possessions.

'Ta-ra, Mam,' she murmured.

'See you keep your nose clean,' Rose said stiffly, not wanting to show the slightest weakness. It had done neither of them any good to show their feelings before. She pitied her daughter, but it was best for all that she left. Kate should be grateful that they were caring for her child. She should expect nothing more, for she had brought this all on herself, Rose thought bitterly.

Kate stepped out into the street alone. There was no one to see her off at the station, not even Jack. Since the time she had been ill after Catherine's birth, he had steered clear of her, avoiding her look, hardly speaking two words. He blushed when she came near him and flinched from her touch as if she was somehow contaminated. Maybe it was just a young lad's squeamishness about childbirth and feeding. Or maybe it was she who now revolted him. All Kate knew was that she seemed to have lost her former ally.

On the train, she managed to stem the tears of loneliness that welled in her throat, but when she passed through Lamesley station and the brown harvested fields around Ravensworth, she broke down and quietly wept. That place had been paradise, but how long ago it all seemed! Where was Alexander now? Happily married? Living nearby or far away? She tortured herself with such thoughts.

324

All she knew from Mary was that he had never been back to the inn. He had disappeared into thin air. If there had been any rumours about him, she knew her sister would have delighted in telling her. Since her disgrace, Mary had lorded it over her on her visits home, making out she was far the better daughter. But there had been no rumours and no news of the coal agent's son.

Staring, heartbroken, at the burnished woods around the castle, Kate felt a ridiculous flicker of hope. If he had married, surely news would have trickled through to the inn? And if he had not, then what was to stop him returning for her one day? Perhaps when his father was dead . . .

She stifled such thoughts. If he had loved her at all, he would have come for her by now. If he had been any sort of gentleman, he would at least have provided for his bastard child. Kate looked away. It was too painful to hope. All she could do was to make the best of her new position and provide for her child herself. Maybe some day she would find a man with a kind heart to take them both on. Unlikely as it seemed, Kate felt a twinge of optimism as she thought of starting anew in Chester-le-Street. She was still young and strong and willing to work.

By the time she stepped down from the train at the Durham market town, no one would know from her ready smile and brisk walk that she carried the weight of the world on her young shoulders, or guess that anything troubled her at all.

To her surprise, Kate found herself enjoying her new job. The baker, Slater, was a bluff, kindly man, and his wife and young family were friendly. The three children took quickly to Kate's warm personality and sense of fun, and the parents were happy with her capacity for hard work. She cooked, cleaned and

325

washed for them, scrubbed down the shop in the evenings and got up in the icy mornings to light the fires.

Towards Christmas, when they were especially busy in the shop, Kate helped out behind the counter. She was cheerful to the customers and did not complain at the long hours. Only at night, in the attic room she shared with the youngest daughter, did she allow herself to think of Catherine and muffle her weeping under the blanket. She fingered her baby's soft lock of hair for comfort and clutched the worn paper package as she fell asleep.

As December came, she began to look forward to seeing her daughter again, although she could not talk about it to her employers.

'I've a baby sister,' she explained to Mrs Slater, having let slip Catherine's name. 'She's bonny – just starting to smile when I left. She'll be crawling by now, I wouldn't wonder – bright as a button.'

'Bet she's a handful for your mother,' Mrs Slater said, with a side-long look. 'Strange, calling her Catherine.'

'Why?'

'Well, with you being named Kate as well.'

Kate went red. 'Me mam likes the name. And the bairn's called Catherine Ann.' She turned away and busied herself with the ironing. She must stop herself prattling on about Catherine, else the woman might guess the truth. She was fairly certain no gossip about what had gone on at Ravensworth had reached down here, but it was as well to be cautious. Kate did not mention Catherine again, but as Christmas drew nearer, her excitement mounted at seeing her once more. She could not wait to see what her daughter looked like after the two long months of separation.

On Boxing Day, the Slaters filled up a large box of bread,

326

cake, pies and groceries for her to take home. They had told her to take two days off for working so hard.

'You've been a grand help,' Mr Slater told her. 'Enjoy yourself.'

'Hope the baby's well,' Mrs Slater said with an encouraging smile. 'But come back to us, won't you? The girls won't forgive us if you don't.'

'Of course I will,' Kate replied, 'you're that good to me.'

She caught the train to Gateshead, meeting up with Mary on the way. Kate steeled herself for the stop at Lamesley, but the thought of seeing Catherine again eased her discomfort at the familiar landmarks of church and inn and distant castle towers.

'I've bought her a rattle and her own spoon,' Kate told Mary in excitement. 'And a blanket for her cot.'

'Thought Mam was to get your wages?' Mary said pointedly.

'I'm just providing for the bairn like they want me to,' Kate defended.

'Well, so you should. I'm glad I don't have to hand over all my wages.' She gave a superior look. 'What you got in there?'

'Cake and that from the bakery,' Kate said proudly, 'for all me hard work. That should please them at home.'

Mary sniffed. 'It'll take more than that for you to please them after what you did.'

Kate felt dashed. Mary was probably right. A mountain of bakery wouldn't let her parents forget the disgrace she had brought under their roof. Well, at least her own bairn would be pleased to see her, Kate thought with spirit.

She was out of her seat before the train pulled into Tyne Dock station and throwing open the carriage door as it squealed to a stop.

'Haway, Mary,' she cried with impatience as they made their way through the town. 'Do you have to look in every shop window?'

'I've been stuck in Lamesley, remember?' Mary retorted. 'Not a proper shop for miles.'

Kate bustled ahead, her parcel from the Slaters weighing heavy in her arms. Some of the windows they passed were strung with colourful decorations and her excitement increased. She loved Christmas. Even when they had been small and there were hardly two pennies to rub together, Rose had always tried to find some treat to put in their stockings. She wondered what her mother had bought for Catherine for her first Christmas.

Reaching Leam Lane at last, they clattered breathlessly through the front door.

'We're back, Mam!' Kate called, rushing into the kitchen.

John was sitting in his chair by the fire, smoking. Rose was setting the table.

'Where's Catherine?' she asked at once. 'Where's me little lass?'

She followed her mother's look and saw her daughter sitting on the hearth rug waving a wooden spoon. She was neatly dressed in a blue serge smock, her auburn baby hair glinting in the firelight. Kate dumped down her parcels and hurried towards her, arms outstretched.

'What a picture!' she cried. 'Come to Mammy and give me a big love!'

She bent down and seized the child, swinging her up into her arms.

'Mind you don't crease her dress,' Rose warned.

'Let me look at you, bonny Catherine.' Kate ignored the plea. 'Eeh, how I've missed you!' She squeezed Catherine to her and smothered her in kisses. Her cheeks felt so soft and warm, her skin smelling of soap and milk. She buried her nose into the baby's neck.

'Stop fussin' over her,' John complained, banging his pipe on the hearth beside them.

Catherine started at the noise and let out a wail of protest.

'There, there,' Kate soothed her, kissing her again. But her daughter screamed louder as she eyed Kate in alarm. Kate bounced her in her arms. 'Now, now, Catherine, don't fret, Mammy's got you.'

'You shouldn't call her that,' Rose scolded, stepping round the table. Catherine caught sight of the older woman and flung out her arms to her. Kate could feel her small body strain away from her with surprising strength.

Rose bustled over and claimed the baby. 'She's not used to you. Shoosh now, Kitty!'

Within seconds, Catherine's strident crying subsided as she nestled into Rose's protective hold.

'It was the banging, not me.' Kate put out a hand to touch her.

But Catherine's eyes widened in fear at the stranger. She buried her head into Rose's broad shoulder and refused to look at Kate. Kate gulped back tears of disappointment.

'She'll come round,' Rose said more gently. 'Won't you, Kitty? This is our Kate. She's come to see you.'

Kate felt swamped by a wave of jealousy. Catherine looked so content in Rose's arms. She didn't even remember her! Two short months and her daughter had forgotten her. Her smell, the sound of her voice, her kisses meant nothing to Catherine any more. Or to Kitty, as her mother kept irritatingly calling her.

'What you call her Kitty for?' Kate could not hide her annoyance. 'Sounds like a cat.'

'Catherine's too much of a mouthful for a bairn this size,' Rose said bluntly. 'Tak your coats off, lasses, and help me serve up the dinner.'

She plonked Catherine on to the hearth again. The baby bleated in complaint but Rose ignored her whimpering. Kate was too wary to pick her up again.

'What you got in that box?' John asked. 'Open it up and let's have a look.'

Kate smothered her hurt feelings. 'I've got a canny lot of food from the shop – they're kind, the Slaters.' She pulled the string and opened up the parcel.

The others crowded round to see as the smell of fresh baking was released.

'That'll do us for the rest of the week,' Rose said in satisfaction. 'Got your pay an' all?'

Kate nodded, digging into her coat pocket and handing over a brown paper bag of money. Rose emptied it out on to the table and counted it.

'There's a bit short,' she said in suspicion.

Kate flushed. 'I bought a few bits for the bairn – Christmas presents.'

'For the bairn?' John barked. 'The little bugger doesn't know if it's Christmas or Easter.'

'I'll buy her things if I want to!' Kate replied hotly.

'Not with wages that should come to us,' he snapped back. 'Your mam'll decide what gets spent on the bairn, not you.'

Kate was furious. She looked at her mother for support, but Rose shook her head. She did not want to take on a fight with John. Or maybe she agreed with him that Kate should have no money of her own to fritter on her daughter.

330

'Help Mary put the pies in the pantry,' Rose said, busying herself with gathering up the money. Reaching up to the battered tin on the mantelpiece, she stuffed it in and replaced the lid firmly. Kate's wages now belonged to the household. She would have to beg her mother for enough to buy soap and boot polish for the coming month.

She ground her teeth with the humiliation of it all and did as her mother told her. Shortly afterwards Jack appeared, slinking in quietly at the back door, glancing at them warily and grunting a greeting, which Mary ignored.

They sat down to a meal of rabbit and braised vegetables, though Kate had lost her appetite and had to force down each mouthful. She watched while Rose fed spoonfuls of watery gravy and mashed potato to Catherine. The child stared back at Kate with cautious eyes. Afterwards Rose removed her to the bedroom for a sleep and Kate did not see her again for hours.

As it grew dark, she walked Mary back to the train and was half tempted to jump on board and go back to the Slaters that night. But she cheered herself with the thought that Catherine might allow her to hold her once she grew used to her face again. She returned to find Rose washing the baby in a small basin of water in front of the fire. Jack had disappeared and John was sitting in his chair with a fresh jug of beer warming on the hearth.

'Let me help you, Mam,' Kate said eagerly, kneeling down beside them.

'I can manage,' Rose replied. 'You can get the tea on.'

'I'm still full from dinner,' Kate protested.

'Do as your mam says,' John growled.

Reluctantly, Kate stood up. How she longed to touch the soft, plump skin and splash her daughter in play. She sounded

331

so contented, gurgling as the warm water ran over her. Kate felt a pang of envy as she went to fetch one of Slater's pies and warm it in the oven. By the time she had finished, Catherine was swaddled and ready for bed. Rose whisked her away into the bedroom. It was obvious she did not want Kate near the child. She was to be her big sister, nothing more intimate. Perhaps Rose believed Kate's badness might be passed on to her daughter if she had too much to do with her. Kate's hopes of two happy days with Catherine disintegrated like ash in the grate.

Jack appeared again just in time for tea, like an animal scenting food. He eyed her as he slipped into his seat, but said nothing. Afterwards, she was left to clear up while Rose went to bed early.

'I get tired with the bairn,' she said, with a look that told Kate it was her fault.

Jack sprawled on the hearth reading an old newspaper, while John supped his way through the jug of beer. When that was finished, he roused Jack with a kick and told him to fetch another jugful.

'Mam said that was to be your last,' he muttered.

John kicked him again. 'Don't listen to her, you nancy-boy. Get up and do what I tell you! Tak some money from the tin.'

Jack jumped to his feet and went out scowling with a coin from Kate's wages. Kate sat down on the settle with a sigh. She could not go to bed until they did, and now her stepfather was in for one of his drinking sessions.

When Jack returned, John turned to Kate and said, 'You can stop your sighing and fetch another cup.'

'Who for?' Kate said irritably.

'You,' John answered, with a sly look. 'And one for the lad

for fetching the beer. We'll all sit and have a drink together and a bit sing-song.'

Kate knew it was best to humour him, so did as he asked. She poured out three cups of the dark ale and nursed hers while watching the men knock theirs back. John wiped his mouth and stared at her.

'Haway, get it down your neck. Tak the twisty look off your face.'

Kate sipped. It tasted bitter on her tongue.

'And again,' he ordered.

She took a longer swig. It frothed in her mouth, leaving a malty taste, more pleasant than the first. She took another. A warm feeling spread through her stomach. She drank again and realised the cup was empty.

John laughed and thumped the table. 'That's it, lass! Knew you'd like it. Makes your troubles fly out the door. Pour us another.'

Kate glanced at Jack and saw that his cup was empty too. They eyed each other and he nodded like a fellow conspirator. Best to keep the old drunkard happy, the look said. She filled up their cups.

After a few more swigs, she began to feel content, even merry. Her head was pleasantly fuzzy. It had just been a temporary setback with the baby. Tomorrow she would be full of smiles for her real mother. Kate would cuddle her and spoon her meals with the second-hand horn spoon she had bought her and bask in her daughter's smiles.

'Give us a song, lass!' John ordered, sloshing more beer into her empty cup.

Before long, Kate was singing her heart out. Irish and north country ballads, popular music-hall songs. The words poured out of her like a river breaking through a dam. She had not sung like this for an age – not since Ravensworth.

It was a blessed release. Kate had a vague recollection of more beer being fetched and more songs sung, until Rose banged on the wall and shouted at them to stop or they'd wake the baby. But they carried on, until the songs became maudlin and Kate could no longer sing for crying.

By the time she and Jack managed to frog-march John to his bed, the fire had almost died out. Kate stumbled back into the kitchen and collapsed on to the settle, her head spinning as she lay. She closed her eyes to stop the room moving. She couldn't remember why she had been crying. Her mind was blanketed in alcohol, her thoughts woolly. The next moment she was deep in sleep and nothing mattered at all.

Chapter 36

June 1912

Peering out of the train window, Kate could just make out the dockside warehouses, but the river was hidden by a sea fret. She had left Chester-le-Street in bright sunshine, wearing a thin cotton lavender dress and a broad hat with large purple bow to match that Mrs Slater had given her.

'You look bonny,' the baker's wife had told her that morning, loading her up with a cake and scones. 'You enjoy your day off.'

She had asked for this Thursday off because it was Catherine's sixth birthday. Kate was coming home as a surprise with a cake and a length of pale blue ribbon for Catherine's long chestnut hair. She had saved up the train fare from the small amount her mother allowed her to keep each month since John and Jack were in regular work at the docks once more.

Several years of slump had hit Tyneside while Kate worked away. Old Charles Palmer, whose shipbuilding and steel empire employed most of Jarrow in the boom times, was dead. There had been strikes over reduced wages and scrapping over what little work there was. For two years hardly a ship was launched from Palmer's, and the McMullens had only survived on the wages and food Kate brought home. Not that she got a word of thanks, she thought bitterly. As far as her parents were concerned, it was her duty and her penance. She would provide for her daughter, even though she was forbidden to be a mother.

In the early days, when she appeared on rare days off, Catherine would totter towards her and hold out her arms, squealing, 'Kate! Kate!' Kate would grab the small girl and swing her round in a boisterous embrace. But Rose was always there to snatch her back.

'What a silly fuss you make! I've just ironed that dress.' And she would plonk her down and straighten the girl's clothes. 'Now sit on the fender, Kitty, and don't fidget.'

Gradually Catherine stopped running to greet Kate, rather giving her a shy, wary smile, and so Kate stopped trying to pick her up. She stifled her urge to hug and kiss until she almost thought of the young girl as her sister. Almost. But there were times when she caught a look of Alexander – in the bold hazel eyes, the glint of copper in her hair – that made her heart leap with bitter-sweet longing. At such moments she wanted to hold her close, for she was the only reminder that her lover had ever existed. Yet at the same time she wanted to shake her daughter until the pent-up rage inside her subsided.

Catherine was pretty but stubborn, and mostly Kate was glad it was Rose who had to discipline the child. She would wander off down the street and be found halfway across Tyne Dock, beyond the dripping archways or escaping up the bank towards Jarrow, swinging on the gates of larger houses.

'She'll be found face down in the Slacks!' Kate protested after finding her playing on the waste ground above Jarrow Slake.

'I'm too old to gan chasing after her,' Rose defended. 'But she gets a skelpin' when she comes home.'

Kate suspected that was frequently. Yet the child showed no concern at either threats or chastisements. She was lively and inquisitive, keen to join in the street games with the older children and capable of throwing a tantrum when told to come in sooner than she wanted. To Kate's amazement, the only one who never lifted a hand to her was old John. Never had she heard that he unbuckled his belt for Catherine. He still threatened his own children with a thrashing, but never the child. He left that to Rose, while he patted Catherine like a pet dog and she sat close to him and shared his meals.

It was a glimpse of the former John who had given them gruff love when they were young. Kate remembered how, as a child, she had tried so hard to please her stepfather, the way Catherine did now. So she made no comment and did not interfere, except over one issue, Catherine's schooling.

'She'll gan to the Catholic school,' John frequently declared, 'be brought up in the Faith.'

But Kate was determined that her daughter would not go to the local school in Tyne Dock where Father O'Neill held sway. So far they had managed to keep up the charade that Rose and John were Catherine's parents, but Kate feared the priest would pick on the child, for she suspected he had guessed all along. She saw it in his sharp look, and blushed at his harsh words about sin. He would see it as his mission to be hard on the girl for her own good, to save her soul from the flames of hell.

So when Catherine turned four and Kate was home in the late summer, she dressed her daughter neatly and marched her up the hill to Simonside parish school, while John was at work. Catherine skipped happily past the allotments and large houses of Simonside village, until they reached the school. It was set by the road, with the church behind and a field to play in between the two. Catherine was delighted and settled in happily.

'Simonside?' John exploded on his return. 'It's full of Protestants! I'll not have her sittin' next to dirty Protestants.'

'It's handy for her,' Kate insisted. 'She can walk herself up the bank.' Then she held her stepfather's look and added, 'And none of the bairns there live round here, so they're not ganin' to talk about what they don't know.'

So reluctantly John had agreed that Catherine could stay. It pleased Kate greatly that Catherine enjoyed going to school and was doing well in her lessons. Already at five she was coming home and reciting rhymes to them on the kitchen hearth. The girl was quick and bright and Kate was secretly proud.

Only when Mary left her job at Ravensworth and came home did trouble start over Catherine. At twenty-three, Mary had tired of chambermaiding and was desperate to be wed. She took a cleaning job at the tram depot and was soon courting a mild-mannered driver called Alexander. Kate couldn't help wondering if she had chosen a man of that name deliberately, but Mary's Alec was kind to Catherine so she said nothing. Her contrary sister was another matter. She alternately vied for the child's attention and punished her for petty crimes.

Recently, Kate had come home to find Mary spanking Catherine hard. For once she intervened.

'The little bugger broke me pearl necklace – the one Alec gave me!' her sister screamed as Kate pushed her aside.

'I'm s-s-sorry!' Catherine wailed. 'Dolly snatched it at the p-party.'

Kate threw her arms around the sobbing child. 'Don't worry, I'm here, pet.'

'She deserved it,' Rose said from her chair by the fire. 'Made a spectacle of hersel' at Dolly Lodge's party – showing off by all accounts.'

Kate ignored the remark and cuddled the shaking girl.

'And what am I going to tell my Alec?' Mary fumed.

'He'll not mind.' Kate was dismissive. 'You shouldn't have let the lass have them if you cared that much.' Mary had only lent the necklace to win Catherine's favour and to spite her, Kate thought crossly.

'That's the last time I give her a lend of anything,' Mary snapped. 'I just did it out the kindness of me heart, so she had sommat fancy to wear for the party – 'cos you give her nowt,' she added cattily.

Kate bristled. She hugged Catherine tight and whispered loudly, 'Don't listen to her – they weren't real pearls anyway.'

'They were so!' Mary cried.

But Catherine turned her face away from Kate's and struggled to be free. 'You smell nasty, our Kate,' the girl complained finally. 'You smell like me da.'

Kate let her go as if she'd been scorched. 'What you mean by that?' she asked indignantly. Catherine rushed over to Rose and squatted between her legs without another word.

'What d'you think she means?' Mary was scornful. 'You stink of booze like Father, that's what.'

'That's a lie,' Kate said, blushing furiously. Catherine fixed her with frightened hazel eyes. 'I just had the one on me way here,' she blustered. 'Bumped into Cousin Maisie outside the station – didn't want to offend her.'

Her mother's look was full of contempt.

'I'm entitled to a bit of fun on me day off,' Kate protested.

'Bad will out,' Mary murmured maliciously.

Kate rounded on her. 'Don't you give me that holy look! You're no better than me – just luckier. I'm the one hands over me wages, not you. So I'll spend me holiday how I like!'

She had stormed out and gone back to the Railway Hotel, looking for her McMullen cousin, who had become her occasional drinking companion on days off. Maisie worked hard at a rope factory and liked 'a bit sup and a sing-song' in her free hours too. It was a respectable hotel back room, not the bar. There was no harm in it.

Maisie had gone, but there were two other women she recognised who stood her a drink or two. Kate stayed until it was time to go back to Chester-le-Street and did not bother to go home again that day.

Kate sighed at the memory as she gathered up her parcel of bakery. Now the train was pulling into misty Tyne Dock once again. This time it would be better. She would go straight home and not be tempted to stop off for a glass of beer, even though the thought made her throat feel dry. She shivered as she stepped on to the platform. The air was cold and clammy after the hot carriage. The sea mist clung to her hair and seeped into her thin summer clothes, making her shiver.

Walking through the streets of Tyne Dock was an eerie experience. She could hear the clatter of wheels as trams rolled past and a dray horse whinnied close by, but could see nothing. The town was draped in a white pall, sounds echoing off unseen walls.

Kate had hoped for a sunny afternoon where she could sit on the step and watch Catherine playing with her friends and she would please her daughter by inviting them all in for scones and cake.

'Our Kate always brings home sommat tasty,' she could hear Catherine boast. 'Works in a posh shop, for the well-to-do.'

Mary called it putting on airs, when the young girl spoke like that. But it pleased Kate, for no one was going to label her daughter a common street urchin like some of the scruffier inhabitants of Leam Lane.

Her footsteps rang as she made her way down to the dockside street. As she approached Number Five, she could see a small figure squatting on the doorstep scoring the stone with a shard of glass.

'Stop that, you'll cut yourself!' Kate cried, dashing forward.

The child looked up in alarm. She had a round pale face and matted black hair.

'Eeh, I thought you were Kitty,' she laughed in confusion. 'Is the bairn indoors?'

The girl stared at her in suspicion. Kate wondered if she was a bit simple.

'Kitty McMullen?' she said impatiently. 'Shift so I can gan in, hinny.'

The child did not move. Kate felt her temper flare quickly.

'Haway, it's the lass's birthday – out the road!'

'Mam,' the glum girl suddenly whined, 'Mam!'

A moment later, a thin dark-haired woman came out clutching a broom.

'What you want?' she demanded.

Kate stood back. 'Sorry, must've got the wrong house – it's like pea soup the day!' But even as she said it, she knew she stood outside Number Five. She could smell the wafts of beer from the pub next door. She stepped forward again.

'What you doing here? This is me mam's house. The McMullens'.'

The woman scowled at her, brandishing her broom. 'This is our house. Don't know of any McMullens.'

Kate gawped in disbelief. Maybe they were all hiding inside, playing a silly trick on her. But then no one knew she was coming.

'Don't be bloody daft,' Kate exclaimed. 'The McMullens have lived here for years. Old John and me mam – and Jack – and the bairn . . .?'

The woman yanked at the child on the step and pushed her inside. 'Well, they don't live here now,' she said shortly. 'This is ours – paid for fair and square.' She slammed the door shut.

Kate stood speechless. What on earth had become of her family? At once, dire thoughts paralysed her. There'd been a terrible accident. They'd been burnt out. Jack had been injured at work, killed. They'd been evicted for not paying the rent. John had gambled it all away on Race Day. They'd had to go to the workhouse. Something awful had happened to Catherine – she was in the isolation hospital dying of summer fever – they all were!

Kate's heart hammered in fright. She could make no sense of it. In a panic she began running up the street, banging on doors and screaming.

'Have you seen me mam? Do you know where they've gone? Has anyone seen the McMullens? Where's our Kitty?'

Finally someone loomed out of the mist. It was Mrs Lodge from four doors up.

'Who's making all that racket? Kate – is that you?'

'Please, tell us what's happened to me mam!' Kate sobbed, fear clawing her stomach.

'Calm yourself down, lass,' Mrs Lodge said, putting out a hand.

'I cannot find them,' Kate gasped. 'Has sommat bad happened?'

'No, nothing bad. Well, not that I know of.'

'Then where are they?'

Mrs Lodge sniffed. 'Done a flit. Up and offed about a month ago.'

Kate was stunned. 'A *month*?'

'Aye, never said a word. But I saw the cart come for their things. That lass riding on top like the queen of the gypsies.' Kate heard the disapproval in the woman's voice. She hadn't forgiven Catherine for spoiling Dolly's party.

Kate swallowed a swift retort. 'Where did they gan, Mrs Lodge? Please tell us.'

'Don't rightly know. Somewhere up East Jarrow. Seen old John and the lad walking down the bank to work.' She jerked her head in the direction of the Jarrow road. 'Fancy them not telling you where they were going.'

Kate went hot with indignation. 'I'm sure they meant to. Ta for your help.'

She turned and hurried down the street, away from the woman's pitying stare. At least they couldn't have gone far if the men were still working at Tyne Dock. She would soon find them. She had a hunch that they had returned to the New Buildings where they had lived once before in more prosperous times. If there was half a chance of renting round there, she knew her mother would jump at it.

But to move without telling her! As Kate toiled up the hill towards East Jarrow, she became filled with anger at their

343

thoughtlessness. She had thought them destitute or dead, had to endure the humiliation of shouting up Leam Lane and their neighbour's disdain. By God, she'd give them hell when she found them all!

She lost her way in the fog and ended up missing the group of houses huddled at the top of Jarrow bank and found herself plunging down to the lip of the Slake. Kate could tell where she was by the stench of rotting rubbish and polluted effluent lapping on the tide. She cursed her mistake as her shoes stuck in the foul mud and backtracked hastily. She could hear the clang of chains and shivered. It sounded like the swinging of an iron gibbet. Was this where the pitch-smeared body of Jobling had hung to frighten the miners back to work? It was just the noise of a ship's rigging, she told herself firmly as she fled up the hill.

Finally Kate caught sight of a street corner emerging out of the mist. A glimmer of sunlight stabbed through the grey blanket, throwing a mysterious pearly light on the brickwork and bay windows. This was Simonside Terrace, the grandest of the half-built plot. Kate stopped to get her breath back. How was she to find them? She could not go yelling round these streets where she was not known. What if they weren't here at all? She panicked. She would have to go back to Chester-le-Street not knowing what had become of them. The thought was too unbearable. She clung to the hope they were somewhere in the New Buildings.

Clutching her now battered box of cakes, she strode down the terrace and turned into Phillipson Street. Peering into the strange hazy light, she could not see a soul, though she could hear children playing somewhere nearby. Their ghostly voices echoed around her. Kate searched the street. She spotted two boys throwing stones at a target on a yard wall.

'Have you seen our Catherine?' she demanded, grabbing one by the arm. 'Kitty McMullen.'

'Na, missus!' he cried, alarmed by the sudden appearance of the angry woman.

Kate let go. It was useless. She couldn't search the whole of East Jarrow in the short time she had left. The sing-song voices of a girls' skipping game came suddenly from very close. Kate spun round and ran to the end of the lane. It petered out into open land where the rest of the street should have been built but never had. Left took her into William Black Street, right into Lancaster Street. The noise seemed to be coming from the left.

Kate swung into William Black Street. She could just make out a huddle of children beneath a solitary lamppost. They were spinning around in dizzy circles, holding on to the end of a rope that was tied to the post. Kate ran towards them. There was something about one of the girls, the glint of long plaits.

She was almost upon the group when she recognised Catherine's startled face. The girl was staring up at her as if she had seen a ghost. Kate reached out and seized her in relief.

'You little bugger! Where've you been?' she shouted, shaking her hard, not wanting to let go. 'I thought you were dead! Don't you ever do that to me again, do you hear?'

'No,' Catherine gasped, looking terrified.

'Where's Mam?' Kate barked.

'In the house.'

'And where's that?' Kate shook her angrily. 'Show me!'

The other children scarpered in her wake as Kate hauled her daughter down the street. She had been frantic with worry all this time, but now she was filled with an inexplicable fury

345

at the young girl. She had been playing happily with her new friends, indifferent to whether Kate returned or not. She probably hadn't given her a second thought since the last time she saw her. Damn the child!

Catherine, half running, half dragged, led her to Number Ten. Kate shoved her through the door. The front room with the best furniture and her parents' bed was empty. Kate stormed into the kitchen. It was cluttered and untidy as if they had lived there for years.

She caught sight of her mother dozing in a chair under the picture of Lord Roberts and threw Catherine forward. The girl stumbled into Rose.

'What?' Rose started from her nap. 'What you doing here?'

'Aye, it's me!' Kate let fly. 'The one you didn't bother to tell. I've been all over bloody Jarrow looking for you. Why didn't you send word? I thought you'd gone in the workhouse!'

'Don't be so daft,' Rose retorted. 'We've come up in the world, not down. Yards are working full time, so we took our chance. Maggie told us this was for rent. There's no need to fuss. You found us, didn't you?'

'No thanks to you,' Kate shouted. 'You should've written, Mam. I nearly went back not knowing . . .!' She burst into tears.

'You know I cannot write letters,' Rose blustered. 'Anyways, I'm too busy.'

'Mary can,' Kate sobbed.

'She would've done in time. I wasn't expecting you. Why you back, any road?' Rose went on the attack. 'Not got yourself in trouble again?'

'No!' Kate sniffed, feeling doubly hurt. 'Came back for the bairn's birthday.' She looked around, suddenly guilty at the way she had taken her anger out on Catherine. 'I'm sorry, pet.' She wiped her face and held out her arms, but Catherine sat rooted to her refuge on the steel fender, watching her warily.

'I've brought you a cake – and a present,' Kate said in a gentler voice. 'Do you want to see what I've got?'

Catherine nodded and sidled over, curiosity quickly roused. She took the paper bag Kate offered her and ripped it open. The ribbon fell to the floor. Catherine bent and grabbed it, running the shiny material through her fingers.

'What you go spending money on posh ribbon for?' Rose complained. 'Cotton rags will do.'

'Do you like it?' Kate ignored her mother.

'Aye,' Catherine smiled. 'Ta, our Kate.'

'Let me tie it in your hair,' Kate offered. The girl held it out. In defiance of her mother, Kate untied the tight plaits that bound her hair and combed it free with her fingers. Then she slid the ribbon under the girl's hair and gathered it in a large bow at the back.

'That looks bonny,' Kate said. But as soon as she had finished, Catherine ran to Rose and stood between her knees as if she sensed they were fighting over her. Kate felt a spasm of jealousy. Suddenly she wished she hadn't bothered to come home. She was better off staying in Chester-le-Street where at least the Slaters treated her like family and no one gave her pitying glances in the street or whispered behind her back as she passed.

She wouldn't come back so eagerly again. Kate got off her knees and straightened out her lavender skirt. Before she could make her escape, Mary appeared.

'Are you ready, Kitty?' she called, then saw Kate and gasped. 'What a fright you gave me! Didn't expect to see you so soon.'

347

'No,' Kate said, 'you weren't easy to find.' She watched Catherine skip across to her aunt and hold out a hand. 'Where you ganin' with the bairn?' she asked suspiciously.

'Promised her a trip to the pictures,' Mary preened. 'There's a Charlie Chaplin on at the Crown.'

Kate felt suddenly defeated. How could a piece of ribbon compete with a matinée show at a picture palace? She should give up trying to win Catherine's affection. She would never be more than the big sister who provided – the one who was good for a laugh when she wasn't arguing, or drinking, or absent. She would be happier if she gave up the battle, went back to the Slaters and got on with life there. It was not such a bad one.

Kate watched Mary fuss over Catherine's appearance and adjust the ribbon in her hair.

'Just as well you've come home,' Mary said, clutching her niece's hand. 'Isn't it, Mam?'

'Why's that?' Kate asked dully.

'Haven't you told her, Mam?'

'Not had a chance,' Rose wheezed. 'Came in here like a bull in a china shop.'

Kate felt nervous at the look of glee on Mary's face. 'Tell me what?'

'Father wants you back.' Mary was blunt. 'Mam can't manage the house any more – not with Kitty an' all. It's up to you.'

Kate stared at her. '*Me?*'

'Aye, it's true, isn't it, Mam?'

'But I've got a canny job.' Kate was indignant. 'Why can't you help around here more?'

Mary was dismissive. 'I'm working too – and I'm courting. I'll be married soon with a place of me own.'

'Has Alec asked you to wed?'

348

'Not yet,' Mary said, colouring, 'but he will. Anyways, it's you that has to keep house – Father said so. Look at Mam,' Mary pointed, 'she can hardly walk across the room, let alone to the shops.'

Kate looked at her mother in dismay. Her face was puffy with fatigue, her breathing laboured and she wasn't even standing up. It struck Kate that she hadn't seen her mother move from the chair at all. Glancing about, she could see now that the room looked messy and neglected. Nothing was polished or scrubbed and clothes were draped over chairs unironed. It was Catherine's birthday, but there was no tea spread out, no table laid.

Rose's dark-ringed eyes looked sad. 'I've tried me best, hinny, but the bairn's worn me out. You have to come home and help us.'

Kate saw the defeat on her mother's face and realised it was true. For six years Rose had looked after the lively Catherine, as well as the men, and it had left her exhausted. Kate had been so absorbed in her own worries that she had not thought how the past hard years had taken their toll on her mother's failing health.

But coming home would mean saying goodbye to the Slaters and her small degree of independence. Gone would be the little freedoms of chatting to the shop customers and occasional visits from her friend Suky on market day. She would be at the beck and call of her sick mother and domineering stepfather. Kate fought the panic rising in her chest.

Then suddenly Catherine piped up. 'Please come back, our Kate. Mam's legs don't work any more. You can put me hair in ringlets and walk with me to school.'

Kate felt her eyes smart. It was the first time Catherine

349

had shown that she wanted her and it made her heart swell. She stepped over and put a hand on her daughter's head.

'That would be canny.' Kate smiled at the child. She turned to her mother. 'Course I'll come back and give a hand, Mam.'

Rose nodded, but there was no smile for her. Her mother seemed past caring.

'That's settled then,' Mary said brusquely, yanking the girl away from Kate's touch. 'Haway, Kitty, or we'll be late for the film.'

Catherine ran to the door without a backward glance. 'Ta-ra, Mam,' she called from the door.

'Ta-ra, pet—' Kate began.

'Ta-ra, Kate,' the girl added as an afterthought.

Kate felt a stab of disappointment. The closeness she had felt a moment before had not been shared by the child. Soon she would see her daughter every day, live together cheek by jowl, yet have to keep up this pretence of being her sister. How could she do it? How long would they all have to live this lie?

Chapter 37

1913

Raking out the fire and carrying the ashes to the midden, Kate stopped to look at the pale dawn light bleeding into the half-dark sky. Midsummer again. She had been home a year, yet it seemed like ten. She stretched her stiff limbs, feeling the familiar ache in her back that throbbed even before she filled the hod with coal and humped it back into the kitchen.

Her mind ran ahead to the long day's tasks. Slops to empty from the bucket by her parents' bed, Jack to turf off the settle, breakfast to make, Catherine to get ready for school, her mother to wash and dress, a midday meal to prepare and leave on the stove. All this before traipsing into Tyne Dock to her cleaning job at the Penny Whistle. Kate felt tired just thinking of it.

Later there would be tea to make, floors to scrub, more coal to fetch, dishes to wash and baking to be done for the following day. Rose to help to bed. Then maybe a sit-down with a piece of mending, her swollen feet plunged in a pail of cold water. Or maybe a small jug of beer to quench the

351

thirst, a tot of whisky to numb the aching. If she took in a bit of extra washing for the Simpsons in Phillipson Street . . .

At least she had resisted taking in lodgers, Kate thought with pride. Her daughter had not had to share with rough seamen or transient workers as Kate had had to do after her father had died. She remembered her childish fear of brawny men smelling of fish and talking in strange accents taking over their kitchen. She still recalled her mother falling to her knees sobbing when it was discovered the lodgers had stolen the housekeeping and the precious bone-handled cutlery and disappeared back to sea.

Sometimes Jack would bring home men he had been working with down the docks, men away from home. Kate would be expected to feed them too, but she did not mind, for some of them brought bottles of beer to wash down their tea and often they would end up with a song or two, calling on Kate to sing. How careful she had to be. She had to gauge her stepfather's mood, keep a careful balance between pleasing him with her singing and provoking his wrath if any of the men showed a spark of interest in her. For she would always get the blame.

'Don't you give him the eye,' John shouted drunkenly when one of Jack's friends pinched her cheek. He was a cheerful Scot called Jock Stoddart and Kate found him good company. He and his quiet friend, Davie McDermott, were stokers off a ship Jack had been unloading. Davie was married to Stoddie's sister and they had come three nights running, spending their pay freely on whisky and beer.

'Such bonny eyes,' Stoddie teased, not realising the trouble he caused.

'Whore's eyes!' John snapped, staggering out of his chair and lunging for Kate. She tried to dodge out of his way, but the beer had dulled her movements and his fist caught her on the side of the head.

She toppled backwards off her stool and landed in an undignified heap on the floor, head spinning. The men looked on in astonishment, Stoddie half rising to help her.

'Leave the slut alone!' John roared, swinging a punch wildly at the Scotsman.

He fended it off easily. 'Sit down, man. I meant nothing by it,' Stoddie said calmly.

But Jack chose that moment to pick a fight with his father.

'You leave the lass alone,' he snarled, rising from the settle and knocking Catherine awake as he lurched round the table. The child had curled up and gone to sleep there without Kate noticing.

'Watch the bairn,' she slurred, nursing her thumping head.

'Come on then, nancy-boy,' John taunted, raising his gnarled fists at his son, 'let's see you fight for the bitch. She's the only lass you'll get. Not even the whores in Holborn look twice at you!'

Jack threw himself at his father, enraged by his words. Kate rolled out of the way as the two of them went at each other with fists and boots flying. Stoddie and Davie tried to intervene, but there was little room among the press of furniture and they ended up getting thumped in the mêlée too.

Catherine screamed and Kate struggled to her knees, flinging her arms out to protect her. The girl buried her head in Kate's shoulder, squeezing her eyes tight shut.

'It's all right, hinny,' Kate tried to calm her. But Catherine refused to show her face, even after the fight died down.

John had a bloody nose, Jack a swollen eye. The seamen departed with a wink at Kate and a ruffle of Catherine's hair.

353

'Sorry, lassie,' Stoddie said, and was gone.

They sailed the next day and Kate had not seen them since. But John made her life hell for weeks afterwards, berating her about her whorish behaviour and threatening her with his belt if she so much as looked at another man.

When in drink she never knew if he would lash her with his foul-mouthed tongue or make lewd gestures and suggestions. Sometimes he would lunge at her breasts and squeeze them with a crude laugh. 'No milk left for me, eh?'

Once, when she had dozed off on the settle waiting for him to come back from the pub, she was woken by his hand thrust up her skirt. She had cried out in shock and scrambled beyond his reach. He had taken offence and started to smash the pictures off the wall with the fire poker. In desperation Kate had run to the bedroom and woken Catherine in the bed they shared.

'Get up, hinny,' she hissed, 'your da needs puttin' to bed. You can stop him raging, I know you can. Tell him one of your poems. Quick, Kitty.'

The sleepy girl had got out of bed, befuddled but alert to Kate's fear. She had crept into the kitchen and up to the ranting drunkard, pulling on his arm.

'Lavender's blue, dilly-dilly, lavender's green,
When you are king, dilly-dilly, I shall be queen.'

She sang it over and over until the words calmed him and the fury drained away. Between them, they managed to coax John to bed. Afterwards, when all was quiet, Kate snuggled close to Catherine, wrapping her in her arms. After the violence, it felt so good to touch her and draw comfort from her warm young body.

'Ta, pet,' she murmured, 'you're me little helper.'

But Catherine had turned her face away and wriggled out of her hold.

'No I'm not,' she said. And Kate was left with the feeling that her daughter blamed her for what had just happened. She felt diminished and overwhelmingly alone.

Certainly, Rose seemed to think all the wrangling at Number Ten was her fault.

'Jack and his da never used to fight like this before you came home,' she told her once, when Kate had complained that John wouldn't leave her alone.

Kate did not believe her, but she saw it was fruitless to argue. Rose had given up caring about anything this past year. She seemed content to play the invalid and let Kate do all the work. Kate was sure her mother could do more for herself than she did, but just didn't want to. She also knew from the sharp words through the bedroom wall that Rose used her ill health to keep John at bay in bed.

'You'll kill us,' she protested. 'Leave us alone.'

'I've a right to it, woman! I'll tell the priest.'

'And I'll tell him he'll be readin' me the last rites, if you don't leave off us!'

So there was little point going to Rose with her troubles, Kate realised. Her mother's sympathy for her had shrivelled up like last year's leaves.

As Kate staggered back indoors with her load of coal and set about building the fire, she thought bitterly how differently Mary was treated. Her younger sister was married now and living in an upstairs house in the same street, at Number Thirty. Poor Alec. He had been tricked into marriage. Mary had been jealous of the way Alec would linger at Number Ten, chatting to Kate.

355

'Don't you turn my Alec's head with your flirtin'!' Mary had accused.

'I just offered him a cup of tea,' Kate protested.

'You'll not have him, he's mine,' her sister had hissed. 'He's not after spoilt goods.'

Kate was hardened to Mary's malicious tongue, but she would give her no excuse to blame her if Alec tired of Mary's bossiness and finished with her. So she ignored Alec when he came to the house and pretended she did not see the lingering looks he gave her across the table. Was it possible he felt something for her? Or did he just see what other men saw – a woman with a bad reputation who took her solace in drink when she could afford it?

Probably she would never know, for Mary had got herself pregnant last autumn and swiftly married. She knew her Alec would no more desert her than run off to Timbuktu. Kate stabbed hard at the fire with the poker. Life was so unfair. Mary had sneered at her for years for going with a man outside wedlock and yet she had done the same. The hypocrisy made her sick! And the others were just as bad. Mary never felt the sting of John's belt buckle for her 'sin', because by the time baby Alec was born in the late spring, Mary had been respectably married and blessed by the priest.

She unbent from her task by the hearth and saw Jack eyeing her from the settle. She thought he had been fast asleep. Had she spoken any of her thoughts aloud? Kate worried.

'Morning,' she said.

He grunted in return.

'Get yourself washed,' she told him, 'then I'll wake the bairn.'

She busied herself with brewing the tea and setting the table for breakfast. Jack swung off the settle and padded into the scullery to douse his bleary eyes. A few moments later, Kate followed him in to peel potatoes in the bucket for the midday hotpot. Startled, she realised he was stripped naked. Since a young boy he had been painfully shy at his sisters seeing him undressed and they had often teased him.

But she stopped and stared at his broad back, the tightly muscled arms from labouring, sunburnt where his sleeves had been rolled up. In contrast his bottom was pale as milk, his legs thick with hair. Kate saw it all in seconds, the body of a fully grown man, and her pulse began to quicken. Then Jack turned and stared at her. She nearly fainted in shock. He was aroused.

Kate stifled a scream and grabbed a grubby towel from a nail on the door.

'Eeh, put that round you!' she cried. 'The lass might see.'

In a fluster, she forgot the potatoes and fled back into the kitchen, heart pounding. Hacking at the bread with a knife, she tried to rid her mind of the image, but could not. Despite the knowledge that Jack was twenty-two and had been a working man for eight years, she had never thought of him as anything more than a lad, her little brother. He might drink and fight like his father, but in many ways he was still boyish. The way he became tongue-tied and blushing whenever a girl spoke to him, his childish enthusiasm for playing practical jokes with his docker friends, his rough-and-tumble friendship with Catherine.

As far as Kate knew, Jack had never asked a girl out, let alone seriously courted one. His family and friends often teased him about his lack of interest. But here he was, bold as brass, showing her that he had manly urges. It was time he *was* courting. Then John's crude drunken words came back to her.

'*Come on then, nancy-boy, let's see you fight for the bitch. She's the only lass you'll get. Not even the whores in Holborn look twice at you!*'

Surely he wasn't aroused because of her? Please, God, no! Kate pushed such unwelcome thoughts away and rushed to get the bacon on. When Jack came back in the room, she barely glanced at him. She went to wake Catherine and her stepfather, plonked breakfast in front of them and escaped to the parlour to see to Rose.

By the time she emerged Jack and John had left for work. She sat down with a thankful sigh.

'Come here, hinny, and I'll untie your rags,' Kate beckoned to her daughter. It was extra work binding up Catherine's long hair every night, but worth it to see a beautiful cascade of ringlets on her shoulders in the morning.

But today, the girl seemed out of sorts. 'Don't want to,' she complained moodily. 'I want to stay at home the day.'

'Well you can't.' Kate was firm. 'Got to leave in ten minutes or you'll be late for school.'

'Don't want to gan to school.' Catherine's look was mulish.

Kate sighed impatiently. 'You like school. Don't be awkward.'

'I've got a pain.'

Kate grabbed the child by the arm and yanked her towards her. She gripped her between her knees while unknotting and pulling out the tight rags.

'Ow!' Catherine complained. 'You're hurting me!' She tried to pull away.

Kate held on to her hair. 'Don't you start,' she warned. 'I've enough to do today without you throwing one of your paddies.'

'I don't want to gan,' Catherine cried, stamping her foot. Kate could see she was working herself up into a tantrum.

358

'Why not?' she asked in exasperation.

' 'Cos Margaret Lodge won't let me skip with her.'

'Is that all? Gan and skip with someone else.'

'Margaret Lodge won't let me skip with any of them.'

Kate swung the girl round. She could see tears welling in her eyes.

'Who's this Margaret? Is she family with Dolly Lodge from Leam Lane?'

Catherine nodded. 'Cousins.'

Something squirmed in the pit of Kate's stomach. Was it possible . . .? Kate swallowed her fear. She stood up and went to fetch a length of rope she used as a washing line in the house when it was too wet to hang clothes in the lane.

'Here, take this. Margaret can gan skip with the devil.'

Catherine's eyes widened at the sudden gift. 'Ta, our Kate,' she gasped.

After that there was no difficulty getting the girl ready and she ran off across the fields at the back of the New Buildings, taking the summer shortcut to Simonside.

To Kate's relief nothing more seemed to come of the incident with Margaret. She was worrying unnecessarily that rumours might have spread from Leam Lane about Catherine's origins. It had just been a tiff among friends.

A few days later it was Catherine's seventh birthday and Kate hurried back from work to lay on a special tea. She had stayed up the previous night baking cheese pies and a ginger cake. She'd taken on an extra decorating job in Lancaster Street to pay for the ingredients and a bag of boiled sweets for Catherine to share out with her friends.

Mary came round with baby Alec to help, but spent most of the time fussing over the small infant and telling Kate of the new furniture they had ordered and the baby clothes Alec's family had bought them.

'Course, the upstairs houses are bigger,' Mary crowed, 'so the bairn can have his own room. And we don't need to sleep in the parlour, so there's room for proper furniture. Matching, of course. Mam, you'll have to come round and see. I'll send Alec round to help you up the street.'

Kate bit her tongue. At least Mary would not be swanning off with Catherine to the pictures this year, now she had the baby to look after.

Catherine came clattering in with a gaggle of friends in her wake.

'Can we eat yet, Kate? We're all ravishing.'

'Where did you swallow that long word?' Kate laughed.

'You mean ravenous,' Mary corrected. 'My Alec says that when he comes home.'

'Ravishingly ravenous then,' Catherine pouted.

Kate shot Mary a satisfied look. 'Aye, tea's ready. Gan and wash your hands.'

She watched them tucking into her food and felt a glow of wellbeing. Thanks to her hard work, her daughter was enjoying a good birthday spread. None of her friends would go home with bad tales about the way Kate ran the McMullen household.

As they finished, Kate handed out the surprise bag of sweets. 'Gan out and play.'

'Ta, Kate,' Catherine said, rushing to the door.

'Hold your horses,' Mary stopped her. 'I've sommat for you, from me and Alec.'

Kate watched as Mary flourished a box from out of her shopping bag. The children crowded round excitedly as Catherine opened it. The girl gave out a gasp of delight.

'Eeh! Our Mary!'

As she held it aloft for all to see, Kate could not believe her eyes. It was a beautiful china doll with a delicately painted face, dressed in layers of white silk.

'It must've cost a fortune!' Kate blurted out, stupefied.

Mary smiled in confirmation. 'And the hair's real,' she boasted.

Catherine clutched the doll to her, stroking the fair hair in wonder. She had never possessed anything so expensive or special. Kate's insides twisted with jealous resentment.

'Careful with it,' Mary fussed. 'Don't squeeze it too tight or you'll break it.'

Catherine cradled the doll in her arms as if it were made of eggshells.

'It's grand,' she gasped in awe, 'the best present I've ever had. Thank you, thank you, Mary! You're me best sister.'

Mary sat back and preened. Kate had to look away. The envy in her eyes must shine out of her like headlamps. She set about clearing the table and resetting it for the men. She could not speak for the anger that choked her. How dare Mary steal the show with her expensive doll? Just because her husband had a steady job and money to spare. It was *she* who had worked her fingers to the bone to lay on this tea for Catherine and her friends, no one else! She might as well not have bothered for all the thanks she got! Catherine did not even love her. Her affections could be bought in a trice by a china doll.

Kate was thankful when Mary left soon after and John and Jack tramped in, dusty and sweat-stained from work.

'There's more work coming in the yards,' John reported. 'New orders on the books from the Government.'

361

'That's grand,' Rose wheezed, looking up from her mending.

'Aye, battlecruisers and that,' Jack said with enthusiasm. 'It's 'cos the Germans are buildin' ships as fast as they can. Maybes we'll have a scrap with them if it carries on.'

'The saints preserve us,' Rose shuddered.

'We'll not fight the Kaiser.' John was dismissive. 'He's related to the King.'

'I'd join up if we did,' Jack said with animation. 'Missed the last one.'

Kate remembered how keenly her brother had followed the Boer War, re-enacting the sieges and battles of distant Africa with a rifle made out of driftwood. She had bought him a book about the war that he had read over and over until it fell to bits with handling.

'You'll do no such thing,' Rose told him sternly. 'Sit down and have your tea. There's cake left from the bairn's party.'

The men were quick to demolish the rest of Kate's baking, though no one gave her credit for it. She stood at the sink washing up, seething with indignation.

'Cut us another slice of cake, lass,' John called over. 'And you haven't put sugar in me tea.'

Kate banged down her dishcloth and stalked to the table. 'Want me to drink it for you an' all?' she muttered.

'Don't give me your lip. You sound like one of them suffragettes.'

'Chance would be a fine thing.' She splashed in sugar and stirred it round vigorously.

'What was that? Aye, unnatural bitches the lot of them. And that one at Epsom – spoilt a good day's racing.'

'Emily Davison?' Kate glared at him. 'She died, for pity's sake!'

'Serves her right, bloody woman.' John slurped his tea noisily. 'Could've killed the King's horse or the jockey.'

'Well, I think she was brave,' Kate dared to say. 'And us women have a canny lot to complain about. It's slavery for lasses they want to abolish first.'

'Kate . . .' Rose murmured in warning.

But John slammed down his fist, already riled. 'Did I ask for your opinion? There'll be no complaining under my roof from you or any other bitch, or it's a good hidin' you'll get. Do you hear?'

Kate swallowed her fury and stormed back to the scullery sink. She knew her stepfather was itching for an excuse to use his belt on her back. She would not give him the satisfaction. Rose mollified her husband by sending Jack out to buy a jug of beer. The nearest pub was a ten-minute walk away and John was less inclined now to go out drinking since moving up the hill, preferring others to fetch it in.

Kate worked on into the evening, rolling pastry at the table in the window, keeping an eye out for Catherine, while the men sat and drank and Rose dozed in her chair. The doors were flung open, letting the evening breeze off the river filter through the stuffy kitchen. As the shadows lengthened, Kate went out and called her daughter in.

Catherine appeared at the top of the lane. 'Can I stay out a bit longer, our Kate?' she called. 'There's no school the morrow and it is me birthday. Please!'

'Just another five minutes,' Kate relented. It was cooler outside and Kate stood for a moment leaning on the back gate, breathing in the salty breeze. She listened to the children racing off up the lane, squealing like seagulls and disappearing into the next street. They were probably playing knocky-nine-doors and annoying the neighbours, but what was the harm in it on such a warm Friday night?

Friday night. When the pubs filled up and wages got spent and the lucky ones went to the picture house or the music hall and had a laugh. And courting couples went arm in arm to the park or quiet fields . . . Kate looked up at the evening star and remembered how it had shone so brightly over the lake at Ravensworth. A deep stab of longing for Alexander went through her. Whatever had become of him? It pained her that she would never know. Most of the time she managed to smother any thought of him. She had long given up believing that he had once loved her, let alone that he might return to discover how she and the child had fared all these years. She had been stupid to think that men did anything except out of selfish motive. They only wanted women in bed or in the kitchen as far as she could see.

But on rare nights like this, when the warm air prickled the skin and the stars beckoned in a violet sky, Kate remembered what it had felt like to be kissed and courted by the most handsome man she had ever set eyes on. For a brief sweet moment, she remembered what it felt like to be in love.

Shouting and a clatter of feet startled her out of her thoughts. Catherine came tearing past her into the yard. The girl doubled over, gasping for breath.

'What's all the noise about?' Kate demanded.

Catherine clasped her knees, her chest heaving. When she unbent, Kate saw her face was troubled.

'What's wrong? Someone been chasing you?'

The girl shook her head and walked unsteadily to the door.

'Too much excitement,' Kate declared as they entered the kitchen. 'I'll make you a cocoa, then it's off to bed.'

But the girl ignored her and went up to Rose, who was yawning in her chair.

'Mam,' she said frowning, 'Mam?'

'What is it, hinny? You look all done in.'

'The missus at Number Sixteen – round Phillipson Street – she was shouting at us.'

'Being a pest, were you?' John grunted, slouching contentedly in his fireside chair.

'You shouldn't be out so late,' Rose reproved. 'It's past your bedtime.'

But Catherine hovered by her, perplexed by something.

'Mam,' she hesitated. 'What does bastard mean?'

Kate flinched and Rose gasped, 'Where did you hear such a word?'

'That missus at Number Sixteen,' Catherine repeated solemnly. 'She said, "You're a bastard on the inside and the out!" What did she mean? It wasn't me who knocked on her door – it was Belle.'

John lurched out of his chair. 'The bloody wife! I'll have it out with her!'

'No, John,' Rose said at once, 'leave it be.'

'No one says that to one of mine!' he growled. 'She'll get a piece of my mind.'

Kate felt nauseous. How could the woman be so cruel? She stared at Catherine and the girl looked back baffled.

'It's what Margaret Lodge said,' Catherine said quietly. 'She wouldn't tell me either.'

Kate's stomach churned. 'They said that to you at school, an' all?' she asked in dread.

'Aye. What's it mean?'

Kate set her jaw. 'Means nowt. You get off to bed. I'll bring in your cocoa.'

'But—'

'Now, Kitty!' Kate ordered. She watched her daughter

365

retreat into the back room, puzzled and subdued. Kate gripped the table to stop herself shaking. When the girl was gone, the argument erupted again.

'I'll not have her bad-mouthed by a bunch of dirty Protestants!' John railed. 'Told you she should never have gone there. Should be at a good Catholic school, learning the Faith. Teachers would sharp beat the bad words out the little buggers.'

Kate felt tears sting her eyes. Why did they ever think they could cover up such a scandal? Their old neighbours in Tyne Dock must have known; now the rumours had followed them here. The poison of people's gossip was leaking out around them like dirty water through fingers. She was powerless to stem it.

'I'm off to have it out with that bitch in Phillipson Street,' John shouted, pulling on his cap.

'No, please.' Kate stood in his way. 'It'll just make it worse.'

'I'll not have her saying owt bad about the McMullens. Get out me way.'

But Kate stood her ground. 'The lass'll hear far worse before she's through.' She looked at him steadily. 'I'll tak her out of Simonside and send her to the Catholics, if you don't go bothering that missus.'

John's bleary eyes narrowed at her suspiciously. 'You will?'

'Aye. But not to Father O'Neill. She can gan to St Bede's in Jarrow,' Kate said quickly. 'They'll not know her there. She can start with a clean slate.'

She watched him working it through in his mind. Finally he nodded and sat back down in his chair.

'Pour us a beer then, lass,' he said with a look of satisfaction. 'We'll drink to Kitty gettin' a proper education.'

Kate did as he asked, relieved that a scene had been averted. Yet her heart was sore that she should have to take Catherine

366

away from the respectable parish school where she seemed happy until now. She could only hope that the move to Jarrow would keep the rumours of illegitimacy at bay – that dark cloud of shame that hung over them constantly, threatening its merciless rain.

Chapter 38

Kate took Catherine away from Simonside school the following week. For the rest of the summer term she had to go to a local school in East Jarrow until there was room for her at St Bede's Infant School in the September. Catherine appeared to take this sudden upheaval in her stride and spent the long holidays roaming the lanes and fields that bordered East Jarrow with her friends.

Kate tried to keep her occupied with jobs close to home: pounding the washing in the poss tub, carrying basketloads of other people's washing back to their houses, running to the shops for soap or flour or matches. But even at seven years old, the girl was fiercely independent, disappearing on adventures and returning triumphantly with nuggets of coal from the cinder tracks or pieces of driftwood for the fire.

'Look what I've got you, Kate,' she reappeared one day, dragging in a huge plank of wood and dropping it like a cat its prey.

'You've not been down the Slacks, have you?' Kate fretted.

'No,' Catherine said, her pretty hazel eyes all innocence, crossing her fingers behind her back.

'You have,' Kate accused. 'How many times have I told you it's dangerous to play down there? You could fall in and drown and we'd not find you – just like Jobling's body

368

disappearin' into thin air. It's a bad place – you stay away.'

Catherine's look turned sullen. She kicked the plank. 'I was just trying to help.'

Kate felt a flash of remorse. 'Aye, well, we'll say no more about it. Tak it out in the yard and I'll chop it up later.'

When Catherine came back in, Kate went to the tin on the mantelpiece and took out a halfpenny. She thrust it at the child.

'Here, gan to the shop and get a twist of sweets.'

Her round face brightened. 'Ta, our Kate.'

'Be quick about it, mind. I need you to help me fold the sheets.'

Kate was not surprised when Catherine skipped back in clutching a comic instead of black bullets, and squatted down on the fender at Rose's feet. The girl had begun to read anything she could get her hands on. Mrs Romanus from upstairs had lent her a fat book by Charles Dickens that Kate had thought would give her a headache with all its words. But Catherine followed the words with her finger in deep concentration. Catherine would pester Aunt Maggie to look at her books too.

Best of all, the girl seemed to like comics and annuals with pictures. To Kate's annoyance she could sit by the fire for hours lost in a story world, oblivious to her pleas for help and blocking the way to the oven. Maybe old John was right and the Catholic teachers would knock some discipline into her dreamy head.

Once Catherine started at the Jarrow school, Kate's limited budget was stretched even further. The girl needed money for tram fares and, as it was too far to come home for dinner, she had to take food with her. As the autumn wore on, the family began to slip into debt.

Kate tried to make ends meet with odd jobs: cleaning, mending window frames, taking in washing. But it was not enough. Her hands and arms were red raw from the scrubbing and possing and wringing of heavy linen through the wooden mangle. Her shoes were rotten and feet sodden and itchy from standing in rivers of filthy water in the wash house. At nights she could not sleep for the burning in her arms unless it was dulled by drink.

This was the only help she got from her stepfather, money towards a jar of beer or whisky, when he had not spent his pay in the pubs on the route home. Jack was little better, for he was drinking hard after his shifts unloading from the ships, and did not see the housekeeping as his problem. At home he was lazy and Kate resented the way Rose always made excuses for her son.

'He grafts hard all day; he deserves a bit beer money. He'll pull his weight when he's got a wife and bairns to feed.'

'He's taking his time about it,' Kate muttered.

'That's his business, not yours,' Rose snapped. 'You're the one with responsibilities, so it's up to you to keep a roof over our heads. Me and your father have done it for long enough.'

At times Kate felt overwhelmed with the burden of providing for them all. She avoided the rent man for weeks on end and began regular trips to the pawnshop in Tyne Dock. She dreaded these trips down to Bede Street and having to pass all the neighbours with her bundles on a Monday morning. It brought back memory of the shame of begging in the streets as a child, the hostile or pitying stares of the better off. She, who had been courted by a gentleman and worked at Ravensworth, was now reduced to trading the clothes off her back at the 'in and out'.

But there was no one else to go. Rose was an invalid, the men would have thumped her had she suggested such indignity and Catherine was too young. Desperate women did send their children, but they had to pester an adult to put goods in for them as by law they should be fourteen. She would save her daughter that humiliation.

As the days darkened early and Kate saw no end to the drudgery in her life, she deadened her pain with the searing golden liquid in the earthenware jar she brought home from the Penny Whistle. Fortified with whisky, she forgot the aching in her limbs and the worries over money. When John lashed her with his tongue or struck out with his fist, she answered back. Many was the time she woke in the morning with a sore head and tender bruises on her body and struggled to remember how she had got them. Then vague memories of late-night drinking degenerating into violent rows would flash through her mind.

Each morning Kate dragged herself out of the warm bed she shared with Catherine and steeled herself to face another day. Sometimes Jack would be impossible to wake and he would miss his chance of work for the day. Her parents blamed it on Kate rather than his heavy drinking.

They all saw Kate as their skivvy, even Catherine, who turned to Rose for a cuddle and night-time story by the fireside while Kate washed up and kneaded bread by the dim gaslight.

Only when her sister Sarah made rare visits from Birtley with her young children did Kate feel a glimmer of self-worth. Her niece Minnie was a year younger than Catherine and never hid her delight at seeing her aunt. She would throw herself at Kate's skirts and Kate would lift her up and twirl her round.

'My, look at the size of you! And your bonny hair. Come with me – I've made you a gingerbread man.'

That summer, Kate had even managed a trip to the new playing fields in Jarrow with Sarah and the children.

'You look knackered,' Sarah had said bluntly.

Kate dropped her cheerful front. 'I am. It's that hard at home. They treat me like dirt. I cannot see an end to it, our Sarah.' She looked at her sister in despair and whispered, 'I see me life running away down a dark hole – like water down the drain.'

Sarah had put an arm around her in comfort. 'Find a man,' she counselled. 'Get yoursel' away from there – from that old bastard. As long as he's alive, you'll never be free.'

Kate stared in misery. 'How can I when Father doesn't even let me speak to lads? And who would have me anyhow? I'm over thirty and worth nowt.'

Sarah had shaken her roughly. 'That's what they want you to think! But you are. You've a loving nature and you work like a slave. Course some lad'll want you. You just have to find him!'

So partly from need and partly from Sarah's urgings, Kate decided by the autumn that they should take in lodgers. They were desperate for the money and maybe one of them might be fool enough to want to marry her and be a father to her child. She told Jack to put the word out around the docks. He seemed disgruntled at the idea of sharing, for Kate told him he would have to sleep with the men. But when she promised there would be more food and drink if he did, he soon found workers in need of a bed.

Kate and Catherine gave up their bed for Jack and two men working on the grain ships. The girl went into the parlour with Rose and John, while Kate slept on the settle. It was often late into the night before the men tired of drinking and playing cards around the kitchen table and Kate dozed off on the settle, too exhausted to care.

One night she fell asleep and dreamt that Alexander came back. It was a sweet dream from which she did not want to wake. She saw again vividly the piercing look in his handsome eyes and felt the warmth of his breath on her cheek as he kissed her. She felt the touch of his hands caressing her and the strength in his arms as he lifted her and carried her around the side of the lake.

'My beautiful nightingale, why didn't you come back to find me?' he asked. 'I waited for you, but you never came.'

And then he disappeared and Kate awoke with tears streaming down her face, engulfed in a terrible sense of loss. The following nights she tried to recapture the dream and the feeling of being loved, but could not. She struggled even to remember her lover's face clearly. It seemed so very long ago.

A week later, lying on the settle, she woke with a start. There was someone leaning over her in the dark, breathing hard. Hands pulled at her shoulder.

'Alexander?' she murmured in confusion.

'Kate,' the man slurred. His breath was warm and sour. He shook her more urgently.

Kate came fully awake. 'Jack?'

'Can I lie with you, Kate?' her brother mumbled.

'Jack, man, gan to bed!' she answered impatiently.

He plonked down heavily beside her.

'Do you remember when we used to climb that tree?'

'Aye,' Kate sighed, 'what of it?'

'Canniest time of me life – 'fore you went off to Ravensworth. Carved your name in the tree, I did.'

'You never!'

'Why d'you have to leave and spoil it all?' he said morosely. 'I could've looked after you, Kate. Not like that fancy man who caused you nowt but bother. I love you, our Kate. Do you love me?'

Kate sat up in astonishment. 'Course I love you.'

His head slumped forward. 'No one else does – no other lasses look twice at me,' he mumbled, 'only you, Kate.' Then, to her consternation, he burst into tears. Jack, who prided himself on being as hard as his father, was blubbering like a child. Kate reached out and hugged him to her. He shook and sobbed in her arms, clinging on to her.

'Here, lie down,' she comforted him, 'just for a bit.'

He curled up beside her under the blanket, as he had often done as a boy. 'You won't leave again, will you?' he sniffed.

'Not much chance of that,' Kate sighed, stroking his head.

'Good,' Jack whispered, then leaned towards her and kissed her on the lips. Kate was taken aback. There was something unsettling about such a kiss. She swivelled away. Jack was drunk and would probably be embarrassed by such a show of affection come the morning. She would not remind him of it.

Chapter 39

In the morning she rose early and left Jack sleeping. When he woke he was as grumpy as usual and hardly looked at her. But over the following days she caught him watching her, then he would glance away awkwardly, as if he remembered.

A week later, he rolled home senseless with drink and shook her awake again.

'Give us a kiss,' he pleaded.

Kate pushed him away. 'Leave us be!' she whispered.

'Haway, Kate,' he wheedled, fumbling at her, 'I just want a cuddle, nowt more.'

'No, Jack, it's not right,' Kate told him firmly. 'Gan to your own bed.'

He sloped off and did not bother her again, but Kate could not sleep. She lay awake worrying over Jack's sudden interest, wondering where it might lead. She knew that deep down he would not wish to hurt her, but he was also John McMullen's son. For too long he had seen his father treat her with lecherous contempt; she could not bear for Jack to go that way too. She wondered if she should tell her mother of her concern. But what would she say? There had only been that one kiss on the mouth and some drunken fumbling. Rose would never believe Jack capable of any impropriety; Kate would be blamed for leading him on. She decided to do nothing.

But a few nights later on his way back from the privy, Jack pestered her again. This time she did not bother reasoning with him, but scrambled out of his reach and escaped to the outhouse.

The next day, worn out with lack of sleep, she made a decision. She would save Jack from making a fool of himself, and herself from sleepless nights. She asked around the Penny Whistle. Yes, there were men putting in new boilers at the timberyard who needed cheap bed and board. Kate went home and told her mother.

'We've three more lodgers the night. They can share the bedroom with the others. Jack can have the settle.'

'What about you?'

'I'll gan up to Mary's. She's plenty room.'

Rose snorted. 'You'll not last long there.'

'I'll tak the bairn with us,' Kate declared. 'Mary'll curb her tongue in front of the lass.'

'As long as you're back sharp in the morning to feed the men,' her mother grudgingly agreed to her plan.

Catherine seemed quite happy to stay at Mary's. She fussed over baby Alec and padded around after Mary, touching and marvelling at the beautifully polished furniture and china ornaments. By the time Kate came in late at night, having seen to the evening meal and cleared up, Catherine was tucked up peacefully in the spare feather bed and asleep.

Alec was reading the evening paper. 'Sit yourself down, lass. Mary'll get you a cup of tea,' he smiled.

'She can get it herself,' Mary pouted. 'I'm off to bed. And you should be too.' She gave her husband a warning glare. Alec shuffled his paper in embarrassment and stood up.

'We'll see you in the morning, then.'

'No we won't,' Mary contradicted. 'She'll be down the road to see to them lodgers, won't you? You can't expect me to feed you as well as give you a bed,' she sniffed. 'I've enough to see to with my own bairn.'

'Aye,' Kate said, too weary to argue. Her sister's carping was a small price to pay for keeping away from Number Ten at night-times.

But Mary quickly resented the attention Alec paid Kate, and after a fortnight had tired of showing off her house to the inquisitive Catherine. She caught her going through her dressing table one day. Kate came in to find her daughter tearful and subdued. Mary had beaten her with a hairbrush for handling her things.

'I want to gan back home,' Catherine whined. 'I miss me mam.'

'And I'm tired of having you round here,' Mary snapped. 'Me and Alec want the place to ourselves.'

'Why you have to gan and spoil things?' Kate accused. 'Let us stay a bit longer,' she pleaded to her sister.

'Why should I?' Mary demanded. 'Those boilermen have left.'

'I'm taking in more,' Kate said quickly. 'You've got room, we haven't.'

'Aye, that's typical of you. Jealous of me and what I've got. Just 'cos I've got a good man and canny things. But I've saved up—'

'And I don't have owt to save up!' Kate said, losing her temper. 'Never will have as long as I've always got to put a roof over the bairn's head. Do I have to be punished for that for ever?' She stopped, glancing warily at Catherine. But the girl was staring at her, perplexed by the shouting. She did not understand Kate's anger.

Kate snatched the child's arm. 'Haway, we're not wanted here. We'll gan back to your precious mam!' She stormed into the bedroom and grabbed their nightclothes. Pushing Catherine ahead of her down the stairs, they almost collided with Alec at the bottom.

'Missed your tram?' he joked.

'We're not stoppin' where we're not wanted,' she said brusquely. They left him standing open-mouthed. Halfway down the street, Kate regretted her harsh words and hot-tempered departure. Alec was a kind man who did not deserve her sharp tongue. Damn her family for making her act this way!

That night she made Catherine sleep on the settle with her, uncomfortable though it was. The next day at the Penny Whistle she asked for her wages in liquor and drank half of it before she reached home. She wandered the streets in a mellow daze, smiling at the Saturday shoppers, putting off returning to the New Buildings.

Just as she turned the corner into Leam Lane, she caught sight of a familiar figure running out from under the vast railway arches.

'Kitty!' she cried. 'Hello, hinny.' She lurched into the child's path, catching her foot on the uneven cobbles. She fell against Catherine and they both bumped against the slimy wall leading into the tunnel.

'Sorry, pet,' Kate said, steadying herself. 'Where've you been, eh?'

The girl averted her face and would not look at her.

'Whas a matter?' Kate slurred, pulling her round. 'Been gettin' into bother?'

The girl muttered, 'No, I've been to the pictures with Belle.'

Kate focused on her. She became aware of another small figure in the shadows. Catherine's friend hovered behind.

'Hello, hinny,' Kate said expansively, waving her forward. The girl stayed where she was. Kate turned back to her daughter. 'That's canny of Belle to treat you to the pictures.'

'She didn't.'

'Oh. Where d'you get the money then? Not been thievin', have you?'

Catherine shuffled her feet. 'Our Jack give us it.'

Kate felt her stomach twist at the mention of her brother. It maddened her that he should spoil the girl when she could afford to give her nothing. She felt suddenly belligerent.

'Well, it's all right for some! You shouldn't be playing round here, any road,' she shouted. 'Gerr off home, the pair of you.'

Catherine darted under her arm and was gone, leaving Belle to catch up. By the time Kate had swivelled round on unsteady feet, the girls were already out of shouting distance. But that did not stop her yelling, 'If I catch you down here again, I'll skelp you!'

She felt sick and dizzy as she toiled up the bank, filled with a rage she could not name. It was something to do with the shame of the half-drunk bottle of whisky that weighed so heavily in her coat pocket and the look of panic on her daughter's face when she caught sight of her under the arches. How Catherine had turned away, pretending she had not seen her or did not know her. The girl was ashamed of her. Even in her befuddled state, Kate knew this. And the lass did not even know she was her mother.

The following week, the lodger, Bill, came rushing back early.

'Been an accident down the docks,' he cried. 'Two lads. I heard one was called McMullen.'

379

'Accident?' Kate's insides jolted. 'What sort of accident?'

'Falling timber – legs crushed.'

Rose gave out an anguished cry. 'Not Jack? Not me bairn! Mary Mother, not the lad.'

Kate's heart began to pound. 'Are they – all right?' she whispered.

Bill shook his head. 'Been taken to the infirmary – that's what I heard. Don't know any more, but thought you should know.'

Rose was whimpering in her chair, half praying, half babbling.

'Don't fret, Mam,' Kate tried to calm her. 'There's dozens of McMullens down the docks – could be any one of them.'

Bill gave a sorrowful look. 'Said he was from the New Buildings.'

Rose gave out a wail of distress. Kate threw her arms around her.

'Father'll be back soon. He can gan down the infirmary and find out.'

It frightened her to see her mother this upset; she was usually so strong and never shed a tear. But as they waited and Kate busied herself to stem her nervousness, she could not silence the voice in her head.

What if it's Jack? If he loses the use of his legs, he'll not be able to pester me . . .

What was she thinking? He was her brother and she still loved him. Besides, she did not want another invalid on her hands, tying her down to this place for evermore.

No. If only it had been her father. If only he would never walk through that door again, making her life a misery.

Catherine returned from school and evening came, but John did not.

'Maybes he's at the infirmary,' Kate suggested as she served up the tea to the lodgers and her daughter. Rose and she did not have the stomach to eat.

'I'll go over if you like,' Bill offered.

Kate nodded. 'That would be kind.'

Catherine kept asking questions. 'How did it happen? Has Jack lost his leg? Will he get a wooden one? What'll happen to his old leg?'

Kate could bear it no longer. 'Shut up! Can't you see the state Mam's in without your daft questions? Gan outside and make yoursel' scarce!'

Catherine scrambled off her chair and escaped into the street. Kate watched her skip over to the streetlamp where her friends were gathered. They swarmed around to hear her news. Judging by their wide-eyed looks she was exaggerating the tale.

Kate went back to clearing the table. She was carrying dishes through to the scullery when she heard her mother's cry.

'Mary Mother, it's you!'

Kate dropped the plates with a clatter and hurried into the kitchen. Jack stood there, large as life, his face still grimy from work but unharmed.

'We thought you'd had an accident,' Rose gasped, holding out her arms to him.

'Not me,' he grunted. 'Me da. Keepin' him in for the night. Leg might be broken.'

Rose heaved a sigh of relief. 'Thank the saints it's not you!'

'So old John's all right?' Bill asked.

'He'll live,' Jack muttered. 'Shoutin' at the nurses for baccy and beer when I left him.'

Kate could not speak, as disappointment engulfed her. Yet she was seized with guilt at wanting harm to come to either man.

Catherine came running in. 'Is me da dead?'

'No, hinny,' Rose said. 'He's in the hospital. Be back the morra more than likely.'

Catherine fell into her lap. 'I'll pray to Our Lady for him to get better, Mam. He mustn't die with his sins unwashed.'

'Aye, you do that,' Rose agreed, stroking her head. 'There's a canny pile to wash.'

'Time for bed,' Kate said abruptly. 'I'll sleep with you the night, Mam. Kitty can go on the desk bed.' She avoided Jack's look. 'We'll not leave Mam on her own, will we, lass?'

'Can I sleep next to you, Mam?' Catherine pleaded. 'Our Kate can gan on the desk bed.'

'You'll sleep where I tell you.' Kate was sharp.

Catherine's look was stubborn. 'I want to sleep with Mam. She doesn't smell of whisky like you do.'

Kate reddened. 'Watch your tongue—'

But Rose intervened quickly. 'She can come in me bed – just while Father's not here. Now off you go, Kitty, before I change me mind.'

Catherine scampered off with a triumphant glance at Kate. Kate swallowed her humiliation and stalked back into the scullery.

The next day, John was brought home in an ambulance. The whole of the street came to their doors to gawp. One trouser leg was ripped to the knee and his leg was heavily bandaged. He groaned and winced as he was helped into the house, but Kate suspected he was enjoying the fuss.

'Fought the bloody Afghans and marched with Lord Roberts,' he cried, 'but I've never had pain like this. Shouldn't

382

have let the bloody doctors near me. Fetch me whisky, lass.'

'You'll drink tea,' Rose told him firmly. 'Get him on to the settle. He can give his orders from there.' Her look was unsympathetic.

Over the next few days, John held court from the high-backed bench. Drinking friends came in with bottles of beer and tots of rum, and sat around listening to the story of the accident. It grew in length and seriousness with each telling.

'It's a miracle you're still here to tell the tale,' Kate said drily, after hearing it for the umpteenth time.

'Hold your gob and pour us another drink,' John ordered.

What was certain was that John had no intention of going back to work. A union official came to see him and talked about trying to get compensation from the yard. Kate watched her stepfather visibly puff up with self-importance after the visit. But even she was excited by talk of lump sums. They could pay off all their debts in an instant. The bairn could have new clothes, she new shoes. Maybe she wouldn't have to slave every waking hour to try to make ends meet. Oh, to be able to put her feet up at the end of the day and just sit for an hour!

Kate's spirits rose in hope. There was another bonus to her stepfather's accident too. As he found it so difficult to move around, it was decided he should sleep on the settle for the time being. Every night, Kate escaped happily to the security of the parlour with Rose and Catherine, knowing Jack would not dare follow her there.

Catherine, she noticed, was lording it over her friends with her injured father. She repeated John's story until it became heroic. He had saved the other worker from almost certain death by taking the brunt of the falling timber.

383

'And he used to fight the Afghans,' Catherine boasted, 'so my da's braver than yours.'

Kate thought there was little harm in it. But one chilly Saturday afternoon while she was standing at the kitchen window rolling out pastry, she heard shouting erupt in the back lane. Catherine had been playing 'shops' with some of the other girls, swapping and trading buttons and bits of broken china and coloured glass.

'You took it!' Catherine yelled.

'I never!'

'You did so – I saw you. Show me what's in your hand.'

'Gerr-off!'

Kate wiped her hands on her apron and went to the back door. She was minding baby Alec for Mary and he was sleeping in his pram in the yard. The last thing she wanted was him waking up before she'd finished baking. On the point of calling for hush, Kate stopped. Something about the tone of the argument made her hesitate. There was menace in the other girl's voice.

'What you going to do about it?'

'I'll tell me ma on you,' Catherine cried.

Belle rounded on her. The look of savage triumph on her young face made Kate go cold.

'She's not your ma!'

'She is so,' Catherine exclaimed indignantly.

'She's not. If you want to know, she's your grandma. Me mam says so.'

'No she's not. I'll hit you—'

'Your Kate's your ma. And she drinks. I'd hate to have a ma who drinks like yours.' Belle thrust her face right at Catherine's.

'No, she's never,' Catherine gasped, horrified. 'I'll get me da on you for saying so – and – and he'll belt you one!'

'Your da?' Belle laughed in scorn. 'I'm sick of hearing 'bout your da – 'cos he's not your da neither. He's your grandda. You've got no da!'

Kate felt thumped in the chest. She staggered back out of view, gasping for breath. She could not bear to see the look on her daughter's face. This was the moment she had dreaded since the day Catherine was born. But for her to find out from other children – friends – was too humiliating. She wanted to rush out and shake them till their teeth rattled for their cruelty. But she could not move. All that Belle said was true. Gripping the table to stop herself collapsing, she listened to the vicious taunting of the neighbours' children who all took up the cry.

'You've got no da! You've got no da!'

Through the window she could see them circling Catherine in the lane, chanting as if it was a game. Kate's throat burned.

'What's all that racket?' Rose asked, turning in her chair.

'They know,' Kate whispered. 'Everyone knows.'

'Knows what?'

Kate looked up, her face drained of colour. 'Listen to them, Mam.'

The high-pitched chorus rang out across the icy yard. 'She's got no da! She's got no da! Kitty McMullen has got no da!'

John paused in his game of patience at the table. 'What them little beggars shoutin'?'

'They're teasin' our Kitty,' Rose said in distress. 'They know we're not her ma and da.'

John thumped the table. 'I'll thrash the little wasters!' he cried, going purple in the face. 'If I had the use of me legs . . .! Get after them, woman.' He waved his stick at Kate. 'Chase 'em off!'

But the next moment, Kate saw Catherine bolting through the yard gate, hands clamped to her ears. Tears were streaming down her face. Running towards the back door, she caught sight of Kate at the window and stopped dead.

They stared at each other for a long moment. Kate saw her daughter's young face ravaged with doubt and confusion. The eyes that gazed at her were Alexander's. How could she possibly deny the truth? There wasn't a trace of McMullen in her. Catherine was Alexander's through and through.

Kate smiled tentatively. Perhaps now the truth was out, they could start again. Mother and daughter. Catherine stood, shoulders heaving as she sobbed. She looked so vulnerable and alone. Kate's heart went out to her. She stepped away from the window to go to meet her daughter, throw comforting arms about her. In that instant, she saw fear cross the child's face. Or was it something else? Disgust.

Kate withered inside. Catherine spun round and dashed into the privy. The door slammed and Kate heard the bolt lock. She crossed the yard and stood outside.

'Haway out, hinny,' she coaxed. 'Come for your dinner.'

'G-go away!' Catherine sobbed.

'You shouldn't listen to what Belle says.'

There was loud sniffing, then silence.

'Just silly name-callin'.'

'Go away – I hate you!'

Baby Alec chose that moment to wake up and start crying. Kate gave up with a heavy heart. She picked up her nephew and took him back inside.

'She won't come out the netty,' she told her mother.

'She'll come round,' Rose said.

But they sat on gloomily throughout the afternoon and the girl did not reappear. Eventually Mary came to claim Alec,

386

and the lodgers and Jack came back for tea. Kate went out into the dark yard and hammered on the privy door.

'You have to come out, Kitty. It's past tea time. The men want in the netty.'

There was no reply. Kate lost patience.

'If you don't come out, I'll get Bill to break the door down and hoy you out!'

She heard a movement inside. The bolt slid back and the door opened. Catherine slipped out, shoulders hunched and face averted. She passed like a ghost, pale and silent. Kate followed her back inside.

'Come and sit by me,' John ordered. 'You can share the top of me egg.'

Catherine shot him a look, then slowly took her customary seat beside him.

'What's wrong with me chatterbox?' Bill asked, unaware of the source of the tension.

The girl neither looked at him, nor spoke.

'There's no need to be rude,' Kate scolded, unnerved by her icy silence.

Catherine glowered across the table. Kate filled with sudden fury. What was she supposed to do? She had protected her all she could. But none of them was immune to the bigoted censure of those they lived amongst. She had had to endure their whispering gossip and contemptuous looks for years. Catherine would have found out sooner or later.

That night, the girl did not go to Rose to have her hair combed or stand between her knees while her grandmother checked for lice. She would not go near Rose at all or speak to her. Her look was full of hurt as if she trusted none of them. She went to bed without a word.

Later, Kate found her curled up on the desk bed, hidden under the blankets. When she bent over her, the child shrank from her touch.

'I'm sorry,' Kate whispered, 'sorry you had to hear it like that.'

Catherine burrowed further into the covers.

'It's not easy for me an' all,' Kate sighed. 'But now you know. I'm your mam and you'll have to get used to it.'

Suddenly Catherine emerged, her face hot and tear-stained. Her eyes blazed.

'Never,' she hissed. 'You're not me mam. I hate you.' Her chin trembled as she gulped back more tears. 'You'll never be me ma!'

Kate reeled with shock at the savage words. Her daughter hated her. She had never guessed how much she was despised. But it was written all over the girl's hostile face.

Something inside Kate snapped, a last cord of tenderness towards her troublesome daughter. If her own flesh and blood loathed her so much, what hope had she for love in this bleak world? Alexander had not only deserted her, he had cursed her with a child who despised her so much she would disown her as a mother! Well, she'd waste no more time trying to comfort the girl. Let her stew in her own misery.

Kate got to her feet, blinking back hot tears. She wished she could tear out the pain inside her, run away and never have to face her daughter again. But she was chained to her for ever, tied to this place that was more prison than home. There was only one way to blot out the overwhelming desolation and rage.

Kate swallowed her pride and begged her stepfather, 'Give us a lend and I'll gan fill the grey hen.'

He fished out a coin from his waistcoat pocket and threw it across the table. Avoiding her mother's withering look, Kate scrabbled for the coin and picked up the earthenware jar they kept for fetching whisky. She hurried out into the black, windy night, her step quickening at the thought of liquor. She would drink until she was senseless. Only then would there be no more pain.

Chapter 40

1914

In the spring, John received one hundred pounds in compensation. The mood at Number Ten was joyous.

'That's me set for retirement!' he declared, propping his bad leg on the fender. 'I'll have a new suit for starters – and we'll buy furniture for the parlour like Mary and Alec got. Brand new from The Store. What about that, eh, Rose? And you can treat yourself to a Sunday bonnet, so you can tak the bairn to Mass.'

'I need a new suit an' all,' Jack joined in.

'Can I have a bicycle?' Catherine asked in excitement. 'Please, Da! I could cycle along the cinder tracks and fetch coal on a bicycle.'

'Aye, you can have a bicycle,' John said expansively.

'Eeh, ta!' The girl squealed in delight and clapped her hands.

'After the rent's been paid off,' Kate added, looking up from the ironing.

John waved a dismissive hand. 'The lodgers cover the rent.'

'No they don't.' Kate banged down the iron. 'We've three months owing on the rent.'

'That's your business,' John replied. 'I'm a retired man. I've signed the papers, haven't I, Jack? Said I won't work at Tyne Dock again. Else they wouldn't have coughed up the money.'

Kate stared at him. 'But you will give us some money for the rent, won't you? You've enough to keep the roof over our heads for the rest of the year – and still have plenty to spend.'

John glared back. 'Don't think you're ganin' to see a penny of this. I'm the one who suffered. I'll never walk proper again.'

'Only 'cos you wouldn't let us change the bandages and got infected.' Kate was scathing. 'Too stubborn to let the doctor see to it. That's why you've got a gammy leg.'

It was the wrong thing to say. John went a belligerent red.

'Doctors! They kill more folk than they cure. It's my money and I'll spend it how I want. The housekeepin's your concern.'

Kate was speechless. He was being handed a fortune, but she was the only one not going to see a ha'penny of it. She appealed to her mother.

'Mam, tell him! It's not fair. I deserve a bit too—'

'You've got more than you deserve,' John barked, before Rose could speak. 'You're lucky I didn't hoy you out on the street years ago. So don't you gan tellin' me how to spend me compensation.'

Kate went puce with indignation. But there was nothing she could do about it.

As summer came, she watched John squander the money on clothes and furniture, drinking and betting. Despite his bad leg he managed trips into town to spend his windfall round the pubs. He and Jack went on all-day drinking binges, so that sometimes Kate was the only one bringing in any wages at all. John's money was locked in the drawer of

Rose's sewing box and jealously guarded. Occasionally Rose managed to slip Kate a few coins which she thought John would not miss. Kate spent them on beer, sometimes pressing a ha'penny into Catherine's hand to buy a comic. She saw how the child waited eagerly for John to buy her the promised bicycle, but the weeks went by and it was never mentioned again.

Instead, most of the money went on drink. The men would stagger up the street swearing at children playing late in the twilight and shout obscenities at the neighbours. Late into the night they would sing and curse and fall into argument over whether Britain would go to war with Germany or not. No lodgers would stay more than a night, so Kate gave up trying to keep them. She lay tensely in bed in the back room, praying for the fighting to stop and silence to fall. For only if they passed out with drink did she feel safe.

Even sharing the bed with Catherine did not keep Jack's unwanted attentions at bay. Fortified with drink, he would sneak into their bedroom and seek her out. She would be dragged out of exhausted sleep by a shake on the shoulder and a pleading whisper. 'Please, our Kate, give us a bit love. Just let me lie with you.'

'Gerr-off, Jack!' she would hiss, pushing him away. 'You'll wake the bairn.'

Sometimes it worked and he slunk away. On other nights he cursed her for being heartless and swore he would not stand up for her again. 'Me da's right, you're just a slut,' he would accuse. Only when Catherine stirred would he stagger from the room.

In the morning he would often look at her with remorse, but neither of them spoke of his night-time visits. If only he could get away from John's malign influence, Kate thought bleakly, he would not be like this. The longer he stayed, the more she feared for both Jack and herself.

Another fear that kept Kate awake at night was debt. She woke sweating and pulse racing from nightmares about being hauled in front of the county court for not paying the rent. It terrified her in the same way as the stigma of ending up in the workhouse did. She might be sent to prison – then who would look after her mother and Catherine?

When fear grew insurmountable, she would parcel up John's new clothes for the pawnshop in Bede Street. One Monday morning, when Catherine was moaning about being tired and the long trek to school, Kate snapped.

'You can stay off then and tak these clothes to the in and out.'

The girl looked at her in shock. 'I – I cannot. I'm not old enough.'

'Here's a penny,' Kate said grimly. 'Ask a wife to put them in for you. Gompertz won't mind, he's a canny man.'

'But I don't want—'

'Be off with you! Haven't I got enough on me plate? Don't come back with anything less than ten bob for that lot.'

Kate steeled herself against the girl's pleading look and retreated to the wash house to start the mammoth weekly wash. When she emerged again, Catherine was gone. It was nearly dinner time before she returned and Kate was getting anxious, going into the lane and peering down the hill for any sight of her.

In triumph Catherine spilt the pawnbroker's money on to the table.

'I got twelve and sixpence!'

'Good lass,' Kate grinned in relief. 'I knew you'd spin a good yarn. Here's a halfpenny to keep.'

After that Kate often resorted to keeping her daughter off school for the pawnshop trips. She would rather face the truancy officer than the county court judge any day. And Catherine was sensible and independent for her years. As Rose said, 'She's got an old head on young shoulders.' Kate had her running errands all over the place, even to the Alkali or the Penny Whistle with the 'grey hen'.

'Gan and fetch some beer, hinny,' Kate would say without looking round. For at times Catherine's look could turn mutinous. Her daughter had grown pious since going to the school in Jarrow where they seemed to teach nothing but retribution for the sins of the parents. Kate knew Catherine disapproved of her drinking, but she would not be made to feel guilty. If she only knew the half of it! She had been driven to drink and it was partly Catherine's fault.

Sometimes, when she caught sight of her daughter staggering back up the hill with the heavy jar, slopping beer on to her boots, Kate felt pangs of remorse. Perhaps she was too hard on the child. What right had she to take out her anger at the world on the lass? But it was a cruel world. She fended for Catherine as best she could like any mother, yet she received none of the love and respect that a mother should. Rose still got that. So Kate smothered her feelings of pity and drank deeply from the grey hen.

In July, to Kate's delight, Jack's sailor friends, Stoddie and Davie, returned from a year at sea. John seemed to have forgotten the jealous brawl over Kate that had precipitated their departure the previous summer and was pleased to have new drinking companions.

After an evening of eating and drinking and tales of their trip to South America, John decreed, 'You can kip here the night. Kate and the lass can give up their bed.'

The seamen ended up staying for the week, spending their pay freely on the household and slipping Kate extra for pickles and tinned fruit and a piece of brisket for the Sunday dinner. She enjoyed having them around the house. Stoddie made her laugh with his jokes and banter, while quiet brawny Davie helped carry in coal and kept the fire stoked.

'You don't have to do that,' Kate smiled.

'Maybe not,' Davie gave a bashful look of his brown eyes, 'but it's done.'

At night they had long sing-songs, with Stoddie playing on the harmonica. Catherine would watch them cautiously from the doorway and resist Kate's attempts to get her to perform.

'Give us one of your poems, Kitty,' Kate cried. 'She's got a grand voice.'

'Just like her bonny big sister,' Stoddie winked.

Kate blushed with pleasure. At least with these men she could pretend to be respectable.

'Haway, lassie, give us a song,' Stoddie encouraged.

After several nights of coaxing, Catherine was persuaded. She stood in front of the fire and recited part of *The Rime of the Ancient Mariner*. The applause was so loud, she grinned and sang 'Sweet Waters of Tyne'. For twenty minutes she went through her repertoire, playing up to her merry audience, dancing on the hearth, her pretty face lively.

'You've a star there, John,' Stoddie cried, and stamped his feet in approval.

'Aye, head's full of stories and nonsense too,' John grunted. But he smiled at the girl, pleased.

'Now it's Kate's turn,' Stoddie grinned. 'She sings like a wee nightingale.'

Kate felt a pang. No one since Alexander had ever said

that to her. She smiled at him and stood up to sing. Soon she was lost in the words and the music. This was the closest she came to true happiness, the room silenced and the music welling up from the depths of her being.

Afterwards, Kate felt bathed in a warm glow of wellbeing and wished such moments could go on for ever, the cares of the day quite forgotten. She noticed how Catherine had crept on to the knee of the gentle Davie, her sleepy head lolling against his broad chest. He seemed to have a way with children, though he had none of his own.

She wished her daughter had chosen Stoddie's lap, for she was aware that her own feelings for the handsome sailor were growing. If only something could come of it, he might be the man to give Catherine a proper father.

But in the morning they left.

'Gone back to Cumbria,' Jack told her. 'Davie's got a wife, remember – and Stoddie's a lass in every port. There's nowt to keep them here.'

Kate flushed. It struck her that Jack might be jealous of his friends. They were experienced men who had travelled the world and were confident with women. Jack was none of these. He was awkward and shy. He admired the older men, yet seemed to resent the attention they gave to Kate. She was saddled with his protective jealousy as much as John's vindictiveness. What chance did she have of walking out with Jock Stoddart?

Then events far beyond Jarrow shook them all out of their daily troubles. The threat of war rumbling in Europe suddenly sparked into reality. In early August the newspapers blared the news that Austria had declared war on Serbia, followed days later by Germany waging war on Russia and France.

'Read it to me, lass,' John ordered Kate. They were gathered around the table for tea.

' "Herbert Asquith, the Prime Minister, was loudly cheered as he gave MPs details of the ul-ti-ma-tum calling on Germany to respect the neutrality of Belgium",' Kate read.

'What's ultimatum mean?' Catherine piped up.

Jack answered excitedly, 'It means if the Hun gan into Belgium we'll fight 'em.'

'Where is Belgium?' the girl asked. 'Is it near Shields?'

'No, Kitty,' Kate reassured, 'it's a long way away.'

'Aye, but the Hun are just across the German Sea,' John said, pointing his thumb over his shoulder. 'They could be sailing up the Tyne in hours.'

Catherine's eyes widened in alarm. 'Shall I gan and look, Da?'

He snorted in amusement. 'Not yet, lass. We're not at war the day.'

But by the next, news spread that Germany had marched into Belgium. People went out into the streets as word went round that war had been declared.

'Didn't I tell you?' Jack cried with glee at his father. 'Said we'd have a scrap on our hands.'

'Well, don't you go thinking of taking the King's shillin',' Rose fretted. 'You're needed here.'

Jack made for the door. 'I'm off out to see what's happening.'

'Can I come an' all?' Catherine asked, jumping up.

'Haway then,' Jack agreed, and she ran out after him.

She came back looking puzzled. 'They've not come yet.'

'Who haven't?' John demanded.

'The Germans. I went down the Slacks to have a look, but there's no soldiers.'

397

John laughed. 'Course not, you daft lass.'

'When will it start?' Catherine persisted.

'What start?' John grew impatient at the questioning.

'The war. Doesn't look like it's started to me.'

John just shook his head and laughed.

Kate tried to reassure her. 'We'll see nowt different round here. The war's a world away – 'cross the English Channel.'

But the long hot days of August did bring changes around the town. Troops marched into Tyne Dock one day and arrested the hapless crew of a ship, *Albert Clement*, that had sailed in from the White Sea with timber. Each Saturday, bands played through the town and posters were slapped to baking brick walls, encouraging men to join up. The sight of men in uniform became common as every workplace, sporting club and social group scrambled to form a company of volunteers.

A wave of patriotism swept Tyneside and the mood was optimistic.

'We'll have 'em beat by Christmas,' Jack crowed.

John shook his head. 'Na. It'll gan on a lot longer. It's never over quick – I know all about war.'

'Aye, war in the Dark Ages,' Jack scoffed. 'But we've got the best fleet in the world and modern guns and that.'

John snorted, 'And the same old generals that don't know their arse from their elbows.'

The arguments erupted every evening like summer storms. As well as John's pessimism over the war, he became fixated about German spies.

'That butcher down Tyne Dock, he's one,' he declared.

Kate laughed. 'Gebhart? He sounds Geordie to me when he opens his gob.'

'That's 'cos he's a spy,' John replied with conviction. 'They're clever like that.'

398

Rose was dismissive. 'He's been there as long as I can remember. Don't think he's even been to Germany.'

'What would you know?' John snapped. He grabbed hold of Kate's arm. 'I don't want you buying owt from that foreigner, you hear?'

Kate threw off his hold. 'Chance would be a fine thing! Can't even afford the scraps off the floor.'

'Well, I'm tellin' ye,' he growled.

Later, when Kate was helping Rose to bed, they laughed about his suspicions. 'Daft bugger,' Rose whispered, 'doesn't even trust his own shadow.'

But when the shock news of defeat and retreat from Mons filtered back, there were outbreaks of violence against businesses and people who sounded German. Windows were smashed and shops set on fire by roaming mobs. Men like Gebhart, who had lived in the town for years, were rounded up and taken away, no one knew quite where. But it pleased John.

By September, there was no more talk of the war being over by Christmas, only an increase in recruitment posters. Everyone would have recognised Lord Kitchener had they passed him in the street. Scores of men were volunteering daily, so many that local councils were giving over schools and public buildings for barracks to house the flood of eager recruits. Rose grew increasingly anxious Jack would do something foolhardy, while John took pleasure in baiting his son.

'He's not got the stomach for real fightin'. Anyone can scrap on a Saturday night round Jarrow.'

Then, unexpectedly, Stoddie strolled in one day dressed in the uniform of the Tyneside Scottish.

'What you doing here?' Kate cried in delight. 'And look at you! You suit a uniform.' She blushed as he pinched her cheek.

'About to board ship when I ran into a couple of the boys. Had a few bevvies and the next thing we're doon the recruiting office . . .!'

A place was quickly set for him at the tea table.

'So why aren't you in barracks?' Jack asked, his look envious.

'They're overcrowded,' Stoddie grinned. 'Giving us two shilling a day extra for bed and board. So thought I'd stay here a week or two.'

'Course you can,' Kate said quickly.

Within two days of Stoddie's appearance, Jack plucked up courage to defy his mother and join up. He had been roaring drunk at the time, according to Stoddie, who was on the same drinking binge. So drunk was Jack that he gave his place of birth as Tyne Dock instead of Jarrow. But he joined the Durham Light Infantry, his father's old regiment, which provoked unaccustomed praise.

'Good on you, lad! You've got some of your father's Irish spirit after all. It'll make a man of ye!'

Rose was only mollified by the thought that he had to live at home for the time being until proper training camps were found. Jack took a new delight in polishing his own boots and strutting around the streets in his new uniform, attracting admiring glances from neighbours who had teased or ignored him for years.

Kate was secretly pleased at the development, for some day soon Jack would have to leave home. In the meantime she enjoyed the mellow late summer days with Stoddie returning from drill and walking her to the end of the lane and back, with the excuse of looking for firewood. Usually Jack tagged along too, like an unwanted stray. Only on Stoddie's last night did he slip out of the pub early and come back to see Kate.

They stood at the end of the street gazing down on the mass of shipping on the river. The yards were working to capacity and there was talk of bringing in men from the south to fill the jobs left by the thousands who had already joined up.

'What time do you leave the morrow?' Kate asked quietly.

'Train goes at ten.'

'Are you – going to France?'

'Aye.'

'I'll miss you,' Kate murmured.

'I'll miss you too.' He took hold of her hand. 'Kate, will you be my lassie?'

Kate held her breath. Was he proposing to her? She did not dare speak, for fear she was assuming more than he meant. She waited.

'Can I write to you, Kate?'

'Aye, I'd like that,' she smiled cautiously. 'But it might be best if you sent any letters to Mary's at Number Thirty. It's just Father – and you being Presbyterian. Mary'll pass them on to me.'

'If you want,' Stoddie agreed amiably. 'And you'll write back?'

'Of course,' she said quickly.

'That's grand,' he grinned. He put an arm around her shoulders and plonked a beery kiss on her cheek. And that was how it was left, with Kate hoping more than knowing that Stoddie was her intended.

Chapter 41

1915

When King George visited Jarrow in May to view Palmer's works, and the streets were choked with crowds come to gaze on their distant monarch, Kate stood in a queue for flour all morning and missed it.

Catherine came tearing in after school. 'They let us go and watch. We got union flags to wave. I think I saw him riding in this big black motorcar, though maybes it was the mayor. Any road, I waved and he waved back – right at me,' she smiled, glowing with pride.

'What you want to see him for?' John ridiculed.

'He's the King,' Catherine answered reprovingly. 'I wish I could see his palace and ride in a that big motorcar,' she added wistfully.

John spat into the fire. 'Down with kings and freedom for the Irish, say I!'

Kate gave the girl a look as if to say, don't bother what he thinks. 'Here, hinny,' she said out loud, 'I got a bit ginger powder from Afleck's the day, you can help me make gingerbread men. We'll give one a crown and call him George, eh?'

Catherine smiled and rolled up her sleeves.

As the evening sun glowed furnace orange over the opposite row, Catherine sat on the fender munching their baking while Rose darned a stocking and Kate read aloud from the *Shields Gazette* to John. It was one of those rare moments of peace that settled on the household when bellies were full and tempers calm. Jack had at last moved into barracks – a converted school – and came home more seldom. He was on coastal watch from Shields down to Whitburn, a more dangerous job since surprise attacks along the east coast had shaken them all. Hartlepool had been bombed from the sea. The war was no longer far away but lapping at their door. Still, arguments were rarer without him there and he seemed happier than he had been for years on occasional visits home.

The continuing war in Flanders had also given John a new interest outside the confines of William Black Street and he was avid for any scraps of news.

'It says here they're wanting lasses at the shell factory,' Kate said casually. 'Short of workers. Listen to this. "The Government has issued an urgent appeal to the women of Britain to serve their country by signing on for war work. The aim is to get as many women as possible doing vital jobs so that men can be freed for fighting." ' Kate slid her stepfather a cautious look.

'You're not ganin' to work in a factory.' John was adamant.

'Why not?' Kate protested. 'They pay canny wages – much better than I can get cleaning.'

'They don't mean lasses like you.' John was disparaging. 'They want young 'uns. Ones that don't have a bairn to look after.' He gave her a sour look.

'I could work while the bairn's at school,' Kate reasoned.

'They'll want you at all hours of the night and day. And who's ganin' to get your mother up in the night? Or make the dinner?' John shook his head. 'No, no. You're not ganin' to work in no factory. Full of foremen from the south takin' all the best jobs and tryin' to steal our lasses an' all.'

Kate clenched the newspaper in anger. All he thought about was his own comfort and keeping her away from other men. He did not care if it meant she could manage the housekeeping more easily, or that she might have some money of her own to spend how she wanted. On a little bit of drink. How she craved a drink now. But even John's compensation was running out and the only time she tasted liquor was when Jack came back and slipped her a few pennies.

She choked back words of protest, knowing it would only make him the more intransigent. Kate's look fell on Catherine's auburn ringlets. They glinted with copper lights just like Alexander's. The girl was writing in an exercise book that Jack had pinched for her from the school where he was billeted. It reminded her abruptly of Alexander, head bent over his sketch book, totally absorbed. It was too painful.

'Kitty, off to bed!' she said sharply.

Catherine looked up, startled.

'What you writing all them daft words for?' Kate cried, venting her anger. 'You'll give yoursel' a headache. And no one's ganin' to read them!'

Her daughter's expression tightened, but she said nothing. She rose, tucking the book under her arm, and stalked off to the bedroom without a word of good night.

Kate felt wretched for her harsh words, but the resentment curdled inside her. Catherine was a like an ache in her side, forever reminding her of her shameful mistake and her deeply buried yearning for the man she had loved. She loved and hated the child as keenly as she did Alexander. Where was he now? Despite the passing years she still wondered about him and what might have been. Did he have other children? Had he enlisted? Was he still alive? So many of the officer class had already been slaughtered on the battlefields of Flanders, according to the long lists of casualties in the newspapers. But she had never spotted his name.

Kate busied herself banking up the fire and tidying the room for the night. Only tiring activity kept such tortured thoughts at bay. She berated herself for even thinking of Alexander. The evenings were long now, but they still had to pull the new blackout blinds against the threat of Zeppelin raids. As John sat and watched her helping her mother to bed, Kate determined that her only chance of escape was with Stoddie.

He had written twice from France; short, cheerful, precious letters that Mary had brought round. She had written back, scrounging the postage from Mary, but heard nothing from him since Easter. Still, he was her hope. By the time Kate had settled Rose comfortably, Catherine was already asleep in the bed they shared. The exercise book was tucked under her pillow. Kate pulled it out and flicked it open. In the dim candlelight she could see pages of uneven, scrawly writing, most of which she could not decipher. Only the title was clear. 'The Wild Irish Girl'.

Kate sighed and smiled wryly. She had been listening to too many of John's fanciful yarns about Ireland. She was a strange, fey child, yet with a stubbornness to match the McMullens when she wanted. Kate felt suddenly fearful for her daughter. It didn't do around here to be different. Everyone was waiting for Catherine to show signs of going the way of her mother, of getting above herself. All this scribbling in notebooks would just give them another chance to tease and point their fingers.

Kate hesitated. Should she simply throw it on the fire now and stem this strangeness? She gazed at the child's soft face, purged in sleep of her troubled frown. How beautiful and innocent she looked. Kate was gripped by a fierce protective pride. Gently she pushed the book back under Catherine's pillow.

In June, war struck at the heart of Jarrow. On a moonlit night the quiet was shattered by sirens wailing and the eerie drone of airships. Then the ground shook as bombs exploded over Palmer's shipyards. Catherine came screaming awake. Without thinking, Kate ran out into the yard to see what was happening. Perhaps they were being invaded. The whole sky was streaked with flames, and acrid smoke fanned uphill on the night breeze.

'Is it the Fritzes?' Catherine wailed from the door.

'I cannot see. Get back inside and hide under the bed!'

The clang of a fire engine's bell sounded below, near the river.

Kate ran back inside and slammed the door. She bolted into the parlour, expecting to find John up and ready to defend them. Both her parents lay sleeping, oblivious to the noises outside. Typical! Kate thought. She'd lost count of the nights he'd dragged them out of bed, brandishing the fire poker and made them stand shivering to attention in their nightclothes.

Yet their sleeping unconcern was comforting and she closed the door so as not to wake them. Crouching down, she joined Catherine under the bed. She sang songs to calm them both, still half expecting the front door to splinter open and

German soldiers to march in. But none came. Eventually the lurid light in the sky died and the dawn came early. They crept back to bed and slept.

The news was all over Jarrow before the evening newspapers told the stark facts. A Zeppelin attack on Palmer's had hit the machine and engine shops. Twelve men on nightshift had been killed. Five others died in the ensuing fire. The town was stunned.

Funeral processions and sombre bands dominated the following week. Foreigners had their shops attacked once more. Gebhart's family put a sign in their window, 'God Save the King', but had their windows smashed anyway.

'They're trying to poison us,' John declared. 'Don't you buy owt from that Boche shop.'

Kate ignored him; they could not afford to anyway.

Playing fields and parks were ploughed up and planted with crops as the queues outside grocers lengthened and supplies on shelves dwindled. Occasionally the newspapers alluded to German U-boats causing losses to shipping and disruption to imports. Catherine went out to watch a huge pontoon dock being towed into the Slake for the repair and refit of battleships and cruisers. The river had never looked more crowded.

Then, at the height of summer, Mary came round with a letter written on wafer-thin paper. Kate sat down with the shock.

'Stoddie,' she gasped. 'He's a prisoner.'

Catherine looked up wide-eyed from the table where she was writing.

'Stoddie's captured?'

Kate nodded, too flustered to mind that John could hear.

'What's he writing to you for?' he demanded.

407

' 'Cos he's courting our Kate,' Mary answered before Kate could. 'Didn't you know?'

Kate flashed her an angry look.

'No, I didn't,' John scowled.

But Catherine butted in. 'Poor Stoddie. How's he managed to send a letter from prison? Is he not chained up?'

'It's been sent by a German chaplain – through the Red Cross. That's what it says.' Kate's eyes smarted. 'He wrote it months ago. He and some other lads were taken at Ypres in April. No wonder I hadn't heard . . .'

'Can I write to him?' Catherine asked. 'I think it's terrible, him being in prison. I heard they give them babies to eat.'

Kate felt sick. 'Don't talk daft.'

'It's true, isn't it, Da? The Fritzes are cannibals.'

Kate glared at her stepfather. Trust him to be filling the child's head full of nonsense.

'Aye, you can write to Stoddie,' she said, daring John to defy her, 'keep his spirits up.'

'I don't think that's proper for the lass,' Mary sniffed, 'writing to a man that's not her kin.'

'It's none of your business,' Kate snapped, 'so keep your big nose out of mine.'

'Well, it's not as if you're engaged,' Mary continued to needle. 'From what Jack says, that man's got sweethearts from here to Shanghai.'

Kate was riled. 'He asked me to be his lass before he went!'

'You never said owt to me about it!' John exclaimed.

'No, she's too sly,' Mary said waspishly. 'Asked him to write to my house so you wouldn't know what she's up to.'

'Mary!' Rose warned.

408

But Mary could see from Kate's thunderous face that she had got the better of her. She could not resist adding, 'You know what she's like with lads.'

'You little slut!' John cried, seizing hold of the poker. 'And with that Scotchman.'

Kate rounded on her sister. 'You can't bear the thought of me having a bit of happiness, can you? Any chance of finding a lad and you'd spoil it! At least my Stoddie's brave enough to join up and fight for his country. I'd rather have him a prisoner of war than have a yella-bellied conchie for a husband!'

Mary went scarlet. 'My Alec's no conchie,' she shouted. 'He tried to join up but his health was bad.'

'Jack was right,' Kate was contemptuous, 'he never tried hard enough. And you wouldn't have let him, 'cos it would mean a bit of hardship. And Alec won't say boo to a goose. People like you just let every other bugger do the dirty work while you stay safe at home!'

Mary flew at Kate, shrieking, 'You bitch!'

They tore at each other's hair and clothes, screaming their hatred.

'White feather! White feather!'

'Dirty cow! I hate you!'

Rose cried at them to stop but to no avail. Catherine jumped back from the table as they crashed into it, scratching at each other's faces.

'Stop it, stop it,' she cried in agitation.

Only John seemed to be enjoying the spectacle, stabbing the poker in the fire and laughing. 'Couple of wild cats you've raised there, Rose Ann.'

The fight only ended when Alec appeared unexpectedly, looking for his wife. He pulled Mary away and she fell into his arms bawling at Kate's savagery.

Kate stood panting and staring at the man she had just maligned so unfairly. She wanted to say sorry, but could not bring herself to be humble in front of Mary. Her sister had started it, deliberately stirring up trouble.

Alec led his wife away, with Mary shouting, 'I'll never speak to you again! Don't think you or your brat can stay under my roof. I'll not lend you a penny neither. You'd only drink it, you drunken slag. Stay away, do you hear?'

Kate stood shaking and trying not to cry. She throbbed where Mary's nails had torn her skin. She cursed herself for losing her temper so quickly. Catherine watched her warily from Rose's side.

'What you looking at me like that for?' Kate accused. 'You can help me clear up the mess.'

Kate bent to the task of picking up the broken plates that had fallen off the dresser, before anyone could see the tears flooding her eyes.

'What did I tell you, Rose Ann?' John said in contempt. 'That one's bad through and through. Should've taken the belt to her before she could answer back.'

Kate carried on, hot with shame at her outburst. Only later did it occur to her that her stepfather might have been maligning Mary and not her. After all, she lorded it over them all. Perhaps he approved that the uppity Mary had been taken down a peg or two. Whichever it was, it achieved one thing. John did not stop Catherine sending chatty letters to Stoddie to comfort him behind enemy lines.

The summer wore on in uneasy calm. There were no more raids on Tyneside, but Mary was not speaking to any of them and sent Catherine away with a sharp word when she tried to visit. The girl contented herself with playing in the street,

410

organising the other children into games during the long evenings and staying closer to home. She showed flashes of affection towards Kate, helping her at the clippy mat when it rained, and buying her a pear on her birthday.

'Me favourite!' Kate cried in delight. 'Come here, hinny, and we'll share it together.'

For a few brief minutes they sat on the step in the sun while Kate peeled the ripe pear and handed half to Catherine. They munched and slurped the fruit.

'Don't waste it,' Kate cried, seizing the girl's fingers and licking them as the juice ran down, before Catherine could wipe them on her pinafore. They smiled shyly at each other. Then Rose's voice came querulously from inside.

'What you doing? Kate! I need helping to the netty.'

Kate sighed and stood up. 'Ta, pet,' she said, resting her hand for an instant on her daughter's head. They held each other's look and Kate wished she could find the words to say how much the gesture had pleased her. No one else had thought to buy her a birthday present. Mary might have if they'd been speaking, but they weren't. The child must have saved up her tram fares to school to buy such a treat and scoured Shields for fresh fruit.

'Kate! Haway and help me!' Rose shouted again.

Kate hurried inside and by the time she returned from the privy with her lumbering mother, Catherine had disappeared to play. Yet Kate was encouraged by her daughter's softening towards her and wondered if it was partly because Mary was absent and not filling the girl's head with spiteful words about her.

Then one Saturday, Catherine surprised her by announcing, 'I'm ganin' to Cissy's party this afternoon. Will you do me hair nice, our Kate?'

411

'Whose party?' Kate questioned.

'Cissy Waller's – round in Phillipson Street,' Catherine said, hopping excitedly round the kitchen.

'You never told me you'd been invited.' Kate was surprised but pleased. The Wallers were a respectable family in one of the grander upstairs houses.

'Everyone's ganin',' Catherine beamed. 'Belle's gone off to get ready. Will you put a new ribbon in me hair? And can I have a clean pinny?'

'No, it needs ironing,' Kate answered.

'Please, Kate!' she begged. 'I'll iron it.'

Kate laughed. 'All right. Pop a coal in the iron and I'll clear the table. Mind you don't burn yoursel'.'

She supervised Catherine's ironing, listening to the child chatter about the afternoon's party.

'We're having games – and cake – and loads of sweets. Cissy said. Best party in the street.'

'Is Belle calling round for you?' Kate asked.

'Aye, she will,' Catherine nodded.

Kate was pleased that her daughter had asked her to do her hair and not Rose. She had noticed how the child avoided standing so close to her grandmother since the sour smell of her incontinence had grown more noticeable in the summer heat. Rose sat with legs swollen and sweating in her chair, trying to catch any breeze by the open kitchen window, issuing fretful orders for cups of tea or help to the privy. As it was, Rose was dozing, unaware of the excitement.

When Catherine was ready she skipped out into the yard and waited by the gate. Kate noticed for the first time how quiet it was in the back lane. Only two small boys were throwing pebbles at a tin can. A sudden unease stirred within.

'What time's the party?' Kate called.

'Two o'clock,' Catherine said, peering up and down the lane.

Kate glanced at the clock on the mantelpiece. It was a quarter past two. Her stomach clenched. From the yard gate it was possible to see into the back of the Wallers' house. She forced herself to go and look. The upstairs windows were open, the net curtains lifting in the breeze. Behind them she could see children running around in some game, the noise of their laughter and excited squeals clear across the deserted lane.

'Look, there's Cissy!' Catherine cried. 'And Belle. She's forgotten to come and get me.' Her daughter turned and grinned.

Kate felt punched in the guts. She stared at her in pity. The poor child did not realise she had not been invited.

'I'm here!' Catherine waved across, jumping up and down to attract the attention of her friends. No one appeared to notice. 'They can't hear me. I'll gan and knock on the back door.'

Kate put out a hand to stop her. 'No, Kitty. It's no use.'

Catherine stared at her in astonishment. Her face creased in a frown. 'I'm missing the party,' she said indignantly, shaking off her mother's hold. The girl ran out of the yard and across the lane. As she clattered up the back steps, Kate could hear jaunty piano music strike up opposite. Her stomach twisted in fear for her daughter as she watched her knock on the neighbours' door. No one answered. Catherine hammered harder.

Suddenly the door swung open and Cissy appeared, flush-faced. Crowding behind, Kate glimpsed other girls, their hair tied up in fancy ribbons like Catherine's. Kate held her breath. Please God, let her in! She was too far away to hear what was

413

being said, but she could read the expression on her daughter's face. The eagerness of moments before had vanished.

Cissy's voice was raised. There was laughter from the others. Then the door slammed shut. For a stunned moment, Catherine stood on the steps gazing red-faced at the closed door. Kate gulped. Damn them for their cruelty!

'Hinny,' she called hoarsely. 'Haway home, pet.'

Catherine turned and retreated, head bent in humiliation. As she came through the gate, Kate put out an arm in comfort.

'I'll give you a penny to gan to the pictures – it's not too late,' she offered.

But Catherine ducked away and would not look at her.

Kate swallowed. 'Never you mind them, hinny,' she said angrily. 'They count for nowt.'

Catherine turned and raised huge tearful eyes at her. The child's look of desolation made Kate nearly choke at such unfairness. She reached out and grabbed the girl, before she could dart away.

'You listen to me, lass,' Kate urged. 'The day'll come when you'll be laughing at them. You're worth twice as much.' She gazed at her forlorn daughter, willing her to be strong. 'You'll see your day with them – get your own back. By God, you will!'

And as she stared past the girl at the house beyond, filled with bitter fury, she vowed there and then, she would live long enough to see that day.

Chapter 42

The winter months that followed the brief spell of calm at Number Ten William Black Street were gruelling. Food queues lengthened and more women left the home to work long hours in the armaments factories along the riverside. News from the front was grim. In December, the Allies retreated from Turkey after huge losses at Gallipoli. Conscription was introduced in January of 1916, and by February the Germans had overwhelmed the French at Verdun.

Prices soared on tea and tobacco and other foodstuffs. When the cheap halfpenny post was abolished, Kate ordered Catherine to stop writing to Stoddie.

'We can't afford the paper, never mind the stamp,' she said firmly. Besides, the Scotsman had only written once to the child and never to her, and Kate knew it was foolish to hold on to the dream that he would return and marry her. Jack had been right: Stoddie had probably said the same to other lasses and had meant nothing by it. Maybe he would never return, for there seemed no end to this war.

When Catherine protested, Kate had sent her off to queue for beer at Daglish's drink shop in Cuthbert Street. Kate did not like to admit that the decision was partly to do with the arrival of a new lodger, Danny MacQuade. He was handsome and genial and liked to spend his pay from the yards on drink. John approved of him because he was Catholic Irish and a Fenian, and many cold dreary nights were made more bearable by Danny's whisky and ready smile. He soon made no attempt to hide his interest in Kate and, to her astonishment, John did not answer his blarney with fists and swearing.

'Let's drink to your beautiful daughter,' Danny would toast. 'The prettiest girl in Jarrow by far, so she is.'

'You could do worse,' John grunted. 'She's hard-working. Bit too fond of the beer, mind. And the lads.'

Danny winked at her. 'I'll drink to that,' he grinned.

'What she needs is a good strong Irishman to keep her in her place.' John gave a lecherous laugh. 'That's where she's gone wrong.'

Kate put up with the jesting because Danny's was good-natured and she looked forward to the drinking at the end of a hard day of scrubbing pub floors, queuing and making meagre rations go round. She enjoyed the attention he gave her and the daring kisses and squeeze of the waist when John had staggered to bed. He began to drop hints that it was time he found himself a wife and Kate dared hope it might be her. Sometimes she felt guilty about Stoddie, but Danny was here and in work and could provide for her daughter now. Stoddie was out of reach and might never return. If there was a chance of becoming a respectable wife she would seize it.

Only Catherine was a problem. Despite Danny being kind and friendly towards her, she was rude to him, pretending she did not hear when he called her over and offered her sweets. After a few weeks she would run off rather than sit on his knee and listen to his jokes.

'Why won't you like him?' Kate asked her in exasperation.

Catherine fixed her with a stubborn look. 'I like Dr Dyer. He gave me a ride in his motorcar.'

Kate was baffled. 'What's Dr Dyer got to do with anything?'

'He's canny and he's got no wife. Why can't you court him?'

Kate looked at her dumbfounded. 'Don't talk so daft! He wouldn't look twice at the likes of me.'

'He thinks you're canny,' Catherine persisted.

Kate was flustered. She liked the young doctor who had delivered her daughter, but he was as beyond her reach as Alexander. She would not make that mistake again and she would not have the girl making a fool of them all with her fancy notion.

'You haven't been making up stories about me and the doctor, have you?' She took hold of Catherine roughly. The girl avoided her look. 'Don't you dare say owt about it. You'll land us all in trouble with your silly tales. There's nowt between me and Dr Dyer and never can be. I'm courtin' Danny, whether you like it or not. He might be your da one day if you're lucky.'

'Never!' Catherine said with a look of horror.

'Don't you go spoiling me chances of a good man!' Kate cried in alarm. 'Even Father thinks he's a canny match.'

Catherine tore out of the house without another word and did not come back until after dark. She grew more wilful by the day, vomiting up the precious food Kate cooked her and refusing to go to school. She woke her at night with strange babbling and several times Kate found her wandering about the yard in her nightdress, letting in the bitter cold air. Kate could not fathom her behaviour and blamed it on the worsening war.

417

Then one raw spring evening, Kate came in feeling mellow after sharing a drink with Maisie after work. At once she noticed that Danny's canvas bag was gone from the settle where he slept at night. Rose's face was in shadow, but Catherine sat at her feet, subdued and quiet.

'Where's Danny?' Kate asked in confusion.

'He's scarpered,' John snarled from his chair.

'What d'you mean?'

'Didn't want you after all,' John sneered. 'More interested in the bairn, the Fenian bastard. Found him out the back when I went to feed the hens – hands up her skirt—'

'John, that's enough,' Rose interrupted, her voice heavy.

Kate's stomach heaved. She stared at Catherine, but the girl looked away.

'I d-don't believe you,' she stuttered. 'Danny's a grand man. He wouldn't . . .'

'Well, I gave him a taste of McMullen medicine,' John said grimly. 'Kicked him down the street. You'll not see him again.'

Kate was stunned. One minute she was courting the handsome Irishman and dreaming of marriage, the next he was gone. It did not make sense. And all over the lass! How could he have done that to her? Kate was filled with disgust and disappointment.

'Are you sure . . .?'

Rose leant forward so that her chiselled, pained face showed in the firelight. 'He was a bad 'un and you're well shot of him. We'll hear no more of it.'

Kate clenched her fists and fought back bitter tears. 'Kitty – I'm sorry,' she gulped, leaning down to hold the child. But Catherine flinched away from her touch.

Kate forced herself to get on with the chores, though she

wanted to run to the bedroom and howl into the bed clothes. She hated Danny for his betrayal, appalled that he could have been molesting her daughter while winning her with sweet words. Danny had thought so little of her virtue that he even took advantage of her child. No wonder the girl had been acting so strangely of late.

Kate fought off nausea to think of it. She would not be so easily taken in again, by God she would not! She was destined to the purgatory of the unmarried mother. Well, if that was her fate, she would let no man touch her heart again.

Danny MacQuade was never mentioned after that, but his memory lay like a festering sore between Kate and her daughter, a source of guilt and resentment to them both. Catherine hardly spoke to her mother, just threw mutinous looks and turned her back. Kate found herself shouting at Catherine all the more for her increasingly unruly behaviour. But the damage had been done. She had not been there to protect her daughter from Danny's lecherous attention and now Catherine seemed to be punishing her for it. Kate lost count of the times neighbours came complaining to her door at the nine-year-old's fighting in the street.

'Look at the eye she's given my Sally!' one woman berated. 'You should keep her indoors till she learns her manners.'

But the more Kate scolded her daughter, the more aggressively Catherine behaved among her friends. Kate saw how the girl bullied the others, pushing them around if they would not do as she commanded. Her tendency to bossiness was now backed by a brawny strength. 'I'll fight ye!' Kate heard the loud threats and despaired to think her child was turning into a wild McMullen. It was as if the wicked things that Danny

419

had done had unhinged her, for Catherine had shied away from fights in the past.

Something else worried Kate. It was months since the exclusion of Cissy's party and Catherine had soon been playing with her friends again as if nothing had happened. But Kate could not help feeling the girl had neither forgotten nor forgiven. She seemed angry and resentful with everyone, but especially with her. Kate could not control her. As summer came, she tried to occupy her with chores, taking in extra washing to try to make ends meet.

Catherine would be sent to fetch the washing and carry it back. She complained bitterly that her back was hurting and tried to get Rose to intervene.

'I cannot carry it, Mam,' she whined. 'Tell our Kate to stop picking on us.'

'Kate, let her be,' Rose chided. 'The lass is all done in after her long day at school.'

Kate flared. 'She's a lazy little madam! And she'll help me with this lot or I'll skelp her backside.'

'She's just a bairn.'

'She's nearly ten,' Kate snapped. 'You sent us out on the street at her age.' She threw her mother an accusing look. 'Is that what you want for Kitty? 'Cos if we don't get this washin' done, that's what it'll come to. I'm the only one workin' meself into an early grave round here. Look at me hands – red raw they are!'

Rose was stung into silence and resentfully Catherine stalked out, dragging the overloaded basket of washing.

But more often than not, she was nowhere to be found when Kate called her to help. She roamed the streets, a law unto herself.

One day she came rushing back in, her dress soaked and rank-smelling.

420

'Where've you been?' Kate demanded.

'Down the Slacks,' Catherine said defiantly, yet her look was shifty.

'I've told you never to play down there!'

'I was looking for firewood,' she muttered.

'Get out of those stinking clothes now,' Kate ordered. 'And if you ever go near that place again, I'll string you up like Jobling, so I will!'

Catherine slunk past her. That evening at tea, she sat subdued without a word to any of them and did not attempt to go out again. She kept glancing out of the window as if watching for something in the dying light. Just as Kate was lighting the lamp, there was a knock at the front door. In an instant, Catherine was out of her seat and bolting for the yard.

'What's got into her?' John asked suspiciously.

Kate went to the door in dread. A man she did not recognise stood in the shadows, grasping his cap nervously.

'This the McMullens'?' he asked gruffly.

'Aye,' Kate nodded cautiously. John loomed at her shoulder.

'What of it?' he demanded.

'I don't want to cause any bother,' the man said, 'but I was told it was your lass did it.'

'Did what?' John demanded.

'Nearly drowned our Billy.'

'Never!' John exclaimed. 'Not our Kitty.'

'She was seen doing it – lad saw her from the Jarrow tram, holding his head under the water. If he hadn't got off and stopped her . . .' The man swallowed. 'Well, our Billy'd be a goner.'

Kate felt dizzy. 'Mary Mother!'

'Can you be sure?' John was still incredulous. 'Maybes your lad's a liar.'

The man frowned in anger. 'I've heard talk of your lass before, always daring the bairns to jump the timbers in the Slacks. This time she went too far and pushed him in.'

'The Slacks?' Kate gasped.

'Aye, missus, that's where it happened.'

Kate knew it to be true. Catherine had made no secret of being at the forbidden Slake. That must be where she went when she disappeared so often. Her blood ran cold to think what the girl had done there.

'Must've been an accident,' Kate blustered. 'Our Kitty would never harm a flea.' But even as she said so, Kate had an image of Catherine's face creased in savage glee as she swung a younger girl around by the arm until she screamed in pain for mercy. How many times recently had she glimpsed her picking on younger children and had turned away, not wanting to see? Too many.

The man's look was pitying. 'The lad on the tram saw it all, missus. He stopped her drowning our bairn. Maybes it was a daft game gone wrong – or maybes it wasn't.' He gave her a warning look. 'But you'll have to do sommat with her, missus, you really will. 'Cos she's got to be stopped.'

'Aye,' Kate gulped, 'I'll see to her.'

The man nodded and jammed on his cap. As he strode away up the street, Kate called after him, 'Sorry for your trouble!'

She returned inside with a leaden heart. What kind of monster had she bred? Maybe the priest was right in thinking no good could come from a child born in sin. John gave her a look of contempt.

'She's your problem – you sort her out.'

Kate watched him retreat to his chair by the hearth. He wanted nothing to do with the punishment, as if it was only

422

her fault for the way Catherine was behaving. She looked to Rose for support. Her mother's haggard look showed she had heard the exchange on the doorstep.

'Fetch her in,' Rose said stonily. 'She'll take her medicine.'

Catherine would get no leniency this time from her grandmother. She had nearly killed a boy. Shame and fury surged through Kate. The girl had been nothing but trouble and heartache from the moment she stirred in her womb! She strode out of the kitchen and down the yard. The door to the netty was locked.

'Are you in there?' She rattled the handle again. 'I know you're in there. Come out, you little beggar!' Kate hammered on the door, but no answer came. 'You can't stay in there all night. We know what you've done. That bairn's da's been at the front door. How could you do such a thing? I'm ashamed of you – right to the soles of me boots, I'm ashamed!'

She hammered some more, but Catherine neither stirred nor spoke. The silence infuriated Kate and her frustration and anger mounted. She itched to get her hands on the girl. But short of breaking down the door, she would have to wait.

'You'll get such a beating when you come out,' she cried as she left, 'you'll not sit down for a week. I promise you that!'

Kate crashed around the kitchen, finishing the day's jobs, fuming at her powerlessness over her wayward daughter. By God, she'd make her pay for all this trouble. What she wouldn't do for a drink! Just one to calm the palpitations in her chest, numb the hateful thoughts in her head. But there wasn't a penny spare for liquor.

Finally it was John who acted. He got up abruptly from his seat and went down to the privy. For an anxious moment, Kate thought he might be going to take the beating into his own hands and with a brief jolt of alarm remembered how long ago they had cowered with their mother in the outhouse, terrified of John's murderous intentions. But then he had been mad with drink and rage; now he just seemed tired and wanting the punishment to be over.

'Kitty, haway out and face the music,' he cajoled. 'Best get it over with, then we can all gan to our beds.'

To Kate's amazement, a few moments later, she heard the bolt slide back and a shadowy figure emerged from the darkened privy. She steeled herself not to weaken at the sight of Catherine's pale, red-eyed face as she entered the kitchen. Grabbing her roughly by the arm, Kate pulled up the girl's skirts and smacked her swiftly and hard on her bottom and legs.

'Don't you ever gan down the Slacks again!' she roared. 'And you leave them bairns alone, do you hear?' She shook her until Catherine sobbed and nodded.

'A-aye . . . I'm s-s-sorry—'

'You'll not gan out to play for a week – you can make yourself useful round here. Now get to bed and say your prayers.' Kate flung her away.

Catherine scrambled round the table and limped into the bedroom, banging the door behind her. Kate stood panting, her callused hands clenching and unclenching as the rage inside her subsided. For a moment she had hated her daughter with every fibre in her body, could have beaten her till there was no more defiance in her tawny eyes. Now, she stood trembling and shocked by the strength of her anger. She was no better than Catherine. They were two of a kind, capable of the worst. Perhaps they were cursed. For the thousandth time, Kate rued the day she had ever set eyes on Alexander.

She pushed back the strands of hair that had escaped their

424

pins and saw Rose staring at her. In the dimness she could not read her expression. Did her mother hate and despise her the way she sometimes did her own daughter?

'Mam,' Kate whispered, 'what shall I do with the lass?'

After a moment, Rose said quietly, 'She's got too much spirit. Kitty needs a firmer hand than most. Go and speak to the priest.'

John snorted. 'She needs teaching what's right and wrong, that's all.'

'She gets that,' Kate said defensively. 'Here and at St Bede's.'

John shrugged. 'Have the lass gan to school closer to home – where you can keep more of an eye on her. A good Catholic school, of course.' His look meant there'd be no nonsense like sending her to the Anglicans again. 'Aye, St Peter and St Paul's, down Tyne Dock.'

'With Father O'Neill?' Kate asked with a sinking heart. Their local priest had aged over the ten years since Kate had came home but not mellowed. 'He'd be too hard on the lass.'

'It's what she needs,' John declared, 'what you should've got at her age if your mother hadn't been so soft. Then maybes things might've turned out different.'

Kate bristled, but swallowed a retort. She was too drained to argue with him. And perhaps there was something in the suggestion. The firebrand priest might be the only one who could tame Catherine's wilfulness.

Kate looked at her mother and Rose nodded.

'I'll gan and see about it the morrow,' Kate sighed in agreement.

Much later, when Kate finally fell into bed, she thought Catherine was asleep, curled up in a ball. Then in the dark she heard her sniff. Reaching out a hand, she felt her daughter's hair. It was wet and sticking to her cheeks with tears.

'Kitty?' she whispered, her anger spent.

Catherine sobbed out loud, 'I'm sorry – I d-don't know why I did it.' Her body shook as she tried to explain. 'They're always teasing me. I just got all angry inside. It wasn't Billy's fault, he was just there. I didn't mean to hurt him, I promise.' Catherine's voice broke as she wept again. 'I'm bad and terrible and I'll g-go to hell!'

'Hush now.' Kate reached out quickly and pulled her into her arms. 'You're not ganin' to hell.'

She rocked the girl soothingly until her sobbing died down. 'Don't you listen to what the other bairns say – they don't mean the half of it. You're not a bad lass underneath. They think you are because of me – but you'll prove them wrong, hinny. You do what your mam and your teachers tell you and you'll make some'at of yourself, by heck you will.'

Catherine burrowed into her side and they fell asleep wrapped around each other, untroubled by nightmares or restless wanderings for the first time in months.

Chapter 43

Catherine appeared to settle quickly at St Peter and St Paul's in Tyne Dock and the bouts of temper gradually abated. Soon John was teasing her for being too holy.

'Here comes St Catherine – say a prayer for me.'

'I do, Grandda,' she would reply seriously, and provoke a roar of laughter.

Kate would find her kneeling at the foot of their bed praying aloud for her family. On Saturdays Catherine would beg her to fetch her boots back from the pawnshop where they went after school on Friday, so that she could go to Sunday Mass.

'Our Lady hears your prayers in the bedroom well enough,' Kate would counter if she could not afford to reclaim the boots.

'But I have to gan,' Catherine insisted. 'Miss Coulthard will ask us what the priest said and I'll get wrong for not knowing.'

'That old battle-axe,' Kate snorted. 'Get one of the lasses to tell you on the way to school.' She was not going to be dictated to by Catherine's censorious headmistress who dared to send her daughter home with her hair bound in plaits after she spent hours grooming it into pretty ringlets. Catherine's wildness may have been tamed by the strict teacher but Miss

Coulthard was the cause of financial wrangles. Apart from more frequent trips to the pawnshop for Sunday clothes, Catherine had thrown one of her old tantrums over a sewing lesson. She needed three yards of flannelette for a nightdress.

'Three yards!' Kate had cried. 'I haven't even got the rent money this week.'

But Catherine had wept and nagged for several nights until Kate snapped. In the twilight, she marched down to Jarrow and, spotting a bale of flannelette in a shop doorway, grabbed it and shoved it under her coat.

To her horror, as she made her escape, she saw that Catherine had followed her and seen it all.

'Run!' she barked at her daughter and they dashed from the street and up the hill, not pausing to stop till they reached East Jarrow. Kate heaved for breath, feeling nauseous from fear. She turned to see Catherine vomiting into the verge.

'See what that witch has gone and made me done?' Kate gasped. 'You better make a canny job of that nightie.'

Catherine said nothing, just looked at her aghast. That night she spent twice as long on her knees at the foot of the bed and Kate imagined the prayers were full of supplication on her behalf.

Kate tried to banish the incident from her mind, for thieving was something she had never resorted to, no matter how hard up they were. She had only done it for Catherine, so that she would not be stigmatised by the other children or picked on by critical teachers. But shortly afterwards, a greater temptation came her way.

Jack came back on leave in June with news that his regiment were to be posted.

'Looks like we're ganin' to France at last,' he said eagerly. Rose was full of dismay, but John was approving.

428

' 'Bout time you saw some action with the Durhams.'

The men went out on a drinking binge which lasted from Friday night through to early Monday morning.

Kate was gathering up clothes for the weekly wash when she felt a large piece of paper in her stepfather's trouser pocket. He and Jack were sleeping late and the trousers lay discarded on the floor where she and Catherine had struggled to undress him the previous night. Her eyes widened as she opened it out to find it was a five-pound note. She had never held so much money in her hand before.

Kate's heart thumped. She thought the last of John's compensation money had been spent over the three days of drinking. He had boasted to Jack that he would treat him to as much whisky and beer as he wanted before he took the train south. This must be the last of it, for the drawer in the sewing box was empty and no longer locked.

She could pay off the rent man with this and have plenty left over for a few treats. Aflecks still had tinned pears on their shelves. Catherine could have a decent coat for Mass on Sundays. She could buy a secret bottle of whisky and keep it under the mattress. Kate glanced through the wash-house door. No one would know if she pocketed it. What was the harm in it? John would not miss it. He had been so drunk he would think he had spent the lot.

Kate stood in indecision while she struggled with her conscience. She deserved it, by God! She had seen nothing of the hundred pounds. For all the years of slaving and putting up with her stepfather's boorishness, this would be her small piece of luck. Kate unbuttoned the top of her blouse and pushed the five pounds deep inside her bodice. She set about the heavy chore of possing the clothes with a savage vigour and sang all morning like a blackbird.

She thought she had got away with her theft until two days later when she walked back in from her job at the pub to hear John swearing and ranting at Rose.

'I know I had it, you stupid bitch! I didn't drink it all. Five pounds I had. You can't have looked proper.'

'It's not in the box,' Rose answered wearily. 'You emptied it on Saturday.'

'Well, I never drank it!' John turned on Jack. 'You knew I had it. Did you tak it? 'Cos if you did I'll knock yer teeth down yer gob!'

'I never touched your money,' Jack snapped. 'You were buying beer like there was no tomorra.'

John swore at him, then spotted Kate at the door. 'Have you seen it?'

'Seen what?'

'Me money. Me five pounds.'

Kate felt her throat drying. 'Me? When have I seen owt of your money?'

'You've stolen it, haven't ye?' he accused. 'Got it hid somewhere. Think I wouldn't notice. What's that you've got? You've been buying stuff with my money!'

He leapt at her, tearing the parcel from her arms. Dirty aprons spilled on to the floor.

'Gerr off!' Kate cried. 'It's washing, that's all.'

John glared at the heap of laundry, his fists bunched. Rose struggled to her feet.

'Leave the lass be,' she ordered. 'She wouldn't take your money. Either you've spent it or it'll turn up. Now sit yoursel' down and I'll make a pot of tea.'

Kate quickly gathered up the dirty washing and hurriedly dumped it in the wash house. When she came back in, the shouting had died and Rose was limping slowly around the scullery fetching vegetables to scrub. She was making an extra effort for Jack's last few days, determined that she would help feed him up and that he should not see her confined to her chair like an invalid.

The women shared the chores in silence, each happy to keep out of the way of the truculent John. As Kate lifted the heavy pan of potatoes, Rose stopped her with a look. Her mother spoke so quietly, Kate had difficulty in catching her words.

'If you did take it, I never want to know.'

Kate felt herself going red. 'Mam, I—'

Rose silenced her with a finger on the lips. 'Just promise me one thing,' she added. 'Spend it on you and the bairn. Not on drink. Promise me you won't drink it away like that devil in there.'

Kate felt a flood of shame that her mother should have guessed, yet her eyes pricked with gratitude that Rose should still be trying to protect her from John. She could not speak, but nodded briefly and escaped into the kitchen with her heavy load. Her mother never mentioned the matter again.

The night before Jack was due to embark for France, he bought two jugs of watery beer and a bottle of rum from a black marketeer at the docks and they drank to his going.

'I'm proud of you, lad.' John punched him playfully on the shoulder and Kate thought how he would boast around the Jarrow pubs till the war ended.

Rose sat tensely, darning a thick pair of John's socks for her son to take with him, for she had heard the trenches were cold and wet, even in summer. Kate drank deeply with the men and sang loudly until Catherine appeared like an apparition and said she could not get to sleep for all the noise.

431

Jack tried to pull her on to his knee but she wriggled out of his hold and darted back to bed.

They went to bed late and Kate fell into such a deep, drink-fuelled sleep that she was not aware of Jack until his hands were on her. She woke with a start.

'Just once, Kate,' he pleaded. 'I'm off to fight for you and England. Might never come back. Just give us a bit o' love before I gan. You'll miss us when I'm gone, Kate. And I'll miss you.'

Kate shook her head. 'It's not right, Jack. I'm your sister,' she whispered.

'I just want a bit kiss and cuddle.'

They tussled. All of a sudden he stopped and leant up. In the blacked-out room she could not see his expression, but she heard the suppressed glee in his voice.

'You took it, you clever lass. You fooled him, good and proper!'

Kate's heart thudded to hear the rustle of the five-pound note in his hand. Jack had pulled it from her bodice. She tried to grab it from him, but he held it high.

'Please, Jack, give it me back,' she hissed. 'I kept it for the bairn. Don't tell on us, Jack man.'

She heard the triumph in his voice. 'You can have it back if you give us a bit love.'

Kate felt defeated. What choice did she have? To give in to Jack's demands or face a vicious beating from her stepfather. She knew the temper of the man and the torture of his belt. Jack would be gone in a day; but John she had to live with till they carried him out in a coffin. If he found out about the stolen money, it would be her body going out in a box, more than likely.

She bargained for time. 'All right,' she muttered, 'but not here. You'll wake the bairn.'

432

'Where then?' Jack demanded, his breath on her cheek.

'The morrow – when she's at school – before you gan.'

'Promise me!' Jack commanded.

'Aye,' Kate said, turning her face from him.

He went, taking the money with him as insurance. Kate lay for a long time unable to sleep, disgusted with her brother for his desires and with herself for not speaking up before about his pestering. But who would believe her? Not Rose, who adored her son whatever he did; not John, who thought him an innocent with women. Shy Jack, a canny lad to the outside world. She would be blamed for leading him on and her life would be made a misery.

The next day she went about her work with a sick dread. As she scrubbed the pub floors of the previous night's beer and spit, she contemplated not going home until after Jack's train had gone. All the family, Mary included, were to travel into Newcastle to see him and the other soldiers on to the train for London. She would never be forgiven for missing the occasion.

She thought of the five pounds and felt a surge of defiant anger. That money was hers and he was not going to cheat her of it! She deserved every penny. Kate knew she would never have the opportunity again of possessing such a lump sum to do with as she wished. It would be her insurance against hard times, an investment in the future that could lift her out of a hand-to-mouth existence.

All the way home she seesawed between hoping there would be no opportunity to be left alone with Jack and determination to get her money back. Jack was polishing his boots on the step, looking out for her.

'Mam's resting before the trip to Newcastle.' He smiled up at her, as if she would be pleased with the news. 'Father's gone into Jarrow.'

'Why?' Kate's heart sank, her courage failing.

'Heard there's war work at Palmer's and they're not fussy about age any longer. Wants to do his bit for the war effort,' Jack smirked. 'Doesn't want me showing him up.'

Without waiting for Kate to reply, he stood up and led the way inside. Kate's pulse hammered. It would be over quickly, she'd see to that. She was following him into the bedroom, when there was a clatter of feet outside and Catherine ran in from the yard.

'What you doing back so early?' Kate asked, startled.

'Miss Coulthard said I could gan to the station to see our Jack off – said he's a grand lad for ganin' to fight for his country,' Catherine beamed.

Kate glanced at her half-brother and saw the alarm on his face.

'You shouldn't be missing school,' he reproved.

The girl looked crestfallen. Kate quickly intervened. She went to the tea caddy on the mantelpiece and fished out a sixpence. She had meant it for a loaf of bread to see them until Friday when she got paid.

'Take this and fetch a jug of beer from the Twenty-Seven.'

Catherine gave her a contemptuous look.

'Just for our Jack – so he can have a last drink before his journey,' Kate coaxed, keeping her temper.

The girl took the coin with a martyred look and plodded out of the house. 'Don't be long,' Kate called after her, 'else we'll miss the train.'

With the girl gone, Kate steeled herself for the ordeal in the bedroom. She lay down on the bed. A cockroach was climbing the damp wall opposite and she made a mental note to clean it with lime and whitewash after her brother had gone. She would fumigate the room and beat the

434

mattress. She would spring-clean the whole house.

Jack made no move towards the bed. Kate looked up and saw the fear in his face.

'I – I can't,' he said hoarsely. Then he covered his face with his hands and began to weep quietly.

Kate got up and went over, putting her arms around him. 'Thank the saints,' she murmured, 'my old Jack isn't dead after all.'

He leant into her and let her comfort him.

'I'm scared, Kate,' he whispered. 'Not of fightin', but leaving home – you and Mam. I can't think what it'll be like.'

'You'll be canny,' Kate encouraged. 'It's what you always wanted, remember? Ever since you had that wooden gun, playing at the Boer War.'

'Aye,' Jack pulled away and smiled bashfully, 'I'm just being daft. Don't tell anyone what I said.'

'Not if you give us the fiver back,' Kate bargained.

Jack scrabbled in his pocket and pulled it out, handing it over.

'Sorry,' he mumbled, 'I shouldn't have took it. If you need any more I'll give it ye.'

Kate shook her head. 'Just take care of yourself. It'll do you the world of good to get away from here.'

He looked at her shyly. 'I didn't mean to do you harm. I don't know what to do with lasses, that's all.'

'You will in time,' she assured him.

'Will you be all right with me da?' He looked uncertain.

'I can handle him,' Kate said stoutly, 'don't you worry.'

Briefly he hugged her. 'I think the world of you, Kate.'

She pushed him away gently. 'Haway, the bairn'll be back any minute.' She walked past him, her heart pounding in relief.

Soon Catherine was back and Kate was helping her mother to rise and make ready for the trip into Newcastle. A brake had been hired to take several families and neighbours into town to see off their sons and husbands. John came back and helped them drink the contents of the 'grey hen', but it was Kate who drank longest and deepest. When Catherine gave her a pious look of disgust, Kate abruptly burst into tears.

'See how much the lass is ganin' to miss you, bonny lad,' John chuckled. 'Soft as clarts, is our Kate.'

Kate avoided their looks, wiped her nose and eyes on her sleeve and hurried outside, pulling Catherine with her. She made the child sit beside her in the carriage and chatted away to the neighbours, so that there was no chance of speaking to Jack.

Her feelings for him were so confused. Part of her loved the shy, vulnerable boy that he still was at heart; the one who had been quietly affectionate and as protective of her as she was of him. Yet a small part of her still feared the flashes of moody, aggressive McMullen that had been fanned by John, the Jack who was goaded into using fists instead of words and thought there was nothing strange in kissing his sister like a lover.

At Newcastle's cavernous station, all was noise and bustle, with bands and buglers playing the soldiers away and families hugging and kissing their loved ones goodbye. No one thought it strange that Kate should be shaking and crying so uncontrollably.

'Take good care of yourself,' Rose told her son tearfully, 'and come back safe.'

Jack hugged his mother in affection and swung Catherine round.

436

'Course I will. I'm a McMullen. We come back like bad pennies,' Jack teased. 'Isn't that what you always used to say?'

'Aye,' Rose laughed, ' 'bout most of them.'

She clung to his arm until the last moment, so that he had to push her gently away to get on to the train. Kate stood back.

'Ta-ra, Kate,' he said, looking at her uncertainly. 'I'll miss you.'

Kate nodded. 'Ta-ra, Jack.'

Then he was swallowed up by the crush of uniforms beyond the ticket barrier. They watched and waved as he clambered with his kit bag into the crowded carriage. Swirls of steam engulfed the train as it lurched away from the platform. Moments later he was gone.

All the way home, Kate sobbed into a handkerchief borrowed from a neighbour, while Rose sat stoical and dry-eyed and John shared swigs of whisky from another man's flask.

'Everyone's staring,' Catherine whispered in alarm. 'No one else is blubbin' like you, Kate.'

But Kate could not stop. She felt as if some beast roared inside, shaking and wailing and flooding her throat and eyes with endless tears. She knew it was probably the drink, yet she did not care if people disapproved for it cauterised her thoughts.

Rose put a consoling hand on her shoulder. 'Don't worry, hinny, our Jack'll be back.'

Kate buried her face in the sodden handkerchief, unable to look at her mother. But which Jack would be back, the affectionate brother or a battle-hardened McMullen? She carried on weeping and letting others comfort her without

437

saying a word. And nobody guessed the real reason for her tears. Nobody knew that she wept for the memory of her young brother who never wanted to be parted from her, but also in relief that John McMullen's son was gone to war.

Chapter 44

Rose seemed to lose heart after Jack went. News trickled through of fierce fighting along the Somme and the family anxiously scanned the lists of the dead and missing. Even when a letter arrived from Jack the following month to say he was well and enjoying life at the front, Rose refused to believe it. Only Catherine could bring a smile to her drawn face, with snatches of poetry or verse she had learnt at school.

Rose no longer left the house, spending the days confined to her chair, battling with painful swollen legs, incontinence and breathlessness. John dismissed it as 'women's troubles', but Dr Dyer diagnosed dropsy. He called occasionally on the family to see how they were faring and never asked for payment for the ointments he left, even though John was working once more at the hard-pressed yards.

Despite the shortages and the worry over her mother, Kate felt her life was bearable. Mary was speaking to her again and young Alec was often to be found standing on a chair in Kate's kitchen, mixing spoon clutched in his small hand, brightening her day with his constant chatter.

Mary loaned her the fare for a trip to Hexham that neighbours had organised and so Kate was able to treat Catherine to a day out. Kate kept her guilty five pounds secret, for she dared not use it yet and knew Mary would be the first to tell their stepfather if she did. They picnicked along the river and the children had races. Kate clowned around with Maisie and led them all in a sing-song. On the way home they sang raucously in the evening air, ' "Pack up your troubles in your old kit bag, and smile, smile, smile!" '

Kate was so infected with good-humour and the pleasure of the day that she grabbed Catherine's hand as they scrambled out of the brake. Lights in the houses were blacked out, but a waxing moon slid in and out of clouds buffeted by a stiff river breeze and cast shadows along the street.

'Haway, kiddar,' she cried, 'we'll race the moon!'

Before Catherine could protest, Kate was dragging her down the lane, whooping and laughing.

'Quick, it's gettin' away!'

Catherine's feet left the ground as they flew across the cobbles and a gurgle of excitement caught in her throat. The moon seemed to be keeping pace with them as clouds whipped across its elusive face.

Catherine laughed and shrieked in joy and panic. 'Stop!' she giggled. 'I cannot keep up. Stop, Mam!'

Kate rushed on a few steps, then stopped abruptly. She pulled the girl round, laughing and panting for breath.

'What did you call me?' she asked in astonishment.

'Nowt.' Catherine looked away.

'You called me Mam,' Kate said breathlessly. 'Didn't you?'

'I said man. Stop, man,' Catherine muttered in confusion.

Kate swung an arm round her shoulders. 'Me da used to race the moon with us when we were bairns – it's one of the few things I remember,' she said softly.

'Me grandda?' Catherine said incredulously.

Kate snorted. 'Not him! No, me real da. He was a canny man.' She tried to recall the tall, kind father of her earliest childhood. She could not really remember his face any more, just the impression of a deep gentle voice telling her stories of the saints, and strong warm hands that played the piano and pulled her down the street to race the moon.

'Kate,' Catherine whispered. 'What's – *my* da like?'

Kate felt her stomach twist. She had hoped the child would never ask. What good would come of her knowing that her mother had lost her head over a member of the gentry? Catherine would never be able to claim Alexander as a father, for his family would never acknowledge his illegitimate child. They had closed ranks against her. He belonged to a remote world shut off from the likes of them. It was better that her daughter never knew, never hankered after such a world as she had once done. She must make her way in life without Alexander. Kate had come to regret ever putting his name to the birth certificate. She had only done so in the wild hope that he might come back. But he had not and her daring act had been no protection against the bigotry to which they had both been subjected.

'Oh, hinny, don't ask,' Kate sighed.

Catherine's face twisted in disappointment.

Kate touched the girl's hair. 'You've his bonny hair and eyes,' she said wistfully. 'That's all I can tell you.'

Catherine seized on this scrap of information. 'Does he live round here?'

Kate drew back in alarm. The last thing she wanted was the girl going around asking questions, trying to find out about Alexander.

'No,' Kate said brusquely, 'he's not from round here and he's never coming back for us.'

'Never?' Catherine whispered, her eyes filling with tears.

'No, he's dead,' Kate said rashly. 'Now, don't ever ask about him again.'

They marched back up the bank in silence, the intimacy of moments before vanished. Kate's enjoyment of the day had been shattered by unwelcome thoughts of Alexander and she slept badly, wondering once more whatever had become of him.

In the spring of 1917, Jack got unexpected leave. Catherine had been writing to him, long letters that Kate had addressed for her but never added to. In return he had sent his niece postcards of Picardy and elaborate embroidered cards that Kate thought more appropriate to a sweetheart. But she kept her counsel as she still felt guilty at stopping her daughter writing to Stoddie the previous year.

'Quick, Kate! Our Jack's coming up the bank!' Catherine squealed, racing in the back door.

Kate clutched her throat. 'Never?'

'Aye, come and see!' The girl took her by the arm and pulled her into the yard.

A crowd of children had gathered at the end of the lane and were calling excitedly to the soldier tramping up the hill to the New Buildings. Kate recognised Jack's lanky swagger long before she could see the bashful look in his dark blue eyes.

Neighbours came out to welcome him home and shake his hand, while children ran behind and fired questions.

'Have you been wounded?'

'How many Fritzes have you killed, Jack?'

'Did you see me da in France?'

Jack brushed them off good-naturedly and strode into the yard of Number Ten. Kate bustled ahead nervously. Rose burst into tears at the sight of her son.

'Eeh, hinny, you're a sight for sore eyes!' she cried in delight and threw her arms around him as he stooped to greet her. 'How long have you got?'

'A week. Then we join a new battalion.'

'You should've said you were coming,' Kate gabbled. 'I've nothing in the larder. Give us half an hour and I'll be back with a ham knuckle – make a broth.'

By the time she had searched Tyne Dock for supplies and trailed home, Jack was holding court in the crowded kitchen. As Kate busied herself preparing a meal, she was surprised to find him so talkative. He had opinions on the war. Generals knew nothing, officers spoke like music-hall toffs and German snipers were fearless. She had never seen him so confident with other adults. He told the neighbours who dropped by to visit that French water gave you the runs and French brandy was nectar.

'Serves you right for drinkin' the waater,' John snorted, pouring them both another whisky that Catherine had been made to fetch.

By the time Mary and Alec came round with their young son, Jack was fulsome about army life and scathing about conscripts who had not joined up voluntarily like he had. Mary took offence and stalked off declaring they would not bother calling again unless he apologised to Alec. Jack laughed at his sister and went out drinking.

Kate was annoyed. Mary would be in a sulk for days and probably take it out on her. She put Rose to bed, but kept Catherine up with her, knowing the men would return soon as liquor was rationed and pubs had to close early. She was still unsure how Jack would be with her once he had had a bellyful of whisky. Her heart began to thump when she heard footsteps outside and loud laughter.

'Look who we found,' Jack cried as he stumbled into the house from the unlit street. 'The Ancient Mariner!'

Kate was astonished to see Davie McDermott striding into the kitchen with his kit bag over his shoulder.

'Needs a bed for the night,' Jack announced.

Davie smiled apologetically. 'My ship's come in for refit.'

Kate was overjoyed. 'Haway in,' she welcomed, 'course you must stay. You can share the bed with Jack like old times.'

She brewed a pot of tea and cut them thick slices of bread smeared with dripping and questioned Davie about life at sea. There was constant danger from German submarines.

'U-boat hit us few miles out – but it didn't explode proper. Managed to see her to port.'

He spoke with quiet understatement, but it struck Kate how hazardous a life he led. Since the start of the war, the newspapers had listed a steady toll of ships sunk in British waters; hundreds of them. She imagined how the McMullen men would make a song and dance about surviving such an attack.

Davie stayed for most of Jack's short leave while he waited to see how long his ship would be in repair. When he discovered it would be another week before it sailed, he packed his bag to return to Cumbria and see his wife.

Before he went, Kate asked him as casually as possible, 'Do you ever hear word of Stoddie?'

He glanced at her shyly, his brown eyes considering. 'Aye – the wife does.'

'Is – is he all right?'

Davie nodded. 'Last I heard.'

'That's grand,' she blushed.

He pulled on his thick greying moustache and added, 'He's started writing to the wife's best friend – she's a widow. My Molly says, if he comes home safe – well, there's an understanding between them . . .'

Kate felt her heart squeeze. Why had he stopped writing to her? If it had not been for wicked Danny MacQuade she might have made more effort to keep in touch too. But he was promised to another now. Davie was trying to tell her as tactfully as possible.

Jack interrupted the conversation. 'Didn't I tell you Stoddie had a lass in every port? Our Kate had this daft idea about her and Jock.'

Kate went puce and Davie glanced away to save her embarrassment. She busied herself preparing his bait tin for the journey. When she handed it over, he touched her shoulder and smiled down. 'Take care of yourself, lass. You do a grand job.'

She nodded, her eyes stinging at the unaccustomed kindness. Then he was heaving his bag on to his shoulder and swinging out of the door into the weak spring sunshine. She watched him sauntering off, whistling last year's hit love song, 'If You Were the Only Girl in the World'. For an instant, Kate had a stab of envy for Molly McDermott, who would soon be surprised by Davie's tuneful whistle and burly figure on her doorstep.

That night Jack left, with some of his McMullen cousins seeing him off from the station. Rose clung to him.

'I'm that proud of you, lad,' she croaked. 'May Our Lady bless you and watch over you always. Take care of yourself, dear Jack!'

Kate felt a sudden wave of pity for her mother; her words sounded so final. Jack kissed Rose quickly, embarrassed at her show of affection.

445

'Don't worry about us, Mam,' he grinned. 'I'm the best shot in the regiment.'

In the doorway, he gave Kate a long look. 'Write to us, Kate, won't you?' he pleaded.

She felt a sudden stab of guilt that she had not been more affectionate with her brother during his brief stay. He had done nothing to warrant her coolness towards him. He seemed so much more confident and happy since his time away. She ruffled his hair. 'Keep your head down,' she smiled.

He smiled back, reassured. 'Aye, I will. I'll come back,' he promised.

Kate turned away with a heavy heart and consoled her weeping mother. Would this hateful war never be over?

Despite the welcome announcement that the Americans had finally decided to join the war on the side of the Allies, the news was mostly bad. In June, a new threat came when London was bombed by aeroplanes for the first time, killing over a hundred civilians in a fifteen-minute attack. Catherine scoured the skies for days afterwards and redoubled her fervent praying. By August, Allied troops in France were bogged down in the Flanders mud, hemmed in as much by ferocious storms as by the enemy. The battlefields of Ypres and Passchendaele were quagmires of cratered fields and bombed-out villages.

The autumn brought defeat in Italy and revolution in Russia. There was grave speculation in the newspapers that the victorious Bolsheviks might sign a peace treaty with the Germans, releasing more of the enemy from the eastern front to fight in France. Only in the Middle East did the Empire's forces seem to be making headway against Germany's allies, the Ottoman Turks.

But Kate read out the bleak reports only to John, for her mother's health was deteriorating quickly and any mention of the war brought on painful wheezing attacks. Through these troubled months Kate's main concern was Rose. Since the late summer, her mother had become completely bed-bound, and Kate had to get Catherine to help lift her to wash and change her clothes and bedding. The once-handsome woman was blotchy-faced and bloated with fluid. She watched them with lifeless eyes, as if she no longer cared what happened to her.

By early December, Rose had to sleep propped up in bed for fear of drowning in her sleep from the fluids flooding her lungs. She sat motionless, the breath gurgling in her throat. John moved out grudgingly, and slept on the settle. But Catherine kept watch from the desk bed, staying close to her grandmother, despite the stench in the cramped room.

'I'll stop with Mam,' she told Kate stubbornly when her mother tried to coax her back to their feather bed.

Dr Dyer came one raw December day and gave Rose morphine to ease her pain. He took Kate aside.

'She'll not be with us long – a week or two. Don't you have a sister in Birtley?'

Kate nodded, too overcome to speak.

'Best to send word – give her a chance to say her farewells.'

That Saturday Sarah arrived with her ten-year-old daughter Minnie. 'I've left the rest of the bairns with Michael's mam,' she explained, hugging Kate in greeting.

'St Teresa!' Kate gasped at her sister's huge belly. 'You've another on the way an' all.'

'Aye,' she gave a sheepish grin, 'if it's a lass that'll be four of each. But they're canny bairns and I've nowt to complain about.'

447

Kate felt a stab of envy for her older sister, who seemed so content with her lot. How she would have loved a large brood of lads. But she did not begrudge Sarah and was comforted to have her as an ally in the house. Catherine was soon organising her cousin Minnie into games in the frosty street while the sisters shared the cooking and tended their weakening mother.

Rose drifted in and out of consciousness, aware that her daughters were gathering at her bedside. On the Sunday morning they were roused with a startling sound.

'What's that noise?' Catherine asked, springing out of bed. Kate had been napping in the kitchen.

'It's church bells,' she exclaimed.

They ran to the door and threw it open. A blast of icy air greeted them and the distant clang of bells.

Sarah and Minnie rushed out of the bedroom. 'What is it? Does it mean an air raid?' Sarah asked in alarm. Kate shook her head.

'No, you get sirens and maroons for that.'

'We're being invaded!' Catherine cried dramatically.

'Don't be daft,' Kate said, though the thought had occurred to her too. 'Gan up the street and ask Uncle Alec.'

But before she had a chance, a uniformed boy with a bugle appeared like a ghostly messenger at the top of the street, shouting the news.

'We've captured Jerusalem! Turks have surrendered to General Allenby. God save the King!' And he blew on his bugle for good measure before racing off to the next street.

The sisters hugged each other and the girls screamed in excitement, waking John from sleep. They gabbled the news to him and Catherine rushed in to tell her grandmother. 'Jerusalem belongs to the Christians now, Mam! Isn't that grand?'

448

Rose was already awake. She looked so pained and tired, Kate wondered if she had slept at all. But she nodded in agreement and replied falteringly, 'You must gan to church – give thanks – pray for all the soldiers.'

'Yes, Mam,' Catherine promised.

'And Kate,' she wheezed, 'light a candle – for our Jack.'

Kate felt a pang at the mention of her brother.

'Course we will,' Catherine assured.

So Kate found herself borrowing a coat of Mary's and trooping off to St Bede's with Sarah and the girls, while their younger sister sat with Rose. It was a rare outing and Kate enjoyed the banter with Sarah, realising how much she missed her sister's company. They paid for a candle for Jack, but it was her mother that Kate prayed for silently and fervently. She hated to see the way Rose suffered, but it frightened her to think of life without her mother.

There were times when Kate had resented her mother intensely. She had sent her out to beg on the streets as a young girl and had been unforgiving over the affair with Alexander. She had taken Catherine from her as punishment. But Rose had shown her a deep, loyal love throughout her life that their hardships and differences had never quite extinguished. Most of all, she had tried to shield Kate from her stepfather and taken the brunt of his excesses upon herself. Kate shuddered to think of life at Number Ten with no Rose to stand between them.

They returned to East Jarrow, to find visitors.

'Aunt Lizzie!' Kate cried, and dashed forward to hug her aunt.

'Maggie sent word.' She smiled fondly at her niece. 'I'm sorry it's come to this.' They looked at each other wordlessly for a long moment, as memories flooded back of happier

449

times when Kate had lived at Ravensworth. They had seen each other seldom over the past twelve years, only at the christenings of Sarah and Mary's children. 'You're still bonny, for all your troubles,' her aunt said kindly.

'How's Mam?' Kate asked.

'Been sleeping mostly since we got here.'

'Aye,' Maggie confirmed. 'Don't think she recognised our Lizzie.'

The aunts and nieces set about making Sunday lunch, eking out the winter vegetables Lizzie had brought from Ravensworth and catching up on family news. George, whose eyesight was too poor for military service, was courting and soon to be wed. Boisterous Alfred was impatient for his next birthday so he could sign up with the Durhams and join Cousin Jack in Flanders.

'Let's gan in and see if Mam's awake,' Kate suggested. 'Maybes she'll manage a bit broth.'

Catherine bounded into the parlour ahead of them. Rose opened her eyes at the noise. To Kate's astonishment, she saw Rose smile for the first time in weeks. Her eyes were fixed on Catherine as she beckoned the girl with a trembling hand.

'Come here, me bonny bairn,' she rasped.

'We lit a candle for Jack, Mam,' Catherine smiled, approaching the bed and letting her grandmother touch her face.

Rose did not seem to register the words.

'Where've you been?' Rose whispered, her eyes filling with tears.

The child gave her a quizzical look. 'Been to church, like you said, Mam.'

Rose frowned in worry. 'Don't run off again, Margaret hinny. You gave me and your da such a fright.'

Catherine glanced round at the others, baffled. Kate came forward.

'It's Kitty, Mam,' she said gently, 'your grandbairn.'

Rose gazed at Catherine, tears oozing down her cheeks. 'You've come back,' she whispered, clinging on to the girl, 'my bonny, bonny lass! Angel child. Just like she said.'

'Like who said, Mam?' Kate asked.

'The gypsy lass, of course,' Rose said with a hint of her old spark. 'Promised me the angel child.' She sank back on her pillows, her eyes still fixed on Catherine. 'And all the time it was you, Margaret, come back to me . . . Don't go away again, hinny, don't go . . .'

Her breathing grew ragged and she closed her eyes in exhaustion. Quietly Kate steered Catherine away.

'Leave her be,' she murmured.

'Who's Margaret?'

'She's gettin' mixed up – it's the medicine.' She glanced at her aunts in the doorway.

'Poor Rose! She's going backwards – thinking of her first bairn,' Lizzie said quietly. 'She died of consumption years ago.'

'Aye,' Maggie agreed sadly. 'Margaret was her favourite. Took it that bad when she died.'

Kate felt her eyes sting with tears. 'I remember that,' she murmured. 'Mam crying and shutting herself away in the room where me sister died.'

'Do I look like her?' Catherine asked.

'Aye, there's a look,' Maggie agreed. The girl seemed pleased with this.

Sarah added, 'And you've got Margaret's bossy streak an' all. Like a mother hen with the rest of us, wasn't she, Kate?'

Kate smiled wistfully and touched her daughter's cheek. 'Aye, from what I remember. Always carryin' us about and being the leader in our games.'

'What did she mean about the gypsy?' Sarah puzzled.

Maggie and Lizzie exchanged looks and glanced towards the kitchen to make sure John was out of earshot.

Maggie lowered her voice. 'Don't you remember going to The Hoppings in Newcastle – before Jack was born?'

Sarah struggled with her memory. 'Aye, I do! Kate, remember the Irish woman who read Mam's palm?'

Kate had a vague recollection of a red-haired woman with mesmerising eyes, touching her hair. There had been a huge row in front of a makeshift tent. It could have been at the fair.

'Well, Rose said this gypsy had spoilt the day by cursing you all with bad fortune. John was that angry and told her never to talk of it again. She wouldn't tell all that the gypsy had said.'

'But she predicted Jack's birth,' Lizzie continued, 'she told us that. And sommat about an angel child.'

'To sweeten her old age,' Maggie recited. 'She always held on to the belief there'd be this bairn like an angel, no matter how bad things got with him in there.' She nodded towards the kitchen.

'Kitty, an angel?' Mary was sceptical. 'Didn't think Mam believed in such nonsense anyway.'

Lizzie shrugged. 'Maybes it helped her keep her spirits up. God knows, she's needed it over the years.'

They all glanced back at the figure in the bed, sleeping fitfully.

'What harm does it do if she thinks Kitty's her special lass come back,' Sarah said, 'if it eases her going?'

The aunts nodded and turned away. Kate looked at her daughter's perplexed face and felt a strange tingle down the back of her neck. Could it be possible that some tinker woman had predicted the birth of her child so long ago? If so, then her daughter must be destined for something special. Briefly Kate rested a hand on Catherine's head and took comfort from the thought.

'Haway, hinny,' she said, 'we'll leave her be.'

The next day, sudden blizzards swirled in from the east and brought trains and trams to a standstill. Lizzie and Sarah had no option but to stay on, but Rose never regained consciousness after the strange incident with Catherine. It was as if, at the sight of the child she mistook for her beloved, long-dead Margaret, she no longer needed to struggle. Their battle-weary, stoical, protective mother had found peace at last.

No one was surprised when, in the early hours of Wednesday morning, Kate was shaken awake by Catherine.

'Mam's stopped making that rattlin' noise. Is that a good sign, Kate?'

Kate rushed to her mother's bedside and held a candle aloft. The eyes were staring and lifeless, her skin already cooling to the touch. Kate closed her eyes for a long moment, squeezing back hot tears.

'Aye, it's a good sign,' she trembled. 'Gan back to bed, hinny.'

Kate sat in the dark, holding her mother's hand. It felt suddenly slim, as if all the knotted veins had unravelled and the thick knuckles dissolved. Rose had a young woman's hands again, she marvelled. Slow painful tears of loss spilt down her cheeks.

'You're with me da now,' Kate whispered hoarsely, 'and me sisters. A happy day for you, Mam.' She leant forward and kissed her gently on the forehead, wishing she could have done so when she was alive.

The next three days were a blur of funeral arranging, with neighbours calling to pay their respects at the open coffin and help contribute towards holly wreaths and sprays of winter jasmine. John sat morosely in his chair, accepting consoling drinks and platitudes about the wife he had once adored but come to despise after years of wrangling and hardship for which they had each blamed the other.

The day of the funeral, Kate bade Catherine say goodbye to her grandmother before the coffin was nailed down. But the child was awkward and ran off. She had been playing up for days, refusing her food and being sick, and this was the final straw.

Kate was too desolate to try to coax round her difficult daughter and left Mary to fuss over the child. She balked at the thought of going to the burial, until Sarah chivvied her with a cup of tea fortified strongly with whisky.

'Get that down you,' her sister ordered.

With false courage in her belly, Kate set out with the family down the hill to Jarrow cemetery. Amid flurries of snow, frozen to the marrow, a grief-stricken Kate clutched her sisters. As the coffin was lowered into the metal-hard ground and the priest hurried over the brief committal, Kate crumpled like a small child, sobbing for her mother.

Soon her sisters and aunts would be gone to their own homes and separate lives. Only she would be left to soldier on at Number Ten with her bullying stepfather and resentful daughter. God give her strength to carry on!

Numbly she looked around for Catherine. Maybe it was just possible that, left alone together, the child might come to love her more and Kate might find more patience. Through

454

her tears Kate saw the girl standing impassively next to her grandfather. She was holding on to his frayed jacket as if it gave her a shred of comfort.

Kate felt sick to the core. For all his hardness and vicious tongue, Catherine was closer to the old devil than she would ever be to her. She felt overwhelmingly alone.

'Oh, Mam!' Kate wailed in distress. 'How can I bear it all on me own?'

Chapter 45

As Kate predicted, John's behaviour towards her grew unbearable. He belittled her every day with callous remarks about her looks and slovenly ways, ordered her around like a servant and blamed her for everything from the lack of food to the bitter weather. He came home reeking with drink and was all too ready to make fumbling grabs at her late at night. He alternately threatened and pleaded.

'I'm a poor widower without me wife,' he whined. 'I've needs. Just give us a little cuddle, lass, that's all I ask.'

Kate pushed him off in disgust, grabbing Catherine to her in the bed.

'You'll keep away from me or I'll leave you for good – and I'll tak the bairn with me.'

She knew even in drink John could not bear the thought of being left to fend for himself or to do without Catherine's uncritical company. But Kate never carried out her threats, despite Mary's goading.

'Don't know why you stop in that house any longer now Mam's gone,' she said with disapproval. 'The lass deserves better.'

'That's as maybe,' Kate protested, 'but where else could I gan? Are you offering to tak us in?'

'We haven't the room,' Mary said at once.

'No,' Kate eyed her squarely, 'and I've not two pennies spare. The only reason I stay is for the roof over our heads.'

But Catherine was anything but grateful for her sacrifices. She grew increasingly rebellious, finally refusing one Monday morning to stay off school to go to the pawnshop.

'I'm not doing it,' she declared. 'Miss Coulthard'll strap me if I'm late.'

'You'll do what I say before that old witch.'

'No I won't.' Catherine glared back. 'It's wrong what you're asking. It's against the law and it's a sin for me to miss me schooling and tell lies about being sick.'

'Don't you preach to me!' Kate went to grab hold of her, but Catherine dodged out the door, running off to school in defiance of her mother. That day, Kate had to make the shameful trip to the pawnshop.

To get through the days Kate found solace in drink. She drank more heavily than she had ever done, blotting out John's abusive words and Catherine's defiance for blissful short hours. She would invite anyone in who might like to share a glass of beer or two and have a sing-song around the fire, to ease the drudgery. No matter how drab the day or great the cares that weighed on her, Kate never lost her love of singing and music.

It was this that gave her an idea, one spring day in 1918, when she had gone with a bundle of clothes to the pawnshop in Tyne Dock. She heard the sound of piano playing in the back of the shop and stopped to listen.

' "Linden Lee",' she gasped in delight. 'Me da used to play that when I was a bairn.'

'My daughter takes lessons,' the pawnbroker told her proudly.

Kate was seized with a sudden thought. Catherine was musical – why should her daughter not have lessons too? It would take her out of herself. She was so moody and distant when she wasn't being defiant, and deep down Kate wanted to please her daughter. She sensed how much the girl missed her grandmother and wanted her to feel better. Kate felt guilty that Catherine had to witness the fights between her and John. Perhaps that was why the child withdrew into her own thoughts so much. All she wanted to do was scribble in that book Jack had given her, filling every inch with indecipherable writing.

But piano lessons were an accomplishment for a young lady. How grand it would be to have piano music fill her home, just as it had in her childhood.

'Where does she have her lessons?' Kate asked boldly.

'At Mrs Dalton's in Hood Street. Her charges are very modest,' he smiled. Kate felt grateful that the man did not scoff at her question. Her daughter had as much right to lessons as the families of the well-off.

But back home again, Kate thought how ridiculous was her ambition. Where would she get the money for lessons, let alone a piano to practise on? Then suddenly she remembered the five pounds. It was still there, sewn into the underside of the feather mattress. This would be the moment to use it. Rose would have approved. It would go towards securing a better future for Catherine.

The very next day, Kate went into town and ordered a piano, using the five pounds as a deposit. It arrived at the end of the week and Kate preened at the astonished faces of the neighbours as the beautiful satinwood instrument was carried in and placed in the parlour. She had not felt so proud in years. But it was her stepfather and daughter's expressions that she could not wait to see.

After tea, she flung open the parlour door and showed

them. At first John was speechless, his mouth opening and closing like a puppet's. Then he exploded. 'You haven't *bought* it?'

'I have,' Kate said with glee. 'It's for you, Kitty.'

'Me?' Catherine gaped. 'But I cannot play . . .'

'You'll learn. You're ganin' to Mrs Dalton's for lessons. It's all arranged.'

Catherine stared at her, wide-eyed in disbelief.

'You're bloody daft!' John shouted. 'You cannot afford it.' He turned on her suspiciously. 'Where've you got the money for this? Been whoring down the docks or what?'

Kate flared. 'No I have not! It's paid for good and proper. Well, at least the deposit's paid and I'll find the rest when the time comes.' She challenged him with a look. 'Maybes some of Jack's pay could gan towards it?'

John snarled. 'You'll not get owt of that for fancy piano lessons. What you want to gan filling the lass's head with ideas above herself?'

'Our Kitty's got an ear for music. She'll pick it up in no time, then there won't be any need for lessons.' She turned to her daughter. 'Isn't that right, pet?'

The girl gave her such a strange look, Kate thought she would burst into tears. She was obviously quite overcome with the gift.

'Go on, have a bit play,' Kate encouraged. 'Show your grandda.'

Catherine sidled over to the piano and lifted the lid. It was like the one at school that the hateful Miss Coulthard banged away on during morning assembly. It reminded her of hymns of repentance. How could they possibly afford it? She touched the keys tentatively. The notes rang out deep and discordant. Her fingers froze at the thought of all those lessons stretching ahead, all to be paid for. And Kate still in debt from the funeral.

Catherine felt bile rise in her throat and clamped a hand over her mouth to stop herself being sick. Her eyes watered as she stared in fear and resentment at her mother. How could she burden her with having to play this monstrous instrument? Just so she could have a sing-song round the piano and get full of drink of a evening! If she'd bothered to ask, she would rather have had a bicycle. That would have saved the tram fare to school and she would have been upsides with Belle and Cissy.

Catherine knew she could not speak without vomiting all over the parlour floor. Without a word, she fled from the room, out of the house and down the lane, throwing up in the stunted grass overlooking the Slake.

Kate was left puzzling her daughter's abrupt departure, vexed at her lack of gratitude.

John laughed at her. 'Doesn't look a willing pupil to me.' He spat into the empty grate.

Kate pursed her lips. 'She'll come round.' She banged the lid shut in disappointment.

Over the following weeks Catherine was sent down to Hood Street for lessons. But to Kate's huge disappointment and frustration, she showed no natural talent or enthusiasm. The noise from the parlour, when it came at all, was hesitant and laboured. Once the longer days came, Catherine was hard to keep in the house and Kate had many a battle trying to get her daughter to practise.

'It'd come easy if you just sat down and played it for more than five minutes,' Kate complained.

'I don't want to play it,' Catherine replied mutinously. 'I'm no good.'

460

As time went on, and the payments on the piano lapsed, Kate sought increasingly desperate ways to pay for the lessons. Trips to the pawnshop doubled, and hearing that Mrs Dalton had several sons to feed, she offered to pay in pie and peas suppers. For some reason Catherine seemed to take offence at this, and would lock herself in the privy when the Dalton boys came up the hill to fetch the meals that Kate had prepared.

The more Catherine played up over the lessons, the more determined Kate was that her daughter would become accomplished at the piano. She coaxed and cajoled and bullied.

'It'll come in handy all your life,' she insisted. 'It's a sign of being respectable. And if you get really good, you could be a music teacher or play with an orchestra or at the pictures.'

'I don't want to be a teacher,' Catherine said sullenly. 'They're old battle-axes and they wear terrible clothes.'

'Well, I'll not have you being a skivvy like me.' Kate lost patience. 'Is that what you want? 'Cos that's all you'll be good for if you don't learn your lessons.'

Catherine glared at her in reply.

A date was set for her first examination, but even this did not spur her on to regular practice. The gleaming piano sat gathering dust and the parlour did not fill with the sweet music that Kate so desired. It was nothing but a source of argument or silent resentment between the two and she grew to regret her foolishly extravagant gesture. It had pushed her further into debt and it was only a matter of time before the prestigious shop where she had bought the piano came to reclaim it for non-payment. What had possessed her to buy such a thing? And at a time of such shortage when even meat, butter and margarine were now being rationed?

Kate had to admit that it was because life was so drab and sorrowful after so many years of war and then Rose's death

461

that she had seized on the idea of cheering them all up. Music would restore their battered spirits and give Catherine an entry into a better world. But her contrary daughter had tossed her generosity back in her face and John made the most out of her mistake, by commenting daily on her stupidity and spendthrift ways.

Shortly before Catherine's dreaded examination, the wrangling household were distracted by a long-awaited letter from Jack. There had been no news from him for weeks during the spring offensive. The Germans had broken through at Arras and Ypres and taken thousands of prisoners. The doom-mongers talked of the British retreating to the Channel and the Germans marching on Paris.

'He's safe!' Catherine cried, the first to read the letter.

'Read it out, lass,' John ordered.

'Dear Father,

I'm writing this behind the lines. We saw a lot of the action along the River Somme. I was on sniper duty. But it is quiet now. Some of the lads are low with influenza, but I'm champion. And this is the best news. I'm being made lance-corporal. Captain Scott says I am a crack shot. I hope you will be pleased with me for getting me stripe—'

'Pleased?' John interrupted. 'The daft bugger! He doesn't want a bloody stripe.' John picked up the poker and stabbed at the fire in agitation.

Catherine stared at him in astonishment. 'But isn't it grand getting a stripe?'

'No,' John exclaimed, 'it's the quickest way to getting his head blown off.'

Kate could see that the girl was flummoxed. 'It's an honour for him being a good shot,' Kate declared. 'I thought you would be proud.'

'I'd rather have him alive than dead with a stripe,' John growled. 'There's nowt wrong with being Private McMullen.'

'Well, there's nothing we can do about it.' Kate shrugged and went back to kneading suet into dumplings.

'Aye, there is,' John replied, scraping the poker against the steel fender so that it screeched for her attention. 'He can turn it down. You write to our Jack and tell him not to take it.'

Kate thought it would make little difference. Jack could be as bloody-minded as his father and more likely to seize the promotion if John was against it. They thrived on one-upmanship and now Jack had found something he was better at than his father. Kate wrote the letter – the first to her brother in two years – expecting the advice would be ignored.

At the beginning of August a postcard of a cheery uniformed soldier came for Catherine, telling her gleefully that her uncle now had a lance-corporal's stripe on his jacket. It happened to arrive on the day of the piano exam and Catherine tucked it into her pocket for good luck. No one expected her to do well and not even Kate wished her luck as she trailed down the hill to Tyne Dock.

It was a futile exercise as the piano had been repossessed the previous week. Catherine had bolted to the privy when the men had come to carry it out and Kate had been left to stand in the doorway, glaring defiantly at the curious stares of neighbours. Afterwards, she had sat at the kitchen table drinking from a secret bottle of rum Davie McDermott had left her and which she kept for emergencies, ruing the money she had thrown away on an impractical romantic whim.

'Well then?' Kate demanded when Catherine returned from the examination.

The girl's expression was guarded. 'It was all right.'

Kate scrutinised her. 'You mean you passed?'

Catherine nodded.

Kate spun round and faced John. 'Do you hear that? The lass passed her test. I told you she was musical.'

'Not much good it'll do you now,' John said disparagingly, 'seeing as that piano's gone.'

Kate flushed. 'I'll find someone else's she can practise on.' She turned to her daughter. 'Eh, Kitty? You can still gan to Hood Street for your lessons.'

'No,' Catherine said in alarm, 'I'm not ganin' back there.'

'Why ever not?'

'No one else pays Mrs Dalton in pie and peas,' she blurted out.

Kate felt winded. The child was ashamed of her attempts to pay for the lessons, but she had no idea how difficult it was to juggle what little they had and make ends meet. Why couldn't her daughter be grateful for the way she tried to do her best for her against all the odds? Kate was sick with disappointment.

When the piano certificate arrived at the end of the month, declaring that Catherine had been awarded honours, Kate sat down and cried.

'You little beggar,' she accused. 'You knew you could do it all along – you didn't try just to spite me. That's the last time I do sommat special for you!'

Catherine ran out with a hurt look, leaving Kate feeling it was somehow all her fault. They hardly spoke a word to each other for days, until a letter came that shattered the tense silence at Number Ten.

'It's Jack!' Kate gasped. 'He's been wounded.'

'What's it say?' John demanded.

Kate read it out falteringly.

'I wish to notify you of the grave news that your son John McMullen has been wounded in action at Miraumont, during the taking of the German-held ridge. He fought bravely and without thought for his own safety. He has been taken to a casualty clearing station where I spoke to him and assured him I would write at once to his family. Your son is awaiting transportation back to England and I pray for his swift recovery.

    Yours sincerely,

    Padre N. Sinclair.'

They sat in stunned silence, then Catherine said, 'But he's still alive?'

'Aye,' John let out a long breath, 'thank the saints.'

Kate felt an assault of conflicting emotions: shock that Jack was wounded and relief he had not suffered a terrible death. She leapt up and paced to the stove, stirring the pot of lentils that was their tea for the third day running.

'We'll need new linen. He might have weeks lying in bed,' she gabbled. 'I'll gan into town the morrow and get some sheets. You'll have to lend us some money.' She fixed John with a look.

He nodded without protest, still in shock.

'I'll make him a card to welcome him back,' Catherine said more cheerfully, the frown of worry wiped from her brow.

The next day Kate trekked far and wide in search of linen and soap that she could afford. She walked briskly to stifle her anxious thoughts. How injured was he? Would he be an invalid for ever? Was he missing arms or legs? Her poor little brother! Then she thought of the years stretching ahead looking after an invalid Jack as well as her stepfather, both demanding her attention and sapping her strength.

She was thirty-six. It might already be too late to escape a lifetime of servitude to the McMullen men. Kate felt herself buckling under the burden of being trapped. In a panic, she turned into Jarrow cemetery and found herself standing in front of her mother's grave, unmarked except for a crude wooden cross and a dead posy of flowers that Catherine must have put there at Whitsuntide.

Dropping her bundle, Kate sank to her knees.

'Oh, Mam! I wish you were still here – I cannot face all this on me own . . .'

She started to weep quietly in the hazy September sunshine as unformed prayers came spilling out of her.

'Please help me. Give me strength to go on. Don't let Jack be badly wounded. I'll take care of him, I promise. Just don't let him be a cripple and a burden to me. I'll help him get better. Please help me . . .'

She did not know if she prayed to Our Lady or her own mother or both, but when she finally got to her feet and picked up her brown paper parcel, she felt an easing of the blackness that pressed around her. Kate walked back up the bank with her spirits lifted a fraction. Jack had survived. He could be her ally against old John now that Rose was gone. They would look out for each other like old times.

When she entered the back door, there was something about the stillness that alerted her. It weighed in the air like flour, thick and muffling. She dumped her shopping down on the table and unpinned her battered hat.

466

'I got the sheets in Ormonde Street.' She turned as she spoke. John was sitting upright in his chair as if to attention, his face impassive, drained of any colour. Catherine was squatting on the fender, her knees pulled up to her chin in a habitual defensive pose.

'What's wrong with the pair of you?' Kate asked. 'Angel walked through the room?'

Catherine started at her words and looked anxiously at her grandfather.

'Tell her,' he said dully, without looking at either of them.

Catherine held out a piece of paper she had been clutching.

'Telegram came while you were out.' Her voice was high-pitched and quavering. 'He died of his wounds. Jack's dead.' Her face crumpled as she said it.

Kate went forward quickly and pulled the girl to her, hugging her in comfort as she cried into her shoulder.

'Poor Kitty,' she gasped, clutching Catherine and stroking her hair. 'Poor Jack!'

Then suddenly she was crying too, weeping for her brave half-brother, dying so far away from home. Guilt quickened her tears that she should have been wallowing in self-pity over her mother's grave. She would have put up with him in any state, just to see Jack home again, giving her a shy smile. Why had she been so off-hand with him on his last visit home?

Kate cradled her sobbing daughter in distress. Jack might have been the only one who could have put John in his place and fought her corner. Now he was dead and gone, and she would never know.

Chapter 46

News of the Armistice reached Tyneside mid-morning on a chilly Monday in November. Hooters blared and bells rang. Workers at Palmer's and along the river downed tools and stopped the machines. People pulled on coats and spilt into the streets to share the sense of relief. Spontaneous cheers went up for the British Army and Navy. No one knew quite what to do.

Later, thousands of war-weary people flooded into the town centres along the river, carrying effigies of the Kaiser. From the New Buildings, Kate could see the crowds set fire to one on Jarrow's old pit heap. The bitter smell of kerosene filled the cold dank air and clung to the washing long after. Children were let out of school and marched through the town, banging tin drums and blowing mouth-organs and kazoos. Catherine improvised with paper and comb and rushed to join her friends.

Kate hurried up to Mary's in excitement. 'Get them blinds down. They can gan on the bonfire!'

'I might need them.' Mary was cautious.

But Kate just laughed and ran around the house ripping down the improvised blackouts. Her joy was infectious and soon Mary was helping her sister throw them out into the back lane along with hers. Within minutes children were

468

scrambling to take them to the heap and pile them on the fire.

'Haway, Mary,' Kate grinned, 'let's gan and watch.'

'But I've washing to do—'

'Oh aye, stop the Armistice – Mary's got her washing to finish,' Kate teased.

Kate rushed back into her house and emerged with a colander secured to her head with a scarf, clanging two pan lids together.

'What do you look like?' Mary spluttered.

'And here's a couple of spoons for you,' Kate said, pulling them out of her apron pocket.

Mary smirked, 'We haven't done something this daft for an age.'

'It's time we did,' Kate grinned, leading the way with a clash of kitchen cymbals.

That night the sky was filled with fireworks and the pubs ignored the wartime restrictions and stayed open till the barrels ran dry. The singing and drinking at Number Ten went on late, John's drinking friends knowing they would be welcome if they came with a tot of whisky to share. Eventually John grew maudlin about Jack and they helped him to bed, weeping like a child.

The celebrations were short-lived. John was soon back to his complaining and bullying. He plagued Kate all day long, for he had given up his war job. Since Jack's death, her wily stepfather was drawing a war pension, claiming he had been dependent on his son's army pay. Not a penny of it did he pass on to her for housekeeping, so Kate was once again forced to take in lodgers to make ends meet.

But as 1919 came, and civilian life resumed, there was no shortage of casual labour needing bed and board. Demand for shipping to replace the losses of the war was high. At least when there were other men in the house, John had to curb the worst of his abuse.

It was Catherine who proved more troublesome. Always one for playing up about tired legs and being sick to stay off school or avoid going to the pawnshop, she was brought back from school one day in a terrible state.

'Lass collapsed in the yard,' Kate was told. 'She cannot walk.'

Kate put her to bed, feeling guilty that she had forced the girl to school that morning, despite her tearful pleading to stay at home. She had complained of a fall a few days previously but Kate had given short shrift.

'Don't think you can skive off school for a scratch on your hip,' she had said dismissively.

But her daughter lay in bed for days, delirious with fever and unable to climb out of bed to go to the privy let alone walk there. Dr Dyer came and ordered complete bed rest, though he seemed baffled by Catherine's symptoms.

'She's lost the use of her legs, though nothing's broken. The girl's in a state of exhaustion – probably run down by the lack of nutrition from the shortages. Lots of rest and a good diet, Kate, that's what she needs.'

While Catherine lay ill and confined to bed, the lodgers went in the parlour and John had to sleep on the settle. He grumbled constantly but Kate was firm that the child must be left in peace. She pawned her daughter's shoes and school clothes to bring her kippers and grapes, trying to tempt her to eat. But Catherine was lacklustre and had no appetite. She showed no interest in the daily comings and goings beyond the half-open bedroom door.

'Eat a bit of pear, hinny,' Kate coaxed, 'you've got to get your strength back.'

Catherine turned her face away, her eyes staring fixedly on the blank wall, and said nothing. Kate was at a loss as to how to break the strange spell of silence that had settled on her usually forthright daughter.

'Well I don't have time to sit here all day talking to me own shadow.' She quickly lost patience and left.

Only at night did the girl find her voice, sometimes yelling out so loud in her sleep that Kate had to shake her awake before the lodgers complained.

'Stop your noise!' she hissed. 'Or we'll have the men banging on the wall.'

Afterwards, Kate tried to pull the girl into her arms and reassure her it was just a bad dream. But Catherine stiffened in rejection and held her face away as if she could not even bear to breathe the same air. So Kate's words of comfort shrivelled on her lips and she fell into exhausted sleep. Sometimes she slept late and it was John who came to rouse her with predatory hands on her thighs and buttocks.

'Get away!' Kate cried groggily.

'Well, you get up, you lazy bitch, and give us breakfast.'

Catherine lay in bed for weeks until gradually her interest in life returned. She found she could get up and walk a few steps. Kate moved her to the settle in the kitchen where she could watch the other children playing in the street. She still seemed oddly detached and did not show any inclination to try to join her friends. But Kate was heartened by her increasing appetite and the occasional spark of defiance.

'You'll be back at school by blackberry picking,' she encouraged.

'I'm not ganin' back,' Catherine announced. 'I don't learn anything useful.'

Kate snorted. 'Tell that to Miss Coulthard.'

471

'I wish she was dead,' Catherine muttered. 'She's always picked on me. I hate school.'

Kate scolded her for such a thought and let the matter drop.

During her long recuperation, Davie McDermott reappeared from sea and asked for lodgings.

'I heard about Jack,' he said with a touch on Kate's shoulder, 'and I'm sorry.'

She nodded and quickly cleared the bedroom for his use.

Catherine perked up to hear the stoker's tales of stormy voyages to the West Indies and America. They sat and played cards at one end of the table while Kate hummed over the ironing at the other. Kate enjoyed his quiet, easy-going presence and he was generous with jugs of beer in the evening. It reminded her of happier moments when Stoddie had flirted with her and made her feel special. She longed to know what had happened to Davie's brother-in-law, but was too shy to ask. Catherine, though, was not.

'Did he come home after the war?' she asked.

'Aye, he's working over Liverpool way,' Davie said, rolling a cigarette.

'Just think of it – after all them years in a prison camp. Can he speak German?'

Davie laughed softly. 'Don't rightly know.'

'D-did he –' Kate floundered, 'has he . . .? Is he wed to your Molly's friend?'

Davie shot her a look. 'Aye, been married six months or more. Taken a shore job to please her.'

Kate felt her heart squeeze. How she envied that woman!

'That's grand,' she forced herself to say. But shortly afterwards, she had to rush to the privy to stop the others seeing the tears she could not hold back.

Later, when Catherine had fallen asleep and John was not yet returned from the pub, she unburdened her troubles to Davie, her tongue loosened by drink.

'I cared for him,' she sniffed. 'I thought we had an understanding, me and Stoddie. But now I've got no one – never will, not as long as old John rules this house. I'm saddled with him and with the lass,' she said morosely. 'Look at her, sleeping with the face of an angel. But I cannot work her out. Sometimes she plays up like the Devil. I've tried to get her to learn her lessons, but she's that awkward. Does the very opposite of what I say, just to spite me. She's got his wayward nature, Mr High-and-Mighty Pringle-Davies.'

If she had not drunk so much, Kate would never have uttered his name. She had never spoken of him in years, had kept his name locked inside her like a guilty, burning secret. Why had she told such things to this quiet seaman, who gave away so little himself?

Suddenly Davie spoke. 'He can't have been worth much, leaving a lass like you to fend for yourself.'

She turned on him with bleary eyes. 'For years I kept hoping he might come back – daft, wasn't it? But I kept telling mesel' something must've happened to him, not to have done. But I was just being soft in the head. Lads just take what they want and hoy the rest to the Devil.' She gave a mirthless laugh.

Davie said nothing, his craggy face impassive, his eyes watchful.

'Sorry,' she mumbled, 'take no notice of what I say. It counts for nothing.'

She stood unsteadily and went to bank up the fire for the night.

The next day, to Kate's dismay, Davie packed his bag and said he was going home. She cursed herself for her drunken ramblings of the night before. She could not remember what she had said, except she knew it had been too much. She had a vague memory of mentioning Alexander, and blushed to think of it.

At the door, he turned to her and said very low, 'Stand up for yourself, Kate. Don't let old John or the lass lead you a merry dance.'

Kate returned inside with a heavy heart, to be greeted by Catherine's resentful look.

'He promised me a game of gin rummy,' she said petulantly, 'and now he's gone.'

Kate felt as wretched as the girl looked, but was not going to be blamed.

'Aye, well, if you're feeling so perky, you can get up and help me with the washing the day.'

To her astonishment, a short while later, Catherine appeared pale-faced in the wash-house doorway, clutching the bag of wooden pegs.

Chapter 47

Something changed within Kate after Davie's visit. She felt a small stirring of self-respect. The tongue-tied Cumbrian with the steady gaze had thought it worth telling her to stand up for herself. For years she had seen herself only as the family drudge, a woman ageing too fast from heavy chores, with a face grown ugly from fatigue, drink and disappointment. But he must have glimpsed something else, something of the old Kate that was worth rescuing. *Don't let old John or the lass lead you a merry dance.*

And oh, there had been plenty of that over the succeeding months!

Catherine had stubbornly refused to return to school. The weeks of absence had grown into months and the attendance officer had called regularly at their door. Even the news that Miss Coulthard had suddenly died did not persuade her mulish daughter to complete her schooling.

'I'm finished with it,' she said dismissively, 'I want to earn me own living. I don't want to be tret like a bairn any more.' How could she tell her mother that it was debt that paralysed her with fear? She wanted to help out so that Kate would be pleased with her and love her more. She longed for her mother to be respectable and not the focus of neighbours' scorn for haunting the pawnshops.

So against Kate's wishes and after a storm of angry words, Catherine found employment at one of the larger houses in Simonside Terrace, cleaning and washing for the family of a foreman carpenter. Her days were long and arduous, but she seemed to thrive on her small bid for independence and the ten shillings a week that she earned.

Kate demanded most of it, but she noticed how Catherine saved the small amounts she allowed her to keep and spent them on more fashionable clothes and a large-brimmed hat that was her pride and joy. After several months of working life, she bought a second-hand bicycle, having hankered for one for years. She disappeared into the countryside on Saturday afternoons with her friend Lily, whom she had met at the church youth club, and the girls would return with ruddy cheeks. Often Lily would stay over and Kate would hear them whispering and giggling late into the night and be reminded of her and Sarah at that age. But Catherine never shared their confidences with her.

At fourteen, her daughter was quick to challenge her over what she wore and the chores she agreed to do. The arguments increased, but Kate watched in astonishment and a touch of admiration as the girl answered John with spirited replies when he cursed the world, especially Protestants.

'I think the Salvation Army are canny,' she declared. 'They're not afraid to shout out their faith in the marketplace.'

Kate had to shove her daughter out of the kitchen as John came after her, waving the poker and baying for her blood. Whether it was Davie's words or Catherine's defiance that prompted Kate to turn on John, she was never sure. But one night in 1921 when he stormed after her drunkenly around the kitchen table, threatening her with the hated poker, she struck back.

476

Without thinking, Kate seized the heavy cast-iron frying pan in which she had cooked his tea.

'Stay away from me!' she yelled, wheeling round to face him.

He sneered, 'You wouldn't dare. I'd kill you first.'

'I dare,' she cried. 'I've had enough of you and your bullying ways. If you touch me again, by God, I'll hit you with this!'

John laughed harshly and swayed towards her. 'You don't frighten me, you slut. Look at you – boozy old hag.'

Enraged, she swung the frying pan above her head and brought it crashing down on his.

He staggered back in surprise, tripped over a stool and crashed to the floor, hitting himself on the table as he fell. Kate stood in disbelief at what she had just done. He lay quite still on the floor. She had killed him! Her heart thumped in shock. Then he groaned and moved. Kate dropped the pan with a clang and ran to the bedroom.

'Kitty, get up this minute!' She shook her daughter awake, terrified that any moment John would come barging after her and beat her to a pulp. 'Quick, Kitty, we have to flee!'

She dragged the sleepy girl out of bed, hardly giving her a moment to throw on a coat over her nightdress. Catherine stopped short at the sight of her grandfather sprawled on the floor, a hand clutched to his head. Blood was trickling through his fingers.

'Grandda?'

'Haway, Kitty,' Kate urged without explanation and pulled her out of the house and into the windy night. They ran up the street and hammered on Mary's door. 'Let us in, Mary! Father's after us! Let us in, for pity's sake.'

A yawning tousled-haired Alec came to the door and let them inside. That night they bedded down on Mary's chintz-

477

covered sofa while Mary's husband went round to see that John still lived. He came back reporting, 'The old devil's got a sore head and a bruise the size of a football. I bandaged him up and got him to bed. But I'd stay away, if I was you.'

So the next day Catherine went off to work and Kate laid low at her sister's house, wary of any heavy footfall in the street below. But John did not come breaking down Mary's door or haranguing them foully for all the neighbours to hear.

'Maybes you've taught him a lesson,' Mary said with a touch of admiration. 'Mam should've done the same years ago.'

Still, Kate kept away, lending a hand around the house and busying herself polishing the many brasses. In the evenings Catherine came in and helped young Alec with his reading. After several days, the sisters were tiring of such close company.

'You'll have to find somewhere else,' Mary decreed.

'Give us a few more days,' Kate bargained, 'while I sort something out.' She thought grimly how they would have to look for cheap rooms in Tyne Dock. With only Catherine's wages and her meagre pay from cleaning jobs they could afford little else. Maybe they could stretch to two rooms and take in lodgers in the second.

As Kate was fretting over their future, she was startled by a rap at the door. Mary peered behind the lace curtain into the street below.

'It's Father,' she gasped. 'You'll have to gan down and speak to him. I'll not have a scene at my door.'

Kate felt sick, but she gripped her skirts to stop her hands shaking and went to answer the knocking.

'Well?' She stared at him, chin raised.

'What you doing hiding here?' he demanded aggressively, though he stood hunched and uncertain. He looked old and ill, his eyes bloodshot and the gash to his head still congealed with dried blood from where he had struck the table. Kate said nothing. 'There's nowt in the house,' he whined.

'So?'

He looked around edgily. 'Come back, lass. Both of you.'

Kate steeled herself against his pathetically pleading look. She would not pity him!

'We're not coming back.'

John peered beyond her. Perhaps he hoped for a glimpse of Catherine.

'Kitty's not in,' Kate told him flatly, 'and you'll not get round her either.'

'Mary'll not keep you for long,' he growled. 'She'll drive you into the madhouse with her bitching.'

'We'll find something.'

John's face sagged. 'Please come home. I promise you I'll not touch you again.'

Kate could hardly keep herself from laughing out loud. How she wished she could believe him! Number Ten might be bearable if only she could go to bed at night free of fear of assault, free of having to placate his drunken outbursts, free of flying chairs and fists.

He must have sensed her wavering for he added, 'Please, for the sake of your dear mother's memory. She wouldn't want me left on me own.'

Kate gave him a contemptuous look. Rose would have left him years ago if it had not been for her daughters. She had thrown in her lot with her abusive husband so as to give them a chance of escape to a better life. Kate saw that now. And it occurred to her that that was what she was prepared to do too.

479

She would go back for Catherine's sake if she had to, but she was determined to hold out as long as she could.

'I'll send the lass round with some bread and bacon,' Kate conceded. Then shut the door on him.

Mary was gleeful. 'That showed the old devil. Never thought you'd face up to him like that. And you the one always trying to please him when we were lasses!'

It was a grudging compliment, but Kate felt encouraged. The next day, she spent a fruitless morning looking for somewhere to rent. There was nothing she could afford. Despite the recent slump at the yards, prices were still high and there was a shortage of cheap dwellings to rent. She balked at the thought of taking Catherine to live in a cheap lodging house and doubted her recalcitrant daughter would follow her.

Kate traipsed back to Mary's to find Catherine already there.

'What you doing back so early?'

'I'm not ganin' to work for the likes of them no longer,' her daughter pouted.

Kate looked at her in dismay. 'They've sacked you?'

'No,' Catherine was aggrieved, 'I gave me notice.'

'What?' Kate exclaimed. 'Are you daft in the head? They're laying folk off at the yards and cutting their wages and you choose this moment to pack in your job!'

'Well, she was that bossy,' Catherine defended. 'I got sick of her telling me what to do.'

Kate was about to start a shouting match, when she suddenly crumpled and burst into tears. Catherine looked at her in alarm.

'I'll find something else,' she promised quickly. 'I'll work hard, but not for those who lord it over me. As Grandda says, no matter who they are, they've all got to gan to the netty!'

The thought of John made Kate cry even harder. To distract her, Catherine pulled on her arm.

'Kate, there's something I want to show you – something you should see. It's in Mary's dressing table.'

Kate wiped her face on her sleeve. What had the girl been up to now?

'You shouldn't be poking your nose into her things. She'll wipe the floor with you if she finds out. Where is she, any road?'

'Out shopping down Jarrow. Haway and look!'

Warily, Kate followed her daughter into Mary's bedroom, where her sister never let her polish. It smelt pleasantly of eau-de-Cologne, and the bed was covered in a pretty pink bedspread. She felt a stab of envy as she watched Catherine pull open one of the gleaming mahogany drawers and reach to the back. She pulled out a muslin bundle tied up in string. Untying it, she held out the contents. It was a wad of paper, grubby-edged. Letters.

Kate's stomach turned over as she took them. She knew the spidery writing.

'Stoddie,' she whispered. 'What's he doing writing to our Mary?'

'Not Mary,' Catherine said quietly.

Then it hit Kate. They were addressed to her. She sat down on the bed before her knees gave way. Sifting through them with trembling hands, she asked in confusion, 'I don't understand. What are they doing here?'

'Look,' Catherine pointed, 'the dates on them. They were written years ago – during the war. For some reason he sent them here.'

481

Kate's insides squeezed. 'I told him to – but I thought he'd stopped. Mary never said.' The full enormity of what her sister had done began to dawn on her. 'She kept them from me!'

With trembling hands, Kate pulled out the top letter from its flimsy envelope, almost reluctant to read it. But she had to know.

Dearest Kate,

How are you? It's weeks since I heard from you. How is the bairn? I keep the picture she drew me in me top pocket. Please thank her. It keeps me cheerful. It's cold here now, but we don't complain. Must be twice as bad for the lads in the trenches. I miss you and think of you always. Write to me when you can and let me know you still think of me.

Fondest regards,

Stoddie.

Kate's eyes welled with tears. He had cared for her after all. She forced herself to read the other six letters. They grew increasingly despondent, reproaching her for not writing back. The final one, dated in the summer of 1916, was full of hurt and regret.

. . . I see from your silence that you never thought of me in the same way I did think of you. I am sorry if my letters have not been welcome. I shall not write another. Send my best wishes to the lassie.

Yours aye,

Jock Stoddart.

'What do they say, Kate? Are they nice letters?' Catherine asked eagerly.

Kate bowed her head in misery. She could have had him! He could have been married to her now, instead of some widow friend of Molly McDermott's. Catherine could have had a proper father. Kate fought down the desire to be sick. Her own sister had hidden these letters from her and robbed her of a chance of happiness! How dare she?

Kate's wretchedness turned to white-hot fury. With a roar of pain, she picked up Mary's bottle of eau-de-Cologne and smashed it against the large dressing-table mirror. Glass splintered into a hundred shards. She launched herself at the row of ornaments and brushes, scattering them to the floor, cutting her hands with broken glass.

'Stop it!' Catherine cried in alarm. 'You're bleeding!'

But Kate could not stop. She turned and set about the bed, pulling off the pink bedspread and ripping it with her chapped and bloodied bare hands. Catherine tried to intervene but her mother shoved her out of the way. Only the sound of the front door clicking open and shut halted the storm of destruction.

Mary stood looking in at them, her hat half removed, her expression frozen in disbelief.

'What you doing in my bedroom?' she demanded in annoyance. Then as she registered the devastation, her face slackened in horror. 'What the devil . . .?'

Kate sprang at her like a demon possessed. 'You hid his letters!' she howled. 'You hid my Stoddie's letters!'

'How dare you go through my things?' Mary went on the attack at once.

'They were mine,' Kate choked. 'You did it out of spite.'

'I did it for your own good,' Mary declared. 'Father would never have let you marry him – he was Scotch and

483

a Protestant. I was saving you from a whole heap of bother.'

'Liar! You just couldn't bear to see me happy with a man, could you? If I'd married Stoddie you wouldn't have been able to lord it over me. You're a selfish, spiteful bitch!'

'You're the spiteful one,' Mary spat back. 'All those cruel things you've said about my Alec being a conchie and a yellow-belly and not doing his bit for the war. I hated you for that – you and Jack – you were the ones lording it over us. And as for Jock Stoddart – he was just a common stoker, a loud-mouth and a drunkard,' she sneered. 'Jack said he was always going with other women. He was just leading you on. Would never have married you in a month of Sundays.'

Kate could not bear such a thought. She flew at her sister, grabbing her linen coat. They tussled and the sleeve tore. Mary screamed and ducked away, but Kate seized hold of her hair and pulled hard, a clump coming away in her hand. Mary jabbed fingers in Kate's face. Blinded, Kate stumbled but took her sister with her. They rolled on the floor, kicking and scratching and swearing their pent-up hatred.

Catherine, appalled by the spectacle, tried to intervene, but got knocked out of the way. She picked herself up and ran out into the street, looking for help. But she could not bring herself to ask a neighbour to intervene. It was too demeaning. So she ran down to Number Ten and roused her grandfather from dozing in his chair.

'Come quickly, they're killing each other!' she panted, pulling him up with all her strength. 'Please come, Grandda.'

John limped up the street to Mary's house, where the noise of their fighting could still be heard. He barged between the two of them, flinging Mary aside and hauling Kate to her feet.

'Your mother would turn in her grave to see the pair of you,' he bellowed. 'What's come over you?'

They glared at each other, but neither wanted to explain to him.

'Get her out me house,' Mary hissed, her hair dishevelled and her face bruised.

'Don't worry, I wouldn't stop here another minute if it was the last house standing in Jarrow,' Kate said contemptuously.

'Haway,' John barked, 'you're coming home with me. I knew you wouldn't last two minutes with her.'

Without another word, Kate hobbled out after her stepfather and down the stairs. Catherine gave a regretful glance at Mary's spotlessly clean kitchen, shrugged at her aunt and followed them out.

Chapter 48

The sisters did not speak to each other again for months. Kate suspected that Catherine called round to her aunt's house occasionally, for she would sometimes wander in with her cousin Alec in tow, pretending they had met in the street. Kate was fond of the boy and fed him scraps of baking, but never mentioned his mother. Her anger eventually died down to a smouldering resentment that flared only in drink.

At such times, she railed against life's unfairness and lashed out at her daughter for ever having brought the letters to her attention. Better never to have known, was Kate's bitter thought, though deep down she knew Catherine had only been trying to please her. The girl had not known the content of the letters and could not have guessed the trouble it would cause by bringing them to light.

Their relationship was as full of quick-fire argument as ever, but Kate was secretly admiring of her daughter's stubborn determination to get on in the world.

Shortly after leaving her cleaning job, Catherine had astonished both her and John by announcing that she was setting up in business painting silk and satin cushion covers and tray cloths.

'But you can't paint!' Kate was disbelieving.

'I can so!' Catherine declared. 'I had a lesson off Amelia at church. I'm ganin' to paint birds and flowers. You can buy these transfers.'

'Where you getting the money for this?' Kate demanded.

'I've got deposits off me new clients,' Catherine said gleefully. 'I'm buying the materials the morrow. Amelia's ganin' to help me chose.'

Within a week, Catherine had completed ten orders for people from church and had begun to canvass neighbours and friends. Despite the creeping slump on Tyneside and the shutdown of Palmer's ironworks, she found more work than she could cope with. She would sit up late at night, eyes straining over her miniature paintings of flowers and fruit in the dim lamplight in order to finish a job in time for someone's birthday. Sometimes, if she was not too tired, Kate would sit up and sew the finished pieces into covers or stitch pieces of lace to a mantelpiece cloth.

At such times they worked together in companionable silence as the gas lamp hissed and rain spat down the chimney on to the fire. Occasionally Kate would sing snatches of songs from the war or old favourites such as 'Thora'. Once, she caught Catherine looking at her with tear-filled eyes. Kate stopped singing.

'What's wrong, hinny?'

Catherine said quietly, 'I wish it could always be like this – just you and me . . .' She broke off unable to say that she wanted her mother to herself, without warring relations or drink or the censure of the outside world – all those things that kept them apart and fed the animosity between them. The shame of her illegitimacy was seared into her soul, but at moments like this Catherine could pretend that they were a normal mother and daughter with no one sneering at them.

'Just you and me?' Kate smiled at her ruefully.

'Aye,' Catherine blushed, and bowed her head.

Kate reached out and covered Catherine's hand with hers. 'You'll always have me, hinny,' Kate said softly, 'always.'

When Catherine glanced up, she saw that her mother's eyes were glistening with tears too. They smiled at each other, and for a moment, all the bad times of quarrelling and accusation receded into the shadows.

Without another word they carried on working, Kate humming quietly, each wishing the closeness they felt would last.

1922 wore on and Catherine turned sixteen. In a week or two, she would be forty, Kate thought. As she stared in the mirror hanging over the wash basin in the scullery, she was startled to see the beginnings of Rose's haggard face looking back. She remembered her own mother at this age, old and care-worn after hard years when John worked little and she lived on the scrapings at the bottom of the pot. They had been living in Frost Street, or was it Napier? One of a series of dismal, overcrowded dwellings they had inhabited briefly like tinkers before having to move on. Rose must have been about forty when work had picked up and they had moved for a while to the luxury of the New Buildings and its veneer of respectability.

And she had been about sixteen – Catherine's age. Kate sighed to think how full of energy and life she had been then, eager to work hard and see a bit of the world beyond Tyne Dock and Jarrow. Eager for love. Always singing. Sometimes she studied her daughter, head bent over her endless paintings, a frown of concentration on her wide brow. Auburn hair glinting. She was far more contrary, one minute playing the clown with her friend Lily, the next anxiously censorious and scurrying off to Confession. The girl could scowl like Father O'Neill yet laugh like a music-hall comic.

What would her daughter do with her life? She had sudden flashes of talent, such as her painting and a head for carrying words. She could recite verse after verse of poetry and song. Yet she did not strike Kate as a happy girl, one that could enjoy life and really let herself go once in a while. Kate blamed herself for much of the shortcomings in Catherine's life, but she would not be blamed for that. She at least had known how to love, to seize each moment of joy, however fleeting. She had regretted bitterly Alexander's abandonment of her, but she had known a man's love and had returned it generously. She knew Catherine was far too cautious and devout to make the mistake she had, yet she pitied the girl if she never allowed herself the thrill of falling in love.

A knock on the back door startled her out of her reverie.

'Come in,' she called, quickly pushing back her tousled hair behind its pins.

The door pushed open and a broad-shouldered figure filled the doorway, the dazzling July light behind him throwing his face in shadow. Kate's heart pummelled in her chest. The familiar wave of hair, the stocky upper body. Alexander! How long had she waited for this moment? An eternity.

'Is it you?' she gasped.

The man moved forward and threw down his bag.

'Kate?' he said quizzically. 'I didn't mean to give you a fright.'

Kate's insides churned in disappointment. It was only Davie McDermott. How foolish of her to mistake for one instant this burly man with his chiselled face still grimy from the engine-room for her long-lost lover.

'Oh, Davie,' she said flatly, 'haway in.'

If he minded her half-hearted welcome he did not show it. The seaman offered at once to refill the hod with coal while Kate made him a cup of tea. She busied herself at the stove, trying to rid her mind of Alexander. How had he come back so vividly to her after all this time? Would she never be rid of this hold he had over her thoughts?

She hardly glanced at Davie or noticed what she should have. Catherine saw it the moment she came in from delivering a parcel of cushion covers.

'Who's died?'

Kate turned from stirring the bean broth. Davie was fingering a black arm band self-consciously.

'My Molly,' he said quietly.

'Your wife?' Kate cried in pity. 'That's terrible. What happened?'

'Heart gave out – she's always been delicate.' He paused and Kate realised he was finding the subject difficult, so just nodded.

'When did it happen?' Catherine asked.

'Turn of the year – I was away at sea.' He shook his head and sighed. ' "Always away at sea when I need you," that's what she used to say.'

'You couldn't help that,' Kate said kindly, 'and you did your best by her.'

There was an awkward silence, which Catherine broke. 'I'll say prayers for Mrs McDermott at Mass,' she promised.

Davie smiled in gratitude and nothing more was said on the matter.

But when Kate's birthday came and Davie was still ensconced at Number Ten, Catherine sparked off a row.

'How long's he stopping?' she demanded crossly. 'I cannot

work with him spreading out his newspaper on the table and lying around sleeping half the day.'

'The poor man's got nowhere else to gan,' Kate pointed out.

'He must've other family,' Catherine retorted.

'Molly never gave him bairns – though I think he would have liked some. He was always canny to you when you were young.'

Catherine ignored this. 'When's he going back to sea, then?'

'I don't know.' Kate grew impatient. 'But I'll not have him driven out by your black looks. He pays his way – which is more than you can say for most men round here now the steel mills are closed.'

'He drinks it all away,' Catherine muttered with disapproval.

'That's his business what he does with his wages!' Kate cried. 'He's a right to a bit of fun after months stuck below deck grafting hard.'

'He's still in mourning.'

Kate was riled by her pious tone. 'Well, we're ganin' down the Penny Whistle to meet Maisie for me birthday whether you and the priests like it or not!'

Catherine stormed out and up the street to Mary's. It infuriated Kate that the girl always turned to her waspish sister when she was angry with her. No doubt Mary fuelled the fire of her daughter's discontent. Maybe it was Mary who had turned Catherine against Davie these past weeks, in revenge for last year's attack over Stoddie's letters.

But when Davie came in from washing in the backyard tub, grinning bashfully in an ill-fitting suit of Jack's, Kate determined to enjoy her birthday. John, who could no longer

491

walk easily into town, was content with the jug of beer Davie bought him before they left.

They came home late, singing and laughing from a merry session in the snug of the Penny Whistle, Kate linking her arm through Davie's to keep her from tripping on the uneven cobbles. At the top of the bank, they stopped and looked out over the dark river and the hunched cranes and gantries of the yards.

'Look at that, Kate,' Davie said with awe in his voice. 'That bit of river never ends, does it? Carries on out to sea – goes on for ever and ever.'

Kate giggled. 'Never heard you talk all philosophical before,' she teased.

He laughed self-consciously. 'That's what I used to think as a lad. Just get on the sea and you can go anywhere you like – free as a fish.'

Kate was suddenly struck by the familiarity of his words. Where had she heard such dreams before? Alexander. He had talked of the sea like that, as a way to freedom. That's how he had probably escaped from her and their unborn baby.

'That's what he used to say,' Kate blurted out.

'Who?' Davie asked.

'Oh, it doesn't matter.' She felt foolish.

He took her arm and pulled her round gently. 'Do you mean Pringle-Davies?'

Kate gasped. 'How do you know his name?'

'You told me once.'

Kate tried to turn from him. 'I shouldn't have been so daft . . .'

Davie held on to her. 'I'd heard the name before – I was sure of it. But I never said anything, 'cos I couldn't remember how.'

Kate looked into his face, her heart beginning to beat uncomfortably. 'Did you ever remember?' she whispered.

'Aye, I did.' He gazed out to sea for a moment. 'It was on a voyage to Russia. We'd put in at Gävle, Sweden to take on timber, but we got storm-bound for a week. There wasn't much to do in the place, so I did what I often do when I'm stuck on land.' He stopped and looked sheepish. Kate feared he would say something shameful that a woman should not hear. But she had to know what he knew about Alexander.

'Go on,' she encouraged. 'I know what seamen are like.'

'It's not that,' Davie said at once.

'Then what?'

'I go and sit in churchyards – cemeteries,' he confessed. 'Read the headstones and imagine the people.'

Kate stared at him, her heart thudding. 'What are you saying?'

He put a hand on her shoulder. 'There's a part of the cemetery in Gävle for foreigners – for all the sailors and them that are taken sick off ships. Some have no headstones or just wooden crosses. But there's one that sticks out – more fancy, with a raven carved on the top.'

Kate's heart jolted. The raven, symbol of Ravensworth.

'And?' she breathed with difficulty.

'The name was Alexander Pringle-Davies from England. I remembered it because it said he came from County Durham.'

Kate felt her knees go weak. She grasped on to his arms. 'Are you sure?' she croaked.

Davie nodded.

'Why didn't you tell me before?' she accused, tears stinging her eyes.

'I wanted to be sure,' Davie said gently. 'Last autumn we

493

put into Gävle with a load of coal and I went to check. It was the name I'd remembered.'

Kate closed her eyes and tried to squeeze back the stinging tears. So he was dead. There was no more vain hoping, however slim. Alexander would never come back for her or Catherine. It was just as she had feared all along.

'Kate,' Davie shook her, 'there was something else on the stone.'

She opened her eyes in dread. Was he about to tell her Alexander had left a devoted wife and several bereft children?

'His dates,' he said, holding on to her. She searched his face. 'He died in nineteen-o-six. July.'

Kate let out a cry of anguish. 'Just after Kitty was born!'

'But don't you see what that means? He couldn't have come back for you. He never even lived long enough to know you'd had the lass.'

She began to shake. 'No, he couldn't, could he? Or sent me money for the bairn.' She gripped him. 'Did it mention a wife? D-did Alexander marry?'

Davie looked at her with compassion in his weathered face. What good would it do her knowing the stone had been dedicated by his 'loving wife Polly'? He could at least save her that extra anguish. Davie shook his head.

Kate felt light-headed with relief. 'So he might have come back in time . . .?' She searched his face for reassurance.

'Aye, he might well have,' Davie comforted.

Kate was engulfed by a fresh wave of desolation. 'He had a blood disease,' she said quietly. 'He must've died of that.'

Suddenly Kate crumpled and gave way to bitter tears of regret. Davie quickly pulled her to him and wrapped his strong arms about her. She sobbed into his shoulder, grateful for his kindness.

After a while, he stroked her hair and said softly, 'Kate, we're both on our own now. And it's like coming home for me when I stay here. Why don't we get wed?'

She pulled away and looked at him in astonishment. But his look was earnest.

'Wed?' she exclaimed. 'What you want to marry me for?'

He smiled bashfully under his bushy moustache. ''Cos I care for you, lass. Always have done – even when my Molly was still alive.'

She stared at him as the full implication of what he had said sunk in.

'All that time?' she whispered.

'Aye. I could see it was Stoddie you cared for, not me,' he said without rancour, 'and I would never have said anything . . . but with Molly passing on . . .' He squeezed her shoulders as if to give him courage. 'What do you say, Kate?'

She was full of confusion. She did not love him, but he was a good man and in time she might grow to be fond of him. Yet she hesitated.

'What about Father?'

'He could live with us,' Davie said generously, mistaking Kate's fear of John's refusal for concern. 'And my pay from sea will keep him happy in drink, I wouldn't wonder.'

'But there's Kitty . . .' Kate was still uncertain.

'I'd be happy to take on the lass,' Davie insisted. 'I've always had a soft spot for her.' He gave her a considering look. 'And maybe in time, we could give her a brother or sister to help care for.'

Kate laughed drily. 'I'm forty years old, Davie man. What you want with an old woman like me?'

He leaned forward and daringly kissed her cheek. 'You're still a bonny woman to me.'

Kate touched his bristly chin in affection. 'I'll think on it,' was all she would promise.

When Kate told John that Davie had asked her to marry him, he blustered but did not say no. Catherine's reaction came as a complete shock.

'You're never going to say yes to him?' she said in horror.

'I might,' Kate was stung into replying.

'What about me?' Catherine demanded.

'Davie's happy to take you on as his daughter—'

'Never!' she cried. 'He's not me da – he's a common stoker.'

Kate flushed in anger. 'Those are Mary's words, I bet. Don't you turn your nose up at Davie McDermott. He's as honest and hard-working a man as ever you're likely to meet. I thought you'd be pleased he wants to marry your mam.'

'Well I'm not!' Catherine said tearfully. 'Where am I supposed to sleep if he moves in with you? On the settle like a lodger? There'll be no place for me.'

'He'll be away at sea half the time,' Kate floundered.

'You just want me out the way, don't you? You'd rather have him than me any day. I bet you wish I'd never been born!'

'Don't be daft . . .'

'Well, don't worry, I'll not stop,' Catherine cried. 'If you marry that man, I'll go.' She gave Kate such a look of anger that her heart went cold. 'And I'll never come back!'

Kate was shaken to the core by her daughter's vehemence against marriage to Davie, and began to have doubts. Perhaps she was better off alone if it would cause such conflict under her roof. When the day came for Davie to rejoin his ship, she told him regretfully, 'I cannot marry you. The lass has taken against the idea. It wouldn't work.'

For the first time she saw his mouth tighten in annoyance and his brown eyes blaze at her. 'It would've worked fine well,' he cried. 'You're just hiding behind the lass.'

'No I'm not,' Kate protested.

'You won't let yourself care for another man,' Davie said angrily, 'one that honestly loves you. Alexander's dead and Stoddie's married another. But I'm here! What are you frightened of, Kate? That I'll treat you as bad as all the other men in your life? 'Cos if that's how little you think of me, then it's best we never marry!'

He seized his duffel bag, swung it on to his shoulder and marched to the door. He turned, his expression desolate. 'We're sailing for South America – a year at sea. When I come back I'll look for lodgings somewhere else.' Before she could say a word, he was striding out of the house, the door banging behind him.

Kate sank on to the settle, trembling. What he said was so true! She did fear marrying him. He was nice to her now, but once he was master in their house, would he not turn tyrant like John? That was how men were with women like her, women held in contempt by all around them, women whispered about behind their backs for their immorality and weakness. They were the drudges that the world believed should be grateful for not being thrown out on the street.

Kate could not stop shaking. When had she turned into such a woman? When had her opinion of herself started to slide until she thought herself unworthy of anyone's love? When she'd first become pregnant? When cowardly Alexander walked out of her life? Or was it the gradual poisonous drip of John's scorn, of Jack's unhealthy interest?

She sat all alone, too numb to cry. Catherine had gone out on her bicycle to avoid saying goodbye to Davie. John was

497

drinking somewhere. She lay down on the settle and curled up like a frightened child, hugging herself and trying to stop trembling. The clock ticked as loud as a hammer. Half an hour passed. Davie would be boarding his ship. An hour. Kate dozed.

The clock struck four and woke her. Davie was gone. How achingly empty she felt. What had he said to her once? *Stand up for yourself, Kate. Don't let John or the lass lead you a merry dance.*

Her head throbbed. What was she doing lying here feeling sorry for herself? If she did not move now, it would always be like this, taking second place to the wants of others. She had done that for too long.

Kate jumped up and grabbed her jacket. When was his ship sailing? Three o'clock, four, five? She dashed for the door and across the yard, not bothering to close the gate behind her. Kate picked up her skirts and began to run. Out of the lane and down the long Jarrow road to Tyne Dock. Her bad foot ached as she pushed herself on, her chest wheezing with the effort, pulse thumping in her throat.

Which quay was Davie's boat sailing from? What was it called? She hurried on, stumbling down the hill, sobs catching in her thoat. If Davie sailed without her ever saying sorry for her churlish refusal, she might never see him again.

As she gained the end of Leam Lane and the familiar streets crowded around her, she remembered the name of the ship.

'The *India Star*!' She stopped a man in passing. 'Do you know where she's sailing from?'

He shrugged. 'Where's she going to?'

'South America,' Kate panted.

'Probably down Shields,' he grunted. 'You'd best get the tram.'

Kate let out a sob. 'I don't have the fare and it sails this afternoon!'

He took pity on her and fished out a penny. 'I hope he's worth the bother.'

Kate took the penny with a cry of thanks and dashed for the tram stand. It seemed to take an age for one to appear, rattling along its rails. Once aboard, she panicked. Where should she get off? Kate asked the other passengers in the dim hope that one of them might know.

'The *India Star*?' a boy answered. 'It's off the Mill Dam – by the customs house. Least it was this morning.'

Kate almost kissed him. Squeezing her way through to the steps of the tram, she jumped off at the stop before St Hilda's pit. The cobbled lane to the Mill Dam quayside snaked down between blackened housing and rough public houses. As a child she had been warned off from begging round there by her mother, in case slave-traders captured her and spirited her away on a ship.

Nothing was going to stop her running down there now. The quayside was a confusion of carts and lorries, men rolling barrels and humping sacks and fishwives calling their wares. How would she ever find Davie in all this crowd? Still, she hurried closer to the quayside, straining over the heads of others to try to see the name of the ships anchored there. There was no sign of the *India Star*.

A terrible thought struck her. Even if the ship had not sailed, Davie would be far below deck stoking up the fires in the furnace of the engine rooms. She would be too late to speak to him. She had missed her chance, her one final chance of happiness.

Someone touched her on the shoulder and she jerked round in panic.

'What you doing here?'

'Davie!' Her heart hammered. Here he was in front of her! Suddenly she was incapable of speech.

'You on your own?' he asked suspiciously. She nodded. 'You shouldn't, it's dangerous.'

She smelt the drink on his breath. Had he been drowning his sorrows or drinking to freedom? Kate had to know.

'I – I thought I'd missed you.' She forced out the words. 'I wanted to say – to say . . .'

Davie watched her with his usual guarded expression.

'I want – I will,' she stammered. 'When you come back from South America – I'll marry you.' Kate held her breath. 'That's if you want to—'

'Want to?' Davie exclaimed. Then his face broke into a happy grin. 'Course I want to!'

He opened his arms wide and Kate fell against him in relief.

'That's grand,' she cried, tears blurring her vision.

'You'll not change your mind?' Davie asked, unable to believe in his sudden change of luck. Minutes ago he had been trying to blot out his failure with Kate with a gutful of rum. Now she was in his arms.

'I'll not change it, I promise,' Kate smiled tearfully.

And right there, in the middle of the teeming quayside, she kissed Davie on the lips like a wife saying farewell to her husband. She did not mind the bitter-sweet taste of rum or the scratchiness of his bristling moustache. For in her mind, she saw their names on a marriage certificate, proclaiming to the world that she was a respectable married woman. Her past would dissolve and she would meet people's look in the street with pride. She saw Davie sitting across the hearth from her, rolling his cigarettes, or lying next to her in the large feather bed, holding her tight in his sleep.

Joy bubbled up inside her. Catherine would come round to the idea. There was plenty of time for her to grow used to it while Davie was away. It was only natural for the girl to be a bit resentful of a new man coming into the family, when for so long she had had Kate to herself. But one day her daughter would thank her for giving her the father she craved. And Davie would be a kind father, given half a chance.

'I'll be a good husband to you, lass.' He smiled at her warmly, as if reading her mind.

Kate thrilled at the words she had thought never to hear from any man's lips.

'Aye, I know you will,' she smiled back.

Davie grinned and hugged her to him tightly. 'I love you, Kate.'

A sob of happiness caught in her throat. 'Show me then,' she laughed through her tears.

Davie kissed her back.

The Jarrow Lass

Janet MacLeod Trotter

Brought up on her parents' smallholding in Jarrow, Rose McConnell knows she is luckier than many in Tyneside during the harsh years of the 1870s. But she can't help dreaming of the world she has glimpsed in the idyllic country estate of Ravensworth where her own mother grew up. And when she captures the heart of handsome William Fawcett, who comes from a respectable family and lives in the well-to-do James Terrace, it seems her dream of a better life is finally within her reach.

As the years go by she is blessed not only with a loving husband she adores, but with a home of her own and a brood of beautiful daughters who she vows will never know the hardships of her own upbringing. But with the poverty of Jarrow never far away it sometimes seems that the security of Rose's new life is as delicate as her childhood dreams . . .

Praise for Janet MacLeod Trotter's previous novels:

'Brings a time and a place vividly to life and makes compulsive reading' *Northern Echo*

'A passionate and dramatic story that definitely warrants a box of tissues by the bedside' *Worcester Evening News*

'A gritty, heartrending and impassioned drama' *Newcastle Journal*

0 7472 6740 5

headline

For Love And Glory

Janet MacLeod Trotter

Growing up in Jericho Street, Tyneside, Jo Elliot has always enjoyed a special friendship with her brother, Colin, and his best friend, Mark. However, when Mark joins the merchant navy, Jo finds herself seduced by Gordon, Mark's ruggedly masculine older brother. It is a secret and short-lived affair: Mark, returning on leave, finds Jo recovering from a broken relationship with a man she now hates and whose identity she will never reveal.

Mark's tender love begins to heal her and their affection flares into a deep passion, but then something comes to light that shatters Jo's hopes for the future and ultimately destroys her wonderful relationship with Mark. As war breaks out in the Falklands both Colin and Mark are called up to fight. It's then that Jo realises that the tragic secrets of the past must not be allowed to affect the future. And that life is too precious to spend it without the man she truly loves – if it's not too late . . .

Praise for Janet MacLeod Trotter's previous novels

'A passionate and dramatic story that definitely warrants a box of tissues by the bedside' *Worcester Evening News*

'A gritty, heartrending and impassioned drama' *Newcastle Journal*

'A tough, compelling and ultimately satisfying novel . . . another classy, irresistible read' *Sunderland Echo*

0 7472 6003 6

headline

Chasing the Dream

Janet MacLeod Trotter

It's 1920 when life in the small pit village of Craston becomes so unbearable that Millie Mercer's mother Teresa escapes with her daughter to the nearby town of Ashborough. They find work at the dilapidated Station Hotel where Millie meets Dan Nixon, a dangerously charming man who is to change her destiny forever. For Dan is the local hero: a professional footballer who sees his future not in the pit but on the pitch, playing first division football for Newcastle United.

Millie can't believe her luck when Dan asks her to marry him. His looks, his passion for the sport and his determination to succeed make the future of his dreams one of happiness and prosperity. But it's not long before Dan's drinking habits and rumours of his womanising threaten to damage both his career and his family. When tragedy strikes and an old, well-kept secret is finally exposed, Millie realises she has spent too long chasing dreams and that true happiness can always be found in reality . . .

'A gritty, heartrending and impassioned drama' *Newcastle Journal*

'A tough, compelling and ultimately satisfying novel . . . another classy, irresistible read' *Sunderland Echo*

'She pulls no punches, tells it like it is and taps directly into your emotions' *Northern Echo*

0 7472 6002 8

headline

Now you can buy any of these other bestselling
Headline books from your bookshop or
direct from the publisher.

FREE P&P AND UK DELIVERY
(Overseas and Ireland £3.50 per book)

The House on Lonely Street	Lyn Andrews	£5.99
A Glimpse of the Mersey	Anne Baker	£5.99
The Whispering Years	Harry Bowling	£5.99
The Stony Path	Rita Bradshaw	£5.99
The Bird Flies High	Maggie Craig	£5.99
Kate's Story	Billy Hopkins	£5.99
Taking a Chance on Love	Joan Jonker	£5.99
The Jarrow Lass	Janet MacLeod Trotter	£5.99
All or Nothing	Lynda Page	£5.99
A Perfect Stranger	Victor Pemberton	£5.99
Where Hope Lives	Wendy Robertson	£5.99
Better Days	June Tate	£6.99
A Rare Ruby	Dee Williams	£5.99

TO ORDER SIMPLY CALL THIS NUMBER

01235 400 414

or visit our website: www.madaboutbooks.com

Prices and availability subject to change without notice.